VIRGINIA KING

The Fourth Door

The Secrets of Selkie Moon

CELESTIAL
hedgehog

First published by Celestial Hedgehog Pty Ltd 2019

This novel is entirely a work of fiction. The names, characters and incidents portrayed in it are the work of the author's imagination. Any resemblance to actual persons, living or dead, events or localities is entirely coincidental.

Virginia King asserts the moral right to be identified as the author of this work.

First edition

ISBN: 978-0-9945923-9-2

This book was professionally typeset on Reedsy.
Find out more at reedsy.com

"Keep your fears to yourself, but share your courage with others."

– Robert Louis Stevenson

Contents

Books by Virginia King

The Secrets of Selkie Moon

The First Lie
The Second Path
The Third Note
The Fourth Door
Laying Ghosts (Prequel)
Leaving Birds (Short Stories)

Glossary

Selkie – sea creature from Celtic folklore that takes the form of a seal in water but
  can take human form on land.

Hawaiian words
  Kahuna – wise person, sorcerer.

Cantonese words
  Feng shui – traditional Chinese placement of objects enhancing the yin/yang balance.
  Gweilo – foreigner.
  Jiaobei – wooden divination tools thrown in pairs to answer a yes/no question.
  Kau chim – numbered bamboo sticks used to seek answers from ancient oracle texts.
  Po po –grandmother.

Prologue

We can't stop touching each other, and the stewardesses giggle behind their hands. They must have seen amorous passengers before. But not in our age-group. Not in first class.

Alister murmurs in my ear, "I keep pinching myself that you're sharing this with me, Selkie. My life. My quest. You've brought me more than love, you know that. You've brought me … hope. Because if I can find you, I can find … him."

He's talking about his long-lost son. Thirty years ago, baby Deshi was kidnapped by his Chinese grandparents, and Alister has been looking for him ever since. Now two separate leads have suggested that the elderly couple are living in Hong Kong. They're the only ones who know where Deshi is. And after years of searching alone, Alister has asked me to join him.

I snuggle into his neck. "I just hope I can help."

"Keep loving me."

"That's easy. Set me a test and I'll pass it with flying colours."

He dozes off and I cast my eyes over the plan we've made. His private investigator supplied a few clues before suddenly dropping the case. We'll navigate through them, and with the help of my psychic twinges, see if they lead us to Deshi's grandparents. It's how I solved a century-old murder in Ireland last year, but this time the stakes are higher.

To calm my nerves, I flip through the in-flight magazine. A previous traveller has scribbled comments here and there. Next to an ad for a gold watch he's written: *Sir buy knock-off Rolex?*

I smile. The words bring back all the sights and smells of my first trip to Hong Kong and the pushy street vendors. That trip was with my ex-husband. I gaze at Alister, his face unlined in sleep, and a muddle of emotions swells my chest: love, excitement. And tension.

What if we luck out on finding Deshi?

After flipping to an article on the English art of tea making, I pour the same beverage from a tiny bone-china teapot into my matching cup. The blue and white willow pattern is exquisite. First class has comforts I could get used to.

Cute little stewardess read my tea leaves, says another scrawled comment. *Said I'd have many lovers. Asked for her phone number ...*

"I read your tea leaves, madam?" The stewardess smiles in encouragement. "It's a company tradition. We combine British custom with Chinese horoscope." She indicates the horoscope booklet under her arm. "It's unique."

Fascinated, I take one last sip before passing her my cup. Her eyes drop and she gasps.

"What's wrong?" I ask.

As she shows me the arrangement of tea leaves, she can barely get her words out. "It looks like ... n-number ... four."

"Four is bad?"

Her smile has gone. "In Cantonese and Mandarin, 'four' sounds like another word. The horoscope won't help."

She hesitates, but reading the tea leaves is a company tradition. I swallow hard.

"Death."

Chapter 1

I t catches my attention.

A scream.

The night market in Kowloon is a mass of movement and noise, so the scream of one child is not remarkable. Or shouldn't be. But this child's cry punctuates the buzz like an exclamation mark. Just for a moment, everything stops. Even the cry. Then another scream follows. The keening of a woman.

As I turn, a woman in a yellow blouse starts running, her arms outstretched, towards two dark figures zigzagging away through the throng. She wails something in Cantonese and her words need no translation. One of the men holds a crumpled form to his chest, not for protection but for speed.

"They've taken my baby!" Every sense tells me that's what she's screaming, but I seem to be the only one who's heard her. Then I start running too, past stalls lit by glaring fluorescent bulbs that dangle from wires strung across the lane like bunting, my eyes on the woman's bobbing yellow blouse as I collide with shoppers who curse when I push past them.

The woman's pace is slowing as if she's out of breath. The market ends in a busy road, where the jostling of cars mimics the human traffic. The thought stops me as I reach the curb. The men have disappeared but the woman has dodged between the vehicles and is stumbling up the pavement on the other side. That phrase. I've heard it but never really thought about it till now—human traffic.

By the time Alister appears beside me, the city has swallowed the incident and I'm staring into space.

"Thank God, Selkie." He wraps his arms around me. "I thought I'd lost you. One minute you were there; then you weren't. I ... panicked."

"I'm so sorry. They kidnapped her baby. She chased them, and I chased her, but they're gone."

His frown deepens. "Take some deep breaths. Then tell me everything."

As I recount what I saw and see the anguish on his face, I try to find another explanation. "Maybe it's a custody battle. The running man might be a father taking his son." I'm sure it was a boy.

Then why two men? The child wasn't going to resist. Unless it was to deal with the woman. I imagine her catching up to them, oblivious to the danger, thinking only of her child.

"Some sixth sense made you pay attention." His pain is palpable. The incident must be triggering every emotion he's tried to keep in check since we left Hawaii.

"I didn't see the snatch, only a woman chasing two men with a baby."

"You still need to report it," Alister sighs.

We're standing on the pavement like rocks in a fast-flowing stream. It's after nine at night, but this is a city that never sleeps. We only arrived this morning. We planned to eat at the market, stall-hopping to satisfy my appetite for street food. But now I just want a family restaurant—preferably upstairs and in a back street—with great home cooking and zero chance of witnessing a crime.

Alister cranes his neck and spots a policeman on the next corner. Grabbing my hand, he pushes us towards him. My expectations crumble when I see how young he is, a junior constable on street patrol. Alister speaks to him in Cantonese and a short conversation follows.

"Would you recognise the men?" Alister asks me.

I shake my head. "They were bulky, thug-like. They had their heads down. Chinese." This is Hong Kong. Most people around us are Chinese.

"A tattoo would be too much to hope for," he says.

I recall the woman. She was Chinese too. I tell Alister about her blouse.

The constable listens, his face blank. If I was expecting him to make chase, it's not happening. I suspect he doesn't know what to do.

"Was there anything memorable beyond her clothing?" Alister asks.

I say that she was short and a little plump, with straight black hair. "There was something else." I try to remember. "I can't think what."

Another glance at Alister's frown reminds me that he was hoping to contact the police on his own terms. They closed the case on Deshi years ago. Will they help us find a thirty-year-old who might not want to be found?

Even though Alister wanted me with him, I'm starting to wish I'd stayed in Honolulu. Trouble has always been my middle name. Now I'm stirring it up again.

The constable mumbles something and Alister hails a cab.

When he asks for the station headquarters on Hong Kong Island, the cab driver blinks, looking as if he might refuse the fare. When he nods, we jump in.

"Not all Kowloon taxis will cross the harbour," Alister explains. "Some of the island taxis stay on their side too."

"Isn't there a closer police station?" It's a long way from the site of the snatch.

"He said we want the Crime Squad. In Central District. On the island."

When I take his hand, I find he's made a fist. At my touch his hand relaxes a little.

"I'm so sorry," I murmur.

"You can't help what you saw. And you're a hero for trying to follow them. It's not a coincidence, Selkie. Our first night here and this happens. Is it a good sign or a bad sign?"

I press myself against his chest and he kisses the top of my head. Good or bad, it's a sign. And wherever it leads, we're in it together.

A tunnel takes us under the harbour, then the busy road hugs the foreshore opposite Kowloon all the way to Central. The cab pulls up outside an imposing complex of low and high-rise buildings.

Inside, another fresh-faced officer takes notes and asks us to wait. After thirty minutes of watching complainants in various body shapes and garbs jabber out their concerns in incomprehensible tones, we're ushered down a corridor and into an office.

The man behind the counter is an expat close to retirement age. His lined face beneath a receding hairline is tired but reassuring. In a British accent, he introduces himself as Superintendent David Butler, head of the Crime Squad.

"Thank you for seeing us," I say.

"We take every child abduction seriously. Tell me where you were and what you saw."

He listens without interruption, only dropping his eyes once or twice to make a note on his tablet.

"The night market in Temple Street?"

I don't know the name. "Parallel to Nathan Road. Near the Novotel."

He nods. "Is that where you're staying?"

Alister says, "We're in a friend's apartment here on the island." He gives Butler the address.

"Ocean View Apartments? Nice." His tone implies expensive. He turns his attention back to me. "Nothing you saw identifies this woman or the child-snatchers."

I know he's right. "Why did they take the baby?" I ask. "Where could he end up?"

"If he's lucky, an adoption to the US. There are legitimate adoptions that start with child abductions. We don't get many in Hong Kong, but it's a lucrative market that requires a steady supply of so-called orphans."

I'm shocked. "And if he's ... unlucky?"

"Not all babies are suitable. They may find new parents here, especially boys. If not, they ... disappear. Possibly sold into slavery."

Feeling sick, I look across at Alister. His face has gone green. Butler notices.

"Are you all right, Mr Sloane?" He realises that Alister can't speak. "Toilets are along the corridor, on the left." Once Alister rushes from the room, the superintendent asks, "What's your interest in abductions and adoptions, Miss Moon? Beyond the fate of this child? Something personal, by the looks of it."

He's not accusing me of anything, but we could be a desperate couple wanting a baby ourselves. I could be spinning a vague story in the hope of getting inside information on local adoption scams.

"Alister will tell you what happened." I hope he's OK. "It was a long time ago—and the case was never solved. This abduction has triggered buried emotions."

"So it seems. And if it's at all related to child trafficking, I'd like to know the story." He looks at his watch. "I'll be finished here at ten and your friend looks like he's going to need a stiff drink." He scribbles an address on his notepad and hands it to me. "Meet me there in twenty minutes. Better if we're not seen leaving together. It's not far but take a taxi."

* * *

The cool air brings some colour back to Alister's face.

As he hails a cab, I ask, "Did you come across Butler the last time you were looking for Deshi? He looks old enough to have been around since then."

"No. And there were so few clues, they didn't take long to lose interest."

"A fresh approach could help us." I take his arm. "And even though it's late, instead of going home, Butler wants to hear your story."

Alister's mouth is a tight line. I know that his past experiences with the Hong Kong Police have made him wary, and thirty years of dead-ends have crushed his hopes that they can help. One of my jobs is to rekindle his optimism and generate new paths to follow. Tonight's abduction is so confronting that it feels like a negative start, but what if it's the opposite?

The cry of that baby is haunting me. I'm sensing that he's alive and crying for his mother. It mirrors my very strong sense that Deshi is still alive too.

The cab drops us off on a narrow street lined with bars, a block back from the harbour front. Sporting a British flag over the door, Churchill's is easy to spot. Inside, the heavily timbered bar with a neon glow is populated by a range of nationalities but few Chinese. I'm guessing that's why Butler suggested it, or it's simply his preferred drinking hole.

Alister is quiet and declines a drink. I head to the bar and order some food—nothing as authentic as the street food we never got to eat, but calamari and chips will do.

Butler arrives. He's changed into a casual shirt and sports jacket but his expression is a little too grim to pass for a tourist.

He orders a beer then pulls a stool up to our table, getting straight to the point. "There's enough noise here to keep your story private, Mr Sloane."

Alister nods and tells the story he's told many times. "My wife was Chinese and we were living in San Francisco. Her parents never liked me but after Fleur and I had a baby, they doted on him. When Deshi was only ten months old, Fleur was killed in a campus shooting. Her parents helped me look after him, until one day they were gone, taking my son with them. I've been looking for him ever since."

"How long?"

"Thirty years."

Butler exhales loudly. "That's tough."

Alister shows him a photo of Deshi with his mother and grandparents, then the lock of baby hair he carries in his wallet.

"He doesn't look very Chinese," Butler says, "but that doesn't mean he'd be easy to spot. Not in a melting pot like this. Maybe he'd stand out in China—if you knew where to look." He hands back the keepsakes. "And the night you arrive here, your girlfriend witnesses an abduction. That's enough to turn anyone green." He takes a slug of beer. "I'm guessing you tried the police here already. Before the handover?"

Alister's nod is stiff. "They weren't very interested. Too much serious crime and nothing much to go on anyway. For the last fifteen years, I've had a team of private investigators on the case. Ads in the papers in San Francisco, here and China. Online. A reward."

"And a lot of tyre kickers hoping to meet their long-lost daddy. You're using DNA?"

"First we use a birthmark, but it could have faded. DNA's sorted the frauds. It's been all frauds until a few months ago. Deshi's cousin came forward. Su Yin. She's in San Francisco with the rest of Fleur's extended family. I got my hopes up, but she doesn't know where he is."

"So why return to Hong Kong now?"

"Are you offering to re-open the case?"

"It's why I wanted your story," Butler says, "but after thirty years, it's not really possible. Your son's an adult. But I've been here for a long time so ask me anything."

Alister hunches his shoulders. "After a lead that they were living in one of the new satellite suburbs, my private eye suddenly disappeared. I wondered if he'd found them—and got paid off to forget it. I've quizzed Su Yin, and she's dropped a few casual questions at home."

"They don't know she's talking to you?"

"No. I was never welcomed by the family. She's had

to be discreet. Her mother is Fleur's cousin, so Deshi's grandmother and Su Yin's grandmother are sisters. It's as close as I've ever come to Fleur's parents, and Su Yin says they've lived in Hong Kong for years. They occasionally fly over to the States for family get-togethers, but never with Deshi. I suspect they changed his identity while he was still a baby—gave him a new Chinese name and applied for a Hong Kong passport."

"An easy way to make him disappear," Butler says.

"But Su Yin has never heard mention of anyone who could be Deshi. She only answered my ad because of the family name—and the reward."

"You're sure about her? She isn't just after the money?"

"The DNA's a match. She even looks like Fleur."

Alister holds my gaze for a long moment. I know that Su Yin gave him a pang when they first met. Her resemblance to Fleur took him back to that fateful morning when he kissed his wife goodbye and never saw her again. But Fleur has been dead for thirty years, and Alister has committed himself to me in heart and body. I have nothing to fear from Fleur's memory or from Su Yin. His eyes brim and I squeeze his hand.

"So now you're going to roll up to your former parents-in-law and ask them for Deshi's address? Why would they tell you anything? You said yourself, he's probably got a new identity."

"And he won't know who I am," Alister says. "I'm more than likely the father who's never been mentioned. No, I won't be confronting them, not until I have some leverage. And I don't mean violence—not my style. But I have to find them first."

The heart of our quest: finding Deshi's grandparents. In a

metropolis the size of Hong Kong.

Butler starts patting his pockets then stops, as if he's looking for cigarettes and remembers he's given up. He takes another slurp of beer.

"You'll need to wring all you can out of the Red Cross and other tracing services," he says.

"Done that. Wong is a common name."

Butler nods. "You're going to need an edge to find them."

Alister doesn't respond. He's so engrossed in his private tragedy that he misses the hint.

"What edge?" I ask.

Butler tilts his head as if to puff out smoke. The action is so automatic, I'm guessing he gave up the habit recently.

He drops his voice. "When I've finished my beer, I'll leave her card on the table. But don't mention my name to anyone except her. I'll deny it anyway."

"Her?"

"She's a banker, but I've used her other skills a handful of times. Unofficially. We met on another abduction case and she impressed me so much that I started seeking her help whenever a child's involved. She's got a ... gift."

A psychic. He's sending us to a clairvoyant. In Honolulu, a *kahuna* named Coral has helped me more than once. She lives in a bus shelter and barks out one-word predictions so I was sceptical at first. But she's been so spot-on that I trust her now. Is Butler's contact Coral's local equivalent?

"Do we use the name on her card?" I ask.

"Call her Miss Tigerlily. Then she'll know I've sent you."

Chapter 2

The cab weaves its way around Hong Kong Island, gradually snaking up ever-narrowing roads that cling to the mountainside behind low stone walls. On our right, we catch glimpses through the trees of a dark expanse of ocean, dotted with the lights of passing ships.

When we arrive at our address, we step out into a stiff wind straight off the sea and hurry to swipe ourselves through the security door. Only a few degrees cooler than Honolulu in March, Hong Kong is surprisingly chilly.

Alister actually owns an apartment in this building, but when he gave up on finding Deshi's grandparents here last year, he rented it out. We're using his neighbour's one-bedroom bachelor pad instead. Rents in Hong Kong, some of the highest in the world, are calculated by the square foot, so it's not surprising that fly-in fly-out executives go for small spaces. Everyone seems to socialise in bars or on the street anyway. Apartments, even the luxurious ones, are for crashing.

We enter the lift and ascend in silence. Even though he didn't witness it, the abduction has taken a bigger toll on Alister than it has on me. His body has visibly wilted and his optimism from the plane has evaporated, leaving a shell.

I take his arm and decide not to bring up the subject of consulting Miss Tigerlily. Not tonight. It's late and the jet lag is catching up with us, but I'm curious about whether he used a clairvoyant in the past. He knows that Coral, the *kahuna*, is accurate and he's open to the psychic world, but he's never mentioned seeking that kind of help to search for Deshi.

Our temporary home is on the same floor as Alister's apartment. As we step out of the elevator, his tenant is emerging from his own front door. Klaus Hofmeier is a German expat, an executive of some kind, and he's shorter and balder than his name suggests. Alister grunts a greeting but Klaus only has eyes for me. His stare burns through my sweater like a blow torch.

"Nice. Let's party some time." He winks as he steps into our lift. "I handpick my housemaids, know what I mean?"

His final leer makes my flesh crawl.

Once he's gone, Alister says, "Sorry about him, Selkie. He had good references, but it seems he uses his posting here to exploit the locals. Morals like his give expats a bad name. Let's hope we don't bump into him again."

After the night's events, it's a comfort to close the door on the world and fall asleep in Alister's arms.

* * *

Something wakes me in the early hours.

I look around wondering what it was. Probably just the jetlag, but I'm suddenly aware of Alister beside me. In the dark, I feel his effect on me more intensely—the power of his presence, even in sleep. It's a sensation that's new to me, a connection that goes beyond the physical. I listen to his breath for several minutes, savouring the sound like music.

We stumbled upon each other by chance early last year, after he attended my business seminar and offered to represent me. The instant chemistry caught us both by surprise. I'd only just escaped from my controlling husband in Sydney, followed by another bad choice of lover, so at first I ran a mile from Alister Sloane. But, after many years searching for the right woman, he was sure about me from the start.

"Do you know about the lunar matchmaker, Selkie?" he asked over lunch one day. "He ties an invisible red cord to the little fingers of two people who are destined to be lovers. No matter where we are in time and space, we're joined by that cord. It will stretch, even get tangled," —he laughed at how much I tied him in knots— "but never break."

The folk tale suits us perfectly and now that we're finally together, I sense our connection even when he's asleep. Snuggling into his naked body, I drift off too.

* * *

It's late morning when we wake and we linger over the pleasures of our bachelor pad—a very private king-sized bed. This is our first time away as a couple and we're still getting to know each other, so our lovemaking is at the romp stage: fresh and fun.

This is different from his Honolulu penthouse. With his live-in staff, it always feels like his space, not mine. I keep finding reasons to continue sharing a humble flat in Waikiki with my hula-dancing flatmate. My best friend, Derek Delaney, insists that my reluctance to settle down is putting too much pressure on the fledgling relationship, but even though I'm crazy about

Alister, do I want to get married again and possibly spoil what we've got?

All these decisions are on hold for now. Here we can share a space that's totally neutral.

"If it wasn't for our quest," Alister murmurs, the search for Deshi never far from his mind, "I'd be tempted to stay here all day. Give our red cord a proper workout."

I roll onto him and whisper, "Another time, Haiku. I won't forget."

The nickname popped up the way nicknames do. Alister is an unusual name in the US, so a close friend calls him Stair, and sometimes Stairway. The Stairway to Heaven is a forbidden hiking trail on Oahu, also known as the Haiku Stairs. Once during our lovemaking, I called him my stairway to heaven. That turned into Haiku. The name stuck.

Hunger calls. Since I'm the one who's starving, I offer to search the tiny kitchen for whatever I can find. Alister probably knows where we can buy supplies nearby, but he's jumped into the shower.

I gaze out the window through the March haze. Perched on the mountainside, this building feels like it's on the edge of the world.

As I look for anything edible, I wonder about the day ahead. When Su Yin called out of the blue to confirm that Deshi's grandparents are living somewhere in Hong Kong, Alister made the arrangements quickly. He wanted me along and, with my next seminar not for another month, I left Derek in charge of registrations and jumped on the plane too.

Last night's abduction is our first lead.

With that thought, a shadow darkens my morning. It descends like nothing I've ever felt before, wrapping itself around my neck. I struggle to breathe and collapse on a stool, enveloped in an invisible bubble of terror. As my chest heaves, I force my eyes to close. It's visceral. Menacing. *Old.* Lurking on the fringes—trying to get in.

Into my head?

Through this suffocating fog, thoughts of last night surface. Everything starts with Deshi's abduction. And last night—our first night here—we were treated to another abduction. It's not a coincidence.

How does it relate to this shadow?

But from the shower, Alister has started singing. His voice fills the apartment with joy, instantly dispelling the threat. After our lovemaking, he's back from the dark places of last night, and my presence here is responsible for that.

Pushing my unease aside for now, I busy myself with finding eggs that even I can cook, coconut water and a mango. A chunk of what looks like sourdough is a little stale, but I slice it and toast it before lathering it with butter. I also find an automatic coffee machine.

When Alister emerges in a terry robe that matches mine, I'm standing beside a platter on the island counter, my chest puffed out like a cooking student at a bake-off.

"Agile in the bedroom and the kitchen." He bends over and kisses me. "I'm a lucky man."

As we tuck in, he notices the business card from Superintendent Butler lying where I left it on the counter. "What's her real name?"

I reach for the card. "Lee Mei Yee, Vice President, Jadeite Financial Group."

"Why does a banker make psychic predictions for the police?"

I've already wondered about that. "As a community service? Butler said she's gifted—and he obviously admires her—so she must have other qualities, like integrity. Maybe she got wealthy by predicting the market and this is her way of giving something back. Or she lost her own child and it's her mission to save other kids."

He takes the card and turns it over, but the other side is blank. "So we ring her direct line and ask for Miss Tigerlily?"

"Do you know another way to contact a clairvoyant?" I laugh at my joke. He doesn't.

"I used one once." His expression is grim. "*She* wasn't giving anything back. She was taking money from desperate people. In spite of what Butler says about this woman, I'm not sure I can do it again."

It's the first time he's told me about this and the betrayal he suffered ignites my anger. "You don't have to do it again. I'll do it."

"See Miss Tigerlily in my place? It's a wonderful offer, Selkie, but you're not the real client. Can a clairvoyant do a reading—a reading that's worth anything—through an intermediary?"

I haven't thought this through. "I could take something of yours to her. Coral reads personal objects—and photos. Or ... what if I check her out for you? Make sure she's legit."

"How will you do that?"

"Ask her to do a reading on me. See if she gets things right."

But Alister is frowning again. "She's a Chinese banker so she's shrewd at reading people. Fake psychics are good at that too. They read your clothes, how you talk, your body language, then they throw out teasers and get all their information from you, but make it look like foresight. You might be ... out of your depth."

Like he was with the psychic who conned him?

"Yeah. I might be. A banker who could be psychic scares the hell out of me. But if there's any chance she's what Butler said—our edge in the search for Deshi—then we can't pass up the chance. So ... I need an edge too."

Alister loses his frown, then laughs. "You've got an idea! Of course you have."

I pick up my phone and start googling. When I've found what I want, I show it to him. He laughs again, then hugs me.

Before we set off, I call police headquarters and ask for Superintendent Butler. He's not happy to hear from me. "I don't know what you're talking about," he says in response to my request.

"OK. That's what you said you'd say, but I need one more favour. Please."

"Make it quick." Alister's story must have touched him. It's what I hoped.

"I need you to call her and make the appointment."

"What's wrong with your own phone?"

"It's complicated. Just ask her for a time, later today or tomorrow. Tell her to expect a woman called Elkie. It's my nickname. A bit like hers."

"Then what?"

"I'll call you back in a few minutes and you can tell me when and where."

He grunts and I hang up, but when I call back it's done. Miss Tigerlily will see Elkie at midday today.

* * *

The cab drops us in the Central District, near the ferries that carry thousands of people back and forth each day across Victoria Harbour to Kowloon. The place I found on the internet is just a stroll from here.

We leave the bustle of traffic, the gleaming high-rises and glitzy shops, and dive into a maze of alleyways, the underbelly of old Hong Kong. It's another world, with narrow buildings, both decrepit and spotless, crammed together as if to save space. Multiple levels of apartments teeter above us, their ancient air-conditioners and poles of washing projecting from every window. At pedestrian-level, each door opens off the laneway into a tiny shop.

We make our way on foot past an enormous tree emerging from the pavement. Amidst the dilapidated awnings, washing poles and aerials, it's the only thing bearing foliage. Beneath it, an old man in baggy pants and a sweatshirt sits on a concrete wall and smokes.

The shop I'm looking for has a flat facade painted orange. Huge funky letters spell the name in English: Empo Retro.

Alister takes my hand and we descend the few steps to the entrance, where we stop, look at each other as if for courage, then giggle like teenagers. We've found a moment of fun in our quest for Deshi, and I'm glad I'm here.

Pushing open the door, we arrive in an Aladdin's cave. The interior is bigger than it looks from the outside, the space divided by aisles with clothing racks on two levels. Luckily there aren't many customers and we move past tuxedos and men's jeans through to the women's section at the rear of the store.

"Should I go for a completely different look? Or confuse her psychic flow with odd things that don't match?"

"I don't think it matters, Selkie. As long as what you're wearing has belonged to anyone but you."

Running my fingers along the racks of retro rags, I hope something will jump out. Designer labels from the fifties, judging by the styles, have price tags that make me blanch. I'm drawn to the club-hopping gear, but Alister vetoes the tiny skirts and skimpy tops, reminding me how cool it is outside. At last, I pounce on a long-sleeved mod-style cocktail dress from the sixties, with big black and pink checks and a boat-style neckline. I have fun teaming it with a matching Carnaby Street peaked cap and hot pink boots.

Alister casts an approving eye over me. "Now your hair. It says too much about you."

My spiky cut and silver streaks are a symbolic link to my aquatic namesakes: seals. Before we left Honolulu, my hairdresser gave me an extra-perky trim.

Alister asks the shop assistant about wigs. She rummages in a box and finds a shaggy blonde one. Almost there.

"Give me all your jewellery," he says. "If she's any good at cold reading, she'll glean a lot from it."

I take off the necklace from my Irish great-grandmother and the blown-glass locket that hangs beside it. The heart-shaped locket was made for me by Fabienne, my French artist friend, and contains a fingerprint from both Alister and me. I hand them over for safekeeping, before taking off the silver bangle that Alister found for me in a French *brocante* market. I ditched my wedding ring over a year ago so my fingers are bare.

As we step outside into a low haze, my body starts to tingle. Excitement mixed with total panic. Alister will follow me as far as Miss Tigerlily's building, where a receptionist will usher me to a meeting room.

"Turn off your phone, just in case she picks up something from it. And remember not to speak." We've decided my voice would give too much away. "Not a word."

In this getup, I feel anything but myself, so that part of the plan is working. But I'm worried that when I sashay down the street, every eye will be outing me as a fake. Luckily the lane outside Empo Retro is relatively free of pedestrians. I remember to breathe.

"Let's separate here," Alister says. "It's probably an unnecessary precaution but better not to be seen together as we get closer to her building."

"And risk losing sight of me in the crowds?"

Suddenly it's back. The shadow I felt in the apartment. It's stronger this time, swirling around my neck with menace. Is it following me? Or Alister? As I gulp for air, I sense how old it is. Chinese? Because surely there's nothing more ancient than this culture.

But Alister laughs at my comment, and it's gone.

Armed with the Nathan Road address in Kowloon, I give him a huge hug.

"I'll follow you onto the ferry," he murmurs. "Remember I'm with you all the way."

Chapter 3

As soon as I hit the main road, it's clear I needn't have worried about drawing looks. Pink and black check frocks with hot pink boots are unremarkable in the melee of garments and styles. If anything, they make me blend in.

I forget about the shadow and relax. I can do this. Crossing to the ritzy shopping arcade, I make my way along marble floors towards the bus terminal and the Star Ferry wharf beyond.

With my phobia of the sea, ferries are not my preferred form of transport, and the waves are choppy from the breeze. I remind myself that even though I can't see him, Alister is connected to me by the red cord. And it's only a few minutes to Kowloon. Keeping my eyes above the white caps, I take in the view. Barges and pilot boats cross paths, along with one traditional Chinese junk bobbing beneath a sail. A tourist cruise, I suppose. On both sides, competing skyscrapers crowd the tiny foreshores, reminding me of Honolulu.

The wig is making my head sweat and the boots are a little too big for comfort, but otherwise the outfit is the easy part. The real challenge will be facing Miss Tigerlily without uttering a word. What will she do? Kick me out as a time-waster? Or guess what I'm up to, then kick me out?

For the first time, I think about my strategy beyond the recycled clothes. If I'm going to help Alister, I need evidence that she's a woman of integrity, a real clairvoyant and not just a reader of body language. If she guesses what I'm up to, she'll have passed the first test. But I'll only know that she's caught on if she tells me. Then not kicking me out will be the second test. Except that might just mean she likes a challenge—and that's already established. She's a businesswoman, after all.

And the third test? This is the big one for us. She'll have to come up with a reading about me that could only come from a psychic. All I have to do is stay mute and keep my nerve. The rest will be up to her.

The wharf on the Kowloon side spills the passengers onto a paved area that leads to another high-rise shopping mall. I head up Nathan Road instead. As the flow of pedestrians channels me under awnings of bamboo scaffolding and past a myriad of shops adorned with paper lanterns, I start enjoying myself.

Every woman should do this. Dredge out a hidden side of herself and take it on an outing. Or maybe something more personal is at play, because I'm loving the invisibility of tinkering with my identity. I remember all the years I spent not being me—when my step-mother and my ex renamed me Elkie—until I reclaimed my birth name and moved to Hawaii. Finding fun in being someone else for a while confirms how comfortable I've become in my own skin. The selkie metaphor makes me smile.

As I near my target, I've got time to duck into one of the many perfume stores and choose a fragrance at random. The tester on the counter produces one that's not my style—way too floral. The shop assistant tries to sell me something else but I decline. I buy a tiny bottle, splash it on my wrists and neck, then toss it into a refuse bin. On the other side of the street, I catch a glimpse of Alister and ignore him.

The Jadeite building is almost opposite a laneway that leads to the night market where the child was taken only last night. With David Butler on the case, I push the memory away and walk between the two marble lions guarding the tiled entrance.

Sweeping across the air-conditioned foyer, I say to the receptionist, "Elkie to see Lee Mei Yee. I have an appointment."

She consults her screen before directing me to the seventh floor, but first I detour to the restrooms. After a much needed stop in the loo, I scrutinise myself in the basin mirror, wipe the sweat from my forehead and upper lip, and add another layer of eye makeup. Making sure my wig's in place, I give my cap a jaunty tug and remind myself to keep breathing. As I take the elevator up, I wonder where Alister has stationed himself.

The meeting room is empty, so I gaze out between the buildings at the glimpse of Hong Kong Island peeping out of the haze. Then I hear the door close behind me and turn to see an older woman looking across the room at me. Probably in her fifties, she's still beautiful and her cream business suit must be silk. A colourful designer scarf, draped over her shoulders like a shawl, adds panache. Around her neck is a single strand of pearls.

She extends her hand and I shake it.

"David Butler said to call you Elkie. Not your real name. But ... a name you hide behind, am I right?"

Bloody hell. But Butler probably told her it's my nickname.

I open my mouth, remember my vow of silence, and shrug.

She gestures to a chair and we both sit down.

"So, Elkie, I understand the nickname. You want to remain anonymous. Let's move on." Her voice is accented but her English is perfect. "David only sends me cases that have hit a wall—or have touched him. What are you dealing with?"

She wants me to tell her the whole story? Alister's warnings come back. Keeping my gaze steady, I say nothing.

After several seconds she says, "I see. Are you going to say anything at all?"

When I toss my wig in a headshake, she looks at her watch.

"I think I know what's going on. The nickname. The silence. It can make my work more difficult—and take longer. Did David tell you I don't charge for this? I trust him, so I'll trust you. I'll give you fifteen minutes and see if we can get anywhere. OK? Then I'll have to put my other cap back on. While you take yours off, am I right?"

She looks at mine and I blink an acknowledgement.

"This is how I work," she says. "I say whatever comes into my mind. A stream of consciousness. Did you bring a notebook?"

Another headshake. She'd see my handwriting.

"Pity." She pauses. "I'll let you record it. Nod your agreement not to share it with the press."

I bow my head. She waits as I pull out my phone and turn it on, risking that it won't tell her anything.

"Pay attention," she says. "Even though it's recorded, your first reactions are the most important. Some of it may be rubbish. Or all of it. Keep an open mind. If something resonates, don't cling to it and dismiss what comes from left field. It could be your own preconceptions blocking the truth. Let it all wash over you, but notice anything that triggers a strong emotion, including disbelief."

She closes her eyes and I'm reminded of Coral in her Honolulu bus shelter. Miss Tigerlily is dropping into the zone. I close my eyes too, doing my best to lose my expectations and empty my mind. Suddenly I'm aware of my disguise. Will vibes from the previous owner muddy her visions and render her insights useless? We were so busy wanting to test her, we didn't consider that these garments might prevent her from demonstrating her gift.

It's more than a minute before she begins. Her voice doesn't change, but as torrents of words bombard me, her accent becomes more pronounced.

"Boots too big. Hair too hot. Scent too cheap. Wait, a shadow! Pink, black, pink, black. Ghost wants to sleep. Can't. Wants to blame. Can't. Changes shape. Sly. Dark. Wants to play. Wants to *win*. Remember your mother. Man waiting. No! Gone. Too much beauty. Skin deep. Save him. *Your* job. Carrying bygones. Can't let go. Stones in the belly. Cut it open. Carry a stone to the mountaintop. Not Chinese enough! Baby called Moses. Touched by the gods. Danger! Danger! Danger! Endless circle. Trapped in time. Look in mirror. Go down to the sea. Speak the truth. Watch out for him. For her. Pray. Burn. White Tiger. Something sharp. Know. Who. To. Trust."

My head is doing cartwheels. Are the words a threat or a warning?

The rapid-fire delivery must have exhausted Miss Tigerlily. She falls back in her chair and inhales deeply, as if she's just been to a place where the air was thin. I know about thin places from my Irish quest only a few months ago. Places where this world and the next collide. The connection feels important.

I have no idea what she's given me, but her words were so

alarming that I'm glad they're recorded. I was supposed to pay attention but right now I remember none of it. I realise how naive I've been. I thought this would be simple. Dress up, see if she'd tell me the name of my first pet and I'd know if we could trust her.

Now I'm confused. Out of my depth. Alister was right about that.

Save him. Your job. Does she mean Alister? Is he in danger? From the shadow? All he wants is to find his son. His job. But Deshi's a man too. Am I to save him?

When Miss Tigerlily opens her eyes again, she's back. She looks at me, then at her watch. She stands up.

"I don't know who you are, Elkie. But whatever you do, stop using this name. Especially as camouflage. It drains your power. But you know that already."

I start to reply but she puts her finger to her lips.

"If you speak now, you'll doubt everything I've said—if you got anything useful. I forget the words as soon as they're out. Your idea to test me was a good one, but there's something about this disguise that got in the way. The clothes are pointing to something. Not the ghost of the previous owner, she's long gone. We know about ghosts around here, the ones who can't move on. This is more complicated. I sense a threat. Be careful."

As she walks me to the door, she adds, "And stop being a blonde. That spiky black cut with the silver streaks is who you really are."

* * *

Minutes later, I'm staggering onto the street as if I've been slapped. The cool air hits me with another punch. I rip off the wig and look for a bin to dispose of it as words from her barrage return for a fresh onslaught: *Danger! Danger! Danger!*

The wig is in my hand along with the pink and black cap. Pink and black. I remember what Miss Tigerlily said about these clothes. After a Google search only a few hours ago, I found the vintage shop and chose this outfit at random. Random. Is anything truly random? For the first time I fear I was attracted to these clothes for a reason. A reason that's hidden from me, as the outfit itself was supposed to hide me.

I scan the passing crowds for Alister. Where is he? *Gone. Danger!* Panic drenches me in sweat. Stepping into a doorway, I check my phone. There's a text message from him and I almost collapse with relief.

Help is here, Selkie. An amazing surprise. I don't want to spoil it. Timing with your visit to Miss T is prescient, but we may not need it now. Sorry to abandon you but I know you'll understand. Meet me at the apartment. I'll be back in a couple of hours. Then you'll know everything. A. xx

My cheeks burn with anger and confusion. I try phoning him but it goes to voicemail. His parting words to me come back: "I'm with you all the way." What kind of surprise took precedence over my meeting? He knows I'll understand. It can only mean he's found a lead on Deshi. But he doesn't know about Miss Tigerlily's warnings.

Where are you? I text back. *What's the surprise?*

And why aren't you here?

I'm standing in the entrance of a little eating house. My legs are barely supporting me and I spot an empty table and sit down. The wig and cap are still in my hand. I'll hang onto them until I know what's going on.

At least a plate of noodles is something I can rely on. I check out what someone at another table is eating and when the waitress plonks a glass of tea on my table, I point to their meal. Only then do I notice my surroundings. A concrete floor full of cracks. Plastic chairs. A tray with chopsticks and condiments on each table. A menu on the wall. Homesickness for the Pearl in Honolulu rises up because I'm suddenly alone.

When my bowl is empty, there's still no reply from Alister. Feeling abandoned, I stumble outside into thick air and retrace my steps to Empo Retro. I left my own clothes there this morning, saying I'd return the disguise. They were happy to receive the purchase price for a few hours of rental, but I've changed my mind. Alister isn't here to talk me out of it.

As I catch the ferry back to the island, words from Miss Tigerlily's outburst pop into my mind. *Too much beauty. Skin deep. Save him. Your job.*

Suddenly I realise that I trust her. Every word she uttered told me something I need to know. Someone is in danger. I don't know the victim or the perpetrator, but there's more at stake than finding Deshi.

* * *

At Empo Retro, the shop assistant pulls a face when I tell her I'm keeping the clothes. "No good. You didn't say."

"I paid the price you sell these for, so I can keep them."

She throws my jeans and sweatshirt at me. "Not retro. Can't sell."

"I might have something retro at home," I lie, sidling up to a question. "Where do you get your clothes? Where did you get this pink and black dress?"

She shrugs. "Ask boss. I only work here. Maybe dead people."

Her words unnerve me but my reaction doesn't make sense. Of course many retro clothes come from dead people. People who kept clothes from their youth, their families sorting through old suitcases in the attic after their loved-ones die.

Why am I freaking out? Because of what Miss Tigerlily said. After a Google search and a browse through a retro shop, I've picked up a dangerous frock?

The thought feels both ridiculous and disturbing, but I decide not to change out of my disguise. The shop assistant's lingering pout suggests she might try to seize it.

Chapter 4

Back in the laneway, I dive into the maze of alleys looking for a street where I can hail a cab. The route looks different from the way I came in, but all these lanes must lead to the main road. It isn't far.

Cramped shops are open for business, selling everything from sporting goods to rice. There are few people about. I pass a young woman facing a hole in a wall, and assume she's making an offering at a Buddhist shrine. Like the roadside shrines in Ireland, one of which helped me save a friend's life only a few months ago, they contain a small statue of the deity being worshipped.

I walk on, but curiosity makes me glance back. Out of the corner of my eye, I catch sight of something that stops me. The woman is holding it.

A red cord.

Intrigued, I double back to loiter outside a doorway opposite the shrine. Peering around the woman as respectfully as possible, I can see a seated statue of a smiling man. He's not a Buddha. He's chubby with rosy skin and thin white hair, fluffy eyebrows, and a long pointed beard. His right hand is visible, holding a staff.

The woman seems to be performing some kind of ritual.

When she moves off, the smiling man beams across the lane—at *me.* In his left hand he's holding a small book—and a bundle of red cords.

He must be the lunar matchmaker, and I can feel his intention like an arrow. He's offering me a red cord, a reminder of my unbreakable connection to Alister, no matter what obstacles life throws at us. In my disappointment about whatever has drawn him away from meeting me, I've forgotten to trust him.

I want the red cord. But I need to make an offering in exchange. The other woman has left a small sweet wrapped in paper. I pat the empty pockets of my retro frock. There's nothing in my bag either. Remembering a stall selling incense, I retrace my steps and buy a single stick.

When I return, an elderly man in a baseball cap emerges from the doorway opposite the shrine. He's carrying a broom. As he sweeps the step, he says over his shoulder, "You find matches in Yue Lao's shrine."

Yue Lao. The lunar matchmaker has a name. I smile my thanks and stand in front of the shrine.

With no idea what the ritual might be, I put the incense stick in the little pot of sand and use a match to light it. As the smoke fills the niche, I bow my head and visualise Alister. My love bubbles up and brims over. Wherever we are in the world, we are joined by the red cord. It stretches, gets tangled, but never breaks.

When I open my eyes, Yue Lao is holding out his left hand. By instinct I whisper our names, so he can write them in what must be his book of lovers.

I take a red cord.

Wrapping it around my little finger, I worry that it might

slip off. Instead I put it into the pocket of my dress, bow my thanks to Yue Lao, and turn away from the shrine.

The man with the broom has gone back inside. I resume my walk, fingering the cord and wondering again if anything is ever determined by chance.

* * *

At the apartments, I can't wait to hear Alister's news and show him the red cord. I punch in our floor, hoping he's already home and has been too busy to text back.

He is. At home. And busy.

Stepping into the living room, I sense the space is occupied. Then a trill of laughter spills from the kitchen.

The laughter of a woman.

When I follow the sound, Alister rushes over and sweeps me up in a hug. "Selkie, at last. I was starting to worry that you were lost. Look who's arrived to help us. Meet Fleur's cousin, Su Yin."

The woman standing beside him is exquisite. Slender and fine-boned like many young Chinese women, but her mane of black hair has auburn streaks. Her facial features have an unusual sharpness, and the glittering light in her eyes adds an impishness to her expression that makes her beauty captivating. Judging by the way she tosses her hair, she knows it.

"We're just back from the airport," Alister says. "Su Yin's flown all the way from San Francisco to help us look for Deshi."

Her arrival made him abandon his post watching over me. He thought meeting her was more important than hearing what happened with Miss Tigerlily. Why does that bother me so much?

"What a surprise," I manage to say, putting out my hand.

Su Yin ignores it and throws her arms around my neck. Before I can pull away, the tips of her fingers are caressing my nape. The act is sensual, like nothing I've ever experienced, and a shiver of pleasure races down my spine, followed by a wave of revulsion. Surely she greeted Alister the same way.

"We need all the help we can get," Alister says, "but I can't quite believe you've made this sacrifice, Su Yin. What about your studies?"

She laughs again. The sound is like water bubbling over rocks. "My dissertation is in psychology. *The Emotional Journey of Loss.* This trip will be my research."

Alister frowns and I'm appalled at how pleased I am. "You want to use me as a case study?"

"Not you, Alister. Deshi. When we find him, I'll interview him."

For a moment no-one speaks. She's very sure we're going to find Deshi, but will they want to share their reunion with this little opportunist? And if she helps, will they have any choice in the matter?

Alister recovers. "Well, I'm glad you're so confident about finding him. It's infectious. But of course, that's not a deal I can make on his behalf in exchange for your help." He turns to me. "Selkie, I thought we'd put Su Yin on the couch, so it's easier for us all to work together."

Really?

"No," I hear myself say. Alister frowns again as I race on. "Just thinking about everyone's privacy. The bathroom is in our bedroom, and Su Yin needs a room that isn't a shared space. I'm sure there'll be another apartment in this building.

Then we'll be close but also have time to ourselves."

As I make eye contact with Su Yin her expression is unreadable, but we both know she isn't pleased. I've been dazzled by her presence—and distracted by my reaction to it—but now I wonder about her real agenda.

Will she help us to find Deshi?

Or is she working towards a different outcome?

An internet search locates a furnished rental several floors below and in a few minutes we've booked it. I offer to see Su Yin to her temporary home, and she glares at me as Alister agrees. He needs some time to himself too.

As we descend, I try to remember Miss Tigerlily's warnings but my mind is like mud. It feels significant that her reading coincided with Su Yin's arrival.

She breaks into my thoughts "You don't like me, do you?"

"I've only just met you so I haven't decided. But I wonder why you're here. We can probably use some inside help to find Deshi, but arriving unannounced like this seems ... odd."

"I told you, my dissertation."

"But if Deshi turns up, he might not want anyone pouncing on him for an interview. He doesn't know Alister, and he doesn't know you either. It's disrespectful to expect it. You assume too much."

Her eyes flash and she tosses her hair. "And you assume that Alister won't be tempted by a woman half your age."

I laugh. If seduction is her only agenda, I can relax. But something else about her is ringing alarm bells. What?

She takes on a sharper tone. "You think you're so powerful in your pink boots. You think you've won. But you don't know *anything*."

She pouts the rest of the way.

Her apartment is on the fourth floor, reminding me of the prediction of the tea leaves. Luckily she's too busy sulking to notice. I enter the access code to her front door. Inside, she drops her bag and looks around. It's the same floor plan as our own, simply furnished for a short-term stay.

She walks over to the window and looks out at the ocean. "It's a good place. Much better than where I live. You're kind. Thank you."

I'm floored. There's something very immature—or very inscrutable—about Su Yin.

"Why did you say that about tempting Alister?" I ask. "If that's your plan, wouldn't it be better to keep me in the dark?"

"Alister doesn't interest me. And all he talked about from the airport was Selkie this and Selkie that. Like you're his princess. I made that up about tempting him—to pay you back."

"For what?"

"You don't trust me."

"And now I trust you even less."

She throws herself on the couch and bursts into tears.

I let her cry and within a couple of minutes she's asleep. Pulling a blanket off the bed, I throw it over her, then let myself out.

Back in the lift, the air feels lighter without Su Yin. I reflect on my impressions of her. Is she just a mixed-up kid who's too beautiful for her own good and needs time to grow up? *Too much beauty. Skin deep.* Or something else?

Another phrase from Miss Tigerlily returns: *Remember your mother.*

My mother was a mixed-up kid with too much beauty. It meant I lost her when I was just a toddler. Is this link with my own past making me wary of Su Yin? For the first time I realise that by losing my mother so young, I have something in common with Deshi.

There's been no chance to review the recording, but the more I think about my encounter with Miss Tigerlily, the more I trust her. She knew who I was under the disguise. But what of her insights? How do they apply to me?

When I enter our apartment, Alister takes me in his arms in a proper embrace. "I'm sorry I abandoned you, Selkie. I had no idea Su Yin was on her way. Her text was a shock. But I thought she was making a sacrifice to help us, so I couldn't just leave her to arrive alone."

"I understand but I'm still pissed off. I came out from the meeting with my head about to explode, and you weren't there. I'd put myself through an ordeal, and you hadn't hung around to hear about it. Then your text sounded like you had a wonderful surprise."

"You don't like her."

"I don't *trust* her."

"She's young. She's flirty. She's ambitious. She's American—and Chinese. It's a potent combination. Almost as potent as an Australian who's named after the Celtic seal people." He gives me a cheeky grin. "But Su Yin's our link to Deshi."

"In exchange for him granting her an interview." I won't let it go. "Even if Deshi says yes in a rash moment, how confidential would it be? She could sell the story to the press. They love stuff like that."

"I had no idea that was her plan. And it's not going to happen. I'm hoping she'll drop it and help us because he's her cousin."

I pull back. "Just don't rely on anything she says. She's either manipulative or unstable. Downstairs just now, she started sobbing on her couch."

He throws his hands up. "You were only gone for a few minutes. What happened?"

"We had words in the lift, then she said she didn't mean them, that she was paying me back for not liking her."

"Do I need to go down and smooth things over?"

"No. She's asleep now. She dropped off like she was drugged."

"She's tired from the flight."

"Or she wanted me to feel sorry for her. With beauty like that, she's used to getting her own way. Just be wary, that's all."

He wraps me in his arms again. "I trust your judgement, you know that. But Su Yin's arrival could be a gift. We need to manage her, but at the same time let's keep an open mind about her motives."

* * *

With concerns about Su Yin muddying my thoughts, I slip into the bedroom where I can finally shed the camouflage and be myself. I've only just remembered how important that is.

When I emerge from the shower, I pick up the frock from the floor. The red cord is still in the pocket, safe for now. I'll surprise Alister with it in bed tonight.

He's at the front door taking delivery of a huge order of dumplings and other finger-food. We sit on cushions and eat off the coffee table while I answer his questions about Miss Tigerlily.

"She guessed why I was silent," I say. "And she knew about my hair."

"She actually described it?"

I blink a yes and wrap my lips around a heavenly meatball slider. "When I was leaving, she told me to stop being a blonde. She knew that my hair's spiky black and streaked with silver. I'm sure she's a true clairvoyant."

Alister laughs. "This is wonderful, Selkie. Miss Tigerlily can help us. If you're right about Su Yin, she might jump on the next plane when I insist on her help without conditions. Did you make an appointment for me to see Miss Tigerlily?"

"No. I wanted to talk to you first, and she wouldn't let me speak in case it tainted my trust. She told me to reflect on anything important that she'd told me. Wait till you hear it: an avalanche of psychic visions. It's all here on my phone."

"Don't play it yet. Tell me what you remember."

I close my eyes and let the words come.

"Ghosts?" He's gone pale. "Does she think Deshi's dead?"

It's the emotional roller-coaster he's always on. Every day he wonders if Deshi's gone, if his thirty-year search will end in heartache. But every time I see Deshi's baby photo, I get a strong sense of his presence. I've learned that photos can carry an essence of a person, and although my psychic twinges are cryptic, they've mostly been proven right. But I've never shared this intuition with Alister for fear of getting his hopes up—and then being wrong.

According to Su Yin, Deshi has never turned up at family gatherings in San Francisco. Why? Do his grandparents exclude him completely, in case his father tracks him down? It explains why Alister has welcomed Su Yin and missed the clanging of alarm bells. But I haven't forgotten that we're in

Hong Kong because of a tip-off from her.

The talk of ghosts makes me wonder what Deshi's presence really means. Am I sensing a living person? Or could he be the ghost from Miss Tigerlily's outburst, the one with unfinished business?

"I'm not sure anything Miss Tigerlily said is about Deshi," I say. "I was in the stranger's clothes. She told me that the outfit was pointing to something, that I should be wary." I tell him about the cheeky sales assistant in Empo Retro. "Of course a lot of pre-loved clothes belonged to people who are gone. In hindsight, it might have been better to buy new clothes from the market."

"I thought someone else's clothes would give her a better test."

"She passed the test. And she did say something about a baby. Not that Deshi's a baby anymore, but that's your memory of him and the way I see him too." I close my eyes again. "*Baby called Moses.*"

"That's Old Testament. Fleur's family isn't Christian."

"*Touched by the gods,*" I say. "I don't know if that fits with Moses. It might."

"Can you type up everything she said, Selkie?"

I'm surprised he doesn't want to listen, but he has another idea.

"I need to see her myself."

He picks up her card and dials her number. Amazingly, he's put straight through.

"You saw my friend Elkie earlier today. Not her real name. She came on behalf of me." He says his name and waits while Miss Tigerlily replies. Then he tells her what happened to Deshi. "We think his grandparents are in Hong Kong, and he could be here too. Superintendent Butler says you may be able to help."

He waits again. "Tonight?" He listens, nods, then scribbles an address on a notepad.

When he hangs up, his eyes are wet. "She's going to see me after work. In a café. She told me to come alone."

"Makes sense."

"She thinks I'm under some kind of threat. She asked me not to tell anyone where I'm meeting her." He rips the note off the pad and puts it in his pocket.

"Makes sense," I say again.

"Including you."

"Oh."

"I don't like it either, Selkie. But if I want her help, I have to do what she says."

Shit. He hasn't met her yet and he already trusts her. Because of me. But what if I really am out of my depth? What if everything I experienced with Miss Tigerlily wasn't what it seemed? I recall her presence. There was something very confident about it. Powerful.

Su Yin's words come back: "You think you're so powerful in your pink boots but you don't know anything."

What don't I know?

"I could wait for you nearby," I say. "Out of sight."

Alister shakes his head. "I don't recognise the address. This café may not be in the main tourist area. You could end up alone on the street. I'd rather you stay here. I'll call you as soon as I'm done."

He leaves the room to look up the location. Before I start transcribing Miss Tigerlily's insights onto my laptop, I notice he's left the notepad on the coffee table. I remove the top page.

It's a crazy idea and I don't have a pencil to do a rubbing over the imprint of the address. Would I really defy his wishes and follow him around the backstreets of Hong Kong?

Instead of answering my own question, I put buds in my ears and start playing back the reading, hoping something makes sense and quells the fluttering in my stomach. This cloak-and-dagger stuff is making me feel threatened. I haven't forgotten the tea leaves from the plane—or the shadow circling my neck.

Soon Miss Tigerlily's disembodied voice is shouting in my ear: *Danger! Danger! Danger!*

Chapter 5

J ust as he's leaving, Alister gets a text from Su Yin.

"She's woken up. She wants to know what we're doing."

"Don't tell her!" I calm my voice. "Sorry. I don't think you should tell her about Miss Tigerlily."

Alister frowns. "At least Su Yin sent a text and didn't just land on our doorstep."

"She's already done that."

"OK, her sudden arrival makes you suspicious, but she's our ticket to Deshi's grandparents. You don't have to like her, Selkie. Just don't rub her the wrong way."

Alister never pulls his punches. Calling it as we see it is how our relationship started, when I refused to sign a contract to become one of his seminar presenters. He turns nobodies into stars, so he hadn't experienced a walkout before. Now after a very long courtship, with some serious cold feet on my part, we're a couple. But a few short hours since arriving here, I'm sharing him with two other women—Miss Tigerlily and Su Yin—and feeling powerless to protect him.

"I won't spend the evening babysitting her."

"She won't bite." He reads aloud as he texts her back. "Order in some food and charge it to the apartment account.

Have a quiet night with a movie. We'll put our heads together tomorrow when we're all refreshed."

"OK." The knot in my shoulders eases.

"Same instructions for you, Miss Selkie."

That name's almost as fake as Elkie, but I say nothing as he puts his arms around me.

"There are no signposts leading to Deshi," he says. "Remember our plan? You're the one who told me that we can't control the helpers who turn up along the way. David Butler, Miss Tigerlily, Su Yin. We just have to grab them and strap ourselves in for the ride."

"Yeah, but I'm missing out on the ride. I don't even know where you're going tonight. At least let me know the district."

He tells me: Mong Kok. The name means nothing to me.

"Luckily it's not mainland China," he says, "where we'd be even more foreign, and the blind alleys would be guaranteed. When Su Yin said Hong Kong I was relieved. At least there's a chance to get help here and not get sucked under by the same level of corruption as the mainland." He pauses. "I hope."

He's remembering his last Hong Kong private eye, the one who we suspect 'forgot' about finding Deshi's grandparents. Alister kisses me and walks to the door.

"And Deshi,"—his voice catches—"might not even be alive."

It's an emotional moment to depart on and Alister is gone.

I stand for a long minute. With Su Yin out of the way, I'm a free agent. I didn't come here to watch movies, and more food can wait. I could call a cab to try to follow Alister, but his own cab will be long gone by now. Another idea pops into my head: eyeliner charcoal.

In the bedroom, I rummage through my makeup bag for the

little pot from my flatmate, Wanda. She's against all 'chemicals' so she mixes her own makeup. The handmade label confirms my memory: coconut oil, aloe vera and activated charcoal. Finding the little brush that goes with it, I wonder if this will work.

Back in the living room, I spread the notepaper on the table, before swishing a tiny amount of eyeliner across the paper. It's a little too moist so doesn't work as well as I'd hoped, but when I squint at it sideways I can just make out the address. A number and three words: 26 New Fan Road.

Without letting common sense interfere with my gut, I call a cab.

Grabbing my tote bag, I leave the apartment and summon the lift. As I wait on the landing, I hear squealing. Playful or panicked I'm not sure, but it's coming from Klaus's apartment. His door flies open and a woman's bare arm darts out. I notice a tiny tattoo on her wrist before she's pulled back inside, followed by another squeal. The door slams.

My only encounter with Klaus tells me he's got the local brothel on speed dial, but I walk to his door and press the buzzer. What if I'm interfering in something private? No answer.

The elevator arrives.

As I descend to street level, I worry about the woman I've just glimpsed. He said he handpicks his housemaids, *wink*. Because they enjoy extra activities? What if she was trying to escape? I decide to call Superintendent Butler, still wondering if the whole affair was between consenting adults. It goes through to voicemail, but before I can leave a message he picks up.

"It's Selkie Moon—the woman who saw the abduction last

night. Any news?"

"One of my men is asking stallholders about it tonight. So far no-one saw it. But a few of them remember you."

"Oh."

"They probably don't want to get involved," he says. "Thugs have ears."

We've landed in a hotbed of corruption and danger. Miss Tigerlily confirmed we need to be careful. Of what I have no idea. I take a breath and tell Butler what I've just witnessed on the landing.

"Klaus Hofmeier is your neighbour?" he says.

"You know him?"

"Professionally. He's the director of a child adoption agency. We cross paths occasionally. I'm interested to know that he lives at Ocean View. How old was the girl?"

"I only saw her bare arm. And the tattoo on her wrist."

"That suggests she's an adult. Women around here look younger than their age. Let it go. Just don't get in a lift with Hofmeier. He's got a reputation. But not for anything illegal."

Not a criminal, just a first-class creep.

In the foyer I pocket my phone in time to see a taxi pulling away. There's a distinctive profile in the back. Su Yin isn't watching movies either. At that moment my taxi arrives, and the driver gets an instruction straight from the movies.

"Follow that taxi."

On the narrow residential roads on our side of the island, taxis are common so it's not conspicuous to keep the other cab in sight. When we hit the traffic on the way to the tunnel crossing, there's no need for a high-speed chase through red lights. My driver stays close without being obvious.

Su Yin is not going bar-hopping in the local precinct where

we met David Butler last night. She's travelling under the harbour to Kowloon. The tension in my shoulders tightens as I anticipate catching her up to no good. She left the apartment after texting Alister. Perhaps she even saw him leave, then called a cab. Her timing seems subversive.

When her taxi turns from the busy highway into a dark street devoid of traffic, we follow. I glimpse the sign: Egg Street. The rear lights indicate her cab is pulling over, so I shrink back in my seat, telling my driver to keep going and drop me around the next corner.

Fumbling to pay the fare, I lose precious seconds. As Su Yin's cab speeds past me, I'm stepping onto the pavement. When I walk to the corner and look back down Egg Street, her shadow is disappearing down an alley.

The atmosphere around me presses in. This is just the kind of dark street Alister warned me about. Narrow and empty, with no shops, more of a warehouse district with only blank walls and closed roller-doors facing the street. I look up but the apartments are dark: no noisy air-conditioners signifying private lives behind curtains; no poles waving friendly washing. No more taxis passing either.

What business could Su Yin have in this place?

Shivering in the cool air, I move towards the light coming from the alley. Rubbish litters a cracked concrete floor and at the far end, light spills from a doorway. I strain my ears but I can't hear any music—only muffled voices and some strange clicking sounds. As much as I need to know what she's up to, there's no way I'm going up there.

Wedging myself into a space between two buildings, I check my phone. No reception.

After several minutes of indecision, wondering what

predicament I've got myself into, I hear voices from the alley. As I shrink out of sight, five figures pass me. Four men. And behind them, Su Yin.

She knows people in Hong Kong. Relatives? But this doesn't look like a family gathering. She could have a lead and be asking around about Deshi's grandparents. Or she's known all along where Deshi is and she's met up with him. But none of these men is young enough to be Alister's son.

Instinct tells me to stay hidden. As I watch the retreating group, a flashing neon sign on the busy road makes me blink. Its light illuminates Su Yin's black hair, turning the auburn streaks to orange, then flame red. As my eyelids flutter, the bizarre happens. She disappears.

I blink again. There's no Su Yin. There are only four men walking away. Did she slip down a side alley? But I was watching her the whole time. Her hair was aflame, then she was gone. Or was it one of my visions and I've imagined the whole thing?

A rumbling engine makes me turn. A cab pulls up. It's empty of passengers and I'm so relieved that I run to the back door and jump in.

The driver looks at me via the rear view mirror. "Where you going?"

I should go home but not if that's where Su Yin's gone. Being with those men was bad enough, but vanishing like that is freaking me out. I've suspected her of hiding her true motives but I've been thinking money—she knows Alister's loaded. Now it appears we're dealing with ... something else.

Phrases from Miss Tigerlily's prediction return in a rush. *Changes shape. Sly. Dark.*

Am I dealing with something surreal?

Wants to play. Wants to win.

Win against … Alister?

New Fan Road. There might still be time to check on him. What's happened here has changed the stakes. I was worried about spying but what about his safety? Miss Tigerlily told him he was under threat, but his focus will be on clues to finding Deshi, not on protecting himself. With a shaking hand I show the driver the note with the address of the café. He looks around for a moment, then drives off.

Sinking into the old leather seat, I try to calm my breathing. This cab turned up at just the right time.

After putting a few kilometres between us and Egg Street, my driver says, "I tell you traditional Chinese story. About wife of Emperor Wu. You like?"

Could a story make me feel better? "OK."

"Madam Li very beautiful," he begins. "But she die. Emperor sad. She come back as shadow. He happy."

Why is he telling me this? A shadow has been following *me*.

"How could his wife become a shadow?" I ask.

"I say wife but she not the big wife. Second wife. Emperor Wu have many wives. Madam Li, she dead, get jealous of real wives. She put soul in shadow puppet, dance behind screen for emperor as *ghost wife*."

With these words something sucks the air out of me and I'm plunged into a living horror movie. As I gasp for breath, my vision starts strobing as ghostly auras flash before my eyes. Slashes of white light claw at my retina, then thunder and lightning explode in my head. A kaleidoscope of colours zigzags across my eyeballs in patterns that make me dizzy. Then bring up my lunch.

"Stop the car," I scream.

Just in time, we pull over. I get the door open and throw up. As my head hangs upside down at gutter level, the feet passing by don't even falter in their rhythm. They're dancing to the beat in my brain.

My driver leaves me alone, but I can sense him watching over me. When I flop back inside and collapse like a deflated cushion, he passes me a paper towel. "You drunk?"

While I wipe my face and mouth, the pounding in my head makes me want to close my eyes, but I'm afraid of what I'll see. A nightmare of bright shadows? But when I lower my lids, the ghosts have gone.

Ghosts. Shadows. I keep thinking about them.

With the part of my brain that's still hanging onto reality, I wonder if this was a migraine. My father gets them after eating chocolate and he's warned me that I might inherit them. He's told me about the strobing, the visual distortions. Except his headaches last for days, not minutes. But after the flashing neon sign, this explanation makes sense.

My first mini-migraine. My day has been stressful enough to cause it.

Pulling myself together, I pay the driver. I don't ask for more information about the shadow wife, but legends carry power. Superstitions always linger from the old days, especially amongst older generations. On my trip to Ireland last year, I had to untangle myself from faerie legends when they got in the way of my quest. To be honest, I attract them. The Irish experience might be useful here: keep looking for the truth amidst the fantasy.

When I look up, I see a sign in both English and Chinese. Shadow Puppet Theatre
NOW SHOWING

EMPEROR WU AND MADAM LI

"This your address," my driver says. "You sick right outside."

As I step out, he leans across and hands me his card.

Winston, Storytelling Taxi Driver.

If I wasn't still recovering, it would make me smile. Never underestimate the business acumen of even a humble cab driver.

"You want taxi, you call Winston." He beams. "I take you anywhere you like to go. And I tell different story next time."

Looking at the street numbers, I realise that the address is not the theatre. The sign is an advertising banner with a life-sized shadow puppet wearing a traditional gown. I'm standing in full view of 26 New Fan Road, an open-fronted shop full of lucky golden cats waving at me. So much for a stealthy approach. But Alister said they were meeting in a café. Was that a smokescreen or did my trick with the eyeliner fail? Then I see stairs leading to the floor above.

At the back of the store, a man on a mobile phone is sitting on a plastic stool. I navigate my way around mountains of what look like funeral goods—incense and hell money. After the prediction of the tea leaves, I can't get away from death.

"Excuse me. Is there a restaurant upstairs?"

He doesn't look up from what sounds like a horse race. I think he hasn't heard me or isn't going to answer, but as I move away, he mumbles a word that sounds like 'secret'.

"What did you say?"

He ignores me.

A secret café. They exist in every city, no doubt avoiding health and licensing laws. A perfect venue for Miss Tigerlily to choose. In her job she'd need to be careful who she's seen meeting up with—especially after her visit today from a blonde in a pink and black frock. Does the Jadeite Group know that she moonlights as Miss Tigerlily, psychic to the police?

While I pretend to browse paper mache smart phones—to burn for your dead relatives to use in the afterlife—I consider my next move. But the decision is resolved by the sound of footsteps on the stairs. Alister appears. The tightness in my chest eases when I see he's OK. I'm about to go after him, when I hear the clatter of a woman's heels. Instinct tells me to wait as Miss Tigerlily emerges from the stairwell.

If I wasn't expecting her, I wouldn't have recognised the woman in the shapeless smock. The floral pattern is like the hundreds hanging in any market stall. Only her posture, upright and confident, gives her away. Beneath the cheap blouse is the same silk pencil skirt she wore this morning.

She pauses on the pavement and looks right and left. Alister has hailed a cab. As Miss Tigerlily moves off, my legs make the decision and I fall in step behind her. We wend our way through the evening throng, and I realise how clever her disguise is. She blends in. Meanwhile, in my jeans and jacket and my own black hair, I look very different from 'Elkie'. It gives me confidence in my role as a tail. But if she's as psychic as she seemed, could she sense she's being followed and recognise me? What will I say if she confronts me?

The question makes me wonder what I hope to discover. As much as I'm following my gut, my actions suddenly feel out of line. Inspector Butler trusts her. I trust her. Alister has consulted her because of my experience. He's no doubt told her everything about Deshi, and she may have done a psychic reading in a quiet corner of the café. I hope she's given him something he can make sense of.

As she turns into what I see is Nathan Road, I wonder if my own possessiveness of Alister and his quest is the real reason for following her. She passed my three tests with psychic flair and gave me a lot of clues to unravel. I'm sure she's the real deal. Then something happened to change my mood.

Su Yin arrived.

As I move through the sea of passers-by and keep up with Miss Tigerlily's brisk pace, I consider my mistrust of Su Yin. How valid is it? There could be many reasons for her meeting with those men. A dark street after hours isn't necessarily sinister. And the simplest explanation for her vanishing act is a trick of the light—the flashing sign setting up the rhythm that minutes later triggered my migraine.

Alister's right. Both Miss Tigerlily and Su Yin have resources that we don't. My desire to be the one who finds Deshi is an obstruction. It's a moment of painful self-recrimination. If I truly want to help him, I need to get out of the way.

My pace slows and I lose sight of Miss Tigerlily. Then she reappears in her silk suit on the other side of the street, almost outside the Jadeite building. She's slipped off her blouse and resumed her corporate appearance.

Instead of tailing her, I should call Alister. He'll be on his way home, expecting to find me there. I stop and pull out my phone, but when I look up, Miss Tigerlily is talking to a woman. A Caucasian woman with wavy auburn hair. Was she waiting? They're deep in conversation until Miss Tigerlily turns away. The woman grabs her arm, but Miss Tigerlily pulls free and swipes herself through a side door into her building. I watch the other woman's body language. Hands on hips, then shoulders slumped.

In the next moment, she hails a taxi and is gone.

Chapter 6

Alister answers my call, his excitement tinged with exhaustion. "Selkie, I'm glad you're still up. I'm in traffic on my way home. Miss Tigerlily was as psychic as you said. A torrent of visions, scribbled in the form of a mind-map. With your help I may even decipher it. And she had a reason for meeting at this particular place, but something happened. I'll explain when I see you."

He wants my help. While instead of being a team player, I've been trying to be the star of the show.

"I'm not at home, Alister. I've done something stupid."

Stepping into a doorway, I take a deep breath and confess to following him. I leave out Su Yin and her vanishing act, as well as my undignified deposit in the gutter. When he makes no comment, I end with an apology.

"Where are you now?" he asks.

"Nathan Road. I'll get a cab."

"Do that. Then we'll talk."

He's angry. I'll survive his fury, but the disappointment in his voice is worse. In anticipation of the showdown we'll have to have, butterflies collide in my belly all the way home. My driver is silent and I almost miss the distraction that another folk tale from Winston would have provided. All my loyalties are getting jumbled up.

But when I open the door to our apartment, Alister is not alone. He's sitting on the couch opposite Su Yin. She's leaning towards him from an armchair, her long hair brushing the top of the coffee table. At my entrance, she looks up and shows me her teeth.

Alister looks at me. "I know it's late but Su Yin was still awake, so I invited her to join us. She has exciting news."

"Great." I walk over and kiss him on the cheek so that Su Yin doesn't detect the rift between us. Luckily he puts his arm around me. "Can I get everyone a drink?"

Drinks are my excuse to slip into the kitchen and find something to eat. After what's happened, I don't think I can join this threesome on an empty stomach. Food first, followed by alcohol. Lots of it.

"There's beer in the fridge," Alister says. "And spirits in that cabinet."

"Perfect." Su Yin smiles. "I'll make beer cocktails."

"I'm game," Alister replies.

As Su Yin follows me into the kitchen, I try to remember my resolution about her. She's a helper. Be nice.

Try not to kill her.

After she grabs three bottles of cold beer, I take over at the fridge door. To my horror, she leans in close and nips me on the ear with her teeth. I'm so startled I almost cry out.

"I know what you are, Selkie." She laughs her rippling laugh. "But you don't know what I am. Not yet."

As she leaves the room, Miss Tigerlily's words come back: *Danger! Danger! Danger!*

But who's in danger? And why am I suddenly cold?

After toasting the last of the bread and lathering it with way too much butter, I feel ready to return to the living room where Su Yin and Alister are sipping their drinks.

I slug back my cocktail and collapse in a fit of coughing. It dashes the last remnants of my composure, but it gives me time to think. I'm going to keep trusting my gut.

"I saw you earlier tonight," I say to her. "On Egg Street."

Alister's answer stuns me into silence. "Selkie, that's the news. Su Yin was on Egg Street for a very good reason. She met up with Deshi's grandfather. He plays mahjong there every Tuesday night with a bunch of friends. It's why she was too excited to sleep when she got back."

And now I've got egg all over me.

"My mom gave me his number." Her eyes sparkle with victory. "She's not happy that I'm over here all by myself." She laughs. "Too dangerous."

In spite of the news, I can't help thinking: dangerous for everyone she meets.

"So Mom told me to contact my family here in Hong Kong. If I'd, like, asked her for their number she would have been so suspicious. Like I haven't seen them since I was a kid, and they're *old*. But I let her think she was making me call them. And when he answered—my great uncle, second cousin, whatever—Mom had already called him and reminded him who I am. He didn't have much choice; he had to see me. But he didn't sound like he wanted me to come to their house. Instead he told me to drop by his mahjong game."

The details sound true. The voices and the clacking sounds fit. The men I saw her with were the right age. So why doesn't the story feel right? But when I look at Alister, his eyes are huge, and I hate myself for my lingering doubts. What the hell is wrong with me? This is the closest he's come to Deshi in thirty years.

I slip my arm through his. "Your father-in-law."

He nods. "Winston Wong."

To say my mind does a backflip is an understatement. Winston. I've heard his name before, but surely I haven't just spent a taxi ride in the company of Alister's missing father-in-law? In a city the size of Hong Kong what are the chances? Except for the fact that he picked me up on Egg Street and that something about the storytelling driver made an impression on me that the old men with Su Yin didn't.

Alister says, "I wonder if I'd recognise Winston after all these years. He blamed me for getting Fleur pregnant, but he let us get married. Then he avoided me as much as he could."

He moves to the bookcase and picks up the dossier of photos he always carries, flipping to a Wong family portrait. A smiling Fleur, uncannily like Su Yin, holds her baby. Her parents stand behind her. I've seen the photo before but now I really look at Winston, who's unmistakable even after all these years, in spite of the receding hairline and fuller face.

"He must be pushing seventy," Alister says. "An old man."

"You got that right," Su Yin says.

I look at her, trying in vain to see something to trust. Even if Winston was playing mahjong before he picked me up, there wasn't time for her to meet with him for more than a few minutes. And where was his cab? I'm sure she's lying. Why? A word returns: *sly*.

"What did he say about Deshi?" I'm hoping to expose her.

She smirks. "As if I'd ask him straight off! But he'll tell me." Her voice takes on the edge of a razor wire. "An old man will tell his sweet little niece anything ... if she's savvy enough."

Poor Winston. Even though he took off with Deshi, I

wouldn't wish Su Yin on him. She should do a psychological dissertation on herself. And do we need her? I've got Winston's number on his business card.

"Su Yin is meeting with him again tomorrow," Alister says. "She's going to get to know him better—"

"— then go in for the kill." Her tinkling laugh mocks her words.

While I've been playing amateur sleuth and treating the local gutters to the contents of my stomach, they've made plans. I removed myself from the discussion, and Alister handed over this most delicate negotiation to Su Yin. If she blows it, he'll lose his chance to find Deshi.

Perhaps his last chance.

But in a few hours, she appears to have done what years of private eyes failed to do. Her results are so targeted that Alister trusts her, while I collided with Winston by chance.

Did he make an appointment with Su Yin, but turned up late? Then he saw me and picked up the fare? Unless he was playing games himself.

It might run in the family.

Alister's tension is palpable. In his excitement, he's forgotten Su Yin's motives. I'm sure that the closer we get to Deshi, the more she'll use the wiliness she's so proud of on us. Unless she's managed to get rid of me by then. I have no idea how she'd do that, but the nip on my ear is throbbing its reminder.

She yawns, gulps down the rest of her cocktail and stands up. "See you tomorrow." She's speaking to Alister.

He gets up and puts his hand on her shoulder. "I can't thank you enough, Su Yin, for everything you've done. You know how much this means to me."

"Yeah, I know. It's the closest you've ever come to finding Deshi. You're more grateful than you can ever put into words."

He laughs and walks her to the door.

When he returns, I've made a call. I tell myself I'm not deceiving him; I'm protecting him with insurance.

"What a night." He takes me in his arms and presses his lips into my hair. "I'd love to take you to bed, but I'm too wired."

"Makes sense." When I kiss him, his warm response says that he's forgiven me for tonight's spying. "Stretch out on the couch. I'll make more cocktails."

"She's something else, isn't she?"

"Yeah." I've got some words in mind.

"It's all happened so fast. Prickly types like Su Yin are often the ones who get things done. They don't waste time being nice. I thought she'd ask me for more money, but she hasn't."

Too savvy.

"Did you show her Miss Tigerlily's drawings?" I wonder where they are.

"No. I wouldn't do that behind your back, Selkie. And after meeting Winston, she was so full of her own news that I didn't mention Miss Tigerlily."

Good.

But there's not a thing I can say to warn him. Not yet. I'm counting on my phone call to do its job.

Alister goes to his coat that's hanging on the hooks inside the front door. He returns with a paper napkin and spreads it on the table.

"I have no idea what any of these symbols mean." He points to the crude drawings. "I won't tell you what she said in case it interrupts your intuition."

With tension blurring my vision, I barely have a chance to

focus before the intercom rings.

Alister looks at his watch. "It's almost midnight. They must have the wrong apartment."

"It's OK. I've asked someone to pop over." Under a pretext.

Alister frowns and folds up the map, but he doesn't quiz me.

I meet our visitor on the landing and invite him in. His expression shows he's wondering what he's wanted for. When he walks into the living room and sees Alister, he spins around as if to run, but I'm right behind him. He stops. Setting his jaw, he turns back.

Meanwhile, Alister has stood up—and dropped his glass.

"Hello Alister," Winston says. "We wonder how long it take you to find us."

Chapter 7

As I rush into the kitchen and back with more beers, Winston and Alister sit down in the armchairs opposite each other, their postures a fixed tableau. Alister is leaning forward like a coiled cobra, and Winston has slumped against the cushions like an elderly teddy bear.

"What's going on, Selkie?" Alister's voice is harder than I've ever heard it.

I tell him how I met Winston. "I'm sorry I didn't explain. It was too complicated and I wanted to get you two together tonight—and save a lot of time."

Alister's tight nod says we won't discuss Su Yin until we're alone.

He turns to Winston and growls. "You've wondered how long it would take me to track you down? After you stole my son? Try thirty years. So let's get this over with. Where's Deshi?"

Winston is staring into his beer. "It's long story, Alister."

"Spare me the bloody story. Tell me where he is."

"I tell you everything. Things very bad for Rose and me. Since Fleur die, things very bad. Since Deshi stolen, things get more bad."

He starts to cry.

"It's called karma, Winston. Bad things come back to bite you. So make them right. Put me in touch with Deshi."

But Winston is shaking his head and Alister springs from his seat. When he grabs Winston's collar, I cry out and he lets go.

"I tell you everything," Winston whimpers. "We do bad thing, but we not hiding. We need help."

Alister's rage has frightened me. He's got every reason to hurt Winston, but it's a side of him I haven't seen.

Then, like a puff of steam, it leaves him. He drops his voice. "I won't hear another word until you tell me where Deshi is. Is he ... *alive?*"

Winston is sobbing now. "I do not know. Rose do not know. We do not know. We think Deshi not dead, we not see his ghost, but we ... *do not know.*"

The colour has drained from Alister's face.

"He *stolen*," Winston says. "We take Deshi from San Francisco, bring him to Hong Kong to be Chinese boy. We hide, change his name to Wong Chi Lung. It's noble name of first king of China, means son of dragon.

"No-one look for us," he continues. "We think all OK. Then Rose go to market with Chi Lung and robbers *steal* him. Rose chase them, but it night time. They gone."

It's exactly what I witnessed last night. The night market. A baby taken. A woman running.

"When?" Alister's voice is so thin it's barely audible.

"Not long after we come back. Rose go to night market, come home crying. He gone now ... thirty years."

Deshi is gone. Only weeks after losing his mother to a gunman, he lost his father. Then, soon after, he was stolen away again. While I wrap my mind around this triple tragedy,

Alister stares straight ahead, his eyes blank. The news has broken him. I go to him and put my arm around his shoulder, but he's far away and doesn't respond.

"After he go," Winston says, "we try to find him but it no good. We put poster in every shop, with photo. You see this baby? No answer. We ask our family in San Francisco if you steal him back. They spy on you but you not have him. Maybe family in China pay good money for baby boy. We know we never find him in China, give up."

They didn't involve the police. Because their custody of Deshi couldn't be scrutinised? But they never let Alister know—even anonymously. To save face that they couldn't protect their grandson, they've sat on their tragedy for thirty years. And let Alister sit on his.

They allowed the not-knowing to corrode his soul.

In the silence that follows, Winston launches into more of his woes. News worse than the loss of baby Deshi?

"After that bad things start happen," he says. "Very bad. We not sleep. Every night we ... haunted!"

Winston's crazed look suggests superstition. They don't think Deshi's dead so who could be haunting them? But this story is too much. To silence him, I put my hand on his shoulder.

I don't know what to do. Send Winston home, now that we've finally made contact? Or wait out Alister's dazed state? What if Winston is lying and my brinkmanship has ruined Su Yin's chances of finding out the truth? What if he goes into hiding again? He might have more to tell us, so I can't take the chance. I order in some food and pour more beer. It's going to be a long night.

* * *

Winston eats and drinks as if he's starving. But Alister just drinks. He's abandoned the cocktails for straight bourbon. Cradling his glass, he stares into space like a man who's lost the will to live.

Eventually, I encourage him to stand up and I guide him to the bedroom. After pulling the door behind us, I put him to bed.

Then I kneel on the floor beside him. "You're hurting and you're empty, Haiku. Winston should have told you the truth long before this. It'll take time to recover. I know it looks like finding Deshi just got harder, but I'm not going anywhere. Together we'll follow the clues wherever they take us."

He's silent. And what am I promising? Not to find Deshi, only to look for him. Alister's been looking for thirty years.

I stroke him until his breathing slows, then return to the living room, relieved that Winston hasn't let himself out.

"What else can you tell me about Deshi's abduction?"

Winston shrugs. "It happen in Temple Street Night Market. I make baby cart for Chi Lung. Rose take him to market. She want to buy fresh lychee, look away from cart. Men take him and run. She chase, but they too fast."

As he talks, a question comes. "What was Rose wearing that night? Do you remember?"

"Rose keep blouse. She put it on shrine with baby clothes and toys. Maybe Chi Lung see her blouse in his dream, know Rose his po po—and come back."

"A yellow blouse," I say.

For the first time I doubt the reality of what I saw. Did I witness a real woman in an old-fashioned yellow blouse? Or a psychic re-enactment of Deshi's kidnapping?

But Winston has a story he's desperate to tell. The other story he's been sitting on for three decades.

"Fleur very angry," he says. "She angry at shooter for kill her. She just young girl and now because of shooter she *dead*. Alister make Fleur angry too. He not say goodbye proper way."

"What do you mean? What's the proper way?"

"Chinese way. He not give her things she need for afterlife. Now she ... *ghost*. Haunt us every night."

He thinks Fleur's the ghost? It fits with their belief that Deshi is alive. It's a comfort to think he's thriving somewhere, but something about this story doesn't ring true.

"If Fleur is angry with Alister," I ask, "why is she haunting you?"

He shrugs again. "Maybe she haunt him too. It's his fault."

"What happened at Fleur's funeral? Why didn't Alister give Fleur the right gifts?"

"He not come. He ... stay home."

I don't believe this and the truth hits me. "You didn't allow him to attend Fleur's funeral, did you? How could you do that? She was his wife and the mother of his son."

Winston stares into his beer. "He's not ... Chinese."

Bloody hell. They didn't want her to marry him, so they excluded him from her funeral, then stole his son. And now that they think they're being haunted, they blame Alister. For a moment I want to leap across the coffee table and grab his lapels myself.

Instead I ask, "How do you know she's haunting you?"

He continues to hang his head. "We make shrine for Fleur. Rose put Fleur's ashes on shrine. I say no, take ashes to temple. If Fleur stay with us, she miss us too much. But Rose too sad, not listen.

"Every night," he continues, "I leave food for Fleur's ghost. She not eat! She bang on pot holding ashes. Bang, bang, bang. Very noisy, wake us up. Last few months, it get very bad. Alister not say goodbye at funeral. Now Fleur is ... angry ghost."

The beer has caught up with him and he dissolves into tears again. I slip a cushion under his head and throw a blanket over him.

I should go to bed myself, but I want to check something. Winston didn't say how he knows the ghost is Fleur. I google the term 'angry ghost'. In Chinese folklore, the spirit of a person who has died an unnatural or unjust death can return as a vengeful ghost to seek retribution. So her murderer is the one responsible for her ghostly state—and he died right after she did.

This should be good news, but it doesn't feel like it. The whole story could just be a manifestation of their guilt, keeping Fleur's ashes and obsessively putting out food, only to lie awake all night imagining they can hear her ghost banging out an angry rhythm on her funeral pot. But I know from personal experience that ghosts exist. It's possible Fleur really is haunting them. Why?

Why would she be hanging around, unable to go to the afterlife? Unable or unwilling? Winston's comment about Fleur's anger makes me latch onto something Miss Tigerlily said: *Carrying bygones. Can't let go.*

Does Fleur's ghost know that her parents kidnapped Deshi, then lost him?

Chapter 8

Alister lies beside me drugged by alcohol. After the evening's revelations, I'm glad he's out of it, but sleep eludes me. Instead of dwelling on the shock of Deshi's second abduction or visions of Fleur in ghost form, I can't stop thinking about Su Yin. I didn't ask Winston about her. Surely there wasn't enough time for her to speak to him in the mahjong room, before he picked me up in his cab.

What else has she lied about?

Her DNA test proves she's related to Winston and Deshi. In every other way she's an enigma. A shadow woman. The sign to the shadow puppet theatre keeps flashing into my mind.

Climbing out of bed, I check on Alister who's breathing deeply. Then I make sure that Winston is still in the living room. He's on his back, snoring softly. Undisturbed by the nightly banging of his daughter's ghost, he's crashed. I won't wake him. He may be a child abductor but he's lived with his own demons into old age. My questions about Su Yin can wait until tomorrow.

Back in bed I snuggle up to Alister, hoping it comforts him, and drop into a fitful sleep. The horrors of the day inspire technicolour dreams.

A baby boy is sailing down a river in a little boat. It's a

Chinese junk with a familiar pink and black patchwork sail. The boat rocks and jerks in a breeze. Something about the baby doesn't fit the scene. The landscape is flat and garish like a painting sold in a market, but the baby is round and real. He's wearing a Carnaby Street hat that slips off to reveal a bald head. Many babies are bald so why does it seem important? Something I'm missing.

My attention is distracted by a huge shadow that appears behind the sail. A mythical creature has risen from the water, the silhouette of its head filling the sail and showing the unmistakable outline of sharp teeth. I can't make out its shape. It moves like a puppet behind a screen, its size making it even more frightening.

The baby gurgles and flaps his chubby arms, unaware of the danger looming over him. But before I can cry out a warning, the child is gone—and I'm weeping with loss and despair.

* * *

When I open my eyes, daylight is leaking around the curtains. But the image of the empty boat lingers. Not just a boat, a junk. Like the one I saw from the ferry yesterday.

Leaning over Alister, I'm relieved he's still asleep. It's the best tonic for last night's shock. I slide out from under the sheets and pull on a robe. I've remembered where else I saw a junk. Not just from the ferry. Somewhere else.

In the walk-in wardrobe, the in-flight magazine is stuffed inside my tote bag. There were a couple of articles about Hong Kong I wanted to keep. Flipping through it now, I see a comment scribbled by the previous passenger. Next to a restaurant directory, he's written:

Find Wind Sand Chicken.

Under other circumstances this reference to the Hong Kong specialty, known for its crisp skin and garlic coating, would make me hungry. Now I keep flipping until I find the story about a handful of old boatmen who still take pleasure cruises by junk. Did this story trigger the boat in my dream? There are several close-ups of craggy faces and toothless smiles, the men's tiny boats behind them, moored between yachts and other vessels.

At a noise from the bedroom, I drop the magazine back in my bag. At least the origin of the junk is solved. What about the monster behind the sail? The baby must be Deshi.

Alister emerges from the bathroom.

I'm so elated to have him back that I make a joke. "How's the head?"

No answer. He looks straight through me, the way he stared last night. When I walk over and wrap my arms around his waist, he doesn't respond.

"We're not going to give up searching," I murmur. "Deshi is out there, and we haven't even started on Miss Tigerlily's map."

As I hold him, Alister's knees crumple. He slips from my embrace and sits on the edge of the bed. When I step back, his head drops into his hands as if he can no longer hold it up. He's in deepest despair, and nothing I say to him is getting through. As I sit on the floor in front of him and stare into his vacant face, I gulp down a whimper.

Helping him back under the covers, I kiss his forehead. "You've had a terrible shock. Give yourself time."

Alister doesn't even blink.

In the living room, Winston is up and checking his phone.

"Where Alister? He OK?"

"What do you think?"

"He not OK. He angry. He got broken heart. He drink too much."

If only it's just an almighty hangover.

"People calling taxi." He moves towards the apartment door with me at his heels.

As he opens the door, the lift bell pings and out steps Su Yin. Winston rears back, lets out a high-pitched wail, and races past her into the elevator just as the doors are closing. Did he think he just confronted his daughter's ghost?

Su Yin and I stare at each other.

"Who's your freaky friend?" she asks.

We all looked at his photo in Alister's album last night, but she didn't recognise Winston. Both their reactions confirm that she lied about meeting him.

"A cab driver," I say. "I met him on Egg Street last night."

She laughs. "Can't help checking up on me, can you, Selkie? But your spy doesn't look too reliable, does he?"

As we speak, I let the apartment door close behind me. She's not coming inside.

"Alister's got a hangover," I say. "Your beer cocktails pack a punch."

The flattery works. And she hasn't come here to see me. She laughs again and presses the button for the elevator, while I imagine it depositing a scurrying Winston into the lobby.

When it arrives, she smirks. "I'll be in touch when I find Deshi."

"Do that."

The promise should keep her busy for a while, especially if Winston keeps bolting at the sight of her.

Back inside the apartment, Alister hasn't moved. His eyes are open and he's staring at the wall. Crawling in beside him, I toss and turn for an hour, my mind churning over the yellow blouse. Why did I have a psychic vision of Deshi's abduction? Is there a clue there I've missed? When Alister gets his old self back, my insights might give us a lead.

Finally I go to the bathroom where I'm shocked by the bags under my eyes. Even my hair has drooped. I take a quick shower but when I'm reaching for a towel, the shadow is suddenly back, this time sucking the air from me. As I claw at my throat and fight for each breath, I'm suddenly aware of what it wants.

Alister.

With that thought it's gone, but I race into the bedroom in a panic.

He's asleep.

I look down at his face, handsome without those glazed eyes, and the love I've never felt for another human being rises up. I didn't get to show him the red cord, but I can feel it, coiling warm threads around my heart and spinning me in its spell. I've made the journey to this moment complicated, but he's the man I want.

A sob escapes. As I stand beside his sleeping form, I recall the power of the shadow. Just as fierce, it's fighting with my love. Gone for now, but what is it? And why is it here?

Chapter 9

Remembering Alister's eaten nothing since last night, I warm up some frozen bao buns. When I offer him one, his eyes are open again, but he doesn't acknowledge it or me.

What if he's ill? Really ill? The thought douses me in dread. I don't know how to help him and until I'm sure he's OK, I can't leave him on his own. I'm a stranger here. Who can I turn to? Who can I truly trust?

The phone rings. I return to the kitchen to answer it.

"David Butler here."

At the sound of his voice, I remember we have an ally. Does he have news about the abduction?

"It's about Miss Tigerlily. She's missing."

I clutch the counter for support. "When? I consulted with her yesterday. Then Alister saw her last night." I give him the address in New Fan Road and tell him how I followed her all the way to the Jadeite building. "I saw her swipe herself inside. Doesn't the building have CCTV?"

"What time?"

"I rang Alister right after." I check my calls. "At 9.17pm."

"She hasn't been seen since. Her housemaid rang me this morning to say she didn't come home last night. She's missed her tai chi and an early morning meeting. She's not answering her phone. It's … completely out of character." His voice cracks and I sense how close they are. He pulls himself together. "I need you and Mr Sloane to come in and make statements."

"Of course I want to help, but that might be difficult at the moment." I update him on Winston's news and Alister's condition.

"I'll put you in touch with a doctor. You two are my only witnesses to her movements last night. Something might have happened at her meeting with Sloane, something that put her in danger."

"She disguised herself in a cheap blouse, but slipped it off as she reached her building."

"So she thought she might be followed."

Was someone following her besides me?

"There was a woman," I cry. "When Miss Tigerlily stopped outside her building, a woman came up and spoke to her. As if she'd been waiting."

He pounces. "What did she look like?"

I think back. "Caucasian. Wavy reddish-brown hair. Stocky build. I didn't see her face clearly but I'd guess around forty? I'm trying to remember what she was wearing. Jeans?"

"It's OK. I know who she is. I thought I'd convinced her to go home. Leave it with me. If she saw something, I might not need your statements. And I'll call you back with the name and number of that doctor."

When Butler calls again, I'm ready for him.

"Dr Lee." He gives me a number. "He's your man for anything psychological."

I think of Dr Tejala Turnbull, a hypnotherapist in Hawaii

who helped me with my own demons. Should I take Alister home?

Butler says, "I spoke to Beth, the woman you saw. She confirmed that she accosted Miss Tigerlily last night. She gave Beth the brush-off, and Beth thought she seemed distracted by something—something on the other side of the street." I was on the other side of the street. "But she only saw what you saw. Miss Tigerlily entering her building."

When he hangs up, I drop my phone on the counter, reeling from the news. I forgot to ask him about the abduction in the market but we've both got other things on our minds.

Everything is getting complicated. These incidents can't be just coincidence. Why are they happening and what do they mean?

Dr Lee's number is on the notepad in front of me. Alister might be all right tomorrow, but what if he isn't? With trembling fingers I make the call. A receptionist called Cindy answers and I blurt out the problem.

"He has been like this for how long?" she asks.

Her respectful tone calms me a little. "Overnight."

She asks for our names and where I'm calling from. "Hold one moment."

It's a long minute before she's back on the line.

"Dr Lee's appointments are full today, also for the rest of the week. He said he is sorry he can't come to the phone, but I told him your friend's symptoms and how urgent this sounds. He said he can make a house call tonight after work."

Relief washes over me. As I give her our address, my emotions overflow. "I can't thank you enough. I've been feeling so alone and helpless. I'll do anything to help him."

"Inspector Butler sent you, and your problem sounds …

unusual. Is there anything else you can tell Dr Lee? Has anything strange happened?"

"Stranger than his symptoms? They're really scaring me."

"Anything out of the ordinary," Cindy prompts. "Anything you can't explain. Before or after he got the news about his son?"

I try to defog my thoughts. "Well, sometimes I ... *feel* things."

"Go on."

"Ever since we arrived here two days ago I've sensed ... a shadow around us. It feels threatening. Something silky seems to wrap itself around my neck. It tightens and I can't breathe. Then it's gone."

"Did Mr Sloane feel this shadow too?" Cindy asks.

"I don't know. I don't think so. Then he got the terrible shock, and now this ..."

"Write down everything that's happened since you got here. What you just told me. Don't leave anything out. Dr Lee is trained in Western psychiatry and traditional Chinese medicine. He knows most things that can happen to the mind. Mr Sloane will be in good hands."

After she hangs up, I close my eyes and replay the conversation. I've been thinking that Alister might need a course of medication and some counselling sessions to deal with the shock about Deshi. But Cindy's questions are worrying me.

If the shadow wants Alister, could it be responsible for his condition?

I think back. In Hawaii, it seemed like we made our own decision to come here together. But now I sense another force at play. It drew us here.

I can feel it now. Pulling. I grip the counter, so I don't get sucked in. Into what? The shadow? Suddenly I know that's a disguise. Whatever this is, it's using the shadow as a cover. Like the spirit wife who dances behind a screen. Like the creature in my dream, hiding behind the sail. It drew us here for its own purpose.

What?

Picking up my phone, I replay Miss Tigerlily's reading, alert for what I've missed. With so many layers to navigate, I let the words wash over me and see what sticks.

"Boots too big. Hair too hot. Scent too cheap. Wait, a shadow! Pink, black, pink, black."

Pink. Black. Pink. Black. That was my disguise. The colours make a powerful statement. Pink is a girly colour—which is why I never wear it. And black? In the west, black signifies mourning and death. Does it in Hong Kong too?

My disguise might have been just an unlucky choice, but Miss Tigerlily said it was pointing to something. Was it infiltrated by the shadow? That bloody frock is hanging in our wardrobe. Is it seeping bad vibes all over Alister?

There's a rubbish room for trash on the landing. Within minutes I've raced into the bedroom, ripped the frock from its hanger along with its matching cap, and stuffed them into the giant communal bin. Back in our apartment, I slam the door and lean against it.

Is it far enough? Or have I just eliminated a crucial clue?

Controlling my ragged breathing, I sit down and return to the recording.

"Ghost wants to sleep. Can't. Wants to blame. Can't. Changes shape. Sly. Dark. Wants to play. Wants to win."

A ghost who wants to win. Winston says he's haunted by the ghost of Fleur. She won't sleep. Surely she's the ghost, which means Miss Tigerlily sensed her presence and even foresaw our meeting with Winston. His problems with Fleur are not our issue, unless she's also haunting Alister. But I can't believe that Fleur would blame him for anything, not with her parents so culpable.

"Remember your mother. Man waiting. No! Not waiting. Gone. Too much beauty. Skin deep. Save him. Your job."

My job was to watch out for Alister, and look what's happened to him on my watch.

Creeping into the bedroom, I check that his eyes are still closed, his breathing slow. His naked body under the sheets already seems thinner, paler. And his presence—always so potent, even in sleep—seems less somehow, as if his very essence is slipping away. As I watch the rise and fall of his chest, my heart swells in mine. Our love is so new and so magical. I'm not going to lose him to a ... predator. The prediction of my tea leaves returns with all its power, followed by Miss Tigerlily's order.

Save him. Your job.

The possibility that we might be dealing with a supernatural force terrifies me, but it sounds like Dr Lee is the right man for the job.

I hold the bedside glass to Alister's lips and his eyes open. He sits up and takes a few sips of water. Relief washes over me at this one small win.

Menus from local eateries are pinned to the fridge by magnets. I call for a delivery: several tubs of chicken soup. This feels like more progress, one step at a time.

Miss Tigerlily's warning returns: *Sly. Dark. Wants to play. Wants to win.*

Not without a fight.

Needing a break from the recording, I remember the reading she did for Alister. With all the dramas following Winston's revelations last night, the mind-map of motifs was forgotten. There must be something there to help us. I find it on top of a bookshelf—a folded napkin from the café.

Leaving the bedroom door open so Alister can see me, I spread it on the coffee table and sit in an armchair. With a cushion at my back, I calm my breathing and allow the tension to leave my muscles. I won't try to interpret the drawings, but look beyond them to their hidden meanings.

My eyes wander over the child-like sketches, stopping at anything that resonates.

Two vertical lines with a hat on top might be a gate. It's an opening. It feels spacious, not dark like a black hole. The space expands inside me, reminding me to trust my intuition.

Next I'm drawn to a u-shaped line. It's powerful. Is this what's pulling us? I feel it now—and resist. But what you resist gets stronger. Where have I heard that?

One circle inside another looks like a plate—something to do with food? Or a hoop? *Endless circle?* But I'm trying to control the message. I allow my breath to slow again. Nothing happens. This one's keeping its secrets. We're outside the circle. That feels important.

My eyes land on several rectangles arranged in a brick-like pattern. A wall? An obstacle, blocking something.

Two circles, with a human face on the top one, look like a snowman. Or a Buddha.

An animal that could be a dog with pointed ears and chin, its face staring out from the page. Staring at me. I jump. Its expression is so canny, I have to look away. When I look back the sensation is gone, but a word remains: red.

My eyes rush on past a simple oval and land on something familiar. It makes me laugh for the first time today—the unmistakable shape of a fortune cookie. Did Miss Tigerlily know about my cookie jar? I didn't consult one before we left Hawaii. Would it have warned us?

A buzz from the intercom announces the soup. After taking the tubs from a young delivery boy, I find a slotted spoon and scoop all the pieces of chicken out of one tub. I want it to be as close to liquid as possible, so Alister can drink it.

With the bowl in my hand, I return to the bedroom. Crouching beside him, I say, "I'm going to save you, Haiku."

His body stiffens. He's responding to my words. Which ones?

"I'm going to save you, Haiku."

The same reaction. All his muscles twitch, then release.

I test a commanding tone. "Open your eyes, Haiku."

He does.

"Sit up."

He sits up.

"Eat this soup."

I push a spoon of the clear warm broth to his lips and he slurps it up. I almost cry out with joy. After a few mouthfuls in this fashion, he takes the spoon from me and finishes the whole bowl.

Then I get the jar of fortune cookies from the bottom of my suitcase and show it to Alister. "Remember what Eugene said, Haiku?" Eugene runs the Pearl, a noodle bar in Honolulu's Chinatown where I'm a regular diner. He knows my love of fortune cookies. "He told me that there are no fortune cookies in Hong Kong. So he filled my jar for our quest to find Deshi." So supportive.

Alister doesn't react.

Choosing a cookie, I crack it open and put the pieces on my tongue. Desperate as I am for answers, I never rob a fortune cookie of its message. The pastry dissolves like sweet cardboard and the sugar works its magic.

I unfurl the paper and read the words aloud: "A dragon with two heads thinks twice." Closing my eyes, I let the meaning soak in. "Thinking twice has two meanings. It can mean changing your mind: I thought twice about going. We didn't think twice about coming to Hong Kong, did we?" It looks like we should have. "But thinking twice also suggests thinking through a problem and coming to the right decision. That's what we need to do."

Alister has closed his eyes again. I return to the living room and close the bedroom door.

The dragon in the message has two heads but I only have one. Alister's head isn't working. Su Yin's is suspect. Miss Tigerlily's is missing. Dr Lee's is several hours away.

Derek.

At the thought of my best friend, I laugh. Just hearing his voice would be a tonic. I don't know what time it is in Honolulu, but if it's after midday, he'll pick up.

"Selkie. A call at last!" It's only been a couple of days since we hugged goodbye at the airport.

Derek listens to our crisis, then to the fortune cookie message that made me think of him.

"No wonder Alister's mislaid his mind. I've always envied his strength. He's never given up on the search for his son, but the poor man's just spent thirty years on the tail of a phantom. The shock has made him flip."

"And he's in no fit state to rescue himself. He's only got me,

DD. I'm his only link to this world."

My words make me wonder where Alister's mind is. He's not present in this reality, so where is he? But Derek's next comment pulls me back to the conversation.

"If two heads are good," he says, "three heads are better. And Nigel's got a better one than most."

Nigel is a former futures trader turned nurse for dementia patients. He's also Derek's partner.

I can hear tapping in the background. "What are you up to, DD?"

"Done. See you tomorrow."

"What?"

"Nigel's on leave. I'm at your beck and call. We both care about you and Alister. And I've been busting to visit Hong Kong."

"DD, I rang for a shoulder to cry on,"—the tears are flowing now—"not to ask you to fly to my side."

"I know. That was my head in action. Give me your address. We'll pick up a cab to your apartment."

He tells me their arrival time and rings off.

As I stare into space, tears stream down my cheeks. Even though Derek and Nigel are unlikely to be able to help with Alister's condition, just the prospect of having them with me has lightened my load.

Chapter 10

As Dr Lee's visit approaches, I do as his receptionist instructed and type up a detailed account of everything that's happened since we landed. I expect the clues to seem less sinister in retrospect, but documenting the events has the opposite effect. My anticipation that Dr Lee can bring Alister back is being eroded by my mounting fear. Fear that he might be the victim of a supernatural force.

Almost as I have that thought, a message from Su Yin pings his phone.

I'm back. With news. Is it too early for cocktails?

I need to keep up with her lies, but she's not getting anywhere near Alister. I type a message as if it's from him.

Hangover bad. Meet tomorrow? Share your news by text?

It's a couple of minutes before she composes the next lie.

Still working on Winston but I think Deshi works with fast food.

Great lead. Did Winston let something slip?

She must have been thinking about her answer.

I kept him talking. He's a fast food junkie.

No way has she talked to Winston who took off as soon as he saw her. But the words trigger something I've seen. In the in-flight magazine.

The receptionist's words come back: "Don't leave anything

out."

Without disturbing Alister, I retrieve the magazine from my bag in the walk-in wardrobe. At the door, I look back at his prone posture. Resolve strengthens my spine. This happened to him on my watch. Nothing else in the world matters but getting him back.

In the living room, I flip through the remarks scrawled on most pages of the magazine, deriding the goods being advertised, until I find the words beside the café directory: *Find Wind Sand Chicken.*

As I read them, something happens. I get a glimpse of Deshi. As a man. Not an abandoned Chinese-American waif who grew up without a family's love. He's happy and confident. Tall and slender. His face is smooth-skinned with fine Eurasian features—and a strong resemblance to Fleur. And Su Yin.

Shit. I forgot to reply to Su Yin.

Sorry, head throbbing. Clever of you. Where does he go to get his wind sand chicken?

Only when my message is gone, do I realise what I've let slip.

She ignores the question. *Just a teaser! More when I see you. Will Selkie be there or has she given up?*

What?

Why would she give up? I wonder if I'm going too far but I can't help it. I hit send.

Don't know, she writes. *Just wondered. Good luck with headache.*

She's planting a seed of doubt about me. Savvy.

The interaction makes my whole body tremble. Why say 'given up', instead of just 'gone home'? I'm sure she wants to get rid of me. Her words feel so deliberate, they suggest that she knows about Alister's trance and how desperate I am to save him; knows she was texting me, not him.

The room goes cold. Something brushes past me. Like a scarf of gossamer silk, it caresses my neck with a menacing touch before swirling away with a flourish. The shadow is taunting me. It's still here. I wasted my energy ditching the frock—or has it found another host?

The sensation is gone, but its presence lingers like an echo—the echo of fingertips fondling my nape.

The fingertips of Su Yin.

Her texts have reminded me that finding Deshi is the reason we're here—and now the key to Alister's return. Because his long-lost son will have the emotional power to call him back like no-one else can. Even me.

The in-flight magazine is open on the table. The directory lists specialty cafés, not fast food joints. My image of Deshi was fleeting but something was tied around his waist. An apron? What's the possibility that I saw him because he works at one of these restaurants? I blur my gaze trying to recapture the vision but it doesn't return.

Find Wind Sand Chicken.

The scribbled comment is an instruction; an order. A clue? Each word begins with a capital letter. What did the writer mean?

Still feeling the chill left behind by the shadow, I flip the pages. Some of the comments could apply to us, maybe even to Alister's predicament. Are they acting like fortune cookies? Which ones? Why?

In the *What's On* section, my eyes land on a blurb about the Shadow Puppet Theatre, with a photo of the same image I saw on the banner. Was it only last night? A screen shows the projection of a puppet in a traditional finely fashioned gown. One arm stretches above her head as if she's dancing, but the passenger has drawn a knife in her hand—pointing downwards in a stabbing pose.

Beside it, he's written, *Madam Li wants her guy. Watch how she does it.*

The chill returns. This looks like murder. But in Winston's tale, Madam Li didn't kill the emperor; she was dead, so she put her spirit in a puppet and danced for him.

On the surface this comment could just be a joke, but it has all the signs of a prediction.

As I finish adding the magazine to my report for Dr Lee, the phone rings again. I'm relieved to see Nigel's name but worried he can't make the trip.

"Selkie, DD filled me in. How frightening for you. How are you bearing up?"

"Much better since ringing the doctor and talking to DD. He's roped you into flying over, Nige, but I'll understand if you can't drop everything."

"I'm coming. Have you seen the doctor yet?"

I update him on my call with Dr Lee's receptionist.

"OK. If he's picked up on the urgency, he sounds like a good man. He'll start by considering post-traumatic stress." Nigel knows the power of PTSD. His cousin suffers from it after the Afghanistan war. "And there's another possibility. It's why I'm calling. It's going to scare the hell out of you, but you need to ask him, in case he hasn't seen it."

A supernatural force? My throat goes dry. "What?"

"Alister's symptoms could also apply to ... dementia."

"No way! He's only forty-seven."

"It's rare, but an extreme shock involving strong emotions

can bring it on at any age. Think of Alister's long-term stress levels in his search for Deshi—now dashed. It's ... possible."

Nigel described dementia to me once: "You're still the same person at your core but you've lost the key to the room where that person lives."

It fits.

Dementia. I stare into an abyss—the keyhole with the missing key. And beyond is the room where Alister is locked away, even from himself. I catch fragments of him wandering about, absent and empty, his identity replaced by a shell.

Nigel's voice is a distant squeak. "I'm sorry to scare you, Selkie, but I had to. You need to ask Dr Lee to assess the possibility, so Alister gets the right treatment. There are medical breakthroughs all the time. Let's wait for the diagnosis."

My fragile control shatters. Collapsing into an armchair, I bury my face in my hands. Dread of a supernatural force has been stalking me, an opponent invisible and invincible. But permanent damage to Alister's mind would mean he's already lost to me.

Forever.

* * *

"Call me Bruce," Dr Lee says, handing me his card. "Blame my English mother. I tried changing it to Bruno, but it didn't suit me any better than Bruce." He chuckles at the story that he probably always tells.

He's short and slight like a teenager, in black slacks and a white shirt. Not a toned muscle in sight. His quirky name makes him a kindred spirit and I like him immediately. But behind his Clark Kent glasses, he looks too young.

Does he have the experience to rescue Alister?

"I'm Selkie." Hiding my tension, I extend my hand. "My mother loved the myth of the Celtic seal people. I tried changing it to Elkie but ..."

"You too?" He shakes his head. "You know it's called 'scripting'? A terrible burden to live up to. But we can compare notes about our mothers another time. I hear Mr Sloane has reacted badly to a shock. What was the news and how did he react at first? Try to remember every detail."

Keeping my voice steady, I bring him up to date on the history with Deshi and Winston's revelation. "Alister had been drinking beer cocktails. When he heard that Deshi had been kidnapped a second time, he switched to straight bourbon and just stared at the wall as if no-one was home. I put my arm around him, but he was already far away. When I got up this morning, he'd gone into the bathroom and I thought he was OK. But ... he was just the same."

"Food?"

"He sipped some water, then fed himself a bowl of clear chicken soup."

"OK. I'll have more questions after I examine him."

Alister is where I left him, lying on the bed and staring at the ceiling.

Dr Lee shakes Alister's unresponsive hand. "I'm Dr Lee, but call me Bruce. You've had bad news, I hear, and it's left you empty and lost, am I right?"

No answer.

"I'll just check you over physically. Then we'll look at how to get you back to your old self."

He takes Alister's pulse, temperature, and blood pressure.

He listens to his heart, then looks inside his mouth and eyes.

"Sit up for me." Bruce slips his hand under Alister's shoulder.

I've been perching on a chair in the corner, but when he doesn't move, I go over and say, "Sit up, Alister." I'll only call him Haiku in private.

He sits up.

Bruce follows my lead. "Swing your legs over the edge of the bed, Alister."

Alister remains passive until I repeat the command. Bruce nods. With a tiny hammer, he hits Alister's kneecaps. Each leg responds with a kick.

"Alister," Bruce asks, "is it your mind or your heart that's shut down? Or both?"

Not even a blink.

"It's OK. You're not able to speak for yourself at the moment. You're listening to Selkie and that's great. I'm just going to check out your energy centres to see what's out of balance."

I ask Alister to lie down again, and Bruce holds his flattened palm an inch above his body, starting at the groin before hovering it over his belly, diaphragm, and heart, then his throat, eyes, and the top of his head. He looks at Alister's left hand, which I notice is clenched in a fist. Bruce lifts an eyebrow at me, and I shake my head.

"OK. Selkie and I will leave you for a while."

We step into the living room and shut the door.

Bruce keeps his voice low. "I'll get to his energy centres in a moment. He's in good physical shape, and you may be able to get him to exercise just by telling him to. You've found a way to get him to eat, so he's not going to waste away. But we've got dissociation which supports a diagnosis of post-traumatic stress. And there's another possibility which has similar symptoms. Sudden-onset dementia."

I'm breathless with dread, but relieved that I didn't have to ask him.

"There may also be something else going on."

Something worse than dementia? Fingers of fear grip my heart.

"But let's not get ahead of ourselves," he says. "I haven't finished my diagnosis. Are you familiar with the concept of *qi*?"

"It means energy," I manage to say. "The energy centres in the body are used in traditional healing."

"Correct. Also called *chakras*. There are seven of them, used to heal disease in practices like acupuncture, *qi gong* and *reiki*. And in Chinese philosophy we each have two souls, the *Hun* and the *Po*. The *Hun* is the ethereal *Yang* spirit that leaves the body after death; the *Po* is the physical *Yin* spirit that's present in the body, even after death.

"The *Hun* spirit," he continues, "is responsible for dreams and sometimes leaves the body when you're asleep. The *Po* spirit never leaves; it keeps you rooted in the earth. When someone is in a coma, the *Hun* spirit has left the body. That appears to be the case here—except Alister's *chakras* suggest there's something more complicated going on."

I brace myself for what's coming.

"The *chakras* act like a map," he says. "In this case they're telling the story of his dissociation. They show he's present in four places. His base or groin *chakra*—his *Po* spirit and his survival centre—is in overdrive, along with his heart *chakra*. Either they're doing battle with something that's trying to take them over or they're trying to make up for the low energy in the other *chakras.* His third eye—the intuition centre on his forehead—is weak but steady, and his crown *chakra*—the connection to the spirit world located at the top of his head—is calm."

"What does the low energy in the other three show?"

"You said something earlier about his reaction to the shock. No-one home. Far away. Why did you use those words?"

It's a few moments before I can answer. "Last night it seemed as if his spirit left. As if the search for Deshi had been keeping his flame for life alive. The news about the second abduction seemed to ... snuff out the flame." I've been keeping my emotions in check, but now a wail escapes.

"Well his life flame isn't extinguished. His *Hun* is far away, but his third eye is still active. And his heart connection to you is very strong. He's still tethered to you somehow."

The image of a tether resonates, but I can't think why. "How do I ... pull him back?" Am I strong enough?

"I need more information before I can answer that. Cindy asked you to make a list of everything that's happened since you arrived."

I point to my laptop on the dining table and offer Bruce a cup of tea.

"Twinings Gunpowder if you've got it."

"A Lipton's teabag?"

He grins. "Good enough. No milk or sugar."

He sits down to read my report.

For the next twenty minutes over our cups of tea, I sit opposite Dr Lee and scan his face for changes in expression. Finally he stretches and looks across the table at me.

"Shadows following you in a strange country? Getting into the taxi of the man Alister's here to find? Do things like this often happen to you? Especially since you changed your name back to Selkie?"

I give him a tight smile. "Elkie was a much safer name. But it was like living in a cage."

"And then there's Lee Mei Yee. I know Miss Tigerlily through David Butler, but this is the first time I've seen one of her readings. Do her phrases speak to you?"

"Yes. Even the things I don't understand. I didn't realise at first, but she predicted something happening to Alister."

He looks at the screen. "*Save him. Your job.*"

"And now she's missing, too."

"David told me," Bruce says. "Not magic, I suspect. Thugs hired by child traffickers who don't like her activities. And saving her is *not* your job. Leave that to the police. You've got to devote all your energy to Alister."

I drop my voice. "I'll do whatever you tell me."

"You're the one with the sixth sense, and the close connection to him. And I've seen that the connection works both ways. You're not going to give up on him."

The same words Su Yin used. "Never."

"Some loved ones do. They don't intend to give up—they don't even acknowledge that they have—but when their relative's *Hun* spirit is no longer present, it triggers the same response as if they've died. The loved one flips straight into grief mode, which overwhelms their fight response. You haven't done that."

It's something I've done right. It brings a glimmer of hope.

Bruce gestures towards the bedroom. "Let's try something. I want you to ask him this question: where are you?"

A spark ignites my being. Could it be this simple?

We enter the bedroom and go to the bedside. Alister hasn't

moved.

"We're back, Alister," Bruce says. "Selkie is with me. And more importantly, she's with *you*, isn't she?"

"All the way." I bend over and kiss him on the forehead.

I'm sure he blinks.

Bruce signals, and my body tenses. I take a deep breath and whisper into his ear, "Haiku, where are you?"

He opens his mouth.

I examine his face for signs of him trying to speak. Nothing comes out. His jaw is open but quite still. I wait for a long minute, fighting back a sense of failure.

"Close your mouth now," I sigh.

I'm drenched in sweat, but Bruce is calm.

"Do you have something—a piece of jewellery he's given you? Like the ring he's wearing. Do you have one to match?"

"We haven't exchanged rings, but he gave me this silver bangle when we were in France. It's special. I always wear it."

"Good. We'll use that. Alister, we're going to do a little experiment. Are you game?"

It's the same word Alister used about Su Yin's cocktails. Game. Why do I remember that?

From his pocket, Bruce produces a silver chain with a hook on the end. With a pang, I take off the bangle and hand it to him. He wraps the chain around it and loops it through the hook before giving it to me and guiding my hand to dangle it over Alister's heart like a pendulum. As I hold the chain perfectly still, the bangle starts to spin.

I gasp. It's exactly like the dowsing I performed in France. At the time I didn't believe in such things but I needed guidance and it heralded the beginning of a journey. A journey that revealed my love for Alister.

As the spinning movement mesmerises me, something happens. Without warning, Alister's fisted left hand flies up and grabs the spinning bangle. The action emits an explosion of light that blinds me, then throws me backwards.

But not before I see it. Tied to his little finger.

A red cord.

I'm still holding the chain when Alister's hand yanks me back. As I fall across him onto the bed, Bruce is beside me.

"Are you OK, Selkie?"

"I think so." Then I burst into tears.

Bruce hovers his palm over Alister's throat *chakra.* "Your energy level is heightened. Your left hand is talking through the bangle. Good job. Did you get the message, Selkie?"

"Yes."

Chapter 11

As Alister falls asleep and loosens his grip on the bangle, Bruce re-tests all of his energy centres. Only then does he pronounce the experiment finished and give the bangle back to me.

Back in the living room, I feel as shell-shocked as he looks. With all the dramas since I saw the lunar matchmaker, I forgot the red cord. When I threw away the frock, the real one was still in the pocket.

"Wow," Bruce says, "that was more than I expected. And I was only watching. Fill me in. What happened in there? What sent you flying?"

I'm still breathing like I've just run a marathon. "When Alister grabbed the bangle, there was a flash of light and I flew backwards. Didn't you see it?"

"Not the light. It was meant for you."

"So you didn't see the cord? On his little finger?"

"No. Have you ever seen it before?"

"I've sensed it, after Alister told me a story about the lunar matchmaker. He uses a red cord to connect two people who are soul mates."

"Yue Lao," Bruce says. "I thought you two were tethered. Was the red cord the message?"

I blow out a deep breath. "Yes."

He listens as I recount my visit to the shrine and my horror that I've thrown away the real cord.

"Don't worry. That cord was just a symbol. The real connection is invisible. Alister was reminding you of that."

As I look down at my little finger and sense the pressure from the cord, the magnitude of our communication dawns on me. As soon as he had the chance, Alister took one decisive action to show me the red cord. It cost all his energy to send that signal. All his *chakras* were in overdrive. Afterwards he was spent and fell instantly asleep.

My tears flow in earnest now—with joy. He's not lost to himself in a keyless room. Part of him is here with me. Waving.

I'm celebrating this revelation, until I realise something's wrong.

Bruce is pacing, his brow furrowed in thought. "You said that as soon as Alister grabbed the bangle, the flash of light threw you backwards. Then he pulled you back."

"That's when I saw the red cord."

"Think very carefully before you answer this question," he says, locking his eyes on mine. "When the light exploded, did something ... push you away?"

Shit.

Every cell in my body is pulsating, not only from the after-effects of the encounter but from the implications of his question. Am I remembering pressure on my breastbone? Or has the question caused my memory to invent it?

It's a while before I can answer. "I'm not sure."

"It's important," Bruce says. "Crucial. Take your time. Go back there and describe what you remember."

I close my eyes and visualise the scene. "I thought it was

the light, flashing and bowling me backwards. Until you asked that question. Now I think ... something pushed me."

"One thing? More than one?"

I think hard. "Two. Two at once."

"A shove."

"Yes."

As I try to get control of my breathing, he holds his palms out vertically, with his fingers pointing towards the ceiling. "Flat, like this?" He rounds his fingers into claws. "Or sharp, like this?"

It all happened so fast, I hadn't noticed until now. "Sharp."

A sharp sensation on my chest.

It's a long minute before either of us speaks.

Bruce's frown gets deeper. "Alister pulled you back against an opposing force. It explains the activity of his other *chakras*. His base *chakra* is working hard, hanging on for sheer survival. That's good and bad. His will is strong, but something is challenging him. His heart *chakra* is overactive, which may mean there's a struggle for control of it. His crown *chakra* was calm before, but just now it was jumping—as if his connection to existence was under threat."

Swallowing hard, I wait for what's coming next.

"A threat explains his fist. He's closed his hand over the red cord—to protect it. The experiment with the bangle exposed a malign force. It appears that something ... has kidnapped his *Hun*."

It's what I've been fearing but not naming. "S-sorcery?"

"Some kind of magic," he says. "I've seen enough cases in my psychiatry practice to study Taoist folklore. It takes many forms and I'm far from being an expert. But Alister's son was kidnapped. Now this. I'm not a fan of coincidence."

As my mind stumbles over the dire implications, Bruce finds Miss Tigerlily's reading on my laptop and reads out the words that I'm starting to know by heart—a sinking heart.

"*Boots too big. Hair too hot. Scent too cheap. Wait, a shadow! Pink, black, pink, black.*" He looks up. "She caught the shadow hovering over you. And you think the rest refers to your disguise, as she was warming up to the full reading?"

With a supreme effort, I clear my head. "Yes, but something about my disguise bothered her."

"Well, you've thrown the dress away and the shadow is still around."

"But it's been targeting me, not Alister."

"Or both of you. If he's not psychic, he didn't get the warning."

And I didn't tell him.

Bruce returns to the reading. "*Ghost wants to sleep. Can't. Wants to blame. Can't. Changes shape. Sly. Dark. Wants to play. Wants to win.*" He stops. "The only ghost we know about is Fleur, although Deshi could also be a ghost. And after what happened to them, blame fits them both." He reads from the screen. "*Carrying bygones. Can't let go.* Is that the ghost? Miss Tigerlily's insights jump around, so phrases that follow each other might not be connected. Either way, there's vengeance here."

With each step, Alister's plight plunges deeper into darkness.

I force myself to stay practical. "What is changing shape? Why would a ghost do that?"

"In the Chinese spirit world, 'ghost' is a broad term, covering many kinds of spirits. There are shape-shifters who are tricksters. The word *win* feels sinister, and *play* isn't much better."

"Power."

"A power imbalance," Bruce says. "That's always danger-ous."

"Winston called Fleur an angry ghost, but Fleur was a beautiful person, inside and out. Why would her ghost have turned malevolent?"

"A lot can happen to a ghost in thirty years," he says. "Fleur was murdered, then her parents stole her baby from his father. She's a ghost with grievances. If Winston's right, she's also a wandering ghost, who's travelled from her burial place in San Francisco to haunt her parents in Hong Kong. She should know where Deshi is, but what if she's looking for him too? A ghost can become ... impatient."

"Whatever pushed me didn't feel like a ghost. It felt sharp." The more I think about that push, the sharper it feels. "Miss Tigerlily said: *White Tiger. Something sharp.*"

Bruce thinks about this. "The reading isn't clear but I suspect the phrases aren't connected. At the White Tiger Festival, you make offerings to the tiger to ward off any evil against you. I've never heard of a White Tiger shape-shifting, especially into a shadow—too subversive. And pushing you would be too petulant for the tiger's noble character."

He refers back to the reading. "*Too much beauty. Skin deep.*"

"That's more likely to be Su Yin. She's subversive and petulant. But I'm not sure she's got the kind of power necessary to hurt Alister." And what would be in it for her?

We move on to Miss Tigerlily's paper napkin of runes. Just looking at it overwhelms me.

"A map," Bruce says. "Each symbol is a signpost. Their meanings will come to you one at a time. In the right order."

He fixes me with a steady gaze. "The clues are in these readings, Selkie. You used the words 'no-one home' about Alister for a reason. His *Hun* has been stolen and you were already attuned to his absent spirit." He drops his voice. "*Save him. Your job.* Use your psychic gifts to find him and bring him home."

On unsteady feet, I walk him to the door.

"Miss Tigerlily's last words are important," he says. "*Know. Who. To. Trust.* You've trusted me because I'm a doctor recommended by David Butler, but you're in a strange place and under siege from unknown forces. Follow your instincts regarding Su Yin. Be careful."

"My friends from Hawaii are arriving tomorrow. They'll help me look after Alister and make wise decisions."

"Good." His shoulders visibly relax. Tonight's events have been tough for him too. "And Miss Tigerlily was also reminding you to trust yourself. Alister's got the right woman on his side."

A woman facing a mountain. "Thank you."

We step onto the landing in time to see a flash of pink and black. It disappears through Klaus's door.

"That's the dress," I scream. "Did you see her?" I'm unsure if I imagined it.

"A Filipino housemaid," Bruce says. "Hong Kong's affluent households run on them."

"She looks so young." Was that her squealing last night? With terror? At the thought of Klaus pawing her, my skin goes clammy.

"How did she get the dress if you threw it away?"

"I used the communal rubbish bin."

"So she was dumping her rubbish and found it," he says. "A

free frock."

The sight of it has shattered my fragile composure. The symbolism of throwing away the red cord is pressing in on me. I think about knocking on Klaus's door and asking the maid to give the dress back. But I threw it away for a good reason, and a young woman on maid's wages has found it. It's gone.

I turn to Bruce. "The red cord from Yue Lao was in the pocket of that dress. I know it's symbolic, but after Alister's message it feels urgent to replace the real one. As a talisman for his return. I need to go back the matchmaker's shrine."

"And you won't leave him here alone." Bruce looks at his watch. "Go now. I'll stay with him till you get back."

"Thank you!" I'm so grateful, I throw my arms around his neck. It's over in a flash so he doesn't comment.

Back inside the apartment, he detours to the kitchen to warm up more soup. I call a cab, then slip into the bedroom. After his ordeal, Alister is still asleep but the connection between us is much stronger.

"I got your message, Haiku." I don't know if he can hear me. "I saw the red cord and I'm going to visit the lunar matchmaker to get a real one. Bruce will keep you company while I'm away. Eat some soup. I won't be long. Promise."

This is the first time I'm leaving his side since he succumbed to this malaise, and I wrap my arms around his unresponsive body with a pang. I know he'll be safe with Bruce but it's still hard. Then returning to the living room, I grab my coat, give Bruce a wave and hurry out the door.

In the back of the taxi, my mind sifts through the evening's events, heralding a new wave of terror. Alister proved that he's with me, soul to soul, but someone—or some*thing*—doesn't want us to connect on that level. Who? Or the even scarier question: *what?* The pressure of those hands—or claws—gets stronger the more I think about them. Do they feel familiar? And I can't bear to consider what they're doing to Alister's *Hun.*

Then the dress turned up—just in time for me to see it—on that vulnerable girl who's living within the same four walls as Klaus Hofmeier, first-class sleaze. But with Alister's situation so dire, her predicament is a battle I can't take on.

* * *

The location of Yue Lao's shrine isn't clear in my memory. Using my GPS, I return to Empo Retro. It's still open, as are most of the other shops. From here, I retrace my way along the brightly lit lane until I'm level with the shrine. No-one is visiting Yue Lao and I'm relieved to have him to myself.

Until I see that he's no longer holding any red cords.

The sight of his hand, empty except for his book, knocks all the optimism out of me. After Alister's supreme effort to remind me of our unbreakable bond, it's such a cruel blow that I'm not sure my legs can hold me up. I lean against the closed door where the man with the broom emerged yesterday.

The door opens a crack. I jump.

The same man pokes his head out and I get a glimpse inside. Lights, statues, coloured flags and urns of incense. It's a tiny temple. Right here in the middle of the shops.

"I go home," he says, "and remember red cords." He must be the caretaker of the shrine, because he holds out a bunch to show me. Then he pulls the door shut behind him. "After sunset," he explains, "must keep out bad spirits."

Slipping past me, he crosses the lane to replenish Yue Lao's stocks.

On his return he opens the door and catches me peeping past him. "Sea Goddess Temple close now," he says. "Come back tomorrow." He disappears inside.

A temple to a Sea Goddess. I've never heard of her but my thoughts go to the selkies—Celtic sea goddesses in their own way. *Go down to the sea.* Miss Tigerlily was reminding me to honour my namesakes and trust my psychic instincts. They're going to be crucial to rescuing Alister.

The incense kiosk is open. I return to the shrine and exchange an incense stick for a red cord. I close my eyes and thank Yue Lao, letting him know that Alister is lost and needs to find his way home. Then I wind the cord around my silver bangle.

* * *

Bruce greets me at the apartment door with his medical bag in his hand. He looks drained after the extra hours we've added to his day but he asks about my excursion. I show him the cord and tell him briefly about the man from the temple.

"A temple keeper. He was working late. Temples usually close at sunset—unless you're a gangster or the police, who keep unusual hours." He smiles. "Taoist temples are tucked away in surprising places all over Hong Kong. I used to visit one on my way home from school—a secret I kept from my mother. The temple keeper was full of stories from the folklore." He steps onto the landing. "Alister woke up and we both ate a bowl of soup. There's one waiting for you."

After gulping down the soup, I ignore my own exhaustion and update my report with the evening's events. When I climb in beside Alister, he's asleep again. Pulling the blanket around us for protection, I then wrap my fingers around his fist.

My dozing mind bombards me with the sights and colours of Hong Kong. Red lanterns twirl under awnings propped up by bamboo scaffolding. Signs flash. Egg Street. Wind Sand Chicken. Shadow Puppet Theatre. Jadeite Group. Empo Retro. Sea Goddess Temple.

Noticeable in the melee, a fat man sits on a step, smoking. His bare chest is flabby, his belly spilling over baggy pants. He's not Yue Lao or the temple keeper. I'm trying to get to the bottom of his identity when Alister appears behind him. He waves at me but as I call out, he fades away.

A sense of desperation chokes my throat, until I see that something is snaking a path from where he was standing.

The red cord.

Chapter 12

"Get away from him," I scream.

I've returned from the kitchen to find Su Yin leaning over Alister. Her hand is around his throat. I launch myself across the bedroom and knock her over.

"Get off me," she snarls.

Grabbing her arm, I drag her out of the room and slam the door behind us.

"What the hell?" I hiss. "How did you get in?"

The apartment is locked. I remember how she disappeared in Egg Street, and the hairs on my nape stand up.

She writhes and pushes. "Let me go."

The shove from last night reminds me to look at her hands. Her fingernails are bitten down. Not sharp.

I'm reeling from this revelation when the air turns icy, a silky sensation swishing around my neck.

Su Yin throws her head back and her wild cackle freezes my blood. "*You'll never have him*," she crows.

I open my mouth to challenge her, but the shadow disappears. Su Yin blinks as if she's waking up. Did that voice even come from her?

Looking down at my hand still clamped around her wrist, she says in her normal voice, "I came to tell him about Deshi.

You're hurting me."

"By choking him?" My limbs are quivering. Did I get her away from him in time?

She puts her other hand on her hip. "What's your *problem*? Alister's text said to visit today. He already gave me the door code so I let myself in. The bedroom door's open, and he's lying on the bed staring at the ceiling so I said 'hi'. When he wouldn't answer me, I went in and took his pulse. Or tried to, till you tackled me."

My perspective flips. She could be telling the truth. In my panic, I thought that she'd walked through the wall. But if Alister thought she'd be staying here, he'd have given her the door code.

And she only had one hand on his neck.

Looking at her pouting mouth, I remember she's a chameleon. Seductive one minute, arrogant as a teen the next.

Now she drops her voice to a whisper. "I might just know where Deshi is."

Bloody hell.

I let go of her wrist.

For the first time, I realise that we only have Winston's word that Deshi was kidnapped again—confirmed only by my so-called vision. What if I witnessed a real baby-snatch? What if Winston is lying?

He was here when Alister took ill. He dropped the bombshell that triggered it. Working in plain sight as a taxi driver, he must have been ready for Alister to track him down. Did he decide to come out of hiding with this story as a careful charade? Winston seems like a man broken and haunted by loss, but he's already shown he'd do anything to keep Deshi away from his father.

Su Yin watches my face as if she can read my thoughts. It's even possible Winston ran off when he saw her because he knew she'd out him as a liar. Has he disappeared? Then I remember she lied about meeting him on Egg Street. She didn't recognise him on the landing. And I'll never forget that cackle.

Know. Who. To. Trust.

Bruce's advice comes back—trust my instincts. And Alister's—keep Su Yin onside. Their words calm me and the panic of the last few minutes ebbs away. Alister only has me to look out for him. I have to keep my head.

If Su Yin's involved in sorcery, which her bizarre behaviour suggests, I need to keep her where I can see her. And change our door code. But if Winston is the sorcerer, I may need her family connection to get Alister back.

I take on a confiding tone. "The doctor came to see him last night."

"What's wrong with him?"

"A very bad hangover. After the cocktails the other night, he got stuck into the bourbon. He's been in this waking sleep ever since."

I can see her mind working. Is she wondering about the text messages we exchanged? Instead she surprises me.

"I didn't spike his drink if that's what you're going to pin on me next."

That stops me. It's something I haven't considered. Bruce didn't mention the possibility either. Chinese herbs are ancient—and potent—medicine. They could have evil applications in the wrong hands. Would Su Yin mention it if she'd drugged him? Or is this her savvy way of deflecting attention?

But Winston was the one who was present when Alister's spirit left his body.

"Where's Deshi?" I ask, flipping subjects the way she does.

"Trust works both ways," she says. "That's for Alister's ears."

I cast around for an angle. "Leave then. I'll call you when he's well."

She knows I'll change the door code. She'll lose the power she's gained. I'm walking her to the front door, hoping she'll spill whatever she knows, when the intercom buzzes.

"Aloha," says a beaming voice. "The gay guardians at your service."

"Mwah and mwah," I scream, pressing the door release then turning to Su Yin. "My friends are here. One of them will be guarding Alister at all times."

"I was only taking his pulse."

I drop my voice. "Why won't I ever have him?"

She snorts. "Oh that? Sometimes words pop out, like a burp. When they're gone, I feel better."

"Why those words, right after you saw Alister?"

"Dunno. Because you have got him, haven't you? In your power. Like, he's not going anywhere."

The elevator pings and I open the front door. Derek sweeps me up in a Fred Astaire pirouette, then Nigel bends for a bear hug that only a man of his height can give.

Instead of escaping, Su Yin hovers. I do the introductions. As the boys carry their bags inside, she presses the button for the lift. When it arrives, I hold the doors open.

"Where's Deshi?" I ask again, but she's not buying it.

"I'll give you a clue." Her eyes flash. "Find the Wind Sand Chicken."

* * *

Racing past Derek and Nigel, I press a finger to my lips in a silent signal. In the bedroom, Alister appears unchanged, breathing steadily.

I nuzzle my face into his shoulder and whisper, "I've got a huge surprise, Haiku. I'll be gone for a few minutes, then I'll be back to show you."

Meanwhile, Derek and Nigel have already scoped out the living space and discovered the sofa bed. They've rearranged the furniture so the bed's in a corner and the armchairs are snug around the coffee table. They've also thrown open the curtains.

"You two are so gorgeous. Thanks for the daylight. I've been living in the dark as if we're under siege. And you may have arrived just in time to stop me from assaulting Su Yin."

Derek says, "I sensed she might be a tad ... precocious."

"More on her later. Let me take you to Alister. He'll be excited to see you, but he won't show it. It's like he's asleep with his eyes open."

Nigel says, "Has a doctor seen him?"

"Yes. I'll update you on everything, but I don't want to keep him waiting."

I open the door to the bedroom and go in ahead of them.

"Look who's arrived from Honolulu. Derek and Nigel. They're going to help me look after you and get you back to normal."

"Hey, Alister," Derek says. "Good to see you. Sorry you're under the weather. My home cooking will fix that, and you know Nige. The man can't help putting on his medical hat. He'll have you bandaged up like the invisible man in no time, even if you don't need it."

Did his lip just twitch?

"Sit up and shake their hands," I say.

He does what I ask without looking at them.

"Alister, I'm just going to take your pulse." Nigel puts his fingers on Alister's throat—exactly where Su Yin put hers. She was telling the truth. But she still broke in uninvited and spat out that sinister prediction.

"You're fine," Nigel says, "but lying here all day, you'll lose muscle tone and bone mass like an astronaut. You need to keep up your physical activity. Selkie, there must be a gym in this building."

I confirm this, then put my hand on Alister's shoulder. "Dr Lee discovered that your body is here, but your spirit is somewhere else. It's my job to find it and bring it back." Whatever that means, but I keep my voice strong. "So while I'm out looking, I want you to do whatever Nigel and Derek ask, OK? Nod your head if you understand."

I hold my breath. He gives me one slight nod. It's the final sign that Su Yin didn't disturb him.

At Nigel's request, Alister gets up and puts on a robe before walking with him onto the balcony for some daylight. As Derek and I follow, my footsteps falter, not only from the view but also from my intense protectiveness of my man.

The city is out of sight, behind our building. We gaze at the sea, feeling dwarfed by the wide expanse of blue, an offshore island peeping out of the mist. It feels like a symbol of the vastness of the human spirit—and a metaphor for my quest. Alister's *Hun* spirit is out there somewhere, on the loose from its physical vessel. Now that the boys are here, it's time for me to leave the confines of this apartment and bring it home.

Chapter 13

Alister's in safe hands with Nigel, so I unknot my shoulder muscles for the first time in two days and make myself turn to practical matters. Derek comes with me into the kitchen to inspect the dwindling stocks of food.

"I'll go shopping," he says. "We need to get him eating more than soup."

He inspects the freezer, warms up some frozen dumplings, and together we carry bowls to the living-room table. After Alister eats his fill, Nigel helps him back to bed.

When Nigel returns, I'm too wired to update them, so Derek reads out my report for Dr Lee. His eyes dance at Miss Tigerlily's reading. He loves this stuff, but the dire implications keep his excitement in check.

When he reads out Bruce's experiment, Nigel whistles. "You've walked into a minefield of powerful motifs, Selkie."

"But not dementia, Nige. Sorcery." I'm actually relieved to say it.

"I've never seen anything like it," he says. "Sometimes folks with dementia become suddenly lucid, as if their old selves are fully back, for a minute or an hour. But they're not in control of when or how, and just as fast they're gone again. Reaching out for your bangle—and your vision of the red cord—indicate a different condition of Alister's mind. A fleeting moment of control." He turns to Derek. "Have you come across the red cord, DD?"

Derek collects Hawaiian ghost stories, but his interest in folklore extends way beyond the archipelago.

"It's a symbol in many Asian tales," he says. "China, Japan, Korea. The old lunar matchmaker does his thing, joining together couples who will be lovers, either by the ankle or the little finger. It's always invisible. Now that you've seen it Selkie, it –"

"– commits me. I know."

I hold out the cord wrapped around my bangle and tell them about Yue Lao's shrine.

"I didn't know he was worshipped like a deity," Derek says. "What do you do with the cord?"

"I don't know. Keep it with me and not throw it away." I tell them about ditching the frock. "Then last night I saw it in a dream, weaving a path for me to follow." I push down a rising sense of overwhelm and move onto Miss Tigerlily's napkin. "It's not literal, but Bruce says this is my map."

Derek runs his eyes over the crude drawings. "You need to copy this, and hide the original in the safe. You don't want Su Yin getting her hands on it."

"She doesn't know about it, but I've photographed it. Can you do it too as a backup?"

They take shots with their phones.

"Why did you almost assault Su Yin?" Nigel asks.

I update them on her actions this morning.

"Self-important and capricious," Derek says.

"Or she has a medical condition," Nigel says. "Spitting

out words she doesn't mean could be Tourette Syndrome. It usually involves a twitch of some kind, and sometimes involuntary outbursts."

"I haven't noticed a twitch," I say. "But don't people with Tourette's swear all the time?"

"In the worst cases, but that's rare."

"She said the words explode from her like a burp; that she feels better after she says them. She said she didn't mean that I'll never have Alister." The memory of that voice douses me in venom all over again. "Then the shadow slipped past, like it was taunting me, and Su Yin blinked as if she'd just woken up. But she's an actress."

"Possessed." Derek folds his arms across his chest. Case solved.

"Don't throw that word around lightly, DD," Nigel says. "Possession is rarer than Tourette's. Selkie needs to be sure of what she's dealing with. She thought Su Yin walked through the wall this morning, then discovered she knew the door code. Now's a time for clear heads."

I'm used to this kind of interchange. Nigel has real experience of the supernatural—he reads auras, bends spoons, and has explored most strange phenomena. On the other hand, Derek's experience comes from collecting recounts of ghost sightings and his avid reading of folk tales. He's a little too addicted to anything woo-woo.

Derek's pursed lips show he's miffed that Nigel has pulled him into line, but his sulk only lasts a minute.

"I can't thank you two enough," I say, "for catching the first flight over here. It's so good to see you I could melt."

"Disasters are tripled when you're away from home and without friends," Nigel says. "Now that we've turned up, you've lost your privacy. But with the shadow slipping around at will, we need to be on the spot."

"What do you think it is?"

"If Dr Lee has dismissed PTSD and sudden-onset dementia, then he's the expert. But I doubt that sorcery finds traction in a vacuum. There may be psychological factors at play. The shadow could be a manifestation of what has befallen Alister. He's a shadow of himself. You're psychic, so you foresaw it as a metaphor."

He knows it wouldn't be the first time that my mind has played tricks on me.

"This is a malign force, Nige. Something has put him in this trance. Kidnapped his *Hun*."

"Then the force will reveal its identity along your journey. And we'll support you all the way."

* * *

The boys need to sleep off their jetlag, and I need some serious rest after the morning's emotional roller-coaster. I leave them to the sofa bed, with Nigel's feet hanging over the end. When I climb in beside Alister, he opens his eyes. It's my first real chance to show him the red cord and tell him about Yue Lao.

"Here it is, Haiku. The physical version of the red cord you showed me last night. It's going to guide me on my journey to find your spirit and bring it back."

His blink feels meaningful. I'm sure he's heard me. Then wrapping my arms around him, I tell him to close his eyes. When I do the same, I plunge into a deep sleep.

The doors all look the same. A row of them, painted red and

framed with gold. I'm not sure how many there are until I see that each bears a number. My eyes move from one door to the next until I get to the end. Four marks the last door. The sight of it causes the same drench of dread I felt on the plane.

Dread rhymes with dead. Door rhymes with four. Four sounds like death. It's a poem for the victim of number four.

Alister's spirit is locked behind one of the doors. To set him free, I have to choose the right one. With Alister's life in the balance, I've only been granted one guess—and just four minutes—to make the right choice. If I'm wrong, he'll be locked away, forever out of reach.

A clock starts ticking.

Time presses down on me like a weight. My first thought is to use the keyholes, but each door's key is in place, preventing me from peeping through. Could the red cord be on the other side of the right keyhole, ready to guide me? I dare not touch any key in case my action indicates a choice. That rules out knocking too. In desperation I call out Alister's name, but the wall of doors deflects my voice.

His *Hun* spirit is silent.

Against my will, I'm drawn again and again to the fourth door. Is it a trick? Is Alister silent behind the fourth door because he's already dead?

The ticking gets louder. Time is running out. I move towards the fourth door, looking for a sign but it's like wading through quicksand. As I pass the other doors, the numbers turn to tea leaves. One after the other, they crumble to the ground.

One gone, two gone, three gone. Quicksand through an hourglass, counting the minutes. I fear that time is killing Alister.

The tea leaves on the fourth door start to flash. The strobing blinds me. I lift my hand to shield my eyes—and feel my bangle pulsate. Alister is calling! But the tea leaves on the fourth door begin to crumble.

No!

As I rush forward to push the door open, my feet are stuck. Not quicksand. Something sharp has shackled my ankles. It's pulling me back from the door, but I reach out and snatch the key.

When the shackles disappear, the fourth door does too. Alister is still in the locked room.

But now I have the key.

Chapter 14

We're back at the table, huddled over Miss Tigerlily's napkin.

"I'm not going to sit on this psychic map any longer. I have to start the journey,"—I swallow hard—"and go wherever it takes me."

"The hero's journey," Derek whispers, "has many perils."

I tell them about my dream.

"Your intuition is your strength, Selkie," Nigel says. "Mine your dreams for clues. Those shackles? Did you get a sense of who or what they represent?"

"They were sharp. Like the thing that pushed me away from Alister. And there's something sharp in Miss Tigerlily's reading."

"Sharp like claws? Teeth? What's this animal she's drawn? Knowing who or what is trying to stop you from reaching Alister would give you power."

Claws or teeth? The sight of the animal makes me shrink, but I remind myself that the drawings are metaphors.

"I thought of the word 'sharp', but nothing penetrated my skin."

"We're being literal," Derek says. "What other things are sharp?"

He finds the notepad and we start tossing out words as they come to us.

"Wind," I say. "Rain and hail can be sharp. Lightning."

"Sharp flavours," Derek adds. "Vinegar. Pickles. Lemon. Ginger. Horseradish."

"Cheese."

"Herbal tea."

I think of tea leaves.

"Some cocktails. Poison." Derek pulls a face.

Was Alister's drink spiked? I rush on. "Sharps in music. Some languages have sharp tones. Anger."

"Anger could be involved here," Nigel says. "Other emotions?"

"Grief. Envy. Revenge. All sharp."

"Thorns," Derek says. "They carry curses in folk tales, like Sleeping Beauty. Anything pointed. The tip of a knife. A skewer. An arrow." Then he adds, "Sharp also means clever. Savvy."

"Su Yin," I say. "Maybe that's what I felt when she scratched my nape with her chewed nails. I sensed her savviness and felt wary."

We stop. We're done. We stare at the list that seems way too big to navigate.

Nigel says, "The list shows the power of the word itself. This could be all about power. You're sensing the power of your opponent. Whatever it is, it's flexing its power over you, hoping to intimidate you into giving up."

"That's what Su Yin said in a text to Alister: Has Selkie given up yet?"

"This thing called Sharp wants you to give up," Nigel says.

It makes sense. "But the shadow isn't sharp. It's dark—and

silky." The memory of its touch makes me shiver.

"If you're sensing only one opponent then it's shape-shifting. Dark and silky are other forms of power. The power to threaten and the power to seduce."

"But what's its motive?" I ask. "Why has it kidnapped Alister's *Hun*? If I knew that, at least I'd know what I'm dealing with."

"There's one person who might know," Nigel says. "He knows more than you do, anyway."

"Alister," they say together.

I'm about to protest that Alister's too fragile, but they're right.

"He should be here with us," Nigel says. "We know he can hear us. He may have more to contribute. And we know he'll find a way to do it."

* * *

When Alister wakes up, I bring him through to the table. Nigel updates him on our opponent and explains why we've named it Sharp. Alister doesn't respond but his eyes remain on me. Pushing aside my anguish over his condition, I focus on the task ahead.

Nigel turns practical. "OK. Alister, you showed Selkie the red cord and she got a real one from the lunar matchmaker. She's going to use it as her guide." He turns to me. "How will you do that, Selkie?"

I'm worrying about that myself. "It showed the way in my dream, but it wasn't a real path." I look at Alister but he doesn't react.

"So you're not picking up how to follow it with your waking

mind?"

"I sense the shadow but not the cord."

"Follow Miss Tigerlily's map while you're asleep," Derek says, "then wake up and act on what you've seen."

"My dreams aren't literal enough, DD. But I suppose we could try to decipher the signs."

We sit in silence and stare at the runes.

Derek says, "What about using the bangle? It's got a foot in both camps—it was involved when you saw the red cord, and it throbbed in your dream."

"DD!" I throw my arms around his neck.

"Ouch," he says. "It's hot."

Now I feel it myself. Sizzling on my wrist. I check the red cord but it's quite cool.

I look at Alister. "It's another message. I wear it all the time, and it's never been hot before."

"Not all the time," Nigel says. "You dowsed with it and Alister grabbed it. Have you looked at the inside of his hand?"

We all lean across the table as I whisper, "Show me your fist, Haiku." It's resting on the table. I take it and turn it over. "Open it, just a little."

He moves his fingers slightly and sure enough there's a scorch mark peeping out from his palm.

"Does it hurt?" My lip quivers.

"It could be a psychic burn," Nigel says. "The imprint of that red-hot moment of connection between you. But let's treat it with some balm."

Derek finds some in the bathroom cabinet, and I use my finger to spread it through the opening in Alister's fist.

"Why was my bangle hot? It's cooled off now. I'm not getting a message from it." I point to the symbol on the psychic map that I've been calling a plate. One circle inside another one. "Is that my bangle? Dr Lee said this map would show me where to start."

Derek peers closer. "Your bangle is an open loop, but this drawing is a closed loop. Why not use your bangle to dowse the map? Tie it to the cord."

It's a great idea, but it means taking it off again. As Alister watches behind unblinking eyes, I tie the red cord around the bangle and dangle it over the napkin. As I move it from one symbol to the next, nothing happens.

"Remember what Nige said about spoon bending?" Derek says. "It only happens when you don't care."

"I care!"

"Give it to Alister then."

Of course. The bangle and the cord are his devices.

But when I try to put the cord in his right hand, he pulls away. Remembering his communication through the bangle last time, I tie the cord loosely around his left fist, and he lets me guide it over the map.

The bangle starts to spin.

I scream.

Derek points at the cartoon face above a huge circle with a belly button.

"There was a fat man in my dream," I say. "The dream with the red cord."

"I assumed this was a Buddha."

"Me too, but the man in my dream looked more like a kitchen hand."

Find Wind Sand Chicken.

"Shit. The clue about wind sand chicken has been flying at me from all directions." I update them on Su Yin's hint about fast food, then we open the in-flight magazine and look at the comment scrawled beside the café directory. "Wind sand chicken isn't fast food but there must be a link here somewhere."

"That's dinner solved," Derek says.

Chapter 15

Derek and I pounce on the intercom, and a reception committee greets the delivery boy when he exits the lift. If I was expecting the man with the bulging belly, I'm disappointed. Our delivery boy is just that—young and skinny, with a strand of straight black hair that he flicks back from his forehead.

He hands over our order, and as he reaches for our offered tip, Derek asks, "Do you do private deliveries?"

"You mean food?"

"Yeah. We'll pay you well for helping us," Derek says. "We want more wind sand chicken from these different cafés." We show him the directory from the in-flight magazine. "Can you deliver them after your shift?"

"OK." A big smile from the boy.

Derek gets his name and they exchange phone numbers. Marty takes a photo of the directory and agrees to bring our orders from the cafés that are open late. Derek and I will check out the early-closing ones.

"We're looking for a fat man with a big belly who works in one of these cafés. If you find the right café, there's an extra tip."

Marty moves off, mumbling, "Chi sin gweilo."

Crazy foreigner. It's the only Cantonese I know.

Back inside, I say to Derek, "What if Marty already knows who we're looking for? He's not silly enough to tell us and cheat himself out of his delivery fee. And the late night cafés are more likely to be less classy. The fat man in my dream looked pretty rough."

"We can't visit them all, Selkie. And we'll know before the night's out." Then he says, "If we find him, what will you ask him?"

It's a good question, and an answer comes. "Does he know a tall Eurasian kitchenhand? It's something that David Butler said and my vision of Deshi matched it. He doesn't look very Chinese."

* * *

We consider doing the café crawl as a foursome, but Marty might return before we're back, and Derek and I will move faster. I'm also nervous about exposing Alister to the outside world in his vulnerable state.

"I'll be back soon, Haiku," I whisper. "And the red cord will stretch wherever I go."

Derek brought a suitcase full of Aloha shirts and has to borrow Alister's coat. "Who would have thought it would be jacket weather in March?"

He's studied a map and numbered the cafés in order of distance. We'll start with the furthest on the northern outskirts of Kowloon, working back to the island and home. The cab is waiting for us outside the lobby.

After giving the driver the first address, Derek asks him, "Do you know the storytelling taxi driver, Winston Wong?"

Our driver shakes his head and keeps his eyes on the road.

"Why did you ask him that?" I whisper.

"Just wondering if Winston has disappeared since he dropped the bomb on Alister. What if he was lying about Deshi? He might have flown the coop. Sorry—too much talk of chicken."

I've wondered that myself. "I'll call him tomorrow. I want to know why he didn't meet up with Su Yin on Egg Street." Or if her story is even true.

"Call him now."

I dial Winston's number, but it rings and rings, finally going through to voicemail. I don't leave a message.

"He might have recognised your number," Derek says.

He grabs Winston's business card, dials the number with his own phone and flips it to speaker.

"Winston, Storytelling Taxi Driver," a familiar voice replies. "Where you like to go?"

"Hey man, I'm over from Hawaii." Derek hams up his accent. "Researching folklore for a college course on Chinese mythology, but I'm after the local stuff. You know, the stuff I can't find in books. I was planning to go into China, but holy moly, I picked up your card in the lobby. It must be fate. How's about a half-day tour of Hong Kong Island, and you can knock yourself out with some of the local stories, throw in some superstition while you're at it."

"No problem. No problem." Winston's voice beams through the phone. "I take you very good tour. Tell very good stories. Special price."

They haggle a bit and make a date for tomorrow afternoon.

"Pick me up at Central—the Mandarin Oriental—the name's Derek Delaney but you can't miss me. I'll be wearing an Aloha shirt—and goosebumps."

He hangs up.

"The Mandarin Oriental?" I ask.

"Yeah, let him think I've got money and will lavish him with a hefty tip. Then he won't bunk off if he gets a better offer."

"What's the plan?"

He hasn't got one but he can't stop grinning. His mission is one I can't undertake myself. "We've got time to come up with a strategy."

"Yeah, but you need to be careful, DD. Even though he hasn't gone into hiding, we still don't know what game he's playing."

We settle back and watch the lights of Hong Kong whizz by. It's a long drive along busy highways, and I'm sure we pass the turnoff to Egg Street. At the memory of Su Yin's vanishing act, I quake all over again.

The first restaurant is a huge room full of large round tables already crowded with diners. A waiter guides us to a small table in a corner. We watch the other waiters scurrying back and forth. Like most waiters the world over, they're all thin.

"He could be out the back smoking," I shout above the hub-bub. "I've just remembered he was smoking in my dream."

"Now you tell me," Derek says. "Was there a sign above his head with his name on it?"

"Wind Sand Chicken." It must have slipped into my dream from the magazine. This café crawl could turn out to be a wild goose chase. "I'll check out the rear exit."

"Watch out for overflowing trashcans and ... wildlife."

Since we're guests confined to the dining area, not health inspectors who can wander through the kitchen at will, we've devised a plan. We split up and use the bathrooms, before getting lost on the way back. I wander along a corridor until I find a door that opens onto a raised outdoor dining area that's closed for the cooler months. Chairs stacked under an awning leave the tables looking forlorn. A single spotlight throws eerie shadows, making the folded umbrellas in the centre of each table look like crumpled humans, down on their luck. No employees are taking a nicotine break.

For some reason I count the umbrellas. Eight. I look across the rail at the low-rise residences lining both sides of the rear lane. It's a rare glimpse of an older and less-developed part of Hong Kong.

When I make my way inside, Derek is back at our table. "I got a look into the kitchen. Hard to see through all the steam but I hovered as long as I could. No fat man."

"No rats either," I say. "Only eight umbrellas."

We leave without placing an order.

The next stop is closer to the action, just off Nathan Road in a short street lined with eateries ranging from folding tables in a covered alley to this mid-range family restaurant at the top of a flight of stairs. The location is around the corner from the Temple Street Night Market, bringing back memories of the child abduction. I wonder if David Butler has been able to confirm if it happened—and if he'll tell me what he's found. Would knowing if it was real help my search? And what's the news on Miss Tigerlily?

This place is buzzing and we're lucky to get a table when two patrons vacate it. The kitchen can be glimpsed through a doorway. On my way to the bathroom, I peer into the tiny chaotic space where woks, steamers and barbecues bubble over high flames. Cooks and kitchen hands wearing singlets sweat. One has a cigarette dangling from his lips, but none of them is fat. As I loiter, a waiter rushes past with a plate of crispy wind sand chicken, the aroma of garlic assaulting my nostrils.

In two more cafés we repeat our unsupervised inspections. Derek gets to see a rodent. But we have no luck with the fat man or any staff member who could be Deshi. The last café at Central on the island is on the third floor of an office building. The clientele are a mixture of locals and tourists. The kitchen is open to a vast dining area and from the queue at the door, we scan the whole room in a few seconds.

My knees are buckling from exhaustion and a profound sense of failure. Finding the fat man would have been a sign that the map has put me on the right track.

Derek senses my mood and puts his arm around me. "Come on. Marty has started sending videos from his list. He might have stumbled onto the elusive FM. Time to go home and eat some chicken."

*　*　*

By the time we've devoured our wind sand chicken—Alister eats a huge plateful—we've got videos from all but one of the other cafés. We watch staff waiting tables, turning skewers on barbecues and sweating over woks. Their body types range from skinny as chopsticks to wobbly as tofu, but there's not a fat man among them.

Derek starts googling. "Maybe there's a café called Wind Sand Chicken and it's not on this list. The passenger could be recommending it."

I shake my head. "It's not a café, DD. My sign was a dream sign. Not real."

"There's something cryptic we're not getting," he says.

"But Marty's got one more café on his list."

With all my hopes now pinned on the last video, it comes up empty too, except for a fleeting glimpse of Klaus Hofmeier dining with a bunch of men. First his arrogant laugh booms out above the hubbub, then his shiny bald head appears. Pushing aside my sinking hopes about the fat waiter, I tell Derek and Nigel about Klaus's permanent leer and how his housemaid found the pink and black dress.

"You've replaced the red cord," Nigel says, "but if you really want to destroy the frock, you could offer to buy it back from her. She probably sends money home to her family. Cash might be more useful than the dress."

"Great idea. But I'll have to do it when Klaus isn't home."

Derek waves his phone. "Like now."

Grabbing my purse, I race onto the landing. But when I buzz Klaus's bell there's no answer. Since it's late, I don't buzz again.

When I return, Nigel says, "These girls work long hours. She probably collapses after all her chores are done."

Talk of Klaus reminds me that he works in the orphan business. I tell the boys. "Would he know anything about what might have happened to Deshi? It was thirty years ago, but the child abduction network might operate in much the same way."

"He'd know all the abduction scams," Nigel says. "There's big money in adoptions to the US. Even if he runs a legitimate business, he must get approached with black-market orphans."

We're talking about children, sold like merchandise. Was that Deshi's fate?

"I feel sick at the thought of asking Klaus for help, and I

don't want him to know our business. But it's a connection I'll have to exploit."

"Make an appointment in the morning and one of us will come with you."

Eventually Marty drops by. He's laden with more bags of chicken and brings them through to the kitchen where we're all sitting at the island counter.

On his way out, Derek gives him a tip.

"Easy money," Marty says. "Makes me fat."

"Have you been eating our chicken?" Derek teases.

"It's a joke. I'm an English student, so I make good jokes. It's hard to explain Chinese characters but fat means rich. Like we say at Chinese New Year."

"Kung Hei Fat Choy," Derek says.

"Yeah. Wish You Get Rich."

Derek returns. "Did you hear that? Our man might not be a fat man. If your dreaming mind was playing with the word, Selkie, he could be a rich man."

"That's Alister." I put my arm around his shoulder. "But I didn't know that meaning, so would my dreaming mind know it? The man in my dream had something to do with a café, or a kitchen. And Miss Tigerlily drew a fat man on her map."

"It could still be symbolic of Alister," Nigel says. "The map starts with him after all. Marty's joke could be a clue."

Symbols and clues are doing our heads in. We need to go to bed.

I'm desperate to wash off the night's adventures, so after the boys have used the bathroom, I take Alister with me into the enormous shower cubicle. Under the water, I wash him and hold him, this empty shell of the man I love, grateful that the spray masks my tears.

Only when I'm cuddled up with him under the covers and almost asleep, do I remember that I didn't change the code on the front door.

* * *

A noise wakes me.

As my eyes spring open, I hear a deep rumble. Is something in the room with us? The sound is so primal, it triggers my protective instinct. I throw my arm across Alister's chest and feel a rhythm quaking his torso, then hear his voice in my ear. The sound is coming from him. He's growling. And he doesn't stop.

Now the shadow swirls past my neck with its taunting flourish.

"Sh-arp," I cry, my voice faltering. "I kn-know your name. What do you want?"

"*You'll never have him*," a voice crows. "*Give up now and save yourself.*"

It fades into a cackle, just as a disturbance erupts in the living room. I don't want to leave Alister's side, but the door is no longer closed. Derek appears in the doorway, holding Su Yin.

Nigel comes up behind him. "Don't try to wake her, DD. If she's sleepwalking, and that's what it looks like, she'll be disoriented. She could lash out at someone—or hurt herself."

"She just threatened Selkie," Derek says. "Thanks to my jetlag, I was counting cobwebs instead of sheep. I heard her creeping about. When she opened the bedroom door, I pounced."

"Thank you," I whisper.

"Let's move her gently to the armchair," Nigel says.

Leaving the door open so I can see Alister, I help them make a kind of bed with two armchairs. We put a cushion behind her head and throw a blanket over her. If the boys weren't here, I might have had other plans for her.

Nigel holds a finger to his lips and we go into the bedroom and close the door.

"Shouldn't one of us keep an eye on her?" Derek asks.

"It's gone now," Nigel says.

"What?"

Nigel and I say it together. "Sharp."

Derek puts his hands on this hips. "You said Su Yin wasn't possessed."

"Possession is a dangerous word, DD. It creates a certain impression—of the mind and body being taken over by a demon. We could be dealing with something much more complex."

"Complex?" Derek sighs and looks at his watch. He loves anything woo-woo, but he also adores his sleep.

"I forgot to change the door code," I say.

"Good that you forgot," Nigel says. "Now we've all seen Su Yin—and Sharp—in action. They're in some kind of symbiosis. But the fact that she's asleep may mean Su Yin's a passive player."

"Possessed," Derek murmurs.

"Alister was growling," I say. "That's what woke me up."

Nigel goes over to the bed and whispers, "It's Nigel. If you can hear me, Alister, open your eyes."

His eyes fly open.

"It's OK, you're safe. Selkie is right here. And Derek. You were growling just now. Why?"

He sits up, climbs out of bed and walks to the door. We all follow him past the sleeping Su Yin to the napkin map still laid out on the table. Guessing what he wants, I take off my bangle, tie one end of the red cord around it and the other end around his fist. He dangles it over the map until it starts to spin.

We all peer at the rune, but by silent agreement we don't turn on a light in case it wakes Su Yin.

"What is it?" Derek whispers.

As a tribute to his couch-surfing days when he stumbled around in the early hours to find strange bathrooms—or pot plants—Derek always carries a flashlight. He gets it now and illuminates the drawing under the still-spinning bangle.

I reach across to lower Alister's fist. He appears unchanged after Sharp's visit. "Good job, Haiku," I murmur.

"It's the animal," Nigel says. "Pointed ears. Four legs. A cat? A dog?"

I stare at it, remembering how it made me jump the first time I saw it. "Before we brainstormed all those sharp things, I sensed Sharp might be an animal. Something with claws. But it seemed too literal."

"An animal from the Chinese zodiac?" Derek says. "A tiger or a dog? Or a goat? That might make it a clue to a particular year."

"An animal fits with the growling," Nigel says. "Without your *Hun* spirit, Alister, you're relying on your base *chakra* to defend yourself. And you've found your opponent on this map."

"A mythical beast," Derek says. "Lots of them in Chinese folklore."

Beside me, Alister is silent.

"Detached from your worldly body," Nigel says to him, "your spirit could be encountering all kinds of otherworldly creatures."

Bloody hell. I've been focused on how to get him back. But while I'm stumbling over clues, he's all alone out there, facing who knows what? If his spirit gets mauled by some supernatural monster, will it be able to return to his body? The possibility makes his rescue even more urgent.

I try to keep my voice steady. "In the reading, something changes shape. Whatever this animal is, it's silky one minute and sharp the next."

Derek says, "Mythical shape-shifters are often animals in their changed form."

"Cats are silky and unpredictable, with sharp claws," Nigel says, "Are there cats in Chinese folklore, DD?"

"There are tigers. Not sure about cats."

"What do you think it is, Selkie?"

I tell them what Dr Lee said—that whatever pushed me away from Alister is not the White Tiger in the reading. Then I close my eyes. "And it's not a cat. Dogs are either fierce or friendly. Like the reading says, this shadow thing is ... *sly*."

We're all silent. We've reached another dead end.

"Let's get some rest," Nigel says. "We can explore more possibilities in the morning."

"Can we take Su Yin back to her apartment?" Derek asks. "I'm not sure I want to breathe the same air as her. And she'll probably make a scene when she wakes up."

Nigel has other ideas. "Her presence here is proof that she broke in while she was asleep. She might have something to tell us."

* * *

The Chinese junk bobs on the river in a strong wind. The animal behind the sail leers, its features clearer now—ears, chin and teeth, pointed and sharp—but not its identity.

It cackles in a familiar voice, "*Steal the spirit and the body will follow.*"

The mast morphs into Alister, his arms stretched high above his head. Powered by the wind, the sail is pulling his body upwards. I'm standing in the boat as it rocks and bucks, trying not to fall over. I grab his ankles but he spirals out of my grasp and disappears like a column of smoke.

In desperation I look down, expecting to find baby Deshi and hoping that he'll cry his heart out and call his father back.

But the junk has morphed into a basket, overflowing with eggs.

* * *

Su Yin wakes with a scream. "You've kidnapped me!" She starts searching the armchair, presumably for her phone.

I've left the bedroom door open, so I'm out of bed and beside her in a flash. "Why the hell would we kidnap you when you turn up here all by yourself?"

"To make me tell you where Deshi is."

"Try this instead," I say. "You broke in here last night. Again. This time you were sleepwalking."

She looks down at her pyjamas.

In the corner of the room, Nigel throws back the covers, leaving Derek motionless on the sofa bed.

"We only met briefly," he says to Su Yin, "but Selkie is

telling the truth. You also made a short speech."

Nigel intimidates most people, but Su Yin puts her hands on her slim hips. "About what?"

"Selkie?" he asks.

I'll never mimic that voice so I deliver the words deadpan. "You'll never have him. Give up now and save yourself."

For the first time, she hesitates. She knows it fits with what she said yesterday. "I've already told Selkie that I, like, say things I don't mean."

"How long have you been doing that?"

"Are you a doctor?"

"Why? Do you need one?"

She yawns. "I have bad dreams. They started about the time I met Alister. They scare the crap out of me and sometimes they give me ideas about things I must do. Then I do them."

"Like telling Alister to come to Hong Kong?" I ask.

"I don't remember. I found out that Winston and Rose were living here, so that might have been my idea. To get the reward. How is Alister? Still hungover?"

We ignore her question.

"And the voice?" Nigel asks.

"What's it to you?"

"I'm a friend of Alister's. You've seen that he's ... not himself. What you tell us might help him."

"His pulse was OK, but he's, like, not all there. 'A bad hangover,' *she* said." Su Yin flicks her head at me.

"You broke in," I say, "so I didn't confide in you. And now you've said something creepy. *Twice.* I don't trust you."

"Whatever. What have you got to eat?"

I warm up the last of the bao buns and we sit down at the table. After Alister's dowsing of the animal rune last night, we put the napkin map in the safe.

Into the long silence that Nigel and I create, Su Yin starts to speak. "I answered Alister's ad for information. I'd never heard of Deshi, but it looked like he might be a relative. There was a reward. Too big to pass up. Sometime after we met I started, like, having these weird dreams, but I didn't make the connection straight away. Then Alister told me that my DNA was a match for Deshi. He sent me part of the reward and asked me to see what I could find out from my family. The reward was for 'information leading to finding' Deshi, so just being his cousin wasn't enough. I had to do more to get the rest of the money."

I know what she says is true. And it sounds like her dissertation was a lie.

"What's weird about the dreams?" Nigel asks.

She does a shoulder roll and flicks her mane. She likes being the centre of attention, but is she telling the truth? "They're scary. Nightmares. But I never scream. Sometimes I stay up late and try not to fall asleep. That never works."

"A recurring dream."

"Yeah." She fixes her eyes on Nigel. It's clear that she's going to tell him more. "I leave my body. I don't want to, but it's like I'm sucked out and straight away I'm lost. It probably sounds peaceful to you, flying around in my sleep, but I'm desperate to find my body again."

"And you do find it."

"So far, but not without a fight."

"What are you fighting?" he asks.

"I don't know. That's why it's scary. After searching for, like, forever I go: shit, there it is. But I have to fight my way back in. I didn't want to leave, and now my own body doesn't want me back!" She starts to cry.

Nigel ignores the tears. "What's your body doing? Just lying there on your bed?"

"No. It's always doing something. Like breaking in here. After a lot of effort, I somehow get back inside. That's when I get a message to do something. Then I, like, wake up."

As if her story makes perfect sense, Nigel says, "So since you met Alister, you've been doing a lot of sleepwalking."

"If you want to call it that. Most times I can see what I'm doing, but I can't control it."

"Where else have you sleepwalked?" I ask.

She hesitates. "Here, the first time I broke in. I'd stayed up really late trying not to fall asleep. It's harder to resist when I'm asleep. My body kicked me out and came into this apartment. When I got back inside, I saw Alister lying on the bed."

"Did you get a message to take his pulse?"

"No. I've got a first aid certificate."

"What about the words that came out of your mouth?" I ask.

"After you grabbed me, I got kicked out again. That happens sometimes. Then my body spoke. They're not my words."

She seems to be genuinely bewildered. A thought pops into my head, and I repeat my question. "Where else have you sleepwalked?"

"Egg Street."

As soon as she says it, I know. I can feel the twinge in the pit of my stomach. Psychic as well as peptic. It's where my quest started and where it resumes—to find Deshi and rescue Alister.

Egg Street.

"I went there to meet Winston like I told you," Su Yin continues, "but when I got to Egg Street, my head started to throb like it was going to explode, and I got sucked out of my body. It went down the alley and into that room full of gaming tables. My body was asking those men about Deshi. I was floating around, trying to get back inside myself, so I knew Winston didn't show up. Then on the street, my body finally let me back in."

At the moment it looked to me like she vanished? The timing fits.

My voice is shaking. "Where were you ... when you woke up?"

"In a doorway. It was dark and the men were gone, and I knew I had to lie to Alister, tell him that I'd met Winston. Don't ask me why, I never know."

"Why would those men know anything about Deshi?"

And if Winston plays mahjong with them, he would have asked them himself. Why didn't he meet Su Yin? He could have been running late, but why pick me up instead?

She shrugs. "The men didn't like the questions about missing kids. They got up and left."

"So you're lying that you know where Deshi is?"

She pauses. "When my body followed the men outside, one of them said something about a café. Then Alister's text asked me about a chicken dish. Did you send that? That's how you follow clues isn't it? Put them together. If I help you find Deshi, I'll get my reward."

I still don't trust her, but I wonder how anyone could fabricate such a story and expect to be believed.

Nigel looks at me. I suspect he's wondering if we should take Su Yin into our confidence. If her bizarre story is true, she's a tool of the force that kidnapped Alister. The force we've named Sharp. But because she sees what her body is doing, she's also a potential spy. We could enlist her to play double agent, but could we ever be sure that she was on our side?

If she's telling the truth, it seems that Sharp is hell bent on finding Deshi. I'm focused on finding him because he might be the only person who can give Alister's spirit the will to fight its way back to his body. But Sharp must have another reason—and the possibility rocks me. To kidnap Deshi too?

My thoughts go to Fleur's ghost. But why would she shape-shift into an animal and threaten Alister? Then try to steal the spirit of her own son? For a fleeting moment Sharp is back, brushing the back of my neck: a silky sensation, then a scratch.

Alister appears in the bedroom doorway, the low growl from last night coming from his throat.

Leaving the table, I run to his side. "It's OK, Haiku," I whisper so only he can hear. The nickname is my code word. He'll always recognise me. "It's gone now," I say aloud. "We're all here. Su Yin is telling us how her body gets kidnapped."

"Kidnapped?" she says.

Compared to what's happened to Alister, it's more like spirit swapping, but I say, "It's like that, isn't it? Your body goes off on its own sometimes, leaving your spirit on the loose."

"Yeah, you got that right."

I lead Alister to the table where he sits and stares at Su Yin.

I say to her, "You'll want to go back to your own place and get dressed."

"Yeah. Then what?"

My decision is out of my mouth before I can reconsider.

"You're coming with me. To Egg Street."

Chapter 16

I walk Su Yin to the door. On the landing, Klaus is emerging from the elevator, looking as if he's been out all night. What was he doing in the café with those men? I expect him to give Su Yin the same X-ray treatment he gave me, but he ignores us and bolts for his front door.

It looks like I won't be talking to Klaus about orphans this morning, but seeing him reminds me to make an appointment. When I return to the apartment, I google him. He's the director of an agency called The Dove. I phone the number, bending the truth with the receptionist to bypass an underling and see Klaus himself. A meeting tomorrow afternoon.

With Alister back in bed and Su Yin gone, Derek gets up. We bring him up to date on her story.

"If she's telling the truth," Nigel says, "she's describing a form of astral travel. I didn't think of it till now, Selkie, but it could be where Sharp has trapped Alister's spirit. On the astral plane. That's where you could undertake your quest."

"Astral travel?" I squeak.

Derek beams. "Nigel's an expert."

"Don't be discouraged by Su Yin's description. By the sound of it, her experience isn't voluntary—it amounts to soul stealing. But you probably astral travelled as a child, left your body to explore your bedroom, looked down at yourself sleeping, and just thought it was a dream."

"I don't remember doing it." But my step-mother suppressed my psychic abilities.

"As a novice," Nigel says, "you'd need to practice on small trips to get your astral wings, if you will."

"You think finding Alister is urgent enough to ... *leave my body?*" Just the thought pushes me out of my depth again.

"With most conditions, a mix of care and speed is prudent."

We drop the subject, and I'm relieved. Returning to Egg Street is enough for now. If the red cord shows the way, the path to follow will be clear.

As Derek makes plans for his cab tour with Winston, I show him a family photo in Alister's album. "He's thirty years older, but still much the same. Heavier build. Less hair."

Derek peers closer. "Fleur was a lot like Su Yin, but something's different. Her eyes are clearer. There's something veiled about Su Yin."

He flips the page to a full length photo. Fleur is sitting on a chair holding Deshi, her parents standing behind her. What makes me gasp are her boots. Pink and black cowboy boots. Is that why Alister was attracted to my disguise? On some subliminal level, did he remember Fleur's outfit from this photo? What if pink and black were colours that she loved?

When I point out the boots to Derek, he looks closer. "They've got a tiger stripe. What if Dr Lee was wrong and that's the animal on the map—a tiger—and the baggage Miss Tigerlily sensed? Your pink boots are resonating with Fleur's."

I flop back onto the chair. "Was I throwing away the dress when I should have been ditching the bloody boots? They could have drawn the attention of Fleur's ghost. She's got to be the ghost in the reading, DD. *Ghost wants to sleep. Can't. Wants to blame. Can't.* It fits with what Winston said. She's angry and restless. And Dr Lee said she could be vengeful, in spite of her character as a living person." Then another possibility dawns on me, stretching my experience of ghosts into unknown territory. "Could she be using Su Yin as her body?"

"Another form of haunting," Nigel says, testing the idea.

"They look alike." I feel queasy. "It all fits, except ... I'm still not convinced that Fleur would ever hurt Alister."

Derek's been thinking. "Of course Fleur can't sleep after what she suffered. But why can't she *blame*? That's much more intriguing than insomnia. It doesn't fit with being vengeful. If she can't blame, she's too noble. Or too powerless. She wants something that she can't have. That doesn't sound like Sharp, who's manipulating everyone to get her own way."

"Has Alister ever tried to contact Fleur?" Nigel asks. "Because surely as a ghost she knows where Deshi is."

"He had a bad experience with a fake psychic. That made him wary of trying anything like that again. It's why I tested Miss Tigerlily with the disguise." Landing us all in a heap of trouble.

"Has anyone else contacted Fleur?"

Derek flips the album back to the Wong family close-up. "What do we know about her mother?"

"Her name's Rose," I say. "That's about it."

Fleur was seventeen when this photo was taken, so how old was Rose? Late thirties? It's hard to tell. With her flawless skin, her beauty comes close to her daughter's.

That's what was distinctive about the woman in the night

market. I only caught a glimpse of her face before she took off after the child abductors, but on a subliminal level she reminded me of Fleur.

Rose would be in her sixties now.

"The Chinese are big on honouring the spirits of their dead relatives," Derek says. "We need to talk to Rose about what she's done to contact Fleur."

"Winston mentioned the shrines in their house," I say. "One to feed Fleur's ghost and a second one to attract Deshi. But if Winston really doesn't know where Deshi is, then Fleur's ghost hasn't told them anything."

"Why would she? They stole him, then lost him. No wonder she's haunting them."

We're no closer to knowing if she's now haunting us, but the pink and black boots must mean something. As much as I want to toss them into the sea, it feels important to keep them. For now.

It's time to collect Su Yin and see if I can find some answers.

"What's the plan with Egg Street?" Nigel asks.

"Eggs, chickens," Derek says. "Its name is not a coincidence."

"After what happened there on my first visit, I suspect it's what the Irish call a thin place. Where this world and the next … almost touch."

"And you're going back there with Su Yin," Nigel says.

"What?" Derek was dozing when we made this arrangement. He puts his hands on his hips and treats me to his best frown.

"It's broad daylight, DD."

"And sorcerers only operate at night?"

"Sharp is targeting both of us in different ways, so she and I need to do this together."

Derek goes to the kitchen and returns with my jar of fortune cookies. "See if the message agrees with your plans."

He's exploiting my weakness but it worked last time. I reach into the jar, choose one in the middle and eat it. Then with a rush of foreboding, I unfurl the paper strip—and gape at the message in shock.

"An egg can make a chicken ... or an omelette."

We're stunned into silence by its prescience. It's a moment before anyone speaks.

Nigel goes first. "An egg that becomes a chicken is a symbol of new life. An omelette is ... a tasty mess."

"Tread carefully or you'll break eggs," Derek says. "An omelette is the end of the road. It's a warning. No more wind sand chicken."

He gets Miss Tigerlily's map, and we stare at the simple oval shape. An egg.

These signs mean they're going to let me go. But I don't tell them that I've read other meanings into the message. Alister's *Hun* spirit is out on the soul plane without the safety of its earthly shell. If it's mingling with other uncontained spirits, does it risk becoming an omelette that can never return? The message escalates the pressure for me to get him back in a hurry.

And what of Deshi? He was kidnapped as a tiny chick. Has he made it to rooster?

My next stop is urgent. Egg Street. I text Su Yin to meet me in the foyer in thirty minutes.

* * *

Derek calls a cab to the Mandarin Oriental, and I remind him to be careful. While we're gone, Nigel will take Alister for a workout in the apartment gym.

After a shower, I spend some quiet time with Alister.

"I'll be looking for the red cord, Haiku. If I see it, I'll know where to start my search for your *Hun* spirit. I'm not sure why I need Su Yin with me, but she's part of the puzzle." He stares straight ahead and I don't know what he's taken in. "And there's a connection to Deshi in Egg Street, so I'll search for clues to him too."

After telling him about Derek's mission, I wonder if I should mention our other discoveries and decide there's nothing to lose.

I retrieve the pink boots from the walk-in closet. "Remember these boots? I wore them to meet Miss Tigerlily. Fleur had a similar pair. Is it possible that your subconscious picked them for my disguise?"

His response is immediate. He gets up, and I follow him to the shelf with the photo album. He flips to the family portrait where Fleur's outfit is clearly visible.

Then he growls.

The sound is deep, primal, and chilling. I don't know what to do to ease his distress but put one reassuring arm around him.

"Who's hurting you?" With my other hand, I point at each person in the photo. Fleur, Rose, Winston.

He suddenly stops.

Are all three of them colluding to destroy him? That might mean that Rose is harnessing the power of her dead daughter's ghost. But why would Fleur join forces with her culpable parents against her loving husband and the father of her son?

I cross my fingers that my trip to Egg Street—and Derek's

time with Winston—will bring us closer to the truth.

Chapter 17

Su Yin is waiting in the foyer.

"Thank you for being on time," I say.

"I have to do what you tell me," she says. "Or else you'll think I'm working for the enemy."

"Are you?"

"I get kidnapped, remember?" She's jumping on the defence that I handed to her. "But you're making me go back to Egg Street, like I'm your guinea pig. Do you even know what you're doing?"

Her comment hits a nerve. Will we find chickens or omelettes? I have no idea.

The taxi pulls up and I tell the driver our destination.

"Egg Street. Bad place," he says. "Ghosts."

"Why is it called Egg Street?" I ask.

"Old market sell eggs. Gone. Now many many ghosts. You like fashion, I know good place."

"We're looking for ghosts."

"Speak for yourself," says Su Yin.

We follow the familiar road over the middle of the island, under the harbour, and through the busy streets of Kowloon, heading north. Traffic is heavy, so it's easy to spot some landmarks from our café crawl last night. At last our driver pulls over as cars whizz by.

"You get out here."

Either he really is spooked or he's worried he'll lose time on Egg Street getting the next fare. I check the street sign, then peer into the shadows at the garages and roller-doors. When I get out, Su Yin stays put. Just as I think she's going to make me manhandle her, she sighs and gets out too.

We cross the busy road that forms a T-junction with Egg Street, then our destination swallows us like a portal.

"I don't like it here." Her voice rises. "I'm going to get kidnapped again; I can feel it."

"What's happening?"

Her chest starts heaving as if she's short of breath. "I ... see lights ... exploding. Colours and ... patterns like a disco. My head ..." She drops her head and wraps her arms around it as if she's in pain.

As I watch she straightens up and stares at me, her eyes dark. Then she turns and walks away from me down the street.

Racing after her, I curse that we didn't arrange anything if this happened again. But what could we have done? With her spirit kicked out, she's not present to implement any plan.

She also might be shamming, but I follow her to the same alley where she emerged last time with the men. When she plunges down the concrete path, I hesitate, staring at the dark doorway at the far end.

Su Yin was right about being my guinea pig. Her body came here last time. My own eyes confirmed that fact. Then in front of my eyes, she disappeared. Now as she enters the doorway, she slips from view again.

I'm about to follow when an inner wisdom plants my feet. There's something to fear in that room at the end of the alley.

I'm not sure what it is, but it's something to do with those men. I can't afford to risk a rash act. I have to find the red cord.

Near the entrance to the alley, I duck into the same narrow space as last time. I'm out of sight of anyone leaving the mahjong game, but with a good view up and down the street. At the other end, Egg Street turns the corner in an L-shape where the taxi dropped me off. That driver wasn't scared of ghosts. Neither was Winston.

Along the length of the street, closed roller-doors press against me—physical barriers but also symbolic impediments. I scan the old apartments upstairs, but their curtained windows shut me out. What are they hiding? The past or the present?

There's so little life in this street. Nothing to suggest there was ever a market here, but eggs resonate with the fortune cookie's message—and the basket of eggs in my dream.

My mind plays with the word. Eggs in the market would have been bought and sold for a range of purposes. Some fertilised and kept warm to incubate chickens, some to cook all kinds of egg dishes—including omelettes. What else?

Something red.

Keeping my eyes open, I soften my gaze and concentrate on the image. It's not the red cord and I'm disappointed. When it comes into focus, I see a red egg. Then a basket of them. Unlike the eggs from my dream, these don't look real.

At the faint smell of smoke, I scan the street but I can't see anything burning. When the smell gets stronger, my legs make the decision to follow it, walking to the corner where the road bends and finding another alley. It's narrow, blank walls lining each side. After walking the whole length without finding the source of the smell, I reach the other end and look across a road at something I recognise. The café from last night; the one with the folded umbrellas. It's linked by this alley to the bend in Egg Street.

Unable to make sense of why I've been drawn here, I turn back towards my hiding place to wait for Su Yin. In the middle of the alley, my bangle feels hot against my wrist. It's a sign to pay attention and I stop outside a closed door. A red door with paint peeling.

Did I pass it before?

There's a window in the door. The glass has been painted over, but scratches in the paint form a Chinese character. Slivers of light escape. Pressing my face to the glass, I glimpse a flame. At first, it blinds me. Is the place on fire?

As my eyes adjust, I see a candle burning. Beside it are sticks of incense in a pot, a tiny vase of frangipani flowers, and other objects. It's a shrine. A small Buddha oversees the offerings.

A flash of red snakes away behind the shrine—the red cord?

I blink to get a better look—and face a brick wall. The thin place just gave me a secret view, but now a barrier shuts me out. I wait but the moment has passed. Even the smell is gone. If I hadn't blinked, I might have seen more. Where was the red cord leading? How can I find it again?

Racing back to my hiding place, I lament the missed opportunity. If I'm going to rescue Alister, I need to be less dazzled by chance moments like this. What was the meaning of the shrine? A glimpse into the past? The shrine of ghosts?

Find Wind Sand Chicken.

Why do these words resonate so strongly? They must have cooked chickens in the egg market. Merchants and customers have to be fed. I imagine farmers in the fields beyond old Kowloon going out before dawn to collect eggs and kill chickens. Later on, cooks behind woks, cigarettes dangling from their mouths, would do a roaring trade in fresh street food.

Did they coat the pieces with granules of garlic and fry them until crisp, inventing the dish called wind sand chicken?

How does it relate to Deshi?

And what do the red eggs mean?

Voices erupt from the alley, and I shrink back out of sight. In almost a re-enactment of last time, Su Yin emerges behind a group of men. So she happened upon another game of mahjong. A coincidence? Or is the place used at any time of day or night for players to drop in and join a game? Illegal high-stakes gambling? Possible. Just like the faeries in Ireland, the rumour of ghosts on Egg Street would keep the police at bay.

But Su Yin's body entered that room today—if it was for the same reason as last time—to find a clue to Deshi.

These men seem younger than the previous group but I can only see their backs. They're not afraid of ghosts because two of them are laughing, their voices bouncing off the hard surfaces. As they walk down towards the intersection, I brace myself for another re-enactment—the disappearance of Su Yin.

But just as she stops and turns back towards me, I'm treated to a different replay. A rush of pain splits open my head. Lights strobe and colours zigzag across my vision. The migraine is happening again.

Now something is upon me, scratching at my eyeballs and wrapping my head in a blindfold.

My spirit is being pulled skywards. No!

In a state of acute panic, I see my body shrink away as I rise.

Watching the top of my head retreat, I kick my spirit legs in a futile attempt to stop the kidnapping. Where is it taking me? Then I hear a voice.

"Was Deshi pretty enough?"

Suddenly I'm back on the pavement, looking into the dancing eyes of Su Yin. She's with me—and I'm with her—but surely her comment about Deshi risks another replay. Our assailant might switch back into her body again.

"Run," I scream, grabbing her hand and taking off like a typhoon towards the intersection.

Do I think we can outrun Sharp, who isn't constrained by physical boundaries? But we leave the thin place behind us and reach the busy road.

A cab picks us up. As soon as we collapse on the back seat, my phone chirps. It's been without reception.

Winston drove me around the island, Derek writes, *and told me a story. It's important. Fridge now full of food. Didn't buy eggs. Or chicken.*

The view from the cab of bamboo scaffolding, shabby tenements, and modern skyscrapers brings me back to the real world after my close shave with Sharp. In our apartment she's only taunted me, so why did she try to steal me now? Because I'm looking for Deshi? And Egg Street gives her extra power?

Her. A malevolent female spirit.

Is that why she's able to invade Su Yin—and now me—but could only steal Alister's male spirit?

Fleur.

Who else could it be? I've been trying to believe otherwise, but this has to be personal.

She's after me now. That makes saving Alister even more

dangerous. But the key has to be Deshi and she's shown her hand.

I look across at Su Yin who's flopped across the seat, breathless from our run. I'm still stunned that her question saved me—not by design but by chance.

"What did you mean?" I ask. "Was Deshi pretty enough?"

Her breath is back. "I want the rest of my reward."

It was always about the reward. "You know Alister will pay you."

"If his mind comes back. If it doesn't, how will I get my money?"

"How much?"

I'm sure the figure she states is ten times what he offered her. Did she see a lot of money changing hands on Egg Street and get greedy?

"I don't have that kind of money and I'll find Deshi without your help."

I sound more confident than I feel, but I sense that offering her more won't increase the odds of her cooperation. It will just make her more manipulative.

Su Yin pouts. "What if I help you?"

"If it leads to Deshi, you'll get your reward."

But if she helps me get Alister back? I'd hand over all my divorce settlement to feel Haiku's presence beside me and hear his voice in my ear; to have the future that was ours until a few days ago. I swallow hard to hide how much I'm hurting for both of us.

Su Yin surprises me with information. "I followed my body into that room. There were a lot of tables playing, more than last time. I watched myself walk up to one table and ask where to find wind sand chicken. You gave me that clue. They didn't like the question and pointed to another table. My body went over and asked the same question. One of the men asked why I wanted to know. I was scared for my body, the way he looked at me. I heard myself tell him I was looking for a missing baby—like without mentioning it was thirty years ago."

"And he told you something about Deshi?" This sounds highly unlikely.

"He said that whatever happens to missing babies—*babes* he said—all depends on how pretty they are. The other men laughed like it was such a big joke."

This sounds true enough to make me shudder. They weren't talking about thirty-year-old abductions. It sounds like the members of a modern abduction ring were doing a little illegal gambling right there on Egg Street. Bringing the ghosts with them.

I wonder if Su Yin has any insights beyond the obvious. "What do you think it means?"

"Don't you get it? If they're pretty enough they get adopted by rich people."

And if they're not pretty enough?

What was Deshi's destiny? Miss Tigerlily's words come back: *Baby called Moses.* I used to know my Bible stories. Did that clue trigger my dreams? First a tiny baby bobbed about in a boat. Then a boat morphed into a basket. But in both dreams, Deshi was gone. Did he ever find a new mother and father? Or did he meet a worse fate? I'm grateful that Alister isn't hearing this.

"Then the guy told me I'm pretty," Su Yin says, "and I should forget about wind sand chicken if I want to stay that way."

"He spoke in English?"

"Yeah. But he had a funny accent."

Not American, but pick your nationality. Plenty of expats who exploit whatever they can in Hong Kong. But what's there to forget about wind sand chicken?

* * *

Back at our building, we enter the lift. As we ride up, I remember the red eggs in my vision and ask Su Yin if they form part of any Chinese traditions.

"We have a red egg and ginger party. To welcome a baby."

"To celebrate its birth?"

"Later. One month, or one hundred days, or one year. It's an old tradition to keep the baby safe, but people suit themselves about the date. The baby's name gets announced, some hair gets snipped off, stuff like that."

Is that when Alister took his lock of Deshi's hair?

"What makes the eggs red?" I ask

"Nothing special. Hard boiled, then rolled in food dye."

She shows no curiosity about my questions. The doors open at her floor and she gets out.

"I won't go back to Egg Street." She flicks her hair over her shoulder. "No matter how much you pay me. That guy with the accent was one mean creep."

For the first time, I sense how frightened she is. Not only by Sharp kidnapping her body—although she seems strangely pragmatic about that—but by her encounter with those men. It was different from her last visit. This time she went at my insistence, and by saying 'Find Wind Sand Chicken' she put herself in danger.

Then with no guarantee that she'd get her reward, she gave

me information that might help Alister.

I follow her to her front door. "Thanks for taking a risk."

"Yeah, like I had a choice."

"You didn't have to tell me what happened with those men."

"If it helps Alister, I get my money."

"You have to find Deshi too. How are you going to do that?"

She treats me to her sly look. "I have my ways."

"Someone else is looking for Deshi," I say. "Whoever is kidnapping your body. Who do you think it is?"

She turns to punch in her door code, so I can't see her eyes. "I told your tall friend I don't know who it is. And I still don't." She opens her front door. "I helped you just now but I don't have to answer your questions."

"We both want to find Deshi—and help Alister. We could work together."

"No promises."

She closes the door.

Chapter 18

When I enter our apartment, the curtains in the living room are drawn. Beyond Nigel, who's hunched over his laptop at the table, Derek and Alister are watching a movie. At the sight of Alister engaged in such a normal activity, little wings of hope flutter in my chest. Is he back? Could it all be over? Did my trip to Egg Street magically restore him?

Then I notice how stiffly he's holding his head, how rigid his torso sits in the armchair. His lack of presence makes him a cruel replica of himself. Derek must be trying to involve him in the thrill of the action, but he's as far away as ever. My fluttering wings falter.

On the screen in front of them, fantasy backgrounds flash and strobe. Characters in animal-hide jerkins spit out spirited arguments in Cantonese, before the scene flips to another surreal tableau. As I watch, it occurs to me that the events of the last few days are like living in a Chinese ghost movie. Then a young woman flies through the air on a jungle rope, lands on a ledge, and pulls a sword from her belt to slash at a swooping dragon. She's wearing a black leotard—tucked into pink and black boots.

They might be in fashion for superheroes, but the sight of

the boots is too much for me. How are they connected to the kidnapping of Alister's spirit?

The volume of the soundtrack allows me to slip into the bedroom without disturbing the others. Suddenly desperate to wash off this morning's encounter with Sharp, I undress and turn on the shower. Under the needles of hot water, the delayed impact of my close shave with the astral plane hits me hard. I start howling. The shower becomes my crying cubicle, a private place to drown my fears, so I can show a brave face to the world.

Because I'm no superhero.

In trying to find a lead on Deshi and rescue Alister's soul, I almost lost my own. This is a moment of deep recrimination for being so careless. And in spite of the risks I took, I'm no closer to discovering if 'Find Wind Sand Chicken' is really a clue—or just a meaningless comment in a magazine. It feels like I've chosen the omelette.

But the hot water works its magic. As my emotions disappear down the drain, my thoughts flow. When my spirit almost left my body, it was exactly like my sudden nausea in the back of Winston's cab. That first time was no migraine.

Sharp must have known I was hiding near the gambling den. After Su Yin vanished from view, Sharp cast her off like an abandoned skin and travelled with me in Winston's cab. The timing fits. Then she tried to invade my body. The explosions in my head were sudden and powerful, but I wasn't sucked out that first time.

Why?

Letting the water massage my muscles, I return to Winston's back seat. My 'migraine' happened right outside the secret café where Alister was meeting Miss Tigerlily. What came first, the migraine or the location? Miss Tigerlily was busy scribbling runes on the napkin. If I include Sharp, five players in the quest to find Deshi came very close together at that moment.

Winston had just finished telling me his Emperor Wu and Madam Li story. I screamed at him to stop the cab beside the banner advertising the shadow puppet theatre.

Madam Li wants her guy. Watch how she does it.

Alister is like Emperor Wu, separated from his cherished wife by death. Fleur is like Madam Li, dancing in the shadows so she can reunite with her man. When Winston told the story, he and I were strangers to each other. But Sharp must have known our identities.

Did the story spark her attempt on my spirit? How?

No matter how much I want to exclude her, the identity of Sharp keeps pointing to Fleur. Did Alister's arrival in Hong Kong trigger her ghost to take action after all these years of waiting? When I travelled to Ireland last year, I discovered the power of ghosts who are trapped by unresolved violence. They remain in the landscape like a memory, poised and waiting, until the deeds of the living re-activate them.

But why try to invade me that first time?

Why stop?

Fleur's ghost must know that Alister has finally found someone to love again. Did she see her chance to slip into my skin where she could lie in his arms once more? On a psychic level, it makes perfect sense, but something went wrong.

For a moment I put myself in her place—and sense the lure of temptation. But by taking over my body, she would have been an imposter, forced to listen to him whisper my name, not hers. As this truth hits me, I'm overcome with empathy for her plight.

But I'm being loyal to Fleur for Alister's sake.

Madam Li wants her guy. Watch how she does it.

Obstructed from being his Madam Li and pleasing him as a spirit wife, did she kidnap his *Hun*—so their spirits could be together ... for eternity?

In spite of the water, I break into a sweat. The stakes are high. If Fleur wants her guy, then nothing will stop her. Especially me. Surely the events on Egg Street an hour ago prove it. Fleur must know that if I find Deshi, Alister's long-lost son could join forces with me. Together we could create such an emotional pull that his spirit will find the strength to leave Fleur and return to us—so she's stepped up her taunts on me to a full-scale attack. It explains why Alister growls when she's around. He's not recognising his old love, but the desperate spirit she's become.

Thanks to Su Yin murmuring the right phrase at the right time, Fleur's real attempt on my spirit failed.

This time.

As I step out of the shower, I'm on high alert. I can't forget that she kidnapped Alister in this apartment, but he was emotionally weak and vulnerable. While the water drips onto the floor, I close my eyes and visualise my little black dress wrapping my body in a protective coating. Made for me by Davina, my psychic Irish friend, the frock fits me like a skin and creates a symbolic link to my namesakes, the selkies. It protects me from psychic invasion—something Derek pointed out when I was having my first strange experiences in Hawaii.

I brought the dress with me, but as a cocktail frock it's not always practical, and the psychic version works just as well. I should have thought of it sooner, but I won't forget again. I'll need it when I return to Egg Street to get a stronger bearing on the red cord.

Back in the living room, the movie is over. Derek is putting a platter of cold wind sand chicken on the table. There's so much news to share, but Derek is bursting to begin. If he goes first, it will give me time to decide how much of my news to let Alister hear.

I smile at my man, looking for a flicker of response in his eyes. When I see nothing, I wrap my hand over his fist, the surge of warmth bringing a fleeting memory of the red cord. Fleur hasn't won yet.

I turn to Derek. "So Winston picked you up. Does that mean he didn't lie about Deshi's abduction?"

"I've been thinking about that theory," Nigel says. "He could be staying in plain sight because he's satisfied that he told you a good story."

"Except as a storyteller he's a taxi driver," Derek says, "in spite of his business card. My hunch is he couldn't spin a convincing lie. I'm sorry Alister but I think he was telling the truth."

Under my fingers the warmth in Alister's fist falters. His remaining *Po* spirit is following everything we say—and responding to the pain.

"What happened?" I ask Derek.

"Winston picked me up at the Mandarin Oriental. I asked him for a tour that would end with the best market on the island. I told him to tell me some folk tales, and he started with Emperor Wu and Madam Li. When I said I already knew that one, he ran through his whole repertoire. But the tour wasn't finished and he wanted his tip, so that's when he got to the interesting one. It must be an urban myth. About a woman taxi driver."

Derek has a habit of getting carried away by tangents. When he googles something, all kinds of red herrings snag his attention and interrupt his research.

"Tell me this is relevant, DD."

"Be patient, Selkie. I'm going to tell it better than Winston did. The punchline is worth it." He takes a breath and begins. "A guy in some far-off Chinese province catches a taxi, and the driver is a woman. This is unusual; she's beautiful; they connect. He goes home and tells his mother about her. Bad move. Mom doesn't like it one bit. A woman taxi driver? For a start, she sounds way too attractive, and therefore manipulative, and how could she be a proper woman who knows how to look after a man if she's picking up fares night and day?

"Mom tells her son to investigate in case this taxi driver isn't what she seems. The guy is under the thumb of his mother—Confucius and his filial piety have got that handled—so he asks a woman he knows to check the taxi driver out, make friends, and stay the night to see if there's anything weird about her. The friend does and ... she discovers something."

"What?" I ask on cue.

"She smells."

Bloody hell. "DD, really. A stinky taxi driver?"

"You haven't asked what the smell was."

"Money? I'll bet she got lots of tips."

"Fox stench. Women taxi drivers have fox stench. Winston said there were even advertisements for ways to get rid of their smell—with deodorants or surgery."

"Surgery?"

"To remove their sweat glands, but alas if you're a fox spirit, they grow back. Of course it's just misogyny. Uneducated women from the countryside not knowing that it's not their place to drive taxis; taking men's jobs; being too attractive and luring passengers away from their mothers, blah, blah. The story must have started with mythology. The fox is a shape-shifter. They mostly change into gorgeous women who seduce men to ensure their own immortality."

"Like vampires?" Derek knows I draw the line at stories with vampires or zombies.

"Energy vampires," he says. "Fox spirits steal a man's spirit."

Shit.

Derek's punchline renders us silent. Except Alister who starts rumbling in the back of his throat. As I squeeze his fist and feel new heat, Nigel gets Miss Tigerlily's map from the safe and spreads it on the table. We stare at the four-legged creature that Alister divined with my bangle. Pointed ears. Pointed chin. And the few pale lines we missed under torch-light now clearly indicate a bushy tail. Sharp's silky taunts and prickly scratches suddenly make sense.

"A vixen," I say. I tell them what happened on Egg Street with Su Yin and Sharp. "Sharp is female; I'm sure of it. I think it's why she can slip in and out of Su Yin's body at will. But because Alister's male, I suspect she can only kidnap him."

"There's a weird logic to that," says Nigel.

"But she might have invaded *you*, Selkie." Derek's voice rises. "You could have come back here with a phoney on board."

"So far she's only taunted me here, and I've just put on the psychic version of my little black dress. I'm protected. But

I have to return to Egg Street, and she seemed to get extra power in the thin place."

They need to hear about my vision of the red cord, but first I tell them what I learned from Su Yin. "This is going to be hard, Alister, but it's more information in our search for Deshi."

As Derek and Nigel listen to what the man with the accent told her, their faces turn grim.

"Could they have smuggled babies into China?" Nigel says. "*Moses in a basket.* I've heard that during the one-child policy, some parents who wanted a son gave their daughters away. That fits with the word pretty." He's avoided the rumours of baby girls being abandoned or killed. "As a boy, Deshi would have been valuable. It might explain why they abducted him."

Inside my hand, Alister's fist turns cold. I should have protected him from this insight. We'd have no hope of finding Deshi in China, unless he answered one of Alister's ads himself.

Then I remember something. "But Superintendent Butler said something important when he saw Deshi's baby photo. And Miss Tigerlily said almost the same thing: *Not Chinese enough.*"

Nigel voices our thoughts. "If he didn't look Chinese enough, questions would have been asked about his origins. Not a so-called orphan from mainland China, but a baby of mixed parentage from across the border. They couldn't risk any kind of investigation. Perhaps that means they found parents for him here."

Could Deshi have been adopted by a mixed race couple here in Hong Kong? Like Dr Lee's parents who are English and Chinese? It's possible and my optimism returns.

"It's an important clue, Haiku," I whisper, resting my

forehead against his cheek. "I haven't dared tell you this before but I'm sure Deshi's alive. And Sharp thinks so too. That's why she took Su Yin into that gambling den. Twice. She was looking for a clue from those child abductors, thinking their treatment of orphans hasn't changed in thirty years. It's not comforting to have Sharp on Deshi's trail, but it confirms that he's not far away."

If Alister suspects that Deshi's close, is his *Hun* spirit more likely to find the will to return? In the silence that follows, his fist warms up. He trusts me. To find Deshi and bring him home. The quest is getting ever more dangerous, but I won't let him down.

Nigel says, "And thanks to your excursion with Winston, DD, we know Sharp is something akin to a fox spirit. Miss Tigerlily's sketch confirms it. Now to discover *who*. And *why*."

"I've been thinking," Derek says. "It seems like Sharp used Su Yin's body to confront those men. Why didn't Sharp go to Egg Street herself?"

"Because she's dead and needs a human body?" I won't name Fleur while Alister's so vulnerable.

Derek shakes his head. "A fox spirit, assuming they exist outside folklore, has the power to change shape. Sharp should be able to take on human form, not have to resort to invading Su Yin. It's demeaning. It suggests she can't shape-shift."

"That brings us back to sorcery by a living person." Nigel says. "That's much more plausible. A medium might believe she's channelling the cunning of a fox spirit, and Miss Tigerlily picked it up."

A living person. What if I'm wrong about Fleur? Completely wrong. What if Sharp is someone else?

A name pops out of Derek's mouth. "Su Yin."

In a 180 degree turnaround, I recall the first time I saw Su Yin—the sudden surge of mistrust. Now I'm seeing her face in my mind: the pointed shape of her eyes and chin, her layered mane of silky hair with auburn streaks. And again I feel her fingers scratching the nape of my neck, bringing on a rush of alarm—and pleasure. Right from that moment she manipulated me.

Now I remember her comment in the lift: "You assume that Alister won't be tempted by a woman half your age." I wasn't worried that she'd seduce him, but her remark bothered me for a reason I couldn't define. Then she said, "You think you're so powerful in your pink boots. You think you've won. But you don't know anything."

Now I'm wondering if she turned up here under the pretext of helping Alister, expecting him to be alone. Then all the way from the airport, he did nothing but talk about me.

What happened between them in San Francisco?

When Alister first laid eyes on her, just for a moment he thought she was Fleur. He told me he was taken back thirty years to the morning Fleur was killed. Then the mirage faded and he remembered Fleur was dead. If Su Yin sensed that surge of his misplaced love, what expectations did it evoke in her? He's old enough to be her father but he's an attractive man.

He's also rich.

Is that what this is all about? His money? The fat man really is the rich man, after all? In the cab just now, all she could talk about was her reward.

But stealing his *Hun* puts his fortune out of reach. Why would she do that? Her motives must be more complex.

Derek breaks into my thoughts. "I've seen nothing to make

me trust her. It would be just like a self-styled fox spirit to trick us into thinking she's been possessed."

My confidence dwindles at so easily being her dupe. "The rescue from Sharp on Egg Street is looking like a charade. Now that I think about it, the timing was too neat. She turned back from the group of men just as it happened. The trick worked. I started to trust her."

Know. Who. To. Trust.

Miss Tigerlily was doing her reading just as Su Yin arrived in Hong Kong. And Su Yin was doing private business on Egg Street when Miss Tigerlily sketched a fox. Was it Su Yin's spirit that followed me in the cab? She admitted later to lying about meeting Winston—but she had to do that because I caught her out. She mixed the beer cocktails that Alister drank; she asked in a text message if I'd given up yet; she broke in here twice and crowed evil phrases about me and him. And she stood over Alister as he lay vulnerable—with her fingers on his throat. What might she have done if I hadn't stopped her?

Derek is on his phone. "The myth would have originated in China and I can't find a Cantonese translation, but fox spirit in Mandarin is *huli jing*. The syllables sound way too much like Su Yin to my ear."

My mind is racing. Is Su Yin even her real name?

She's the one who answered the ad and contacted Alister, but surely his investigator checked out her background. Because of her family's hostility towards Alister, they've had to keep their contact secret—giving her way too much power.

Only a few minutes ago I was sure Sharp was Fleur. Now I can't get my head around this sudden flip. I look at Alister. He isn't growling. Is blaming Su Yin too simple?

I pick up the phone. "Let's talk to her now."

No answer. I send her a text asking if she's OK after this morning's brush with the child abductors. No response. She might just be ignoring me, so I go down to her floor and buzz. After knocking and calling, I use the code to open up. Then I run through the place, wondering if I'm hallucinating. Her stuff is gone. The wardrobe is empty. The bathroom is devoid of her makeup.

After returning from Egg Street, Su Yin packed up and moved out.

Shit.

Chapter 19

"Her ears were burning," Derek says. "We've been giving her a pretty bad rap."

The timing feels ominous. If Su Yin really is some manifestation of *huli jing*, the fox spirit, then leaving without telling me looks like an escalation.

"Where the hell has she gone? All the way back to San Francisco?" But I don't believe for a minute she's given up. Whatever is motivating her hasn't changed.

"This doesn't prove she's Sharp," Nigel says. "She might be in trouble."

That stops me. I navigate another mental turnaround. If her sleepwalking story is true, then should we be worried about her? Has the invading spirit made her pack up her things? Either way, her disappearance means trouble—and it's going to be bad for Alister.

Nigel turns to Derek. "DD, you called Winston's fox story an urban myth, but could he be talking about a real taxi driver? Someone here in Hong Kong?"

Derek is already googling it. "Women taxi drivers. The South China Post." He scans the article. "Of the 40,000 licenses only 6,000 are women. Too dangerous. Too much competition. Long hours and—get this—they're slow at changing tyres. Nothing about fox stench. Why would a taxi driver use sorcery to target Winston's family?"

"Maybe he's been spreading his fox stench story around the other drivers," Nigel says. "Those comments about changing tyres suggest a culture against women drivers—so what if the online bullying started? And snowballed? But the 'who' will lead to the 'why'. Who else?"

Letting go of Su Yin for now, I think of the only other female with a stake in Alister's quest. "Rose. But Alister hasn't told me anything about her."

"Maybe the fox stench story is about Rose and Winston," Nigel says. "They could share the cab and take shifts. What if they met in rural China, then ran away to San Francisco to get away from the local prejudice? Winston might not usually tell anyone about their history, but he ran out of stories with you, DD, and you were safe, being a tourist."

"What's her motive?" Derek asks.

"Rose blames Alister for Fleur's death," I say. "I know that much. A grieving mother can hold a grudge for thirty years, especially so she won't have to blame herself for losing Deshi. When Winston was here he barely mentioned Rose, only the shrines she's made for Fleur and Deshi. Do they show she's some kind of medium, DD?"

"Every Buddhist household has a shrine," Derek says.

Like the shrine in my Egg Street vision?

"We have to talk to Rose." I say. "Winston's not answering calls from me. You call him, DD. But how will you get him to take you home?"

"Tell him you'll pay good money to meet a fox lady for your research," Nigel suggests. "If he takes the bait, we can follow in another cab. And hope it's not a scam."

Derek nods and sends Winston a text. Within minutes he gets a reply.

Fox lady very private.

Derek sighs. "Money talks in this town." He doubles, then triples his offer.

Fox lady say OK. Meet at secret place. Monday ten o'clock. I take you. Triple price for taxi.

"Not till Monday?" I cry. "If Rose is our sorcerer what will she do to Alister over the weekend?"

The phone rings. It's Dr Lee's receptionist.

When Cindy hangs up, I exhale with relief. "Dr Lee will call in again tonight. We can quiz him about fox spirits."

Derek's pleased. "I want his advice about Chinese healing foods for Alister. I asked discreetly at the market and got con-flicting answers. They thought I was asking about something … unmentionable. It might be illegal but one joker tried to sell me a powder labelled 'rhino horn'."

"Welcome to Hong Kong," Nigel says.

"Dr Lee will approve of your trip to the gym, Nige," I say.

"Alister was willing. Half an hour of interval training while you were out. Then we lifted some weights and arm wrestled. After that we went for a walk."

"You took him … outside the building?"

"Don't look so worried, Selkie. Just along this road there's a walking trail that goes right up to the peak. We wandered through the vines and got some great views across the harbour. I figure that Alister's spirit is more likely to come back if his body is enjoying all the benefits of living. Come with us next time."

Enjoying all the benefits of living. I've just thought of something that his body is not enjoying. My cheeks flush.

Nigel notices. "What?"

I'm embarrassed to answer, but these boys are like my sisters. "Alister and I haven't ... made love since this happened."

Nigel thinks about this. "Keeping the base *chakras* limber—and connected—seems like the best exercise at a time like this. For both of you."

I look across at Alister, his eyes dark and empty. My throat constricts. I reach out and touch his hand. "Not without your consent."

Everyone is silent, until Nigel looks at his phone. He hands it to me. "A little corny but you can't beat Ravel for mood creation. It's ready to play."

Derek gets up. "Show me that hiking trail, Nige. I've been in Winston's cab all morning, listening to his awful stories. I need to come up for air and stretch my legs."

As they leave the apartment together, my heart swells with love—for them and their respect.

"We're good at this, Haiku," I whisper, wondering if we can do it—and fearing what will happen if we can't.

Then taking his hand, I lead him into the bedroom and shut the door.

* * *

This room should feel like our own space, but Sharp's intrusions have created an air of violation. As an antidote, I throw open the curtains on the high windows, allowing a private view of the sky. Golden rays stream through the clouds and illuminate the king-size bed.

Aware that Sharp might somehow be witnessing our every move, I remind myself to focus on Alister, on *us*. I slip out of my clothes first, grateful that the virtual little black dress will protect me. Alister needs help because he's still making a fist with his left hand.

When we're both naked, I pick up Nigel's phone. We've never needed props before—it's always been slow and steamy or fast and fun, whichever way the mood took us. I remind myself that music is the language of the soul; that it might work its magic on Alister's *Hun*; that at the very least it will enrich our connection. As I turn it on, the room fills with the drum beat that heralds the Bolero.

Drumming is my music and I begin to move. On a wave of longing, I'm overtaken by a hunger that I realise I've suppressed till now. Then a flute pipes its haunting melody, followed by the clarinet, and I flip from Alister's protector to his lover, with a need to consume him and be consumed by him in return. It's been missing since his spirit departed—our bodies uniting and living the red cord's promise.

At first he stands passively, until the music acts like a spell. He remembers the mechanics of movement, and as I brush against him, he joins me in a slow dance. It takes me back to the night we lost ourselves to the music on the banks of the Loire River in France and I imagine us back there now.

When we fall onto the bed, I wrap myself around him and press my lips to his. Gazing into his vacant eyes, I will him to show me even a glint of his soul's presence, but the depths remain dark. I persist, hoping the power of his base *chakra* can open up a chink. Instead it makes the next thing happen.

By a miracle of body memory, we meet and move together. Tears of tenderness roll down my cheeks. But his physical self is going through the motions while his spirit is trapped somewhere else—and the emptiness of our coupling hits me like a blow.

There has to be a way for me to reach his spirit. As my body wraps him in my love, I press my bangle gently against his chest. When his eyes stare blankly, I try to tease his fist open with my mouth but he only squeezes it tighter.

At this rejection, my rhythm falters and at some level he senses it. He looks at me with eyes still dark and hollow, but there's a flicker of movement in their depths. I fall in.

What I enter is like a dreamscape, filtered and hazy. The near dark is punctuated by a rectangular frame of light. I hear my name.

Selkie.

His voice.

Selkie. You found me.

I'm with him. I'm really with him. But his words are floating like dry leaves about to fly away and I sense his struggle to hold them together. Dizzy as I am with joy, I open my mouth to ask where he is.

Don't speak! It's not safe.

With every cell of my being, I will him to tell me who has taken him. Where he is. And why.

Deshi is the key ... He's fading away. Follow the red cord ... Never forget I love you ...

As I choke back a sob, the frame of light vanishes along with his presence. I've lost him again. A wave of my love surges after his retreating spirit, but another wave drowns it.

Malice. Sticky as tar.

A brush appears.

Unable to tear my eyes away, I watch its tip draw something black and wet from a pot. In painstaking calligraphy, it makes shapes on a strip of white paper. The emotion behind the action is suffocating, but still I watch as my chest heaves in each breath. Expecting Chinese characters, I see letters form in English, and when the final letter is done, it reveals the name that I knew was coming.

Alister Sloane.

I gasp, then stifle the sound, as Alister warned. Human fingers, not claws, are clipping the paper to a string beside three others. Like prayer flags, four identical strips of paper bearing Alister's name flap in a light breeze. I'm mesmerised with horror as a lighted match touches each corner and ignites them. Under an orange flame that turns quickly to black, the papers shrivel his name to ash.

And beneath my naked body, four wisps of Alister's remaining spirit ebb from our lovemaking.

In the midst of us sharing the deepest connection possible, something evil is performing a ritual with brush, paper and match. And sliver by sliver by sliver by sliver it's burning away his *Hun.*

Alister has slumped beneath me. His eyes are closed. After making sure he's still breathing, I cover him with a blanket, throw on a robe and race into the living room. The boys are just creeping back through the front door.

"He spoke to me," I cry, collapsing into Derek's arms. "Soul to soul. But she's burning his name, DD. She's killing him."

He holds me as my body shudders in great racking sobs of despair, but even his hug can't console me.

Nigel is just behind him. They guide me to the armchairs where with juddering breaths, I give them the details of my vision.

"Alister's sleeping now. But I was with him. In a dark place. Then my vision faded and I saw her burning his name. The papers were flapping, then they went up in smoke. Four times she did it." My voice rises. "Four means *death*! Just like the tea leaves on the plane predicted. Little by little ... she's *killing* him!"

"Are you sure of what you saw, Selkie?" Nigel asks, him voice steady. "Could you have slipped into his dream?"

"I'm sure. Alister made love to me with his body, but I hoped it might bring back ... a glimmer of his ... spirit." I can barely get the words out. A wail escapes. "When I realised how absent he was, his body sensed my reaction. Then somehow he opened a window on his soul and ... spoke to me. I was with him! That wasn't a dream. And he couldn't have dreamed the burning, it was too graphic—and filled with hate."

Derek purses his lips. "Write his name and burn it? That's sorcery 101. Some kind of curse. For a fox spirit, Sharp's tactics are straight out of the beginner's manual."

I rush on. "Don't you see? This makes finding him more urgent than ever. He said finding Deshi is the key, but that was before she burnt his name. First I have to find Alister. I've got to go back to Egg Street. That's where I saw the red cord. It was gone in a blink and I missed the chance to follow it. I've got to find it again before it's too late. I've got to find out where he is and stop her." How, I have no idea.

I finally tell them about my visions on Egg Street.

When he hears about the shrine, Nigel says, "The cord did its job. When you're close to something relevant to Alister and his quest, the red cord appears. Alister's shown he'll give you more if he can, but that's too uncertain. Use Miss Tigerlily's psychic map, follow your intuition and allow the cord to confirm the clues. You know how to do this, Selkie."

He's talking about the time I was staying with them in

Honolulu and collected a bunch of objects in my sleep. They turned out to be a psychic map and I had to travel to France before the clues fell into place, but it took months of clumsy sleuthing.

"I haven't got the luxury of time, Nige. The longer I leave him in her clutches, the greater the risk that ... he won't come back."

"I know. But you won't get there by rushing around in circles. Don't be the chicken without a head. It's all about ... being sleek."

Being Sleek is my business seminar. It uses the wisdom of seals as a metaphor for trusting your intuition. *Go down to the sea.* Just like Miss Tigerlily, Nigel is reminding me to call on all my skills.

"I get it," I say, steadying my breathing. "I nearly lost my own soul on Egg Street but I had a vision. I saw the red cord. What the hell was it trying to tell me? Is there a whiteboard around here?"

"Voila the fridge!" Derek says.

I find a whiteboard marker in my laptop bag and my audience of two sits up at the island counter.

"Egg Street." As I write it on the fridge door, the action evokes a surge of confidence. "Thin place. Old egg market. Two visions: Red eggs for baby. Baby Deshi?"

"And a Buddhist shrine," Nigel adds.

I list what I can remember from the shrine. "Candle. Incense. Flowers."

"All offerings," Nigel says. "The Buddhists believe in reincarnation. Giving in this life adds brownie points to your karma for a better life next time."

Time to flip my thinking to analytical mode. Alister's life

depends on it. "So what have we got? The shrine looked like a place of worship, of making offerings. Those pieces of paper with Alister's name on them looked like prayer flags, the way they flapped. Do the Buddhists burn paper as an offering? Could this sorcery be a Buddhist practice turned evil? Is that why I saw the shrine?"

Nigel thinks about this. "Paper offerings do get burned in Buddhist temples but it's an ancient Taoist practice that the Buddhists tolerate from their Chinese worshippers. The Chinese believe in burning death money and paper images of worldly goods. The idea is to bring comfort to the deceased in the afterlife."

I remember the store beneath the secret café, its stacks of death money and paper mache replicas.

"These paper strips weren't for Alister's comfort," I say. "I'm sure they were ... killing him."

"Some kind of crude folklore, like DD said. Not death money. A curse."

A Taoist curse. I stare at the words on the fridge and wonder what I'm missing.

Meanwhile, Derek is googling. "OK, the number of Buddhists and Taoists in Hong Kong are about equal; a million or more in each group. There's a Taoist temple in Kowloon that also embraces Buddhism and Confucianism—Wong Tai Sin Temple. Worshippers and tourists can get their fortunes told. That means they speak English." He looks at the time. "We could go there now and tell them what you saw, ask what it means and how to reverse it."

"Thanks, DD. It's a good idea. Stopping the ritual is so urgent, I can hardly think straight, but I need to focus my energy on the right actions. Now that Dr Lee's coming, I'll make myself wait and get his advice."

Derek nods and returns to his phone. "This came up in the same search. The White Tiger festival is on this weekend—the same tiger in Miss Tigerlily's reading. The South China Post must be pleased with their headline: *Make a Curse, Break a Curse.*" He reads out part of the article. "*After its long winter hibernation, the White Tiger wakes up this weekend and wants to be fed. Devotees will congregate under the Canal Road flyover at Causeway Bay, to feed the White Tiger and dispel evil and bad luck. Amidst joss-sticks, incense papers and candles, paper effigies of the deity will be feted with offerings of raw meat, lard, uncooked eggs, mung beans and sesame seeds.* Uncooked eggs. These could be your eggs, Selkie."

The thought pushes me over the edge. "Is that what I've got to do to stop the attack on Alister?" I cry. "Offer raw eggs to a paper tiger? Don't I have to know why she's doing this to him?" I get control of my voice. "Sorry DD, I keep seeing those strips burning—and reliving what they're doing to him."

"And it's corrupting your intuition," Nigel says.

The truth behind his insight hits me. I stop. And suddenly see what I've missed.

"My god, Nige. I've been thinking the vision was Alister's cry for help; that he was showing me what she's doing to him. But he'd just expended all his energy to reach out to me, so how could he have energy to show me anything else?" I start pacing. "Our lovemaking *was* calling his spirit back, so Sharp whipped out that bloody calligraphy brush and pulled me right out of it with that vision. She tried to steal my spirit on Egg Street, and when that didn't work, she started chipping away at my intuitive powers by playing on my weak spot—my commitment to Alister."

Derek says, "No wonder it looked like curse-making for toddlers. The vision was bogus, designed to discombobulate you. Now she sounds like a fox spirit. A trickster to the core."

"Did you see the red cord during your lovemaking, Selkie?" Nigel asks.

"No. And Alister kept his fist closed like a vault. I feared he was rejecting my attempts to touch his soul, but he was keeping me safe the only way he could." I remember his words. In his depleted state, he was still protecting me. I collapse on a stool. "Fleur, Su Yin, Rose. Which one? Who else could care so much about Alister's quest—and his connection to me—to be carrying such a grudge?"

Derek is scanning the rest of the article. "You need to listen to this. There are more powers attributed to the White Tiger: *It's believed that this powerful deity can subdue wandering spirits. Appeased with food, the White Tiger will rid worshippers of backstabbers who spread malicious gossip, and energy vampires who wish them harm.*"

"Energy vampires? Are they hiding under every rock around here? We've stepped into an epidemic. All we want is to find Deshi."

Derek puts down his phone and puts on the kettle for some tea. "Don't dismiss effigies as just folklore, Selkie. They're powerful magic. Even if Sharp *was* burning Alister's name to distract you from your own wisdom, the ritual still carries the force of her intention. If she's got hold of even a sliver of Alister's *Hun*, then burning his name may be sending his spirit right back to him, poisoned by all her malice."

Is that what I felt when Alister seemed to ebb from me? Spiritual poison tainting his soul? My panic about rescuing him returns in a double dose. A moment ago, I was relieved that she was just trying to trick me; now it seems that even her tricks are deadly.

"Thanks DD. I couldn't do this without you two. You and Nige are making sure I miss nothing. What else does the article say?"

"The rest is about old ladies called villain hitters who work under the flyover. You can pay them to feed the tigers for you, or to cause bad luck to your enemies. They hit paper effigies with a shoe. There's a video."

"Dr Lee will know if I should consult them."

Everyone's exhausted. Derek and Nigel settle into the armchairs for a doze, while I look in on Alister. He's in a deep sleep. I want so badly to get him out of here, but Sharp's an enemy we can't escape by running away. I spend a few minutes typing up notes for Dr Lee. Then I climb in beside my man, grateful to drop into a dreamless sleep.

* * *

When I wake, Alister is still asleep. I tiptoe into the living room and tell the boys.

"He's had a big day," Nigel says. "I hope you got some shut-eye."

"Yeah. And thanks to you two, my intuition is back. We don't know where Su Yin and Rose are, so we can't confront them yet, but we must keep looking for Deshi. Alister told me that he's the key. Those men on Egg Street know something or Sharp wouldn't be so interested."

"You're not going to confront *them* instead, I hope," Derek says.

"No, but if I report them to David Butler he may be able to

help us."

"I bet the cops already know about the gambling den," he says. "They might be turning a blind eye—or the ghost stories are deterring them."

David Butler takes my call and listens to what the men said to Su Yin. "Egg Street. A mahjong gaming venue will be illegal. You spoke to these men? Were they Chinese or expats?"

"Alister's niece spoke to them. And the ringleader had a funny accent." I give him Su Yin's number. "She may not reply. Right after we got back from Egg Street, she vacated her accommodation."

"Leave it with me. How's Mr Sloane? Was Dr Lee of any help?"

"He's making his second visit tonight. He's worried that Alister's stress about his missing son made him vulnerable to ... sorcery."

Butler is quiet for a moment. He's been in Hong Kong long enough not to be surprised by such practices. "Right after you both consulted Miss Tigerlily."

"Yes. When we looked back at her readings, she foresaw it."

So why didn't she foresee her own kidnapping? At this observation, I stop. Of course she foresaw it. She wore a disguise. Is that why she disappeared?

"Is there any news on her whereabouts?"

There's a long pause before he answers. "Not that I can share, even off the record. And we're keeping it out of the papers. We don't want a rush of hoax ransom demands."

A ransom. My thoughts return to Alister. By most people's standards, he's rich. Is that the meaning of the 'fat man' after all? Kidnap his *Hun*, burn some paper strips to generate panic, then demand a fortune to give it back?

Returning to the subject of the gambling den, I don't let on that I think Miss Tigerlily has gone into hiding. "I'm sure finding Deshi is the key to everything that's happened. It was thirty years ago, but what if the child abductors are still using the same system? If we can find Deshi, he might be able to help you prevent further kidnappings. I've made an appointment with Klaus Hofmeier to see what he knows about the local abduction rings, but isn't there something you can tell me about their practices?"

"Please don't speak to Hofmeier."

"Oh?"

"Cancel the appointment. I'm not at liberty to say more, or to give you any information about abduction rackets. I'm sorry. But I'm sure Beth will talk to you, the woman you saw with Miss Tigerlily."

"Has Miss Tigerlily been helping her?"

"Yes."

I sense a lead. "Please give her my number."

When he hangs up, I cancel my appointment at The Dove, wondering just what Butler wouldn't tell me about Klaus.

Chapter 20

When the intercom finally rings, I pounce on it.

Dr Lee enters the apartment and shakes hands with Nigel, who towers over him, reinforcing the impression of a schoolboy. Derek emerges from the kitchen, wiping his hands on an apron. The action reminds me of my recurring sense that Deshi works with food. Derek introduces himself.

Dr Lee turns to me. "You must be completely overwhelmed, Selkie, in spite of the awesome support you're getting from your friends."

Alister chooses that moment to appear in the bedroom doorway. His curly brown hair is crumpled from sleep, and he stands there blinking vacantly. He's also completely naked, and my insides ache for his predicament.

"Good to see you're out of bed, Alister." Bruce lifts his hand and shakes it. "But I see your *Hun* is still AWOL. Let's check you out. Then your support team can tell me what's been happening."

When Dr Lee's finished his examination, he reads my brief report. Then everyone sits down to hear his assessment.

"Congratulations on getting Alister back in the saddle as a lover, Selkie. That took courage, and what a payoff! I would never have expected he could speak to you. His *Po* is maintaining his strong connection to you through his base *chakra*—and perhaps the red cord, that he's protecting so strongly, turned into words in that moment. You say you could only see a rectangle of light, but no other sense of where he is? That could mean he's safely contained in some way, but we can't rely on him staying like that without knowing the sorcerer's agenda.

"I prescribe a regular dose of the best sex you can both manage, given the pressures you're under. But you may not hear from him again."

"I'm terrified about damaging his *Hun*. After seeing that cursing ritual, I've been thinking we shouldn't try it again. I suspect our lovemaking inspired it."

"Probably, but you've heard from Alister so you know he hasn't got lost somewhere. And you've glimpsed the enemy." He pauses. "In spite of her sorcery, Alister's spiritual condition has barely changed."

All I hear is one word. "What do you mean? Has something changed?"

"It's a time factor. The longer he's absent the weaker his link to his body becomes. It's what happens when the *Hun* is absent. Meanwhile, she's using all her tricks to keep him under her power. But you've got so much strength in this anti-curse cabal of yours that she's not making much progress. It might not feel like it, but all this psychic activity is a good sign. It means you're in the game."

A game that she'll win if I take too long to find him.

"But you're exhausted," Bruce says. "In spite of the time pressure, it's essential that you sleep whenever you're tired. Use tiredness as a sign that you need time for renewal—and to get psychic messages."

"OK." I push down the urgency that's churning in my stomach and turn to my list, asking Derek to update him on Winston's urban myth.

"I know about fox spirits," Bruce says. "When I was a boy, there was a famous furore. The shape of a fox head appeared in the new facade of the Windsor House shopping centre. It was in one of the marble panels—like the Turin shroud. Crowds blocked the street and the rumour mill generated a lot of angst, blaming the fox spirit for the death of several children. After a couple of days of public panic, the builders replaced the offending marble in the middle of the night.

"But this taxi driver angle is new to me. Google probably hasn't heard of it either. That doesn't mean it's not a strong belief in rural China. If it's given you the clue you needed from Miss Tigerlily's map, then the story might have done its job."

"Why would a fox spirit be interested in Alister?" I ask.

Dr Lee thinks about this. "Chinese fox spirits shape-shift, usually into a woman. In folklore they steal men's spirits to gain immortality, but this attack on Alister seems personal. A female in his circle would be my guess. There's also a belief that by worshipping a fox spirit, you gain the charm of the fox. It may be how our fox spirit gets her power."

That sounds as sinister as I feared. Pushing the thought aside, I ask Dr Lee about the shrine I saw in my Egg Street vision.

"That could be one of two things," he says. "A message about a shrine—any shrine, as a symbol of service. Or a shrine was once located there—like the shrine to Yue Lao you found—but now it's been paved over and turned into a warehouse. With all the modernisation in Hong Kong over the last thirty years, many of the old places are unrecognisable. But the spirit of the past remains. I'm a lapsed Catholic, with some Taoist coaching from an old temple keeper, so I still believe that. Someone with your gifts can feel it."

The spirit of the past remains. It matches my experience in Ireland.

"Could there have been a shrine in the old egg market?" I ask.

"Egg market?"

"A taxi driver said that's why it's called Egg Street."

He smiles. "I remember the Egg Street Market. It sold everything, not just eggs."

I put my faith in that taxi driver's English. But the eggs in my dream came first.

"Shrines can be portable," Bruce says. "The stallholder in the market sets it up in the morning and folds it away to go home. Or there was a humble temple right there in the market and it's since succumbed to the bulldozers."

Whatever it was, I need to focus on what the shrine was showing me.

Finally, I ask Bruce about the value of visiting the White Tiger Festival and consulting a fortune teller at the Taoist temple that Derek found—to understand the cursing ritual and get advice about countering it.

"The festival's this weekend, is it? Under the Canal Road flyover? Spring's arrived early this year." He thinks for a moment. "Miss Tigerlily listed the White Tiger in her reading, so the timing fits. If you decide to consult a villain hitter there, go on Sunday. There'll still be plenty of stalls to choose from, but fewer worshippers. The die-hards and the desperate will go on Saturday and the queues will be serpentine. It's dark and smoky enough underneath the flyover without adding human sweat to the mix. And the villain hitters will give you more attention on Sunday.

"If you visit the Wong Tai Sin Temple," he continues, "the fortune tellers have refined their system for tourists and it might look like a gimmick, but the bamboo divining sticks and the messages themselves are ancient. You may get psychic guidance from their advice. Trust it."

Bruce claps his hands. Then looks at his watch. "Any other questions?"

"Healing foods for Alister," Derek asks.

"Good that you're thinking of that. With his *Hun* spirit absent, he's missing his *yang* energy. Give him warm foods. They'll help his libido too. Ginger, onion, garlic, chicken, lobster. Google a list."

"We've got a freezer full of wind sand chicken." I want to see if Bruce reacts.

"Fat, garlic and chicken—all perfect for Alister. And you've got my stomach rumbling too."

"Please stay for a bite," Derek says, heading for the kitchen.

* * *

After Dr Lee leaves, my phone pings with a text from Beth. It's crisp.

Got your number from David B. Can meet 8pm tonight. Fat Waiter Secret Club, 26 New Fan Road. There's no sign. Give taxi address and take stairs beside funeral store. Beth.

It's where Alister met Miss Tigerlily—and it's called the Fat Waiter! We've been visiting cafés, but not this one. If Alister knew the name, he never said. A club? It must be where she met Beth too—a private place to do her readings? Perhaps meeting me in her office was unusual. What did Alister say on the phone after meeting her? She had a special reason for going there.

I google the name without expecting a website and find one mention in a blog about secret haunts. A poorly lit snapshot shows odd-matched chairs and tablecloths, the walls covered in black and white murals of waiters with bellies bulging over aprons. It's hard to see, but the odd mix of painting styles suggest that patrons can add their own drawing to the mural. Under other circumstances, I'd find it quirky. The blogger boasts that it's only available to savvy diners who know how to ask around. The food must be very good. Or very cheap.

"I'll come with you," Nigel says. With his height, bulk and shaved head, he makes a great body guard.

"Thank you, but Beth might get freaked out and clam up."

"I'll enter separately and sit at another table."

It's a good compromise and I send her a reply, agreeing to meet up.

It's Derek who notices it. "Is it a coincidence that the Fat Waiter Secret Club begins with the same letters as 'Find Wind Sand Chicken'?"

Bloody hell. "Was it one of the cafés in the directory, DD?"

"Nope. I think we'd remember that name since we've been looking for a fat waiter."

I get the in-flight magazine anyway, while Derek checks the videos of Marty's shopping expeditions.

When we come up blank, he says, "These pop-up places don't advertise. Being clandestine is their attraction."

Another text from Beth clinches it. *There's a password for entry. Cute! Same letters as club name: Find Wind Sand Chicken.*

I can't wait to tell the others. "Alister must have used it when he met Miss Tigerlily. He wouldn't have thought it meant anything. It just sounds like a fun entry code. What's the chance that Deshi is one of the waiters?"

"Miss Tigerlily uses that place," Nigel says, "but the clues on her map are cryptic. If Deshi works there, surely she'd have sensed a stronger link to Alister when they met."

I turn to Alister. "You said she had a reason for meeting there. Was that it? She sensed a connection to you?" Except it appears she met Beth there too. "Then something happened. That's what you said when I phoned you afterwards. Does anything on this rune-map give us a clue to what happened?"

I try him with the bangle on the red cord but nothing happens.

"It's not just a passcode," Derek says. "If Su Yin was telling the truth about the child abductors, they reacted to the words 'Find Wind Sand Chicken' with a threat. Why?"

They threatened Su Yin and a few hours later she was gone. Could she be in that kind of trouble?

* * *

Nigel uses the bathroom while I get dressed. When I emerge, Alister and Derek are watching another movie.

"Research," Derek says. "I've read the blurb and it could be useful. It's called *Painted Skin*."

I don't ask for more. I'm sure he's being secretive because he's missing out on tonight's adventure.

Nigel comes out of the bedroom and looks me over. "If this club is at all related to the abduction ring, you'd be wise to disguise yourself. You can't do much about your accent but your hair ...”

"The blonde wig?"

"Perfect."

Derek adores women's fashion. He pauses the movie and follows me into the walk-in closet.

"It's only a wig, DD. My neighbour snaffled the frock."

"Snaffled? Sounds too much like 'snafu'."

"I hope not."

Along with the wig, we find the boots.

Su Yin's voice echoes in my head: "You think you're so powerful in your pink boots." Where is she? I wonder if she's just gone to stay with Winston and Rose, and I'll wake up in the morning to a text message from her. I never thought I'd look forward to that.

Derek helps me with my coif and when I walk into the living room, Nigel whistles. Alister looks around from the frozen image on the TV screen and stares at me.

Walking over, I whisper, "It's me, Haiku. I'm wearing the blonde wig. The one you helped me choose." Does he relax slightly? Since he spoke to me, our connection feels stronger. I savour it.

As Derek farewells us at the door, I'm suddenly very glad that Nigel is coming with me.

Chapter 21

The cab driver hears the address with no visible reaction. Winston didn't seem to know it either. Maybe the Fat Waiter Club is new and word hasn't got around yet. Unless these secret venues change locations, they probably don't stay secret for long.

Traffic is relatively light and the driver takes a route I don't recognise. We don't go past Egg Street, and I wonder if the former market is a red herring. It reminds me to double check the facts before I get carried away. Did the story about the egg market inspire my vision of red eggs? I'm not sure that I can trust it.

The banner advertising the shadow puppet theatre comes into view and we let Nigel out. He's going in first. Then I get the driver to drop me around the next corner. After he drives off, I walk back, past the funeral goods store and up the stairs.

At the top, I knock on the door. A pair of eyes peeps through a slit like a mail-slot.

"Password," he barks with a Chinese accent.

"Find Wind Sand Chicken," I say.

The door opens and I step inside.

The place has a sprinkling of patrons, in couples and small groups, mostly young and on their phones, oblivious to new arrivals. I scan the room. Under a pendant light with a cheap rice-paper shade, Beth's wavy shoulder-length auburn hair is glistening. I recognise her immediately, but with my blonde wig or not, she won't know me.

She looks up as the waiter lets me in, and I wave before making my way towards her. The route takes me right past Nigel, who's chosen a table in the middle.

I put out my hand and she shakes it. "Thanks for meeting me." I sit down.

"No problem. Pleased to meet you. With Miss T on the missing list, I'm at a loose end. You're saving me from another night of my own company. What would you like to know?"

A waiter interrupts and points to the menu written on the wall. I'm itching to ask him about Deshi, but I'll wait until Beth and I are finished. I've already eaten, but I order some dumplings and a glass of wine.

"I saw you talking briefly to Miss T the night she disappeared," I begin. "David Butler asked if I saw anyone and he recognised my description of you. He mentioned that you've consulted Miss T about an orphanage issue. She's done a reading for me too."

"You got an orphanage issue too, huh?"

"Sort of. A small boy I know about. He was abducted from a stroller in the night market here in Kowloon. I'm wondering what might have happened to him."

"Adopted to the US," she says. "They steal 'em and ship 'em, call them orphans. It's seamless and lucrative."

It's a strong answer. I get the impression that Beth is on her second glass of wine.

"How do you know?"

"My own daughter. I adopted Chloe from China ten years

ago through an agency here in Hong Kong. She's such a sweetie. Of course she knows she's adopted and about a year ago she started asking where she came from. Broke my heart, but I said I'd do my best to track down her Chinese family. It can't be that hard these days."

"Brick wall?"

"The opposite. Straight away, the agency sent me a copy of the entry from the Chinese orphanage, signed by the man who found my baby. She was in a basket at the side of the road. I flew over here, thinking I could get in touch with the orphanage through the agency; then fly into China and thank the man; maybe find out more about Chloe's origins."

I recall another baby in a basket: *Baby called Moses.*

Beth lowers her voice and continues. "The agency wasn't keen on my plan. They said they only knew what was on the form. I'm thinking, really? Pull the other one. The woman I was interviewing got called from the room for a minute, so I leaned over her desk and flipped through the file. I only saw the forms for three other orphans before I heard her coming back. Three was enough. All of them were found 'in a basket at the side of the road'—by the same man. He's a busy guy. Lucky too, the way he keeps tripping over those baskets. After a lot of googling, I discovered who he is. The deputy director of the orphanage."

"You think he's buying stolen children."

"Yep. Chloe … will never know … where she came from." She blows her nose on a napkin. "What am I going to tell her?"

This is a shock. David Butler said that legitimate orphans can begin as abductions, but does he know that some orphanages are involved in these rackets themselves?

"It must happen here too," she says. "Why not? At least the

little guy you're talking about has probably gone to a family who loves him. Like my Chloe."

"I'm sorry for you and Chloe," I say. "But I do have one question. I don't know if you'll have any idea –"

"Ask away. I'm not going anywhere till tomorrow."

"If the abducted child has one Anglo parent and one Chinese parent—if he doesn't look very Chinese—would a western family want to adopt him?"

"Oh honey, he's your baby? Kidnapped around here? You poor thing. You're so calm, I thought you must be asking for someone else. No wonder you were desperate enough to consult Miss T." She takes a gulp of wine. "I don't know about anyone else, but I can't lie to you. My Chloe had to look Chinese. She had to be the real deal, you know? A perfect little Chinese orphan. I'm so sorry. Maybe it's different for other people—or with boys?"

I let her see my distress. "If he wasn't suitable for adoption to the US, could he go to an orphanage here in Hong Kong? To be adopted locally? It's what I'm hoping."

"I don't know anything about that. I've been dealing with an agency."

"Of course. Does David Butler know what you discovered about the orphanage?"

"I told him but I'm not sure he believed me. He thinks I'm a flighty female, clucking over my precious chick."

My dumplings arrive, but I'm not hungry. As I share them with Beth, I sip my wine and stare at the mural of fat waiters.

"Were you hoping Miss Tigerlily might give you a lead on finding Chloe's family?" I ask.

"Uh-huh. Wasn't that a waste of time? I met her right here and she seemed distracted. I thought she's one of those mediums who get their messages when they're thinking about something else, whatever that's called. Then she did a few scribbles on one of these napkins and handed it to me. I'm thinking, that's it? I said to her, 'An address would be helpful.' She didn't like that, so that made two of us."

Beth must have been asking for more outside the Jadeite building when Miss Tigerlily turned away. I imagine Beth could be one pushy woman where her Chloe is concerned.

"Last time I saw her," she adds, "she was still distracted. This time by something across the street."

Me? Or someone else?

As the parent of a Chinese orphan, Beth's opinion supports our thoughts about Deshi's looks. What happened thirty years ago when they unwrapped his baby shawl and saw that they couldn't adopt him out as 'the real deal'?

Find Wind Sand Chicken.

This meeting has reminded me to trust my intuition. The fat man in my dream was sitting under a sign bearing these words—both clues pointing to this club. Miss Tigerlily met Alister here for a reason. How are they connected to Deshi?

Beth and I are done. What happens after we stand up confirms Nigel's advice to wear a wig. Our waiter admits another customer.

Klaus Hofmeier.

Without glancing in our direction, he strides across the room, only stopping to bend over two young women at a table and say something that makes them blush. Then he guffaws and sits down at a table of men. Not a business meeting, judging by the late hour and the track pants and T-shirts of his companions.

Beside me, Beth stiffens. She tosses some cash on the table, gives me a quick hug and whispers in my ear, "That bald guy who just came in. He was here when I met Miss T. She kept checking out that group of guys."

Then she's gone, and my knees are trembling. Did Beth tell David Butler about Klaus and his companions?

The waiter starts clearing our table. Keeping my voice low, I ignore Klaus and sidle up to the question I came to ask. "How did the club get its name?"

"Joke," he says. "I work at restaurant in temple. Buddha, he fat. Waiters, they not fat. Work too hard, smoke too much."

I smile. "In a temple? Were you a monk?"

He laughs. "No way. Monks get sick, they need waiters. Monks get better, I lose job. Then I start this café."

"Your password is clever."

He beams. "Use same letters from café. Keep away bad people. Serve good chicken. This place above funeral store make bad luck. Name from temple make good luck."

"Does the temple serve wind sand chicken?"

His eyes jump for a moment, then he smiles in understanding. "No meat at temple. Only vegetables. No garlic too."

The men in the corner have started chatting noisily as they pass their phones around and laugh. Their antics suggest they're sharing porn.

The noise masks my next question. "I'm looking for a Eurasian man who works in a café." I show him the baby photo of Deshi. "He'd be about thirty now."

The waiter takes the photo and stares at it. "My waiters all Chinese."

Suppressing my disappointment, I cast around for another question. But a patron knocking on the door draws the waiter away. The man barks the password and enters, then walks to the far corner to join Klaus and his group.

As the waiter lets me out, I give him my card. "In case you meet anyone who might be the Eurasian man I'm looking for." Then I add, "You're busy tonight. That's a big group in the corner."

His mood flips from garrulous to guarded. "Good customers."

At the bottom of the stairs, I loiter in front of the lucky waving cats, replaying the waiter's comments. It was too much to expect that he'd know Deshi, but was there something cryptic that I'm missing? After Nigel walks past, I fall in step a few paces behind, following him for a block. When he hails a cab and jumps in, I jump in too.

At this hour it's a quick trip along a highway lined with sparkling modern high-rises, the occasional old tenement wedged between. They remind me of the tiny temples, crammed into the old places, and what Dr Lee said about the rebuilding of Hong Kong. The past is gradually disappearing under concrete and glass. Was there once a temple in Egg Street?

Thinking about Klaus, I text Derek to send me the video Marty took. I forward it to David Butler with a message.

Here's KH meeting a group of men in a café last night. Tonight he was with another group at the secret club where I met Beth. Beth said they were there the night she met Miss T. Was he there the night she disappeared?

His reply is brief. *Thank you.*

Nigel and I save our debriefing until we're back inside the apartment. Alister is sleeping so after ripping off my wig, I can talk freely about Beth's research.

"*Baby called Moses,*" Derek says. "Was Deshi found in a

basket too?"

"A basket turned up in my dream. Not a baby basket. A shallow basket full of eggs."

"It's so simple," Nigel says. "Put a stolen baby in a basket and say you found it on your doorstep. The deputy director of the orphanage looks like he's getting away with it over and over."

Derek says, "Baby Moses was saved by his basket. What if Deshi was left in a basket and the people who found him kept him?"

"I love this theory, DD, but when Winston and Rose kidnapped him, he was ten months old. Old enough to climb out of most baskets."

Derek sighs. "A basket of eggs, then. For the White Tiger."

We move onto my conversation with the waiter.

"I was so sure the club's name must be the fat waiter in my dream, but when I asked about Deshi, he said his waiters are Chinese. Thinking back, that feels evasive. What about cooks or kitchenhands? But after seeing Klaus, I'm afraid to go back and ask." My shoulders slump in frustration.

"I saw Klaus," Nigel says. "Those guys in the corner had been horsing around till he turned up. When Klaus first arrived, they sat up straight like schoolboys in trouble. After a while, they relaxed."

"Could you hear what Klaus said?"

"Too far away. And he spoke with an accent."

We all stop.

"He's German," I say. "He's a creep but he works in child adoption, not ... abduction." Except the two can be connected.

Nigel says, "Meeting a group of local men at night suggests he might have something going on the side."

"Pornography and prostitution would be more his style. You saw how they were passing their phones around."

I think of his Filipino maid and hope he's leaving her alone.

Nigel is thinking. "If the men in the gambling den reacted badly to the phrase 'Find Wind Sand Chicken', we now know it's the password for the secret club where that group of men was meeting tonight. Do you remember exactly what Su Yin told you the guy with the accent said to her?"

I think back. "Whatever happens to missing babes—he used the word 'babes'—all depends on how pretty they are."

"Babes could mean trafficking of a different age group. Teens."

"I didn't think sex slaves needed to be pretty," Derek says. "Young and Asian are enough."

"We've got nothing much to go on," Nigel replies, "but Klaus has an accent and he was in the secret club that uses that password. What if he's handpicking underage girls as high-class call-girls? Lucrative. Plenty of expat customers with the dough. It would explain the clandestine meetings. They bring photos into the secret club and he chooses the prettiest ones. Either they don't risk sending images—even encrypted ones—or he enjoys choosing the girls in person." Like he handpicks his housemaids? "He'd have a turnover to manage, as they get too old."

Having met Klaus—and seen the squealing girl reeled back into his apartment—it all sounds way too plausible. Is he the man with the accent? Is he selling young girls like chattels? I feel sick. And the waiter's reaction, when I mentioned the men in the corner, sounded defensive: good customers. As if he knows they're up to no good and he's turning a blind eye. With his new unlicensed premises, tainted by superstition about the funeral store below, it could come down to money. He's happy for the regular income.

Trafficking teens might also explain why Miss Tigerlily was distracted by the men when she did the reading for Beth. She sensed what they were up to. Or was she watching them for the police? With all the eateries in Hong Kong, Butler couldn't know that Beth would suggest we meet there.

I still think the club must be connected to Deshi somehow. The map of runes suggests the link is cryptic. The waiter didn't know anyone like him but he could have been lying. Why? Did Alister show him the same photo? Is Deshi in some kind of trouble, and the waiter is protecting him? These are wild stabs in the dark. I regret not telling him why I was asking—and now it feels too dangerous to return.

Derek has waited as long as he can. He's bursting with news about the movie. "We watched *Painted Skin*. It's about ... a fox spirit."

"You got some insights into Sharp?" My trust in the process surges.

"You bet. And before you ask, the fox spirit doesn't burn any parchment or cast any spells. She does seduce men and eat the hearts of a lot of them—on her quest for immortality. Don't worry, I'm getting to the point." He draws breath. And slows down. "In the movie, the fox spirit has been frozen in ice for centuries, but now she is thawed. She's a beautiful woman who meets a princess with a scarred face. To hide her disfigurement, the princess always wears a mask of pure gold. It happens that she now wants to lie with the man she loves but she's afraid her face will repulse him so,"—he pauses for effect—"she *swaps bodies* with the fox spirit."

"DD, you're a genius! This proves that Su Yin's so-called

'sleepwalking' is in the folklore. Add that to my experience on Egg Street and it confirms she's telling the truth."

Is Sharp responsible for Su Yin's disappearance? Is that the direction we should take? If we can track down Su Yin's location, will we come face to face with Sharp—and Alister's spirit?

Chapter 22

As I toss and turn, desperate to join Alister in slumberland, my thoughts swirl. What am I missing? The waiter talked about a temple. And a restaurant. The password gives him luck. Sick monks. Buddhist shrine. The red cord. A temple in the old market. No chicken. Only vegetables. Red eggs. A basket of eggs.

Finally I get up and find my phone.

The Po Lin Monastery has a vegetarian restaurant beneath the giant Tian Tin Buddha. Lantau Island, Hong Kong. The Buddha is impressive, towering over the human ants, but as I stare at it and let my eyes lose focus, no visions come. Am I trying too hard?

Getting the rune-map from the safe, I carry it into the kitchen where I can turn on a light with minimum disturbance to the boys. As I spread it out on the counter, the two concentric circles draw my attention. A plate for a vegetarian meal? The fat man could be the fat waiter in the club's name, but the talk of a temple could indicate other meanings. Could he be a Buddha after all? The humble Buddha in my shrine vision?

Needing a sign about where to go next, I bring my laptop into the kitchen and revisit the transcript of Miss Tigerlily's reading, looking for things I've forgotten.

Boots too big. Hair too hot. Scent too cheap. Wait, a shadow! Pink, black, pink, black. Ghost wants to sleep. Can't. Wants to blame. Can't. Changes shape. Sly. Dark. Wants to play. Wants to win. Remember your mother. Man waiting. No! Gone. Too much beauty. Skin deep. Save him. Your job. Carrying bygones. Can't let go. Stones in the belly. Cut it open. Carry a stone to the mountaintop. Not Chinese enough! Baby called Moses. Touched by the gods. Danger! Danger! Danger! Trapped in time. Endless circle. Look in mirror. Go down to the sea. Speak the truth. Watch out for him. For her. Pray. Burn. White tiger. Something sharp. Know. Who. To. Trust.

What about the stones? The endless circle? But these words stand out: *Burn. White Tiger. Something sharp.*

On the quest to find Deshi, the club's password is a crucial piece in the puzzle. But I have to balance it—with protecting Alister from further attack.

The next stop is quite clear: the White Tiger Festival.

* * *

When the boys hear about my nocturnal insights, they support my plan to visit the White Tiger Festival tomorrow, as Bruce suggested. But like the ticking clock in my dream, time is running out and nothing we've discovered has got us any closer to rescuing Alister. As the day stretches ahead of me, I will my intuition to give me some tangible guidance.

Derek has been searching the online news for anything about Miss Tigerlily's disappearance.

"Nothing." He pockets his phone.

David Butler said they were keeping it out of the papers. It supports my hunch that she's gone into hiding. I wonder if Klaus was in the secret club the night she met Alister. What if Alister greeted him? Klaus would know he was no longer an anonymous diner. If Miss Tigerlily suspected the men in the corner of involvement in some kind of human trafficking, she might have asked Alister for Klaus's name. If Klaus knew her connection to the police, did that make her vulnerable? It's possible. What if one of his men followed me when I was following her—and she looked across the street and recognised him? It would explain why she cut Beth short and disappeared—to put herself out of danger.

It's a theory I can't confirm, but if she's safe somewhere and I can contact her, would she be willing to help us? It's Saturday so David Butler might be off-duty, but I leave a message on his voicemail, asking him to call.

Derek's got his own plans for the day. I sense he's inspired by his success with *Painted Skin* and a little miffed about missing out on the excursion to the secret club—especially since he's the one who noticed the acrostic link to 'Find Wind Sand Chicken'. Derek loves puzzles and folklore, and last night I was torn about excluding him. But Nigel is the best available body guard and someone has to be with Alister at all times.

"I'm off to the Taoist Temple," Derek says. "Let's see what I can find out about folk sorcery—and get my fortune told at the same time."

"Great, DD." I look out the window at a misty day. "It's drizzling."

"Then the temple might be less crowded."

He takes his turn in the bathroom, then borrows a sweatshirt and jacket from Alister, along with the umbrella that came with the apartment.

When he's gone, Nigel settles down with headphones in front of the TV, while Alister and I go back to bed.

As I throw open the curtains and let in a sky of silver clouds, I remind myself to be calm. I undress us both, this time to the music. It all happens more easily than yesterday, confirming my decision to repeat the same moves. Music and dance until we're energised, then a tumble onto the bed.

This time I lose myself in the arms and loins of my man, knowing that he's focusing everything he's got on me. No longer hijacked by what's missing, I connect to every little sign that he's with me. As much as I ache for it, he doesn't speak to me again, but the rhythm of our bodies binds us together like a memory—bringing back the depths of everything we've shared. It's magic.

Sharp doesn't intrude, and I refuse to be troubled by what that means.

Afterwards we shower together. Under the water I shed some tears—for our history and our future. Our lovemaking has reminded me to manage the present, one challenge at a time.

* * *

While Alister dozes in a chair and Nigel catches up on his business interests on his laptop, I leave a second message on David Butler's voicemail, this time spelling out why I must speak to Miss Tigerlily and how urgent it is.

Then I start my own research into Chinese sorcery. Surely there's something to learn that will link all the clues we've collected so far, and even lead us to Deshi or Sharp. As I flip through a dozen sites looking for something reliable, I'm conscious of every minute slipping away—and Alister slipping away with it. The pressure makes my fingers fumble on the keyboard.

I've just found a blogger, who calls himself a Chinese *wu*, shaman and medium and investigates cases of sorcery across South-east Asia, when the phone rings. Thinking it's Butler, I pounce. But Derek is on the other end, breathless with excitement.

"You need to get over here, Selkie. To the temple."

"What's happened?"

He won't tell me, saying I need to hear it myself. He gives me the address and I call a cab.

Nigel agrees that we shouldn't wake Alister, so I take the drive north alone—to the edge of Kowloon near the New Territories.

* * *

All these door-to-door journeys by cab are convenient, especially on wet days like this, but they put a pane of glass between me and the local culture. Not knowing what Derek's discovered, I push away my anxiety and recall my previous visit to Hong Kong. It was years ago with Andrew Tabrett, my ex. He was always a total control freak, but when he came down with a tummy bug and slept for hours in our hotel room, I was able to escape for a while. I couldn't go shopping because Andrew would deride anything I bought without his approval, so I taught myself to use the local subway, then people watched.

The memory reinforces how different Alister is. His love infiltrates my soul and winkles out every inch of the real me that I had to hide from Andrew. Over the years of my marriage, I forgot who I was. The starkness of the comparison sharpens the urgency to bring Alister back—before it's too late. Has Derek found the clue we need?

The route isn't far from Egg Street and I act on a sudden urge to make a detour. As my cab enters the thin place, a hollow of trepidation opens up in my belly. But I give the driver some money and ask him to wait. When I step into the rain, the atmosphere feels less sinister. Just melancholy. And without Su Yin around, I feel invisible to Sharp.

What if I'd come alone last time? Would I have seen more of the red cord? It's why I've come back today.

Along the laneway where I had the vision of the shrine, I stand and face the wall. Half-closing my eyes, I will the door—and its window revealing the red cord—to appear again. There's something here, some strong connection, but it eludes me. Even when I persist, nothing comes. After several minutes, I return to my taxi and notice the garage that's at the corner of the lane. Its roller-door is firmly closed, like all the others along the street, but a moment of curiosity makes me wonder what's inside.

* * *

The temple entrance is a grey gate with four pillars, reminding me of the sketch on the rune-map. Is this where Miss Tigerlily was sending us? Up the path, I'm confronted with red and gold. At the top of a flight of stairs, a pagoda stands on red pillars draped with red lanterns, then the temple itself is impressive beneath a traditional red tile roof with upturned corners. The lower courtyard is guarded by human-sized statues of the zodiac animals, standing upright beneath their animal heads. On the next level, the courtyard in front of the temple is busy with visitors but not over-crowded.

When Derek taps me on the shoulder, I jump. He's been lurking under an umbrella. "I thought you'd never get here," he says. "You need to meet my fortune teller and hear what he told me about fox spirits."

I want share his excitement but part of me wonders how a fortune told to Derek could apply to Alister's quest. He's already pointing to where you kneel in worship before the main altar, light an incense stick, then shake a cylinder of bamboo sticks until one falls to the floor. Several people under umbrellas or rain hoods are taking their turn.

"It's called *kau chim*," Derek says. "You have to ask a question first. The sticks are all numbered and each one matches a fortune. You take your number through here. The message is cryptic, so you choose a fortune teller to interpret it for you."

"What question did you ask the sticks, DD?"

"Don't laugh. The first thing that came into my head: Who's the best fortune teller around here?"

We've come to a long corridor lined on one side with open-fronted booths. Many are empty of customers, but Derek directs us to the kiosk where a Chinese woman is just leaving. He ushers me onto a stool at the counter and pulls out a second stool to face the fortune teller on the other side.

"Here's my friend," Derek says to a Chinese man wearing a Western-style blue shirt. "Selkie, this is Robert."

Robert is around fifty. He's very thin like a monk, with a long face that conveys wisdom. He tilts his head in greeting and reaches for a piece of coloured paper from the pigeonholes on the wall beside him, each slot containing multiple copies.

Getting straight to the point, he says, "Your friend received the most inauspicious number. Forty four."

Number four is haunting me like the shadow. I silently curse those tea leaves on the plane.

Robert translates from the Cantonese characters on the paper. His voice is accented but his English is formal and perfect.

"Beware. You feel threatened, but the hostile force that undermines you may not be what it seems. It may be reacting from its own anxiety. Your inner strength is being tested. Remain detached and your inner light will keep burning, even if you lose sight of it for a time."

I'm stunned by the prescience: *hostile force, reacting from anxiety, remain detached, inner light.* Dr Lee assured me that Alister's flame hasn't been extinguished, and this prediction agrees. Relief blossoms in my chest, easing the tension that's always there. But I'm confused.

"Is this your fortune, DD?"

"It took me a while to get it," Derek says. "When Robert read it to me, I looked over my shoulder to see if he meant it for someone else. As far as I know I'm not under threat, but Alister is. Was I channelling him?"

Derek would love to channel something, but I know it's never happened.

Robert cuts to the chase. "He is wearing the coat of another person, with a photo in the pocket. Its energy drove the bamboo sticks to fall as they did."

Derek reaches into the inside pocket of Alister's coat and brings out a small pouch. It contains the close-up of Fleur holding her baby, with her parents standing behind.

"I didn't know I was carrying this," he says, "until Robert suggested I might have something that affected the *kau chim*. I checked the pockets and found it."

Before I can wonder if these fortune tellers have to be psychic, Robert explains. "I read palms as part of the service, but the man who owns the coat is absent, so I've read the photo." He begins to repeat what he's already told Derek. "I see three people and a baby with Chinese ancestry. It's an old photo. I sense that the young woman was killed by a violent hand and is now a restless ghost. The married couple are living, but he is weak from sadness. She is also weak, but anger makes her act strong. The baby is now a man. He has a warm heart."

He's rattled it off and it's a lot to take in. I'm relieved to know that Deshi is alive, but the description is so accurate that Alister's fear of psychics returns. How much did Derek give away unwittingly?

"How do you read things from an old photo?" I ask.

"The photo carries the energy of each person from the past, but energy always flows forward like a river. Whatever these people are doing now it's possible to tap into it—with the gift of sight and Taoist training. In this case I sense their shadows. Only two. The man is too weak to cast a discernible shadow and the baby-now-man has a light that's too bright. The shadow over the young woman is ghostly and agitated; she has unfinished business."

Fleur. What business?

"The other woman has a living shadow, like smoke from a simmering pile of resentment. It hangs over her like a stench."

Rose.

"What kind of stench?"

"I already thought of that," Derek says. "I asked Robert to point to the fox spirit."

Robert says, "Your friend refers to *huli jing*—or *wu lei xing* in Cantonese—but its origins are in China so I'll use its Mandarin name. It is a shape-shifting fox spirit that can appear in two forms. The spirit can be pure, descended from an ancient mythical lineage. Or the spirit may have succumbed to its negative urges and invaded a human host. I sense neither manifestation in this photo. Just four people, with and without shadows, one of whom is now a ghost."

No fox spirit? How can that be? Have we been pushed off course by Winston's urban myth and Miss Tigerlily's sketch? What the hell has Alister lost while we've been chasing phantoms down fox holes?

Then I remember the person who's not in the photo. Su Yin.

But Rose's fug of resentment must be a clue. If Robert's reading can be trusted, what else can he tell us about that?

"Why did you use the word 'stench'?" I ask. "Does resentment carry a smell?"

He picks up the photo and smiles for the first time. "Ah, I see what you mean. I didn't see it before. It's just appeared. You should take the Taoist training. Her shadow now has a shape. Pointed ears. Bushy tail. But,"—he gives the image close scrutiny—"there's no lineage. And I detect no invading spirit. She's creating a fox shadow from her resentment. It takes all her energy, so she can only maintain it in bursts."

Shit. "A fake fox."

Suddenly I can see a room, lit only by a flaming torch in a wall sconce. Rose is hunched over a table of trappings and tools. She's dressed in a faux-fur jerkin, and her hair is pushed back with a headband bearing ears. It's how Deshi's grandmother transforms herself into Winston's 'fox lady'. Fuelled by decades of bitterness, she's conjuring up the power of *huli jing* to spew out spells of folk magic.

The hostile force may be reacting from its own anxiety.

She might be a fake, but the vision is so real that I want to pounce on her and set her den alight with her own matches. Would Alister's spirit come flying home if I did?

"Fox spirits are mythological shape-shifters," Robert is saying. "In that sense they're already fake, as you put it. Belief makes them real."

I need to know more. "Fortune 44 talks about a hostile force. Is she dangerous or not?"

"Let the fortune speak for itself."

He hands me a copy of the fortune sheet covered in neat rows of Cantonese characters, turns it over and passes me a pen. Then he repeats the reading while I make notes:

"Beware. You feel threatened, but the hostile force that undermines you may not be what it seems. It may be reacting from its own anxiety. Your inner strength is being tested. Remain detached and your inner light will keep burning, even if you lose sight of it for a time."

There's hope here. Alister is certainly 'detached' in all senses of the word, but by showing me the red cord and whispering to me, he's reassured me that he's still here. Is he protecting his inner light? It's such a comfort that I embrace it with all my being. But as I put the paper in my pocket, the fortune's first word is a stark reminder: *Beware.* Even though Dr Lee said this ancient divination is trustworthy, I won't relax my vigilance based on a printed prediction and a soothsayer in a kiosk.

"Is there anything else you'd like to ask me?" Robert says.

"Your friend gave me a sizeable payment. I like to give value."

Derek, ever the guardian angel. And there is something.

"I'm surprised that Fortune 44 doesn't predict death." A double dose. "It seems to predict the opposite."

"In Cantonese and Mandarin," Robert says, "the word for four *sounds like* the word for death. Because of that tonal similarity it is inauspicious, but it doesn't *mean* death. It's a superstition, a kind of fake omen that can impart bad luck on the person who believes it." He smiles again. "Like thirteen in your culture."

"I see."

Robert keeps smiling and waiting. Into my agitated mind, another thought comes. I pull out my phone and scroll to a photo of Alister.

When I show it to Robert, he shakes his head. "I can read nothing from a screen. I believe there is a print shop nearby."

On a hunch, I pick up the photo folder. It's like an old passport wallet and the family close-up has stuck to the plastic on the viewing side. I open the end and see there's another photo behind the top one. When I pull it out, Derek and I gasp. The colours have faded but a young Alister is clearly visible, lounging on a beach towel with his wife and baby. They're laughing for the camera. A potpourri of sentiments stings my throat.

Passing the photo to Robert, I murmur to Derek, "No prompting, DD."

As I hold my breath, our soothsayer rakes his eyes over the image.

"There is much happy energy from that time," he says at last. "Love. The baby is now an adult who is happy at his core but lately he is learning about other emotions. Anger?

The man is happy but ... lost. I see his energy searching for something, a path to follow? I'm getting more from the ghost. She is still restless; yes, she has unfinished business. But without the energy of the older woman, her purpose is clearer." He picks up the first photo. "Here she is restless and ... in much turmoil. Her energy is churning like a typhoon. In this second photo, her restlessness is different. I sense she's ... waiting for something. She's been waiting for a long time and she's impatient."

It's what Dr Lee said. Does impatience make her vengeful? Or have we always been dealing with Rose, the faux fox spirit with a chip on her shoulder the size of the giant Buddha?

"I don't understand why you're getting different energy from the same ghost if you're reading the energy she has now."

"She's just like a living person," Robert says. "Her energy changes depending on who she's with. Different company inspires different reactions."

"So when she's with her mother, she's like a typhoon."

For a fleeting moment, I can relate to Fleur's ghost. My step-mother Stella has the same effect on me.

"Yes," Robert says. "It makes her purpose hard to read."

Then who is she with when she's waiting—and getting impatient? Someone in the other photo: Alister or Deshi. Or both.

Robert has finished with the photos but he's still in service mode. After a minute of silence, he offers to read my palm. I extend my hand tentatively. He takes it in his cool fingers and notices the red cord tied around my bangle.

"You have asked Yue Lao to find your soul mate?"

"No, the man in the second photo is my lover. We are already connected by the red cord. But something has stolen his spirit. I am waiting for the red cord to guide me to him—and bring him back."

"Then give Yue Lao the right message. He is here at Wong Tai Sin. To the right of the main altar. After my reading, go to him. Don't bother with the usual ritual. Say a silent prayer to tell him what you want, then tie your red cord to the rope of cords. This action will send him the message."

"Thank you. I saw a small shrine and asked Yue Lao to write our names in his book. But I didn't know what to do with the red cord. I just knew I needed to have it."

"The symbolic cord has the spiritual power. Let this one do its job."

Robert is still holding my hand and as he turns it over, I'm struck by a moment of extreme reluctance. Will hearing my own fortune interfere with my focus on Alister?

But he's already begun the reading. "You are lucky. You have a strong inner light and you are surrounded by the light of others. You have love in your life and you are on the right path in your work. I sense an animal spirit." He lifts his eyes and smiles. "A true lineage but it frightens you. Embrace it. Let it guide you. You love food. Trust your gut. Feed it—and listen."

Chapter 23

As we emerge into the drizzle, I'm grateful that Derek got me over here and didn't try to play reporter. "You made the right call, DD. I needed to hear Robert's reading myself. And he's given us so much more."

Derek brushes off my thanks. "The man believes in good food. Feed your gut, then listen to what it says. And he doesn't mean word-burps. He's my kind of guy."

That's all we're going to say. By silent agreement, we won't discuss what we've heard until we're with Nigel and Alister.

We cross the pavement in front of the main altar, to where several steps lead to another level and a life-size golden statue of Yue Lao. Unlike the chubby figure in the shrine, this one is noble in appearance, draped in a flowing robe and standing on a plinth under a crescent moon. On either side of him, the golden statues of a woman and a man are connected to Yue Lao by two enormous red ropes. They're as curved and thick as elephant trunks and made from thousands of red cords like the one on my bangle.

Even in the rain, single girls are going through a ritual, presumably to ask Yue Lao to lead them to their soul mate. My request is different. I wait my turn, then approach him and bow my head in silent prayer. Making my intention clear,

I ask for his help to locate Alister's stolen spirit and bring it home. When it's time to tie my own red cord, I hesitate about which rope to choose. The male rope for Alister? But because I'm making a woman's request, I follow the other women ahead of me. It's a simple action but it carries the weight of purpose. And love.

Turning away, I take Derek's arm and a trail of bobbing umbrellas leads us out of the temple precinct, through modern high-rise Hong Kong and down the stairs to Wong Tai Sin Station. I suggest we catch the train as far as Central. The subway map shows we only have to change once, ironically—or presciently—at Mong Kok, near the Fat Waiter Secret Club.

It's mostly locals surging into the carriages, and my love of everything Chinese returns in a rush. With the threat looming over Alister, I've been viewing their culture with suspicion and fear. Praying to Yue Lao and taking a simple trip by subway provides a sudden antidote—and an insight. The answers to the riddles we're facing will come from the culture itself.

The train proves speedier than a taxi in traffic and we arrive at Central in record time. As we move to the exit, I notice the signs to the Tung Chung line that goes to Lantau Island, the home of the big Buddha. Even though we've nailed the Fat Waiter, it hasn't led us to Deshi and my thoughts keep returning to the Buddha. But so far, my fleeting vision of the red cord has only shown me a humble shrine. Where does it lead?

Above ground, it's still raining. As we hail a cab, David Butler returns my call.

"Beth has flown home," he says. "You met her at the secret club. Don't go there again."

Before I can remind him of my message about Miss Tigerlily,

he hangs up. I say nothing to Derek in front of the cab driver as we take the snaking road to our building.

* * *

While Derek rustles up a wok-full of fried wontons, I jump in the shower—to warm up from the chill of the day and our news.

When I join everyone around the coffee table, I update them on Butler's call.

"Why did Butler warn you off?" Derek asks.

"He didn't say, but it must be because of Klaus and his merry men. I think it's why Miss Tigerlily went into hiding. What if someone followed her the night she met Alister, because he recognised Klaus? If she was already suspicious about the activities of the men in the corner, suddenly she knew who their boss was—and where he lived."

But why did she risk meeting Alister in the Fat Waiter if she suspected its patrons of trafficking? Alister said she had a reason. It had to be compelling. Surely the club is related to Deshi, and she picked up the connection. Did the club owner lie? Or is the link to Deshi more cryptic?

"Just to be on the safe side," Nigel says, "if any of us bump into Klaus, play it cool."

The thought that I might have had a meeting with him makes me shudder.

Derek's the storyteller. He takes Nigel and Alister through Robert's insights as they were revealed. The most explosive news is about Rose.

"Rose is using all her energy to call up the magic powers of *huli jing*," Nigel says.

I agree. "It looks like she dresses up and transforms herself from Rose into Sharp."

We sit with this for a while, the machinations of our minds almost audible. Something doesn't feel right.

Nigel begins unravelling her motives. "So why has she kidnapped Alister's *Hun*?"

"To stop him from finding Deshi," I say. "Keeping Deshi away from his father is her life's work."

"But he's been looking for Deshi for thirty years. Why curse him now?"

"Selkie's with him," Derek says. "Alister turned up in Hong Kong accompanied by his own psychic."

I look across at my man, fearing again that my presence here is responsible for his condition.

"So why not kidnap Selkie's *Hun*?" Nigel asks. "She tried it on Egg Street, but that was after she targeted Alister."

I tell them about my so-called migraine in the back of Winston's cab. Did she target me first, and when that didn't work, she turned her sorcery onto Alister?

But Rose's mountain of resentment is a crucial clue. "I think I'm just a complication," I say. "Rose hates Alister for marrying her only child—and blames him for Fleur's death. When Deshi got abducted on her watch, her warped mind pinned that on Alister too."

Nigel drops a bombshell. "Then who screams the words, '*You'll never have him?*' Doesn't that sound like something your rival would spit out in a fit jealousy? Sharp doesn't want you to have him, Selkie. Is that coming from Rose?"

"Rose doesn't want Alister to be happy with anyone," Derek says. "She regards it as a betrayal of Fleur. Even in death, Fleur is still his wife. That's the Chinese way."

But I think Nigel's nailed it. It's what I've been fearing but not naming.

"There's more than one of them," I whisper.

It's a breakthrough, but the revelation weighs me down like a boulder. I've been thinking that, fake or not, Robert's sense of Rose was a game-changer; that at last we had a glimpse of our opponent. Now it seems that Rose is not alone. She has an accomplice.

"So we still can't exclude Su Yin—or Fleur," Nigel says. "And Alister and I have some news that might help. While you two were at the temple, we did some sleuthing of our own."

"Where?" Derek asks for both of us.

"In Su Yin's apartment. She left in such a rush, I figured she might have left something behind. She did."

It's an idea I hadn't thought of. My disillusionment flips to expectation.

"We found the door code on Alister's phone," Nigel continues. "I put him on carpet duty, looking for anything lying on the floor, while I searched everywhere else. He found a dead match. That led me to the trash and two spent tea-light candles; then on a side table I discovered some sprinkles from an incense stick that she hadn't wiped up."

"Incense?" I say. "She doesn't strike me as the type to meditate."

"They could be leftovers from a shrine."

"To worship Buddha?" I'm still sceptical, but the shrine on Egg Street was pointing to something.

"Or a Taoist shrine for an ancestor," he says. "She might be honouring a dead relative."

If Nigel's right it could be anyone. Su Yin's grandmother is

Rose's sister. She may have died. Otherwise, I know nothing about her immediate family.

"Fleur," Derek says.

"Why would she honour Fleur," I ask. "The aunt she never knew?" The murdered wife of Alister. The woman she looks just like. Something feels off. Not *honouring* Fleur. Something else. "What else could she use a shrine to an ancestor for?"

Derek says, "Channelling. Spirit possession. Villain hitting. Sorcery. I told you I don't trust Su Yin."

A pact between Su Yin and Fleur? I've wondered if Fleur could be haunting Su Yin's body against her will, but this is something else. I let out a heavy sigh. "Are they our two opponents? Fleur and Su Yin? Is Rose just playing with her magic in that den of hers? Full of fake-fox fury, but powerless?"

"We don't know," Nigel says. "The incense suggests that Su Yin's up to something, but we can't discount Rose's ability to curse Alister. That stinking pile of resentment sounds pretty potent to me. What's got me intrigued is the energy Rose is losing to create her fox persona and maintain the masquerade. Pass me the fortune card from the temple, Selkie."

"*The hostile force may be reacting from its own anxiety*," he reads. "It sounds like Rose is carrying her own baggage. This so-called sorcery could be fuelled by mental illness."

In caring for people with dementia, Nigel sees the results of childhood baggage. Sometimes it pops up in ugly ways. Devout church-goers morphing into foul-mouthed cuss-merchants, much to the horror of their families, usually because they spent a lifetime using an emotional anvil to suppress their childhood issues, instead of facing them and diffusing their power. I've had to deal with some exploding baggage of my own.

"Not a real fox spirit," Nigel says. "A ... pretender. You pretend to be something powerful to mask low self-esteem."

I close my eyes trying to get a vision. "She must have been born in the fifties. Something in her childhood? It feels like she's worked hard at covering it up. For a very long time. But why choose *huli jing?*"

"Fox spirits are female and powerful," Derek says. "Chinese girls had no power back then, so she might have fantasised about shape-shifting into a fox spirit."

"I had lots of childhood fantasies about power,"—I suppress an urge to empathise with Rose—"but I didn't grow into a deranged sorcerer." My step-mother might disagree.

Nigel says, "I think we're onto something, Selkie. But until we can confront Rose on Monday, speculation about her secrets won't help get Alister's spirit back. I don't want to divert your energy this weekend, just because I'm intrigued by her psychology."

"If she's Sharp, Nige, then understanding her psychology could prepare us for Monday. We might discover the chink in her armour that will bring Alister back."

I recall the times when the shadow first taunted me. I can almost feel it now. Sleek. Old. And red.

The fox.

"Let's see what comes up in my dreams." I'm confident that the day's events will inspire more insights. "I've already had a vision of Rose at her workbench. Robert's confirmed she's the fox spirit, so she's involved. Now we've got to pin down the other malign force. Are they working together? What do you think, Alister?"

Derek gets up and goes to Alister's coat, now back on the wall hook. He brings over the photo pouch and shows Alister the photo of Fleur and her parents. Within seconds he's growling the way he's done before. But when he sees the photo of himself with Fleur and Deshi, he stares at it without a sound. Derek goes to take it away, but Alister stops him with his hand. His right hand. His fist is for me, his right hand must be for Fleur and Deshi.

Derek sits down again. After a few moments of silence, a single tear falls from Alister's eye. I get up and wrap my arms around him, feeling utterly helpless to comfort him. Without his *Hun* spirit, he's caught up in the deep emotions carried by his body, the raw and visceral emotions from the past. A long howl might be cathartic, but he only sheds the one fat tear.

When I lead him back to bed, he drops instantly to sleep from the impact of it. I climb in beside him for a while—hoping to soothe him and glimpse the red cord. No visions come. As my mind reviews the day's revelations, I remind myself that the photo shows the living Fleur, just the way Alister remembers her. An exquisite orchid preserved in amber.

Fleur's ghost is another entity altogether.

* * *

The light in the room has a yellow tinge. A photograph of Rose lies on her work table. Into the smoky air, she rises from it and gains another dimension. Her now solid form bends over something white and powdery, and as she inhales, her shadow takes on the unmistakable shape of a fox. By the light of the torch flame it looms large, taking on the fine details of a shadow puppet, the serrated outline of its coat shimmering against the wall. Her sense of identity swells to fill the space.

This is who she is.

Then the shadow splits into two foxes. To the breathy melody of a bamboo flute, the twin shadows dance together, swishing their tails in a mockery of swing style. As they move, they overlap and merge into one, before dividing again.

The dance becomes hypnotic until one of them loses its rhythm. It falters, bends, then resumes its dance position, this time brandishing something pointed. With lightning speed it raises a blade and brings it down on its twin. In a moment, just one shadow remains. It no longer needs to dance.

As I sit up in bed reeling from the dream, the music lingers. The flavour of the instrument is familiar. I remember its name. Shakuhachi. A bamboo flute. From Japan.

Chapter 24

Causeway Bay is on the northern shore of Hong Kong Island, opposite Kowloon. Beneath towering skyscrapers and alongside designer stores, a paved apron dotted with massive pillars huddles under the Canal Road overpass. It's another cool morning threatening rain, and the cab deposits us in a place that's dark and gloomy. Gloomy, and already choked with the smoke of incense, but not spooky—too many early morning shoppers jostling and chattering in the side streets, and a constant flow of traffic zipping by overhead. On a scale of one to ten, the ambience of the White Tiger Festival is zero. We decided that coming early might mean fewer people, but at eight thirty the place is as crowded as a market. The patrons who are lined up or milling about are almost exclusively Chinese.

We're all here, including Alister, because I need Derek's knowledge of folklore and Nigel's muscle if anything unexpected happens. As fearful as I am for Alister's safety, the boys have reassured me that our curse-curbing cabal is stronger as a team.

They wait together while I dive into the melee and move between the assortment of cheap cupboards that mark the spots of the stallholders. Each one has opened her cupboard doors and set up a shrine on a makeshift table in front of it. Perching herself in squat position on a low plastic stool, each villain hitter greets her customers.

My plan is to observe a number of them in action until I find the right one. I stop and watch the ritual that I've viewed on several videos. This place has become a tourist attraction, with travel bloggers often filming it, although there's only a sprinkling of Western faces here so far. Being familiar with the process, I'm looking beyond the actions being repeated at each stall, to the character of the villain hitter herself. What I'm looking for I'm not sure, hoping I recognise it when I see it.

The first woman is about fifty and talks a lot. I don't know what she's saying, but it seems by all her hand-waving and the nodding from each customer that she's dishing out advice. It must be working because her queue is long. The next villain hitter is in a rush. Onto a block of wood, she slams down the paper strip that's printed with the generic outline of a male or female person, before whacking it furiously with a slipper. Within seconds she's setting fire to it, then smearing some folded tiger effigies with pork fat to create another conflagration, all in record time. I guess she's offering a budget special.

The third stall catches my attention for a different reason—not the villain hitter but her customer—a young Filipino woman in a pink and black retro frock and matching cap. My timing is perfect—she's just sat down—and I move as close as I can without appearing to eavesdrop. As I watch, she takes a business card from the pocket of the dress and places it on the block.

"Klaus Hofmeier," she says, as loudly as she dares. "Very

bad man. First he trick me, tell me I beautiful. Then he hurt me, make me cry."

The villain hitter nods and starts laying into the business card with a slipper. When that doesn't shred the stiff cardboard, she changes weapon to a heavy boot. Finally she sets it alight and follows the rest of the process.

When my neighbour leaves the stall, I waylay her.

"I'm staying in the apartment next to you."

Her eyes widen in alarm.

"It's OK," I say. "I know Klaus is a bad man. I know he hurts you."

She presses her lips into a line. "You spy on me."

"No, no. I saw your dress and hat. I threw them away and you found them in the rubbish bin."

When I grin, her lips widen into a smile. And she is beautiful—youthful and unsophisticated, with flawless tanned skin, broad features and pointed chin.

"I like it," she says, brushing her hands down each sleeve.

That's when I notice the tattoo on her wrist. It was her bare arm that I saw that night.

"Dress make me brave," she says. "Brave to come here."

"Good. I hope the villain hitting works. I hope Klaus stops hurting you."

She drops her head and nods. "Do not tell him you see me. Please. Today my day off."

"Let's both keep it a secret."

The bastard. I hope David Butler can pin something on him.

"I found this in pocket." She beams, pulling out the red cord. "Help me find boyfriend."

Before I can comment, she moves away and a young man takes her hand. "You ready to go now, Pia?"

Her friend looks familiar. I think he's the waiter who runs the secret club. As they disappear into the crowd, I worry about the connection. I hope he's not spying on her for Klaus—and I'm glad I look different without the wig. As I move to the next stall, a more benign explanation occurs to me. If Klaus sent Pia on an errand to the club, she could well have met the young man there.

The fourth villain hitter should be the one to avoid, given the number, but she's the one who attracts me. She's very old, her skin wrinkled like an ancient turtle. She also has no teeth. Her hair is cut very short and she's dressed in black pants and a peacock blue polyester blouse that's buttoned to the neck, cheongsam-style. There's something about her concentration that catches my attention. It's intense. Her mouth is a tight line, her movements are slow and deliberate. She's in the zone in a way that the first three were not. Perhaps because of her lack of speed, her queue is shorter. I watch for about fifteen minutes and notice she varies her routine depending on each patron. I'm sure she won't speak English, but I'm guessing from her variety of approaches that she's an intuitive.

Returning to the boys, I guide them through the throng. After joining the queue we start to watch, but there's something very intimate about each person's relationship with our chosen villain hitter. We turn away and I tell them about last night's dream.

"One fox stabbed its twin," Derek murmurs. "Like Madam Li in the in-flight magazine."

"I suppose that's where my dreaming mind got the idea. It was still shocking. It woke me up."

Then I mention the shakuhachi.

"Did you recognise the melody?" Nigel asks.

"No. Only that it was a flute of some kind. Then I remembered the name. It's a distinctive sound. Japanese."

"Twin Chinese fox spirits dancing to a Japanese flute," Derek says. "One kills the other one. I wonder if Rose was conjuring up a folk tale."

"It sounds political," Nigel says. "No love lost between China and Japan."

Derek does a quick search on his phone. "There are fox spirits in Japanese folklore. *Kitsune*. They originated from Chinese mythology. They've got paranormal and shape-shifting abilities, but they're loyal and kind, unlike *huli jing*."

We reach the top of the queue. When it's our turn, the boys help Alister onto one plastic stool while I perch on another and take hold of his fist. The old woman looks deep into my eyes, then Alister's. He gazes at her while she looks back and forth between us and I'm sure she picks up something of what's happened.

It was Derek's idea to sketch a copy of the fox from Miss Tigerlily's map. Although we feel sure after Robert's reading that Sharp is Rose, the revelation that there's also another force at work has complicated things. This lack of certainty made us avoid using photographs. I pass the fox sketch to our villain hitter, then make jabbing movements towards Alister's chest to show that he's under attack, before swirling my arms upward from his shoulders to mimic his spirit flying away. She watches intently, then hands each of us a lighted incense stick that has no perfume, but makes a lot of smoke.

She places the fox image on her wooden block, before turning to a rack full of single shoes. She moves her hand over each shoe until she gets a reading. I gasp when she selects a pink boot. With great concentration she carries it to the block. Then in a kind of trance, she incants some words while bringing the boot down over and over again on the image.

What is happening to Sharp at this moment I have no idea. As the hitting continues I keep remembering the impact that burning Alister's name had on him. Effigies are powerful magic and I love the intensity of this wonderful old woman. She's focusing everything on driving the curse on Alister all the way back to its perpetrator. Folk sorcery against folk sorcery. I hold Alister's hand, trying to sense his reaction, and add my own intention to the mix.

When the fox image is shredded, she sets it alight and holds it with reverence. The flames leap up the paper and she only drops it into her ash can when they're about to burn her fingers. Next she lines up paper effigies of the white tiger, folded to give them a 3D effect. She takes her time to arrange and rearrange them in a special pattern. When she's satisfied, she smears each tiger mouth with pig fat, then pushes a morsel of meat into each one. I wonder if she's going to make an offering of raw eggs. She doesn't. This is not the meaning of the eggs. She sets the tigers alight.

Her final act is to take two curved blocks that fit in the palm of her gnarled hand. Called *jiaobei* or moon blocks, Derek looked up their purpose before we came. They act like simple dice to determine if the magic has worked. Closing her eyes, she tosses them onto the ground before getting up from her stool on bandy legs to check how they've fallen. One curved side up and one flat side up mean 'yes'.

At the exact moment that she grins toothlessly and pronounces the job complete, a commotion breaks out at the far end of the festival. People are running and shouting.

Nigel can see over the crowd. "A villain hitter is lying on her rug. Someone is giving first aid."

After several minutes of chaos, a taxi pulls up. The driver leaps out and directs people to help. They quickly pack up the shrine and throw her tools of trade into a plastic bin, while he helps the woman to her feet.

That's when I get a glimpse of his face.

"It's Winston." I'm stunned that he's here. "The villain hitter looks like ... Rose."

Derek whistles. "No wonder she knows her folk sorcery."

On hearing their names, Alister starts towards them. We pull him back.

"They don't know me from Adam," Nigel says. "I'll follow them."

He gives Derek a hug and runs to the one-way street beside the overpass where taxis are tail-to-tail, dropping off and picking up. We watch Nigel climb into a cab and drive off before Winston does. There's only one way out so he'll get his driver to wait along the road, before following.

We're hidden by the surging crowds, and Winston is too busy to notice. We get glimpses of him putting his arm around his wife and walking her bent form to his cab. Returning for her things, he throws them in the back and roars off.

"Shit," says Derek. "I know she's thirty years older than that photo but Rose wasn't looking too good. Did we do that? Send her a taste of her own medicine?"

"You said effigies work, DD—and I'm sure our villain hitter meant business back there. One minute Rose is plying her trade, the next minute she's horizontal. The timing fits."

I put my arm through Alister's and notice how tense he is. He relaxes at my touch. I can only hope that the success of our curse-curbing doesn't backfire on him.

* * *

We catch our own cab back to the apartment, while Nigel keeps us informed with texts and photos. They've left the island and are heading through Kowloon towards the New Territories.

Traffic busy but driver keeping Winston in sight.

Now on highway hugging coast.

He sends a photo of a bay, dotted with distant pleasure boats.

Signs say Tuen Mun. Driver says it's a new town. Many tower blocks. If that's where they're going, we'll lose them.

"The name rings a bell," I say. "I think it's the satellite town that Alister's private eye mentioned before he dropped the case. Too crowded to be a useful lead."

I turn on my laptop. Derek starts googling.

"Tuen Mun used to be a fishing port," he says. "That photo must be Castle Peak Bay. Now it's mainly residential, a dormitory town to Hong Kong, housing thousands of mainly Chinese. Not a tourist area. Nigel's going to stand out like a giraffe at a rabbit wedding."

Not going to Tuen Mun. Turning off into So Kwun Wat Road, in direction of Buddhist wat.

Now Derek is doing his best to track Nigel. I can feel his tension. He's worried about his man.

Winston's pulling into parking lot ahead. We're stopping, hidden by tiny Taoist temple.

Derek pulls up a photo of Tin Hau Temple, a humble grey brick box with few trappings.

"Tin Hau is the Chinese sea goddess," he says.

Like the tiny temple opposite Yue Lao's shrine. Another

example of what might have been in Egg Street before the bulldozers? How does it relate to Deshi?

Cruising past now. Winston getting out of cab. Row of old buildings looks like shops with flats upstairs.

His photo shows a line of four shabby concrete boxes, the white paint stained with age. Downstairs they present a row of red doors—exactly like the ones in my dream.

Door of shop opened by guess who? Su Yin.

This revelation is trumped by what happens next.

Nigel calls me. "I'm going in. My phone's on speaker. Stay tuned."

"Oh my god," Derek whispers.

The three of us huddle around my phone, stomach butter-flies bouncing between us.

"Hello, Su Yin," Nigel calls. "No need to rush inside. I've already seen you. Winston, I'm Nigel, a friend of your son-in-law, Alister. Can I give you a hand with Rose?"

"Go away," Winston says. "Rose not well."

"That might be down to the villain hitting. Selkie engaged an old lady at the festival to drive away the curse that someone's put on Alister. She turned the curse back on the sorcerer."

"Rose got headache, that all. No talking now."

We hear their feet crunch across the pavement.

"More than a headache," Nigel says. "Rose collapsed just as our villain hitter announced the effigy burning had worked. I followed you here. I'm a nurse."

There's a pause before Winston says, "You better come in."

Derek is waving his arms above his head in a victory salute, when we hear rustling, the sounds of movement, and a shout from Nigel. Winston calls out in Cantonese. Feet pound the pavement. With a sudden crack, the phone goes dead.

Chapter 25

Derek is pacing, his tight expression a mirror of my own.

"He's in trouble," he cries. "He looks tough but he's still *human*. He might be able to bend spoons but he can't fight *sorcery*. I should never have let him go, but since when does he do what I tell him?"

"There wasn't time, DD. He jumped into that cab and followed Winston before any of us thought it through. We all believed he could look after himself."

"And we were excited by the chase! While we've been getting an adrenaline rush, he's walked into a trap."

I'm worried too. The noises before his phone died are forming vivid images in my mind. Nigel cried out, followed by what sounded like a scuffle. The crack was probably his phone hitting the concrete. Did he fall? Did Rose whip around and throw a potion in his face? Or Su Yin? I can only hope that my imagination is getting carried away, that Nigel won't come back as a shell like Alister.

"We've got nothing to tell the police," Derek continues, "and by the time we call our own cab and drive out there, anything could have happened."

He's right. There's nothing we can do but wait for news.

To keep him busy, I point to the fridge and tell him to make a mountain of dumplings. Cooking is Derek's soul work these days. Alister sits beside me on a stool at the island counter, while I open up Street View, hoping Nigel's location might trigger an insight.

Four ancient narrow shopfronts huddle together, sharing common walls. Their upstairs windows are smeared and grimy. Only the fourth one has a typical old Hong Kong air-conditioner, which makes the others look empty and forlorn. There are no signs suggesting business names or goods being sold. No numbers either. On the day the Google crew took the photo, all the front doors were shut tight—just like the doors in my dream. My eyes are drawn to the fourth door. Surely that's where Winston and Rose are living. Now Su Yin. And Alister's stolen spirit?

What are they doing to Nigel?

Street View is keeping my dread at bay. Using the panoramic function, I spin the view from the shopfronts to show a clump of trees at one end of the parking lot. At the other end there's a glimpse of the tiny Tin Hau Temple behind a couple of buildings, including the more elaborate Buddhist wat that's given the road its name.

In front of the shops, the lot borders So Kwun Wat Road. The concrete is cracked and weathered. It's empty of cars and dotted with polystyrene boxes growing herbs. Does Rose use them for her evil potions? Across a broad barren area opposite, the distant skyline is dominated by the shiny residential towers of Tuen Mun. The cultural contrast of this mini ghost town, lurking on the fringe of the teeming populous, makes me shiver. The word *old* returns, with all the stealth of a curse.

Hoping to pick up something useful, I move the view along

the road, past industrial sites with trucks and containers behind mesh fences. A few stunted trees. I'm about to give up when I chance upon a lonely cottage, overgrown with weeds and set back behind a ramshackle fence. I move the view to get a better look. Its architecture suggests the same vintage as the row of shops. When the photo was taken, the hut door was open and a plastic chair sits under a faded fabric awning. Household litter dots the front yard. I look for electricity wires and find none. Although the other properties along this road have a hotchpotch of purposes, including two temples, this hut feels out of place. An isolated dwelling surrounded by a remnant patch of wild trees. Something about it snares my interest. I bookmark the location.

My phone rings. Derek and I pounce.

"I'm mostly OK," Nigel says. "So's my phone. We hit the deck together."

His voice is normal.

"Which part of you … isn't … OK?" Derek's composure teeters.

"We'll see when a doctor looks at it. I twisted my ankle and grazed my arm. I don't think the ankle's broken, but I'd better get an x-ray."

His injuries are only physical. We're both fighting back tears.

"Someone tripped you?" Derek asks.

"No. Su Yin took off across the lot and hailed my cab. I'd thrown some money at him so he'd wait for me, but when I chased after her it must have looked like she was under threat. He picked her up. I was trying to dance between some tubs of herbs …"

"Dance?" Derek says. "You've got two left feet."

"Yeah. I never learned to foxtrot."

The jokes feel good after the panic, but Nigel's not out of danger yet.

"How will you get to a doctor?" I'm imagining him lying where he fell. "Did you hit your head? Is there somewhere to hide while we come and get you?"

"It's OK. Winston's going to drive me to the hospital at Tuen Mun, after he puts Rose to bed."

"You've made friends with Winston?" I'm gobsmacked.

"He saw the whole thing. He's put me in his cab to wait and he's just brought some ice for my ankle. I get the feeling he's the good guy, Selkie. He seemed genuinely ignorant when I mentioned the curse on Alister. He asked after his health."

Surely this confirms Rose and Su Yin as the duo we've been looking for. Putting Fleur's ghost in the clear. For Alister's sake, I'm relieved.

"He's not taking Rose to the hospital?" I ask. "What's her condition?"

"Hard to say. Very pale. I only saw her for a second before Su Yin did her jackrabbit routine."

"So Su Yin doesn't care that Rose is sick. So much for her first aid training. Too busy looking after number one. What's Winston said about her?"

"Nothing. I'll quiz him on the way to the hospital."

Nigel rings off, with a promise to keep us updated and not to do anything else to give us palpitations. His ankle will prevent it anyway.

"Idiot," Derek says. "He sounded way too casual for the panic he's just put us through." His mock anger flips back to worry. "Do you think he's safe with Winston?"

"I don't know. He seemed truly grief-stricken about Deshi

that night—weak and broken, like Robert said. If we trust Robert's reading of their shadows, then Winston's too sad to be a bad guy. But how could Rose hide her activities from him? If they live in that tiny shop, there aren't many secret places." Except the other shops seem empty.

"He's out night and day, driving his cab for hours at a time. She might keep all her sorcery stuff in the cupboard she uses for villain hitting. It's a legitimate cover. Those villain hitters interviewed by the South China Post believe they're doing noble work. They're proud of their self-imposed ethics about who they'll target. After Rose works herself up into a fox spirit, she probably pretends she's doing good in the world."

"In my dream she was sniffing a white powder."

He slaps his hand on his forehead. "Of course. Nostril-delivered delusion. It would give that resentment pile of hers a regular boost." He thinks for a minute. "If she's a serious user, Selkie, that might have contributed to her collapse at the festival this morning. Too many people around for her to give herself a top-up."

Rose's collapse has made me think that the villain hitting worked, but what if drugs had already weakened her? Now I look at Alister and realise there's been no change to his condition. Rose might have gone down, but there's no corresponding return of his *Hun*. Nothing.

And because of Nigel's injury, Rose is going to be alone behind the fourth door, with her favourite fix—and Alister's *Hun*. It explains the rectangle of light I saw. He's trapped somewhere behind that door. Now that she knows we're onto her, what could her drug-induced fox spirit do to escalate her hold on him?

But my door dream had another message: I've got the key.

Where?

Looking across to the mind-map on the fridge, I realise I've been dancing through the clues the way Nigel danced through the tubs of herbs. Clumsily. Yes, we needed to know who and where Sharp is, but that's come to dominate my sense of urgency. What the hell do we do now that we know?

With Winston waylaid at the hospital, we could barge in on Rose within the hour, and find her weakened by the villain hitting. Then what? How do we exorcise Alister's spirit—and return it safely to him? In spite of Miss Tigerlily's readings, the input from Dr Lee and Derek, and my prayers to Yue Lao, I've been completely outplayed by Rose and Su Yin.

Su Yin. What if she hasn't abandoned her collaborator? What if she's taken off to a secret location to carry on the work? Nigel didn't say which way the cab took her. Back towards Tuen Mun—or along the road to that cottage?

At that moment, Nigel texts: *My cab just went past going towards town. Looked empty, but she could have ducked down out of sight.*

The cottage. That's the direction the taxi took her. I click on the link and look at it again. A creepy place—even a thin place—and cold at this time of year. Not a residence; a place for spells. Widespread superstitions about ghosts would keep the inquisitive away.

Ghosts. Su Yin had a shrine in her apartment. To Fleur? Is she using Fleur's ghost in some way that I don't understand? I concentrate on the thought, trying to tease out an insight, but my fear about Alister's new vulnerability is getting in the way.

Then something Dr Lee said pops up and steadies me: we're still in the game. As long as we keep at it, Alister's only risk is time. Our activities are warding off further attack. As I wrap my arms around him, and murmur reassurances in his ear, our deep connection embraces me. He's not giving up on himself or me.

With tears clouding my vision, I see Derek busying himself with the dumplings. Keeping Alister close beside me, I turn to my laptop. It's time to get informed about folk sorcery.

"The Chinese shaman I found yesterday,"—I've opened his blog—"says he's dabbled in *feng shui*, exorcism and astrology, and witnessed cases that range from animal- and dream-magic to necromancy and psychology, from Tibetan ritual to Taiwanese folklore. There's even a category devoted to Hong Kong. He ends each post with a summary that looks like a healthy mix of wisdom, scepticism and common sense."

"Sounds promising," Derek says. "Let's hope he knows how to handle fox spirits. Use us as your fake-filter."

"OK. He's prolific. There's a lot to read."

According to this shaman, what's happened to us has elements of standard 'spirit possession'. I start a file, copying and pasting anything that resonates.

"Here's something. There's a practice used in Hong Kong known as 'fairy borrowing'. A person summons a spirit to possess them, in order to boost their luck. The so-called fairy *will change or split the host's personality*. In this case study, a woman wanted to be desirable, famous and rich, so – "

"– she invited a fox spirit to possess her, right?"

"Yep. And the fox caused so many problems in her private life that she wanted it removed." I scan the page. "Listen to this. *It's difficult to exorcise fox spirits because they can read their host's mind and hide their presence from the medium.* In this case, the fox prevented the woman's visits to the temple where she planned to exorcise him—it caused her to have three car accidents en route. But finally a medium coaxed it from her body and interred in an earth urn *for good.*" The blogger does not describe the exorcism process.

Derek joins some dots. "So if Robert was right about Rose and she's not of a *huli jing* lineage, we can't discount the possibility that she's been dabbling in 'fairy borrowing' and invited a fox spirit to possess her. That could be what Robert and you have witnessed in your visions."

"Except Robert didn't detect a fox spirit of any kind, only Rose's fake shadow." I read on. *"With any kind of 'spirit possession', help can be made more difficult if the spirit and the human host have developed a co-dependent relationship."*

That means if she is possessed, there's no way that Rose will ever willingly give up her fox spirit. Judging by my dream, it gives Rose her power. I'm no psychologist, but if she started fantasising about the power of fox spirits as a child and invited one to possess her, then it could have grown into a full-blown identification. Scary.

I say to Alister, "We won't get your spirit back by appealing to Rose's goodwill."

A factor in the next example chills me to the bone. "A man, who'd been hoodwinked by a self-styled Taoist into being possessed, couldn't shake off the invading spirits. He tried different Taoist masters and finally went to a Buddhist shaman, who said, *'No wonder you've got spirits coming and going at will. The minor chakra at your nape is wide open like a door.'"*

Is that what Su Yin was doing with her greeting scratch at my nape? I tell Derek and Alister about it now.

"I never asked if she did the same to you, Alister, but now it looks like she was opening up our minor *chakras* for spiritual attack."

Derek says, "That means she was already working with Rose before Alister picked her up from the airport. What if she hadn't just arrived that day but had already been staying in that cottage, after urging Alister to fly to Hong Kong? If Winston isn't a party to their sorcery, then his news about Deshi played into their hands, weakening Alister for the *Hun* stealing."

"And for some reason it hasn't worked on me—even before I protected myself with my virtual black dress." I return to the blog. "The possessed man asked the shaman what he could do to close his nape *chakra* and he said, *'Choose a proper religion! Listen to advice and be persistent.'"*

There are no other details so I send a text to Dr Lee.

At last the blogger gives a glimpse of the exorcism process, but he won't provide a detailed guide for novices. Although everything he describes is hard to believe, his ethics inspire trust.

"Get this." I've moved on to another case study. "A woman went to a medium for help to shake off 'a ghost' who'd possessed her. But she resisted the medium's attempts at exorcism, quaking so much in her chair that she scratched him. So the medium *brought out an effigy of a woman and coaxed the spirit into it.* Suddenly the woman returned to her old self again.

"But soon after, she showed signs of ghost possession again, *perhaps because of co-dependency*, and the process had to be repeated. Then the medium asked the woman if she'd like to take care of the ghost lady in the effigy—and she agreed. The medium taught her some mantras to chant and showed her how to worship the ghost lady with offerings of rice, tea, flowers and lipsticks."

"A shrine," Derek says. "To a ghost. Are you thinking what I'm thinking, Selkie? Su Yin's tea-lights and incense. What if she added some kind of doll to entice Fleur to visit? Doesn't that creep me out?"

"I've been sure Su Yin couldn't be honouring Fleur's ghost, but in the battle for Alister's spirit what might she gain by doing it?"

Then I consider the fact that Su Yin is the spitting image of Fleur. I don't want to say it in front of Alister, but is she a living effigy? Her sleepwalking might be by arrangement with Fleur—the split personality that comes from 'fairy borrowing'. What if Su Yin offered herself to Fleur's ghost as a human host? On a promise of something—opening his nape *chakra* and delivering Alister's *Hun*?

But Robert said Fleur is waiting and getting impatient. Waiting for what? Impatience suggests that there's something Su Yin hasn't delivered yet. Alister's spirit? In spite of the open nape *chakra*, did something go wrong?

The voice from Su Yin's mouth echoes: "*You'll never have him. Give up now and save yourself.*"

Did Rose and her fox-sorcery interfere with their plans, stealing Alister's spirit herself?

Or is that the voice of the split personality—and Fleur's unfinished business is ... with *me*?

But the blogger's final opinion of the woman with the effigy brings all my theories back to earth. He suggests there was no ghost, just a *mind demon*. The woman was only after attention. He says the border between the mental and the supernatural is a line that wobbles.

At the implications of this assessment for our predicament, every hair on my body stands up. As Fortune 44 from the *kau chim* predicted, there's mental illness at work behind the sorcery. Whose?

When my phone rings again, it's Dr Lee.

Chapter 26

As I recount my research into folk sorcery, I can hear Dr Lee's thoughts churning.

"The minor nape *chakra*." He blows out a breathy whistle. "Whoever is doing this knows their energy centres inside out."

"We need to close them. How do we do that?"

"Not if Alister's nape is the escape route of his *Hun*, Selkie. If we close it, his spirit won't have an entry point to return."

A new wave of panic drenches my body. I'm remembering the fairy borrowing. "What are the dangers of keeping it open? Spirit invasion by … hitchhikers?"

"Afraid so. But I think you can relax. When Alister spoke to you, you thought he was contained in some way. It makes sense that she'd keep his spirit captive, not let him loose. And his body isn't doing anything to attract passing spirits, like consulting a medium. That would be an invitation to the lonely and the desperate."

But we exposed him to the festival this morning, with villain hitters sending curses flying. I've been worried about his spirit's vulnerability out there on the astral plane, but invasion of his body by passing souls is a threat I've never considered. I look across at Alister, watching Derek folding pastry and seemingly his empty self. As crazy as it sounds, I'm relieved.

"And your nape *chakra*," Bruce says. "If it was ever open, I suspect you've closed it again with your intention not to succumb to his fate. Or the neck scraping didn't work on you."

Because I was already wary of Su Yin from the moment I met her? The ripples of pleasure from her touch didn't seduce me. They made me watchful.

"I can check you over next time I'm visiting. Meanwhile, do this: visualise your nape *chakra* like a clam, then use your mind to close it tight."

"Thank you. And thanks so much for returning my call on a Sunday."

He chuckles. "It's my Hippocratic duty. And I've got a ringside seat. I'm rooting for you to beat the sorcerer."

"Sorcerers," I say, with emphasis on the plural.

Bruce listens to my updates on Robert's readings and the White Tiger Festival. Then I drop my voice in front of Alister to share my inkling about Su Yin's shrine. The tsunami of folklore stuns him into silence.

"You're lining up for a showdown," he says at last. "You know that don't you?"

"With Rose and Su Yin?" They've been running rings around me for days.

"And the ghost of Alister's wife."

"You think Fleur really is involved?" Not two sorcerers, a trio? "I've been hoping my theories were fanciful."

"Your impressions about her are strong, Selkie. Trust them. Even without Su Yin's possible pact with her, Fleur's ghost must be haunting her parents. No self-respecting ghost would be idle, not after their criminal incompetence with her child. Look at what Robert at the temple said about her: 'waiting' with 'unfinished business'. That's family business. Including the lost son and Alister—and now you."

"You'll never have him! Give up now and save yourself."

Fleur.

I've been suspecting her, circling the possibility, being convinced, then blaming others and letting her go out of respect for Alister. But now that I think about it, those shadowy sensations have been spectral from the start. The silkiness swirling around my neck—always my neck—morphing into something sharp and spiteful. Surely it confirms that she's been trying to open my nape *chakra* and compromise my spirit. This also fits with the almighty shove to keep me away when Alister grabbed my bangle. Not a sorcerer. A ghost. A ghost with unfinished business. Bruce is giving me permission to name her.

Does that confirm that Rose is working against Fleur?

In spite of her drug use, Rose must be engaged in some kind of sorcery or she wouldn't have collapsed when the villain hitter shredded the fox image. She's always hated Alister. Could she be working to stop Fleur's ghost from reuniting with her long-lost love? It would explain Robert's insight into Fleur's shadow when she's with her mother—churning like a typhoon as she wrestles with the raging Rose. That makes Su Yin a spy in Rose's household. A spy for Fleur.

So who is looking for Deshi?

Su Yin was after clues when she went twice into the gambling den. Her comments about that, including the so-called sleepwalking, could have been a ruse. But if it's true, and she was trying to rope me into sharing my information, it suggests that Fleur doesn't know where Deshi is. As a ghost, why wouldn't she know?

Bruce breaks into my thoughts. "The real conundrum to unravel is: why steal Alister's *Hun*? You say he's become prosperous since the family tragedies happened, so if getting a cut of his wealth is the goal—and never underestimate money as more powerful than love in this culture, even for ghosts who want comfort in the afterlife—how does Alister's current state of limbo allow them to tap into his funds?"

"I've wondered if the kidnappers are waiting till I'm totally beaten, then they'll demand a ransom to return his spirit."

"An interesting theory. Assuming you've got access to his money."

Su Yin used her reward to quiz me about that. Savvy.

Then Bruce gets a thought. "Or they'll lend his body an obedient spirit long enough to facilitate a bank transfer."

Bloody hell. It's the vulnerability of his open *chakra*. One step further than spirit abduction is spirit *possession*. Sending another spirit to take over his body would be the ultimate violation.

I turn away from Alister, so he can't overhear me. "I've thought that he's safe from possession by Sharp because she's female—and therefore couldn't invade his male body."

Bruce knocks this theory on the head. "It's more difficult to possess the opposite gender, but if the intention is ardent enough, it's not impossible."

The lid I've been keeping on my emotions slips. A wail escapes. "How can I ... protect him?"

"You're keeping watch on his body, while all your psychic activity is creating confusion. The villain hitting would have surprised them, but even if Rose is disabled, it sounds like Su Yin is still active. And then there's Fleur. Because she's freed from physical constraints, Fleur's got the most spiritual power. Even if she needs a human host from time to time." He adopts a more earnest tone. "There is one way to protect him, Selkie, and fight for him at the same time. You'd be able to prevent malign invasion and direct his body while his soul is absent. It's dangerous and no-one would expect you to consider it."

Do I know what's coming?

"Possess him yourself."

Racing further out of earshot, I take refuge in the bathroom. My mind is reeling. Just as Bruce announced those words, I swear my soul took flight. For a split second I was on the ceiling, viewing the tops of our heads from above. Derek's new bald patch that's only visible when he bends. Alister's brown curls, unkempt and tangled. My spiky cut as I held the phone to my ear. It was just how Nigel described it. Astral travel. Then in a blink I was back.

"Are you still there, Selkie?" Bruce asks.

"I am now." I tell him what just happened.

"So it's possible," he says.

"To enter Alister's body?"

"To leave your own."

"But I've never left before, not by my own volition, only when Sharp tried to suck me out." As I recall how very close I came to losing my soul that day, I imagine it curling into a tight ball for protection. "Nigel warned me that astral travel needs practice, and I don't have time to learn it."

"He suggested possessing Alister?"

"No. He thought I could go to the astral plane and bring his spirit back with me."

"A living spirit looking for another living spirit amongst all the ghosts? That might work. If Alister's out there. But it would be dangerous too."

"And what if he's imprisoned? In ... an *effigy?*"

"It's a convenient way to contain a spirit." Bruce's matter-of-fact manner is keeping me from losing it. "The symbolism of an effigy is also powerful. You can choose any object to represent the person whose soul you're storing. Once contained, escape is difficult."

Do I need to visualise where they've hidden him? The idea is so repugnant, I don't think I can do it. What if they've created some kind of mannequin to imprison him, while they're planning to cajole him into signing over his assets?

The idea of a ransom is suddenly appealing. Let them have Alister's wealth, if I can walk away with ... all of him. But that would mean trusting them to fulfil their side of any bargain. Bringing him back myself would be much more certain than doing deals.

"You said that going to the astral plane would be danger-ous," I ask Bruce. "More dangerous than ... what you're proposing?"

"Yes and no. On the astral plane, you're far from your body and you're mixing with millions of lost souls in various states of desperation. The ones who are happily dead have gone to their version of heaven."

The image of the omelette returns.

Bruce continues. "But seeking him on the astral plane is less dangerous than possessing Alister's body yourself, because —"

"— I might get trapped there."

"And never be able to return."

That's when I lose it.

As Dr Lee suggests thinking it over, and hangs up, my

grip on reality finally abandons me. The perils to Alister's soul—and my own—are so overwhelming that my knees crumple beneath me and I collapse on the bathroom floor.

Chapter 27

"Selkie!" Derek shouts.

Pulling myself together, I'm back at the island counter in a flash. Derek is holding Alister in a bear hug. As I throw my arms around them both, Alister's body bucks off the stool.

"He started growling," Derek cries. "Then his head flew back like he'd been punched, and he doubled over from an invisible belly blow."

We've all landed on the floor, where we keep holding Alister's jerking body. I'm terrified about what's happening to his spirit. That's when I sense his voice: *Knife.*

"He's being attacked with a knife."

Madam Li wants her guy. Watch how she does it.

But Derek cries, "Su Yin! On the loose in Rose's den?"

Bloody hell. The sorcerer's apprentice. Reaching into my back pocket, I grab Alister's phone and dial Su Yin.

No answer. I text her: *Stop!*

Everything goes still.

I'm running on instinct. *How much do you want?*

Alister?

Selkie. You're hurting him.

Her reply: *You'll know how much when I'm good and ready.*

What are you doing?

Rescuing him. I want my reward.

Rescuing him with a knife? *If you damage his spirit, you'll get nothing.*

Silence.

I can almost hear her mind working. Her disregard for Alister's safety is hiding something. I sense she's out of her depth—and she knows it. It's a chink I can exploit.

Taking a deep breath, I dial her number again. She answers.

"There's a lot at stake, Su Yin. Alister's life."

"That's all you care about," she snorts. "Him. And Deshi."

"I don't care about the money."

"You'd care if you didn't have any! So would Alister. He's loaded but no way would he give me the whole reward. I answered his stupid ad and stuck that swab in my cheek for the DNA test. It proves who I am: Deshi's cousin. But that wasn't enough, was it? He wanted *information*. Like, I'm supposed to spy on my own family—for money. He's waving tens of thousands in my face so he thinks he can tell me what to do."

"Isn't that what the ad promised? A reward in exchange for information that led to Deshi?"

"You still don't get it do you? It's because I'm not *Fleur*. I saw the way he looked at me that first time. He even called me Fleur. Shit, that was freaky. Then he changed and went all business-like about the money. Like it's my fault that I'm not his dead wife."

She sounds a little drunk. It's made her garrulous. That doesn't mean reliable, but at least she's stopped using the knife.

I need to keep her talking. "But you contacted Fleur."

"No. *She* visited *me*."

"When?"

"Right after I met Alister. While I was asleep, Fleur came and sat on the edge of my bed. It was so real, like she was my twin. She told me her spirit had been trapped for thirty years. I remembered the number when I woke up. Thirty. Fleur said I'd helped her escape and she was so grateful. Now she could find her son Deshi and when she did, she'd help me lead Alister to him—then I could get the rest of the reward. She told me to set up a shrine to her, so she could visit me."

This sounds like wishful thinking. Everything leads to the money. "Why did you believe what she said? It was a dream."

"Fleur thought of that. She picked up a lipstick from my nightstand, painted her lips and kissed me on the forehead. She said I'd know it was true in the morning. I nearly passed out when I got out of bed and saw myself in the mirror. Her lip-print was right there where she kissed me."

"Did that scare you?" I wonder if this led to a pact.

"What do you think? I just kept thinking about the money. But I haven't seen her again. I set up the shrine with the same lipstick like she told me to, but she hasn't come back."

If this is true, something tells me Su Yin got impatient.

"What did you do next?"

"I'm the one who helped Fleur escape—I don't know how, but that's what she told me—and because of me she could find Deshi. But what was I getting out of it? A kiss and a promise—from a ghost! And now she was ignoring me. I felt used—by Alister; by her. So I told my mother that I'd seen Fleur in a dream—like, Fleur's her dead cousin. Mom said Rose would want to know about that because Rose was looking for Fleur's ghost."

Winston said Fleur was haunting them. Someone isn't

telling the truth.

"Mom rang Rose," she says.

"And you told Rose you'd met Alister."

"Yeah. Was she angry. Never get on the wrong side of Rose. She might be old but she's scary. She said it was Alister's fault that Fleur died, and I was betraying our family by contacting him. She told me to get on the next plane to Hong Kong because she was going to need my help to sort things out."

"You stayed with Rose and Winston in that old shop?"

"No, there's a wreck of a house along the road and I had to stay there—with the tarantulas. Rose said I couldn't stay with them because Winston would freak out that I looked so much like Fleur. I think it was my punishment for talking to Alister, but Rose got used to having me around. She even likes the way I look. I'm like her long-lost daughter. She gave me some spirit training, then I rang Alister and told him to fly over."

Spirit training. To open Alister's *chakra*?

"Is that when the sleepwalking started? After the training?"

"Yeah, but that's Fleur. Rose says Fleur's trying to use me to look for Deshi—and to give her a human body to sleep with Alister. Then you came along and spoiled everything. Rose told me not to contact Fleur because she's turned into an angry ghost."

Angry with Rose. But Su Yin kept her shrine to Fleur anyway, setting it up in the apartment. It's a reminder that Su Yin doesn't do what she's told.

"You said that I care about Alister and Deshi," I say. "And you care about your reward. What does Rose care about?"

"Haven't you figured that out yet? She wants Deshi for herself. That means keeping Alister away from him—and Fleur too. If Fleur finds Deshi, she'll poison his mind against his grandmother."

"Why is Fleur so angry with her mother?"

"The stupid cow let those men kidnap Deshi in the night market."

"Anything else?"

"Yeah. She kept Fleur's ghost locked up in a pot for thirty years."

Shit.

The revelation hits me with a flash of understanding. After Fleur's murder in San Francisco, her spirit could have visited her mother for a final farewell, either warm or hostile. Did Rose coax Fleur's ghost into a container, with promises to give her daughter the right send off into the afterlife?

Then Rose kidnapped Deshi and took her whole family, including Fleur, back to Hong Kong. But Deshi was abducted. Did Rose fear the wrath of Fleur's ghost so much that she kept her imprisoned while she searched for him? And when she couldn't find him herself, it was too late to enlist Fleur's help—and the threat of her daughter's retribution meant the lid of the funeral pot could never be opened.

But Fleur escaped, because of Su Yin. How?

When Alister met Su Yin—about seven months ago—he reached out to the woman who looked like Fleur with all the power of his living love. What if Fleur felt it? It sounds like that intense moment of unconditional love gave her the strength to fly.

I don't have time to delve deeper. I'm sure Su Yin just tried to prise Alister's spirit out of the effigy Rose has put him in. Her amateur sorcery could cost him his life.

What I say next will be crucial. Derek is sitting beside me, his arms cradling Alister. My phone's been on speaker and he gives me the thumbs up to keep following my gut.

"So because of your help, Fleur escaped," I say. "Now you're trying to do the same for Alister."

"Then he'll give me my reward." She doesn't want to sound like she cares about anything else.

"We need to handle this carefully, so his spirit doesn't get lost or damaged."

"*We?*" She snorts. "What do you know about Chinese sorcery? Nothing."

"Only what I've read. And I've wondered about a few things. I've wondered if Rose is ... a fox spirit."

She's shocked into silence, before her savviness kicks in. "What ... makes you think that?"

"She's been leaving clues." I'm not sure who's who, but I'm winging it. "I've felt silky fur around my neck and sharp claws on my chest, and I've seen the colour red. I didn't know what they meant, but a psychic did a drawing for Alister—of a fox. When you sleepwalk, I think that Rose sends a fox spirit to possess you."

She laughs. "You got that wrong. She performed a ritual on me. Fleur wouldn't join the lineage, but I've joined. I'm a real fox spirit now. The red streaks in my hair prove it."

Beneath her pride, I hear bravado. "What happened to Fleur?"

"She walked onto that campus and got shot. A fox spirit would have been too savvy to do that. Instead of honouring her ancestors, she rejected her family lineage and married Alister. Bam, she's dead."

That's why Rose blames Alister.

"I've never met Rose," I say, "so you'll have to judge this for yourself. I don't think you're a fox spirit. I think she's tricked you. I think a fox spirit controls what you do—and it comes from Rose."

She's silent again. If she's telling the truth about the sleepwalking, she knows that something is controlling her. "That's Fleur."

"Is it? Think about what you just said. If you're a fox spirit, no-one could control you. Fleur's a ghost. Now that she's escaped, she can go anywhere she likes. She doesn't need your help to find Deshi. You said yourself that ever since the dream she's been ignoring you."

Su Yin must have already been suspicious of Rose's control over her. It explains why she took off to the old cottage as soon as Rose was out of action. Now I can almost hear her allegiance flip.

"Rose lied to me about being a fox spirit." She exhales loudly as the penny drops. "She's using me. When I get the reward, she'll find a way to take it. She wants Deshi—and the money."

It's unlike her to admit vulnerability. I don't want her to turn on Alister because she's lost face.

"Only you can be sure of that, Su Yin. But someone sent you into that gambling den where those men might have hurt you. Someone who's looking for Deshi. I can't see how that could be Fleur."

Through the long silence that follows, I start to worry that I've blown it. What if she takes revenge on Alister? But he's fallen asleep against Derek's chest. It's a sure sign that her amateur sorcery has stopped.

At last Su Yin speaks, her voice firm with decision. "I'm looking at a small cupboard. An old shrine with compartments and little doors. Rose put Alister's spirit inside one of the compartments, but something's gone wrong. She can't open the door. It's locked and we don't have the key. I just tried to get it open with a few tools. It won't budge."

A spark flickers in my chest. "How many doors?"

"Four. He's behind the fourth door."

With a supreme effort, I keep my voice steady. "Thank you. Can you text me a photo? I'm on my way." Then I remember what Alister said: keep Su Yin onside. "Do you believe in luck, Su Yin?"

"Of course. Luck is everything. Good luck can change bad fate."

"Well, luck is something you create. You helped Fleur's ghost escape. Now you're choosing to help Alister. This is luck at work. Recovering Alister's spirit goes way beyond the reward for finding Deshi. When he's back to his old self, he'll decide the value of what you've done for him and how much he wants to give you by way of thanks."

She's quiet again. "Rose is sick but she might feel better soon and come here before you can get the shrine—and me."

She wants to be rescued too. Before I can respond, there's a noise as the phone is banged down. Su Yin calls something in Cantonese and a woman's voice replies. Su Yin laughs and answers in a voice that sounds too bright to my ears. Then she starts singing a little song. The words are just loud enough for me to hear, but I recognise the melody from my childhood: 'Who's afraid of the big bad wolf?' The connection is cut.

Every muscle in my body is screaming. It can only be Rose. She must have asked who Su Yin was talking to. Su Yin thought fast, saying she was just singing, at the same time letting me know she's afraid. Afraid of Rose.

That makes two of us.

Chapter 28

Derek has heard everything. "Don't panic, Selkie. For the moment he's safe inside that shrine. I wonder if he's using his spirit to keep the door shut."

Could he be locking the door against their entry?

"He'll run out of energy," I wail. "And the shrine must be small enough to carry. If Rose is suspicious, she could hide it." My voice rises. "Then we might not be able to find it and rescue him, before she figures out how to open it."

All my optimism from learning about the shrine has been sucked into a black hole of despair. I look across at my man, his face serene in sleep, and hope that his spirit is as undisturbed as his body. It reacted wildly when Su Yin was attacking the shrine door with a knife, so that means it's still potent. And there's a small comfort in knowing that it's contained and not out on the astral plane tangling with desperate souls.

Derek is frowning. "Rose knows we turned the villain hitter onto her. Nigel told her. Unless she was too sick to notice."

"Not sick enough to stay in bed for long. She's gone straight to her den and found Su Yin there on her own. Her fox spirit could be picking up Su Yin's change of allegiance."

Rose has shown she's ruthless. How safe is Su Yin?

"Su Yin didn't flip sides because of you, Selkie. She was

already playing on more than one team. Her real loyalty has always been to herself."

"You think she knew all along that she wasn't really a member of Rose's fox spirit lineage? Maybe she just said that to get me to back off. Or she made it up on the fly when I told her my hunch about Rose." A sudden thought makes me stop. "If Su Yin was telling the truth, I didn't tell her that there's no lineage."

"Does she need to know?" Derek asks.

I think about this. "Lineage keeps family members loyal, even Su Yin. So she'll be more committed to us if she knows Rose is a fake *huli jing*."

"We can trust one thing," Derek says. "She'll look after her reward—and that means looking after Alister's *Hun*.

Derek slides out from under Alister, leaving him resting on the floor. We've just put a cushion under his head, when the door to the apartment opens.

Nigel limps in. "Good news. It's just a sprain. And getting ice on it early has helped the swelling. Winston insisted on driving me home."

To my surprise, Winston comes in behind him. "I go now. Nigel home OK. I look after Rose."

"She's out of bed, Winston," I say. "She's with Su Yin at the old house."

"Old house?" He looks genuinely confused. He comes into the living room and sees Alister asleep on the floor. When he recognises Derek, he flops onto an armchair.

"The house is further down So Kwun Wat Road," I say. "It's where Rose has her fox den—and does her magic."

Nigel says, "I've been telling Winston about Rose's activities, but he doesn't believe me."

"Rose *sad*, not bad."

"Winston, she's kidnapped Alister's *Hun* spirit and locked it away in an old shrine. We have to get it back before she destroys it."

"Who tell you that?"

"Su Yin. We need a taxi to drive us to the old house. Will you do it?"

Derek is waking Alister and helping him into his coat. Winston watches, frowning. If he didn't believe that Alister's the victim of sorcery, his own eyes confirm it.

"Su Yin look like Fleur." He shakes his head. "But she not beautiful on inside. She selfish."

"That's true, but a fortune teller at the Taoist temple told us that Rose is pretending to be a fox spirit. She's kidnapped Alister's *Hun* to stop him from finding Deshi."

Winston throws his hands in the air. "Fox spirit. Too much talking about fox spirit. I tell Rose to be villain hitter, make her forget fox spirit. Rose and her sister, Su Yin's po po, their mother talk about fox spirit lineage; she fill their heads."

This information might help us beat Rose, but we have to get to the shrine before she does something rash—and permanent.

"Winston, tell us the story on the way."

Nigel has already summoned the elevator. We're out the door.

* * *

Winston navigates the Sunday traffic like a taxi driver, and I'm relieved not to have to push him to drive faster. He ducks in and out of other cars, making the best time possible. In between answering his phone, he lives up to his title: Winston, the storytelling taxi driver. The story he tells is a shocking one.

"This story start with Rose po po. She just girl, live in Nanking, big city in China. It 1937. Japanese soldiers come. It very bad. They rape and kill many people. Rose po po, she get raped but she clever. She hide, not die. Later she have baby girl. But baby is half Japanese, so Chinese people see her and remember terrible time. They treat her bad. Not her fault. She very sad, have no friends in whole world."

I vaguely remember hearing about the massacre in Nanking before World War II. Now a glimpse of that atrocity fills the cab. While the horror sinks in, Winston takes another call, snaps something in Cantonese, then resumes his story.

"Rose mother, she that baby. She stay home, live in dream world. She read Chinese stories about fox spirit, then find out Japanese have fox spirit too. She tell herself she have fox spirit lineage from China and Japan; it make her special. That why Chinese people not understand. When she grow up and move away, she find husband, have two daughters: Rose and her sister. She tell them they got special fox spirit powers from ancestor."

As he draws breath, we're all silent. It explains my dream of the dancing foxes.

Winston continues. "When I meet Rose, she very young. She tell me she fox spirit, but I say it not true, just story. She not listen. She tell Fleur she fox spirit too. Then Fleur meet Alister, she want to be American, not fox spirit. She have baby Deshi. Then Fleur die. Rose blame Alister." Then he adds, "Rose not bad, just very sad. Fleur very precious. Rose got rocks in belly, only have one baby."

Did Rose have a medical condition that stopped her from having more children? *Stones in the belly. Cut it open.* She lost her only child, then her grandchild. She's one grief-stricken woman. Grief and blame are a powerful mix, further fortified by her childhood brainwashing about fox spirits. The depth of her anger plus her possible psychosis make it all the more urgent to get that shrine. Through the cab window, I see the first sign to Tuen Mun. We're getting close. Relief washes over me that Winston is helping us.

Alister is sitting between me and Derek. He's listened passively to Winston's story, but when Winston makes a call I feel him stiffen. He's the only one of us who can understand Cantonese.

"Rose good mother to Fleur," Winston says. "She good po po to Deshi. Just have bad luck."

"Who did you phone just now?" I ask him. When he doesn't answer, my heart starts pounding. "Did you call Rose and tell her we're coming?"

"I tell her leave shrine behind, but run away from you."

"No!" I throw my arms around Alister, as if my embrace will save his spirit.

"She give *Hun* back to Alister," Winston says. "All OK again."

Of course his allegiance is to Rose, and I blame myself for not predicting it. As I press my head against Alister's chest, my tears of rage soak his shirt. He remains stiff beside me. Does he know how much more precarious his situation has just become?

∗ ∗ ∗

By the time we arrive at the old cottage, I'm beyond despair. Just like in the Street View photo, the door is open. We all trudge across the yard and into the single dark room, burdened by the weight of failure. It's empty. Rose and Su Yin have gone.

After a search, it's clear that the shrine is gone too. Winston's call gave them plenty of time to ring their own cab and be far away.

"She's taken the shrine." My voice is flat. "You had the chance to save Alister, but you couldn't believe Rose would hurt him."

He flops onto a plastic chair. "Su Yin tell lies about Rose."

"Then why didn't Rose tell you about this place?"

Winston looks around in a daze, taking in the trappings of Rose's sorcery. A central table fills the bare room, strewn with candles, joss paper and incense sticks—and some remnant white sprinkles that I suspect transform her into a fox spirit. I go through the motions of examining each item as if she might have left a clue, but I saw them all in my dream. She's beaten me again, and my power to save Alister is draining away like the hourglass in my dream.

I consider telling Winston that Rose kept Fleur's ghost trapped for thirty years and lied that she was haunting them. But that would either break him with the ultimate truth or further his disbelief and make him more loyal. Neither reaction will help us.

He pulls out his phone and makes a call. No answer.

"Where would she go?" Nigel asks. "Su Yin must be with her."

Winston manages a shrug.

"We need your help." I resist the urge to shake him. "We only want the shrine. Where could she hide it?"

He thinks for a minute. "She have cupboard for villain hitting. It stay under Canal Road flyover, got padlock. Not safe, get robbed."

She wouldn't risk it. Even if she's not planning to ransom it, she wants his spirit in her control. Derek has gone right around the room looking for trapdoors and niches. Then I remember the blogger's story of the fox spirit interred in an earth urn. Leaving Nigel watching a passive Winston, Derek and I take Alister outside to search the ground for something recently buried.

"Alister might have a sixth sense about finding it."

We do a thorough search around the cottage and the over-grown garden but come up empty.

"No obvious hidey-holes or disturbed earth," Derek says. "But taking it with her is a risk. It could still be hidden on site and we haven't found it."

There's a small wooded area behind the cottage. We do a wider search, checking the ground, scouring the bases of the tree trunks, looking behind the perimeter wall, finding nothing.

"Su Yin's apartment?" Nigel asks, when we return.

"I don't think so," I say. "That would give Su Yin too much power over Rose, but let's check when we go home. Rose will need somewhere to set up a makeshift sorcery table."

I send Su Yin a text, not expecting an answer. If she's still on our side, she won't do anything to arouse Rose's suspicion.

"We need to see your shop, Winston."

He nods and we get back into the cab.

The row of shopfronts is just like the photo on Street View, looking abandoned and vacant except for the one occupied by Winston and Rose.

Nigel waits inside the front door, while Derek, Alister and I search their humble home—a rectangular space that's a living room-cum-kitchen, and upstairs a bedroom and a storeroom. Winston watches us, his shoulders slumped in resignation.

When we don't find the shrine, panic clouds my thoughts about what to do next. But Alister has stopped at the ancestral shrines to Fleur and Deshi. Side by side in the corner of the living space, their photos from thirty years ago are framed and focal.

Fleur's shrine holds a crude pottery urn with a lid. A funerary pot for her ashes? It should have gone to the temple, Winston said, but Rose was too sad to let it go. She let him think she was only motivated by grief, but it must be where she kept Fleur's ghost captive. Winston thought that Fleur was banging on the outside of the pot, but it must have been her nightly demand to be set free.

The pot inspires an insight. If Su Yin is telling the truth about helping Fleur escape, then the location of the container isn't crucial. Fleur's ghost was trapped here in Hong Kong, but Alister's loving look in San Francisco gave her the impetus to escape. If the emotional pull is strong enough—from me and Deshi—I'm counting on Alister's living spirit to find the same strength.

That means we don't need the four-door shrine to get Alister's spirit back. But we've just made Rose believe that's what we think. It could make her focus her energy on hiding it—and whichever side Su Yin's on, we can trust her to guard it—while we increase our efforts to find Deshi. A surge of relief restores my power. The distraction could give us an edge.

Decorated with faded baby toys, Deshi's shrine evokes a

wave of sadness. The yellow blouse I saw in my vision hangs on a peg, a stark reminder of his second abduction. Reconnecting Deshi with his father is still the key to everything. The key to the fourth door.

Remembering Alister's emotional reaction to the old photo of his family on the beach, I move away to allow him space to reunite with them through the shrines. But would either of their spirits be visiting this hostile place?

He stands still for a minute, then suddenly throws his right hand out from his body. Thinking he's reaching for me, I take it but recoil. His ring is hot. Scorching. Now Alister is shaking his hand. I race over to the kitchen sink and return with a bowl of water. He plunges his hand into the bowl.

Winston comes over and looks at Alister's hand.

"That his wedding ring. Fleur get one too."

He's been wearing it on his right hand all the time we've been together, but it's never bothered me. No longer on his wedding finger, it's a memento of his first love, the mother of his son, and never a threat to our relationship. An inexpensive silver band, it's tight on his finger, hard to remove even with soap. But through the ring, he's kept an emotional link to Fleur all the years since her death.

And just now it got hot.

She was here, connecting with him through his ring. And he wasn't growling. My eyes scan her shrine. Is she still here?

Alister is wiping his hand on his jeans. The moment has passed.

"What happened to Fleur's ring?" I ask Winston.

He hangs his head. "Rose take ring off Fleur's hand before funeral. It engraved and she do not want ring in funeral pot with Fleur's ashes. She do not want Fleur married to Alister in afterlife."

She's one serious woman. "What did the engraving say?"

Winston knows the answer. "Endless love. Rose do not like it last forever."

Endless circle. The two concentric circles on the map. Miss Tigerlily knew about the ring.

"Do you still have it?"

Could I use it to contact Fleur, ring to ring? Would she help me rescue Alister?

"Rose ... throw it away. It gone ... thirty years."

"Where?" But I already know.

"In ocean. Even Fleur's ghost never find it."

Rose has thought of everything.

Chapter 29

I t's time to leave. Winston offers to drive us home, but I don't want him to know our movements.

On the way back in our own taxi, my head is in turmoil about Fleur. What was she saying to Alister? And whose side is she on? The route home takes us through Mong Kok where I see another advertisement for the Shadow Puppet Theatre.

Madam Li wants her guy. Watch how she does it.

Fleur's ring alerted Alister's *Po* spirit to her presence. She's staying in touch with him from the afterlife. Why?

I ask the boys, "If I wanted to get in touch with Fleur's ghost, how would I do it?"

Derek says, "You contacted your great-aunt in Ireland last year. Try the same process with Fleur."

"But my great-aunt wanted me to contact her. Would Fleur want to talk to me?" I turn in my seat and face Alister, taking hold of both his hands. Then I lean in and press my lips to his ear. "Can you ask Fleur to contact me, Haiku?"

At first he stares at me blankly, then he shifts in his seat. Slowly lifting his right hand, he reaches across, and touches his ring to the bangle of my wrist. They meet with the softest ping, but the soundwaves reverberate through me like thunder.

The air is suddenly thick as the cab jerks to a stop. Our driver doesn't respond in any way. Does he even know what's happening?

"Are you h–here, Fleur?" I ask, wondering if she stopped the cab. "Can we talk about Deshi? And rescuing Alister from Rose?"

Derek and Nigel are looking at me, waiting for something else to happen. Nothing does.

Nigel points to the stairs beside the funeral store. "We're outside the entrance to the secret club."

"The club is connected to Deshi," I say, "but I still don't know how."

"And Alister is staring at something," Derek says.

Alister's gaze is directed through the cab window at the shop opposite the funeral store. Its facade is festooned with umbrellas, all open and showing their patterned domes.

"Umbrellas." I saw umbrellas on our restaurant search. "What do they mean?"

Alister doesn't answer. The cab is suddenly moving again.

Derek brushes his hands down his arms. "That was woo-woo."

The moment has passed, but the club is a clue. I remind everyone that its name and password came to the owner after he worked at a Buddhist restaurant when the monks got sick.

"There's a restaurant at the Po Lin Monastery," I say, "under the giant Buddha. But I didn't sense that the red cord wanted me to go there."

The red cord didn't appear just now either. Because it was Fleur?

Derek is looking at his phone. "The South China Post. October last year. *Monks Succumb to Flu. Early in Season.*

Southern hemisphere visitor blamed. Po Lin Monastery."

"I've got to talk to the club owner again." I signal our driver to pull over.

"Remember what Butler said, Selkie?" Nigel says. "The police might have an operation going on. He doesn't want Klaus to recognise you."

"My turn." Derek jumps out. "I'll get my own cab home."

"Thanks DD," I call after him, still reeling from what's happened. Did Fleur just send me a message? I'm not sure.

* * *

Su Yin's door opens to the old code. She hasn't been back. She and Rose—and Alister's spirit—are holed up somewhere else.

Back in our apartment, I grab Alister's hand and take him straight to the napkin map.

I point to the concentric circles. "It's your ring. It matches the endless circle in her reading. This is your connection to Fleur—and Deshi." I hold him and look into his vacant eyes. "Rose has got your *Hun*, but if I can contact Fleur and find Deshi, I think our love could rescue you before Rose even notices you've escaped." I choose my next words with care. "But I'm worried Fleur might be ... possessive of you. What if she's getting ready to take your spirit with her ... to the afterlife?"

Nigel cuts through my fear. "If that was Fleur in the cab, she may have been reaching out. You need a medium, Selkie. A Chinese medium. Dr Lee must know someone."

"I know someone," I say. "Miss Tigerlily."

Superintendent Butler has ignored two messages from me, but saving Alister's life trumps everything. I leave an urgent message, telling him that I sense that Miss Tigerlily has gone into hiding from the traffickers. I stress that Alister's life depends on getting her help—to contact his wife's ghost and retrieve his spirit from the sorcerer.

When I hang up, I realise that if I'm right about her disappearance, showing herself to help us will put her own life at risk. Will she do it?

While we wait, I'm so jumpy that Nigel suggests updating the fridge whiteboard. He picks up the marker and adds Fleur's ring. Followed by an umbrella, in case it's a clue. Then he draws a shrine with four drawers.

"Could your vision on Egg Street be a symbol of the old shrine that's holding Alister's *Hun*?"

"No. I'm sure that was about Deshi and the old market. About eggs and chickens—and offerings."

My eyes brim at the thought, and I look across at Alister. If we get close to Deshi, could Alister's *Po* spirit sense their connection and guide us?

"Buddhists are vegetarians, but eggs could be offerings." Nigel slaps his hand on his leg. "We've wondered if someone put baby Deshi in a basket—to save him like *Baby called Moses*. What about this? Babies born out of wedlock are sometimes left at the door of a church. What if they left Deshi at a shrine or a temple? Like an offering?"

"It fits the clues, but Deshi was nearly a year old, remember? Rescuers wouldn't put him in a baby basket, and he'd climb out of any other kind."

"One-year-olds still sleep a lot. Shrines and temples are busy places. If he was asleep, someone would find him before he woke up."

It feels like a lead. "What would happen to a baby left at a shrine? Where would they take him?"

"A monastery?" Nigel says. "They have orphanages. Monks live to a good age and often stay in one place all their lives. A senior monk might remember a baby left at a shrine thirty years ago. It's worth asking."

Just then Derek sends a text. *On way to restaurant at Po Lin Monastery.*

Nigel says, "The big Buddha is a long way from Egg Street, but its restaurant is linked through that flu epidemic to the Fat Waiter Club. A monk at Po Lin restaurant might have worked near Egg Street in the past."

My energy returns in a rush. "Let's go."

On the way, I text Derek that we'll meet him there. *What time does the restaurant close?*

Just checked. 4.30pm.

We've got almost two hours, but it's at the top of the mountain.

What have you discovered?

Nothing. Owner of Fat Waiter not there so I couldn't press him about knowing Deshi. But flu epidemic was at Po Lin. Plan to ask around.

My buoyant mood sinks. He hasn't got a lead. But it still feels like the closest we've got to Deshi.

* * *

The quickest way is by train, then cable car. In the cab to Central, I'm worried about Alister's stamina—heaven knows I'm exhausted myself—but his eyes are wide open as he watches the sights fly by: first the ocean view from our road, then the high-rises and shops of the commercial district.

At Central we dive underground and take the Tung Chung line to Lantau Island, emerging opposite City Gate, a multi-storey shopping centre of factory outlets surrounded by shiny towers of apartments. It's an incongruous gateway to a monastery. As we follow the signs to the cable car, David Butler returns my call.

"She's going to help you," he says, without saying Miss Tigerlily's name. "I advised her against it, but she insisted. She feels responsible, as if her predictions caused what's happened to Mr Sloane. She'll call you later on a prepaid phone."

"I can't thank you enough," I gush.

"Thank us both by following her instructions to the letter. These people she's hiding from are ruthless."

"I'll do everything she says."

"Good." I'm about to hang up when he adds, "And stay away from your neighbour. And his maid."

"Is he involved in ... all this?"

"I can't say more. Just keep your distance from him—and the secret club."

The Fat Waiter feels like the hub for everything that's happened.

My optimism returns. With Miss Tigerlily as my medium, I'll know soon enough whose side Fleur is on. And if the monks at Po Lin lead us to Deshi, I'm hoping that when he hears his family history, he'll feel connected enough to the father he's never met to participate in bringing him back. But the bombshell of his lost family could easily overwhelm him. I've been worried that we'll never find Deshi, but what if we find him and he refuses to help?

Holding tightly to Alister's arm, I focus my intention on our quest. With or without Fleur and Deshi, I have to trust that Miss Tigerlily's skill, together with the power of my love, will be enough to bring him home.

** * **

The giant Buddha sits atop the mountain, this afternoon shrouded in mist. We enter the building for the cable cars and buy our tickets. There's a shorter queue for the more expensive 'crystal cabin' with a glass bottom and within minutes we've taken our seats. Nigel and I sit on either side of Alister, and three European tourists take the opposite seat.

After my conversation with Dr Lee, I'm tense about his nape *chakra* in public places like this, and the possibility of a spiritual invasion. I stare at our fellow passengers, as if their faces will reveal their spiritual integrity. They ignore us and gaze at the view. But should we do a process to close Alister's *chakra* until we can meet with Miss Tigerlily? I'll ask her.

Is he vulnerable to Fleur's ghost? She was present in his ring today. She could be with him all the time—a possibility I now can't forget. I've slipped my arm through his. As he gazes between our feet at the emerging sights of forested hills and waterways below, I monitor his face for any sign of new distress and find none.

And what about Rose? After chasing her out of her den, I'm expecting more from her than hiding. She's had time to plot her next move. Even though I've convinced myself that we can retrieve Alister's spirit without the shrine, while she possesses it there's a constant risk she'll get it open. What if she finds a stronger hiding place—or does something else to harm his *Hun*?

In other circumstances this would be a spectacular ride, above Tung Chung Bay and past Hong Kong airport, then up the slope to the Buddha. But my whole body is taut with expectation. The sights fly by. When we finally arrive, it's a short walk to Ngong Ping Village, lined with eateries and souvenir shops. We pass some cattle grazing between the paved areas and glimpse the towering Tian Tin Buddha high above us through the mist. Some visitors are lighting giant incense sticks and placing them in huge sand-filled urns. The action reminds me of offerings—and our new theory about baby Deshi. Turning left under a gate similar to the one on the rune-map, we follow the signs to the temple restaurant.

At the entrance Derek is lounging against a red pillar, his posture oozing dejection. "I've asked the waiters on duty if they know where to find wind sand chicken. Their English is limited. Each said that this café doesn't serve chicken. I guess they get tourists asking for meat dishes all the time, but I was hoping for more."

"How old were these waiters? We're looking for a monk who's at least forty five. Older would be better. We need to show him a photo of Deshi."

Nigel fills him in on our updated theory.

"You think Deshi became a monk?" Derek asks.

"We wonder if monks might have found him," I say, "and helped him to get adopted or something."

"But an orphan boy could be brought up by the monks," Nigel says. "They take in young novices and train them. They might have seen a baby left at a shrine as a gift from heaven."

"Deshi, a monk." I test the sound of the words on my intuition—and on Alister. He's staring at the red lantern above Derek's head. "A gift from heaven fits with Miss

Tigerlily's reading: *Touched by the gods.*"

"The waiters serving here aren't monks," Derek says. "They're mostly women."

It's a blow, and our hunch is thin. It's getting close to closing time but I won't leave here until we've ruled it out. Inside the air-conditioned dining room, the circular tables draped in pale green cloths are largely empty. I ask a passing waiter if we can speak to a monk.

She says, "Monks in kitchen. No English."

"It's important." I show her the photo of Deshi. "We are looking for this missing baby."

Her face sags with empathy. "So sorry."

"Is there a monk who is the boss?" I ask. "Can we show him this photo?"

She walks briskly to the end of the room and through a doorway. We follow, then wait. After a few minutes, she returns. It looks like she's alone, and I'm ready to barge into the kitchen, when a young monk appears behind her. He's draped in orange robes and barely older than a boy, too young to remember back thirty years.

"Can I help you?" he asks.

She's brought us a monk who speaks English. I tell him that we want to show the picture to an older monk.

"No babies here," he says.

After I explain the time lapse, he asks us to wait. Beyond the doorway, we're getting glimpses of the kitchen where the last meals of the day are being prepared. The young monk returns with a much older monk whose lined face is devoid of expression. As he stares at the image without reacting, my body tenses. The young monk is talking in Cantonese. A conversation follows, then the older monk shuffles away.

"He said a baby left at a shrine in Kowloon might go to the nuns at Chi Lin Nunnery. They have an orphanage. Po Lin is too far away."

It makes complete sense, but something brought us all this way.

"Thank you for your help." I can't keep the disappointment from my voice.

It's when we turn to leave that Derek tosses the password over his shoulder. "Find Wind Sand Chicken."

The monk stuns us. "He ran away. He won't come back."

"Who?" I turn back, excitement parching my throat.

"Wind Sand. We didn't find him."

"Wind Sand? A monk called Wind Sand?" I can't believe it.

"His nickname." His face crinkles with emotion. "I miss him."

"When did Wind Sand come to Po Lin? When did he leave?" I suppress the urge to grab his robes and shake them.

"He came here as small boy, before I came. He was called Wind Sand Chicken. Then he changed to Wind Sand when he grew up. He worked in this kitchen. But after many monks got sick last year, he left."

He looks over his shoulder, and I'm worried he's being pulled back to his work. The existence of Wind Sand could still be a cruel coincidence.

"Why didn't the other monk remember Wind Sand?" I ask.

"Wind Sand lived here for a long time, since small boy. Then he ran away. The other monks are not happy. They meditate to lose their bad feelings. They forget him."

My next question comes out in a rush. "Where do you think Wind Sand is?"

"He didn't tell me, but a waiter called Charlie worked here.

They are friends. Maybe Wind Sand stays with Charlie. Maybe Charlie got work for him in a kitchen in Kowloon. Wind Sand is a good cook!"

As he starts to move away, I waylay him a moment longer.

"This might be Wind Sand." I show him the photo again. "He would be thirty-one year's old. He has a Chinese mother and an American father. What does Wind Sand look like now?"

The young monk looks up at Nigel, then at Alister who is average height. "He is this tall." He indicates a height between them. "Not old, but older than me. Not Chinese or Western. Both. He left four months ago. Not a monk now. He has long hair now, for sure. If you find him, tell him,"—his voice catches—"Bo says hello." And with shoulders slumped, Bo turns and resumes his duties.

Unable to believe our luck, we stumble out of the restaurant into a stiff breeze.

I reach up and hold Alister's face between my hands so he looks at me. Does he understand what's happened? "It's got to be Deshi," I say. "We're getting close."

Just for a moment, I wonder if Fleur is with us. It's a fleeting thought, whipped away by the wind.

Chapter 30

As we hurry back to the cable car, we're full of what to do next.

"The owner of the Fat Waiter must be Charlie," I say. "He met Wind Sand here when the monks got the flu, then Wind Sand saw his chance to escape."

"If Deshi's been here since boyhood," Nigel says, "the monks are his family. He'd have no experience of living in the outside world, so he'd be very reliant on Charlie, at least for a while."

"But he can cook," Derek says. "He'd be at home in any kitchen. Maybe he's the chef at the Fat Waiter. They might have opened the place together."

"But Charlie said he didn't know him," I say. "He must be lying. Because it explains the joke of the password. 'Find Wind Sand Chicken' applies to Wind Sand himself. If the monks tried to find him, Charlie might have been protecting him—and he might not know that they've given up their search."

Nigel says, "Thinking about your dream, Selkie, was Deshi found in a basket of eggs? Is that why they named him after a chicken dish? Did he spend his first few years at the nunnery? Then the nuns passed him over to the monastery when he was old enough? Maybe the old monk was giving us a clue, after all."

"If we find him, he can tell us. But Butler has warned us away from the club." Frustration swamps my excitement. "We've got to talk to Charlie."

We reach the cable car and stop talking until we've taken our seats in the next one, this time having it to ourselves.

"Don't even think about it," Nigel says. "If Butler's men are watching the club, there's no way any of us can go there. You got away with it this afternoon, DD, but you can't risk it again. Even following Charlie home after work would be a bad idea."

"So we know who Deshi is," I scream, "and probably where he works—and we can't do anything more?" But when I look at Alister, his passive face conveys a sense of calm. It's a subtle change and for the first time, his empty expression soothes me. "We'll find him, Haiku," I murmur in his ear. "Promise."

"The nunnery," Nigel says. "That's our lead. If they brought him up from a baby, he probably keeps in touch."

Derek is googling. "Chi Lin Nunnery. Home to about 60 nuns. Right in the middle of north Kowloon, near Diamond Hill station." He's running his eyes down the screen. "And get this, in 1988 they lost some of their old buildings for the Tate's Cairn road tunnel. Built a whole new complex on the site."

"Is that near Egg Street?"

He leans over and shows me the map. Egg Street is on the other side of the motorway but before the redevelopment it would have been close.

"It says that the nunnery runs orphanages," Derek adds, "so why keep one baby?"

"*Touched by the gods,*" I say.

"A baby in a basket, maybe surrounded by eggs," Nigel says. "Left at a shrine or the nunnery door. That would stir up all kinds of feelings about gifts from heaven."

Just like the feelings they're stirring up in me. Alister's son, Wind Sand. As a monk, he must have struggled with his calling, enough to grab the chance to run away. He could still be struggling, just to survive. Then I remember how Robert at the temple described him. Happy at his core, but lately learning about other emotions. Anger? If we find him, how will he react to meeting the father he was stolen from, the father could have given him everything?

* * *

Without meaning to, I doze off in the cable car, only aware I'm asleep when I see the red cord and follow it into a darkened room. Suddenly I'm colliding with objects and falling over them one after the other, but I can't see what they are. Then with a flash, one wall lights up, revealing an enormous shadow like the fox behind the sail in my boat dreams. But this time it's the outline of a woman, holding something long and pointed above her head. I'm mesmerised, as I recognise the knife from the in-flight magazine. Then there's another flash, accompanied by a whooshing sound. The knife has changed shape. Into an umbrella.

My phone wakes me up.

"No names," are the first words Miss Tigerlily says.

I flip my phone to speaker, glad we're alone in the cable car. Even with a prepaid she's being extra cautious. It reminds me how high the stakes are.

"Tell me exactly what you need," she continues. "I can only meet you once."

"I want to speak to the ghost who turned up in your reading." I summarise the facts, finishing with Rose. "She's keeping my friend's *Hun* spirit locked in an old shrine—to stop him from finding his lost son."

"But you're close to finding him?"

"Yes. We think he's an ex-monk, possibly the chef at the secret club where you met my friend."

"He doesn't work there," she says, "but he's connected to it in some way. And you hope that with my help as medium, his mother's ghost will get his father's spirit back from his grandmother?"

She understands what I'm asking. "Yes."

"Is the ghost ... supportive?"

"I don't know. She may see me as a rival. She may want his spirit for herself. It's a risk. But I'm hoping their son will help."

"Using the power of love?"

"Yes."

"Who else is involved?"

I describe Winston and Su Yin.

"A weak grandfather and a capricious cousin. Good to know where everyone stands. Now read me what I said to you in the reading. I don't remember."

I recite the words from memory. "Boots too big. Hair too hot. Scent too cheap. Wait, a shadow! Pink, black, pink, black. Ghost wants to sleep. Can't. Wants to blame. Can't. Changes shape. Sly. Dark. Wants to play. Wants to *win*. Remember your mother. Man waiting. No! Gone. Too much beauty. Skin deep. Save him. Your job. Carrying bygones. Can't let go. Stones in the belly. Cut it open. Carry a stone to the mountaintop. Not Chinese enough! Baby called Moses. Touched by the gods. Danger! Danger! Danger! Endless circle. Trapped in time. Look in mirror. Go down to the sea. Speak the truth. Watch out for him. For her. Pray. Burn. White tiger. Something sharp. Know. Who. To. Trust.”

When I've finished, Miss Tigerlily says, “No mention of umbrellas, but the mirror means I foresaw the exorcism.”

The umbrella in my dream? Alister was staring at umbrellas from the cab.

She rushes on. “How many days since his *Hun* was taken?”

I think back. “Five.”

“After the seventh day, retrieving it will be harder. That might be why the grandmother has gone into hiding. What time of day did he lose it?”

“Close to midnight. After midnight tomorrow will be the seventh day.”

“Chinese midnight is 11pm on the Western clock. That's when we'll do it.”

“Tonight?”

“Too soon. There are several things you must do and there's not enough time. Tomorrow night.” She pauses to think. “Find the son. It's not safe to go to the secret club but I sense he's close. The stone in my reading is about him. You have friends helping you?”

“Yes.”

“Good. Don't give up. The next thing is harder. The four-door shrine must be present when we exorcise his spirit.”

My voice betrays my distress. “I don't know where it is. Can't you call him back without it?”

“Since the escape of her daughter's ghost, our sorcerer

will be extra vigilant over the shrine. And once we start the exorcism, she'll realise what we're doing and run interference. We have to have the shrine."

"She'll never agree. It's a symbol of her fox power."

"Find a way, even if it means bringing her with it."

My mind is reeling, dancing across impossible ideas, then sinking into mental quicksand.

"The ghost may also be against us," she says. "I'll need another medium to double our spiritual force."

Dr Lee said he's got a ringside seat. "We've been consulting a doctor," I say. "You know him. He's familiar with Taoism and sorcery."

"Will he do it?"

"I'm sure he will. I'll phone him."

"Good. We'll meet beforehand to prepare. Now for the place. A neutral location, public but also private. Available tomorrow night."

I was just dreaming about it, stumbling over the rows of chairs. "The shadow puppet theatre. I've just had a dream about the shadow of the emperor's concubine." I'm even afraid to name Madam Li. "She was holding an umbrella."

"That's the place. It feels auspicious. I will get our mutual contact to arrange it. Tomorrow at 11pm will be well after their evening performance. Meet there at 9.30pm."

"Thank you. Anything else?"

"Bring two large mirrors. And eight umbrellas for the points of the compass. We'll use them to summon and manifest the ghost. Any other objects that have significance?"

I tell her about my bangle and Alister's ring.

"We'll need both. Does the ring come off?"

"I don't think so." I tell her its engraving matches the

endless circle in her reading.

"She's committed, this ghost. We'll harness that commitment—and redirect it if we must."

As my head swirls with worries, I remember Su Yin's shrine to Fleur.

"If the ghost requested this shrine," she says, "she may choose to use it instead of the umbrellas, with the lipstick as her message stick. Bring both."

It's a hell of a lot to do.

Miss Tigerlily is about to terminate the call when I recall Alister's nape *chakra.* I tell her how I think Su Yin opened it. "Should we close it until tomorrow night, to avoid … invasion?"

"He's got this far with it open," she says. "Let's not make any drastic changes that might stir up the players."

Players. Dr Lee called it a game. A game of life and death. Amidst the euphoria of getting close to Deshi, Alister's life still hangs on a thread.

* * *

Derek and Nigel start talking at once.

"Twenty nine hours to find Wind Sand and the shrine," Derek says, "and get them to the theatre. A walk in the park."

"Let's go straight to the nunnery now," Nigel says. "It's late, but call them, Selkie. See if you can get an audience with the head nun. Tell them you've got Wind Sand's father with you. If they brought him up, that should open doors."

I'm dialling Chi Lin's number when my phone pings with a text. The timing isn't a coincidence. It's from Su Yin.

Come to Egg Street. Rose will give you the shrine if you tell her where Deshi is. You have to come alone.

"How does she know we're closing in on Deshi?" I gaze around the cable car, trying to sense the shadow.

"She thinks Fleur's helping you," Nigel says. "She's guessing. But she's opened negotiations."

"I can't use Wind Sand's identity—and his possible connection to the club—to haggle over his father's spirit. Not when his grandmother is one crazy sorcerer. And not without his permission."

"And not on Egg Street," Derek says. "She'll get you there and steal your spirit too."

"Was it Rose who tried that last time? Or Fleur?" I'm still not sure. "Right now, I'm more useful to Rose if I'm in my body, DD. She wants news of Deshi, but what will she do if I refuse?" She could set fire to the shrine, or throw it into the sea. Terror tightens my chest. "She has to keep Alister's spirit safe until tomorrow night."

I craft my reply with care. *We haven't found Deshi yet. Rose needs to look after Alister's spirit until I have news.*

After a minute, Su Yin replies. *Rose doesn't trust you. The exchange is off. If you want your man back in one piece, bring Deshi to Egg Street.*

Derek says, "Don't believe her, Selkie. Rose won't want Alister to get his old self back and have a relationship with his son. She'll take possession of Deshi. He's a man now, but he's still a baby to her. You saw her shrine for him. It gave me the creeps."

"She has to think I'll do a deal."

I'm in her power as much as Alister. The power of the fox spirit is no match for me. I'll do whatever she asks to get his spirit back.

At that moment, Alister falls to the floor of the cable car

and starts coughing, his limbs jerking in terrible spasms. The three of us grab him and hold him. *Incense*, I hear in my head. *Smoke.*

"She's suffocating him with incense!" Fighting back another wave of terror, I brush the hair from his sweating forehead. "Rose is letting me know she can damage your spirit. When we find Deshi, I promise not to hand him over to her. But what about you? What's she going to do to you?"

"She's playing games again," Derek says. "Smoke from incense is more uncomfortable than dangerous."

"Trust Alister to withstand the pressure until tomorrow night," Nigel says. "We'll come up with a way to get Rose and the shrine to the theatre."

Alister is calm again. Rose has made her point. We help him up and onto his seat.

Something in Su Yin's texts snags my attention. "Su Yin mentioned their location twice. Egg Street. What if she's giving me a clue to where they're staying? I saw the red cord, down the lane and through the scratchy window, snaking away behind the Buddhist shrine. When I went back, I wondered about the roller-door on the corner of that lane." I stop. I'm thinking aloud. "It's a long drive out to the old shop in Tuen Mun, so it's possible they use the lockup on Egg Street to park their cab between shifts—and sleep. They might even share it with other drivers. It could be where Winston's cab came from when he picked me up."

Nigel thinks about this. "It would explain how Rose knows about the traffickers gambling just down the road."

"But why did she need Su Yin to ask the traffickers about child abductions?" Derek asks. "If she's trying to get a lead on what happened to Deshi, why not ask them herself?"

"They're dangerous men," Nigel says. "She wouldn't want them to wonder why she wants to know. She'd be protecting Winston too. Su Yin is dispensable."

And Su Yin is with her now. I never thought I'd worry about her, but I hope her wiliness is keeping her safe.

With the latest attack on Alister over for now, we agree to focus on Wind Sand. But when I ring Chi Lin Nunnery, the call goes through to voicemail and a message in Cantonese. Cursing under my breath about the time lost texting Su Yin, I leave a message asking for an interview tomorrow. Then I remember Dr Lee and send him a text. He phones me straight back.

"Let's not use any names over the phone." I explain the plan.

"I'll be there," he says. "Has she asked for any props?"

"Two mirrors and eight umbrellas."

"I can guess what she's planning. For the umbrellas, choose eight different colours or patterns. It makes the process easier. She'll explain. Anything else?"

I tell him about Alister's ring.

"So the ghost is involved, but you don't know what her agenda is?"

"No."

"OK. Remember all the possibilities we discussed for rescuing your friend's spirit? Be ready to trust whatever happens, no matter how scary. Once the process begins, cold feet won't be an option."

"I understand." But fear is seeping through my bones like poison. "See you at 9.30 tomorrow night."

When I hang up, I turn to Alister. In spite of Rose's attack on his spirit, his expression has softened since our conversation with Bo at the monastery. Has the news of Deshi activated his loving instincts? Because I have the strongest sense that more of him is with me.

"How am I doing, Haiku?" I whisper.

To my surprise, he wraps his arms around me. Love surges from his body in a way that's entirely new, even before he was kidnapped. Like a river of warmth the red cord snakes between us, binding our souls together. And in that moment, I know that his ordeal has made him stronger, allowing his deepest feelings for me to flow, those feelings that exist beyond words. With my face buried in his chest, I let go of all my anxiety as endless waves of my love mingle with his.

Chapter 31

We stay on the train until Diamond Hill station. The nunnery gardens are open till seven, so we're hoping to find someone there who can speak to us before tomorrow. Huddling together in the carriage, we discuss what we know. It's not much.

"Miss Tigerlily said the stone in her reading refers to Wind Sand," I say. "*Stones in the belly. Cut it open. Carry a stone to the mountaintop.* Winston said Rose had rocks in her belly so could only have one child. I'm guessing fibroids and a hysterectomy. That leaves: *Carry a stone to the mountaintop.*" I've been trying to get a vision from the words but nothing has come.

"Carrying stones can be a Buddhist practice," Nigel says. "An act of contemplation."

"And we've just been to a mountaintop," Derek says. "It could refer to Po Lin and the big Buddha."

At the nunnery gates, we enter the Lotus Pond Garden. The Tang Dynasty architecture was recreated when the place was rebuilt around 1990. It's stunning, but I only have eyes for the signs everywhere telling visitors that the nunnery itself is closed to the public. Part of me wants to bang on doors until someone opens up, but it's not the kind of approach that will lead to an audience. If I want the head nun to talk to me, I need to show some respect and phone first. I've done that. We stand in our group, exasperation flowing between us.

Two women are wading in the pond in rubber boots. On a whim, I crouch down until one of them is close.

"Excuse me, we are looking for a man named Wind Sand. He used to be a little boy growing up here." It sounds like a long shot even to my ears. "Do you speak English?"

She turns down her mouth in apology. Shopkeepers speak English, but gardeners don't need to interact with tourists. She points to the footbridge that leads to the gardens next door, adding a comment in Cantonese.

"The Nan Lian Gardens are open till nine," Derek says.

"There must be someone there who speaks English," I say. "If Wind Sand really spent his early years here, he probably played in the gardens. The older workers might remember him."

Our lead is tenuous, but we need to explore everything until we can get an audience at the nunnery tomorrow. We race up the steps to the elevated pedestrian bridge and cross the road that separates the nunnery from the gardens. Once inside, we split up. Nigel and Derek take off along in different directions, leaving Alister with me.

With their landscaped vistas and groomed shrubs and trees, the gardens require intensive maintenance. I stop several workers, asking for English. No luck. Then at a grassy quadrangle, dotted with carefully placed rocks and trees, an old man with a wrinkled face smiles at my question, showing gaps in his teeth. He's old enough to have been here since the redevelopment. As I repeat my request about Wind Sand, my pulse quickens.

"We know Wind Sand," he says. My heart pirouettes. "We

very sad he go to Po Lin. Just small boy, he need mother."

I keep my voice steady. "The nuns were his mothers."

The man grins again. "When he go, nuns cry. Not want to show feelings, but we know. We cry too."

The gossip of gardeners is gold.

"How did Wind Sand come to Chi Lin?"

"We find him in basket at front door of old nunnery, before all this." He waves his arms around. "He just baby, lying with chicken eggs, a lot of eggs, like baby chicken. We call him Wind Sand Chicken. Nuns not like name, but it stick."

He notices that Alister is staring at him intently.

I take out the photo of baby Deshi and show it to him. "We think this is Wind Sand."

"It look like him," the gardener says. "He not look Chinese so we know he special boy, sent to us by gods. We all care for him."

"Wind Sand is grown up now."

"We not see him long time. Po Lin on Lantau Island. Long way."

"Does he ever come back here to visit?" I ask.

To my disappointment, the man's face droops. Then I realise he'd be expecting Wind Sand in monk's robes.

"He is not a monk now," I say. "We asked for him at Po Lin. They said he ran away."

The gardener's gloved hand goes up to his open mouth. "I not know this."

"We are looking for him. We have news about his real parents. If you see him, please give him this number."

As I give him Alister's business card, he looks at Alister, who is still fixing him with a steady gaze. Some kind of message passes between them.

"What you want?" the gardener asks.

Alister leaves the path and steps onto the lawn. At one of the border gardens, he picks up a small stone. The gardener takes the stone from him, brushes off the dirt, then hands it back to him. I'm sure this is against the rules.

"This just like eggs in basket with Wind Sand."

Then Alister points to the back of his own thigh, and I remember Deshi's birthmark.

The gardener nods. "It other reason we call him Wind Sand Chicken. He have mark on leg, look like egg." He points to the pebble and pats Alister on the arm. "You find him, you give it to him? Then he know who you are."

They exchange another look. Then the gardener turns to me. "Nunnery closed now. Not answer door. Come back tomorrow. I hope they know where is Wind Sand."

He bends over and picks up his trowel.

I say nothing to Alister about the stone. If Fleur is working through him to lead us to Deshi then I welcome it, in spite of the emotions warring in my chest. We meet the boys beside a stunning waterfall that screens the entrance to the restaurant.

"We've lucked out," Derek says.

I bring them up to date on our news. "It's possible he comes back to see the nuns, but we can't visit the nunnery till tomorrow. What if I can't get an audience?"

"You will," Derek says. "Now you know Wind Sand grew up here, and you've got his father with you. Alister, you're the entry ticket."

Alister proffers the stone on the palm of his right hand.

"Carry a stone to the mountaintop," Nigel says.

"The gardener was happy for you to have this, Alister," I say, "even though souveniring pebbles must be forbidden. Maybe

Wind Sand likes rocks. Maybe he liked them as a boy."

"Part of his Buddhist practice," Nigel suggests, "even though he's no longer a monk? It could be something he does daily, weekly. The mountain could also be symbolic."

Derek looks at the stone. "Its egg shape makes me hungry. We have to eat, Selkie. The restaurant is just about to open. And we can ask the waiters about Wind Sand."

We take a table beside the waterfall. The sound of falling water should be calming, but it feels like time slipping away. We've had a breakthrough with Wind Sand, but what can we do to speed up our search?

"I hope one of the nuns speaks English," I say.

The nunnery website has no English version, and I forgot to ask the gardener if Wind Sand learned English. What if we finally meet him and he only speaks Cantonese?

"Here's one who speaks English." Derek waves his phone. "Penelope Styles was born in the UK, came here as a banker, then flipped to Buddhism and became a nun. She published a memoir about her time at Chi Lin."

"Could she be old enough to know about Wind Sand?" I cry.

"This article's a few years old, but she's too young. Late thirties. At least you can talk to her. Fingers crossed she's still here."

It's the best news. I've been worrying about the phone call, fearing the gatekeepers not understanding me and putting up a wall. There's a wall on Miss Tigerlily's napkin map. Is it the wall where I saw the shrine in Egg Street, or are we going to meet an obstacle? But I can ask for the English nun. If we can get to talk to her, she might know the whole story about Deshi or agree to act as interpreter.

I try the nunnery number again in case someone answers,

leaving another message, stronger this time. First thing tomorrow morning, I'll be knocking on their door.

Feeling like things are starting to fall into place, I allow myself to look at the menu. It helps me manage my disappointment when the waiters who serve us don't know anyone called Wind Sand.

Over our meal, we come up with a plan.

We'll get a cab home, but in spite of our exhaustion, we'll make two stops on the way. The second stop is the umbrella shop in New Fan Road. It's near the secret club, but after Alister's reaction earlier today, we all agree he has to choose the eight umbrellas there. And getting them now will leave tomorrow as free as possible for finding Wind Sand.

The first stop is Egg Street. It's just on the other side of the motorway.

"The taxi can cruise through," I say. "I want to confirm my hunch about the lockup. And we might see something that will help us."

* * *

When the taxi turns into Egg Street, the driver starts shouting in Cantonese. I lean forward and peer through the windscreen, hoping the police aren't invading the gambling den. At the far end, red and white road-work barricades have blocked off the exit. The laneway where I had my vision is on the other side.

As the driver's outburst fills the cab, I try to focus on the laneway. The roller-door next to the lane is closed, but beside me Alister starts humming. A tuneless chanting without words, it gets louder and louder.

"You're connecting with your *Hun*," I cry. It's the closest he's been to his spirit in almost six days. "The shrine must be in there."

I throw some money at the driver, grab Alister's hand and jump out of the cab. Nigel and Derek follow. Looking ahead down the lane, I catch a movement. A flash of orange. Then a burst of white light throws me back against Nigel.

"I think I just saw Wind Sand." The words rush out before I understand them. "A vision of him in saffron robes, then a flash of light blinded me."

"It makes sense," Nigel says. "Alister, his *Hun*, and the area where we think Deshi was left in the basket, all came together just now. Add the strong intention of all four of us to find him."

"Maybe he knows we're looking for him," Derek says.

"Your ring's hot," I say to Alister. "Fleur's here too."

Allowing my feet to guide us, we enter the lane. Halfway along I stop, hoping to see the door. There's only the brick wall.

"The door was a vision," I say, "showing me the Buddhist shrine and the red cord. There must have been a door here once."

"This might be the wall on the rune-map." Derek runs his eyes over it.

"A door covered over by a wall," Nigel says. "Good clues to a hidden key."

While Alister hums, we check the bricks at our respective heights. When I reach down to the area just above my ankles I find a loose brick, its lack of mortar barely visible to passers-by. When Derek helps me jiggle it out, he finds a key.

We race back to the roller-door, where Nigel unlocks it and pushes it up to reveal an empty garage. We're in luck that there's no taxi driver taking a nap, and no Rose or Su Yin either. The shrine must be hidden here.

We move to the rear wall and start looking. There's an old cupboard containing mugs, tea, coffee and a biscuit tin. Derek runs his hands under the shelves, then Nigel tilts the cupboard to look under it and behind it. A kettle sits on top of a small fridge. I check the fridge. No shrine. But Alister is still humming.

There's a water tap in the corner above two empty plastic buckets. A single mattress is leaning against the wall. We check it over on both sides for secret cavities. In a plastic bin beside it, we find two old sleeping bags and carefully shake them out.

"We don't know how small it is," I say.

Doing a circuit of interior walls that are completely bare, we find no niches of any kind. After another search we come up blank again. At Nigel's suggestion, we form a line and move across the concrete floor, checking for cracks that might be hiding a hollow.

I gaze around the space. Something brought me here.

Our optimism of a few minutes ago has evaporated. I was right that the lockup is a home away from home, but the shrine isn't here. We'll have to invent a ruse to get Rose to bring it to the theatre. And I'm worried now that she might return at any minute and be angered by the break-in. Angry enough to hurt the shrine—and Alister.

"Let's lock up."

We return the key, and I face the brick wall, willing another vision to guide me. When nothing happens after several tense minutes, we give up and walk the length of Egg Street without passing another human being. At the intersection,

Alister stops humming. Did he sense his *Hun* spirit or was he connecting with my vision of Wind Sand? I allow the possibility that he'll know Deshi when we find him to soothe my feelings of failure.

Crossing the road, we hail a cab to the umbrella shop.

* * *

It's early evening, so we're confident we won't run into Klaus and his contacts outside the secret club. So far, they've preferred the late shift.

What are the chances we'll run into Wind Sand? After our experience on Egg Street, I hope Alister and I will recognise him. When the cab stops outside the umbrella shop, I scan the street which is buzzing with pedestrians. My eyes are drawn to the banner advertising the shadow puppet theatre. Everything hangs on our success tomorrow night. After not finding the shrine, the tasks ahead seem impossible to achieve in the next twenty-four hours, but I have to trust that the confluence of players is already starting to speed things up.

The shop is crowded with goods and a few customers. The boys wait on the pavement, while I ask Alister to concentrate on the selection of open umbrellas festooning the walls. As he points at the display, the shopkeeper reaches into a drawer and puts a pre-folded version on the counter. Each choice has either a solid colour or one colour with a pattern in white or black. One has pink and black tiger stripes. For Fleur? I ask the shopkeeper if he also sells mirrors and he produces two square ones in plastic frames, one black, one white. He's pleased with the sale and shows no indication that he knows what we're planning. When he offers a discount, I accept.

Within twenty minutes, another cab drops us back at the apartment. In spite of coming up empty on Egg Street, we agree we've achieved a lot in a few hours. Tomorrow's going to be a big day and we're all exhausted.

Wondering again how much our discoveries are down to Fleur's invisible guidance, I take Alister to bed. As I drift off, I'm overcome with worry about waiting till tomorrow night. What if all the elements don't come together and we miss the timing window to bring Alister back? What if I could talk to Fleur tonight? I could touch my bangle to Alister's ring to see what happens. Surely making a connection with her couldn't jeopardise tomorrow's plans.

In spite of my intentions, I fall instantly asleep.

Chapter 32

Minutes after 9am, we're back at the Lotus Pond. The ambience of the nunnery grounds is calming my nerves. I dial their number.

When a female voice answers in Cantonese, I state in clear English, "I left two messages yesterday. I need to speak to Penelope Styles, the English nun. It's about the monk called Wind Sand."

She replies in her language, before the phone is switched through to another female. More Cantonese. I repeat my request. More switching noises, then the phone is answered and put down. I can hear interior echoes of a room with wooden floors, perhaps a hallway. Footsteps come and go. When my new-found serenity has all but evaporated, another woman answers.

"English nun not here." Her accent is Cantonese.

She's about to hang up, so I shout down the phone, "I need to speak to someone in charge. Please. It's urgent." Then I repeat the magic words. "It's about the monk called Wind Sand."

Her intake of breath hisses in my ear. "Wind Sand not here."

"I know. He used to live at Po Lin Monastery but he ran away. I need to find him. His father wants to see him."

"He not have father. He come to Chi Lin from heaven."

"His earthly father is here in Hong Kong. He can prove it." Alister is standing beside me and I point to my thigh. Even in his current state, I trust that he can draw the birthmark.

"Where are you now?" she asks.

"At the Lotus Pond."

"Wait."

My feet do a little jig. We're in.

The Chinese woman who meets us is not dressed in robes. I don't know how a nunnery operates, but judging by her erect posture and Western business suit, she's some kind of manager. She casts her eyes over our little group, then introduces herself as Nancy Long.

"Nunnery private. Not open to public. We talk here."

I make the introductions, explaining our mission to find Deshi and describing Alister's current state as post-traumatic stress.

"Twenty five years I am office manager at Chi Lin. I know Wind Sand from little boy, before he go to Po Lin as novice monk. Everyone here ... love him." She clears her throat.

She was fond of him herself. Good. I show her the photo of baby Deshi. "We are sure that Wind Sand is Alister's missing son. He has a birthmark on the back of his left thigh. Alister can draw it."

I bend and dip my finger in the pond. Alister copies me. Then with great concentration, he draws an oval shape on the path. In a moment it's gone, just like Wind Sand.

Nancy visibly relaxes. It's the confirmation she needed. "It another reason why the gardeners name him Wind Sand Chicken. He have an egg mark on the back of his leg."

"We need to find him, Nancy," I say. "We went to Po Lin

yesterday and discovered that he ran away a few months ago. He needs to know about the family he lost when he was kidnapped as a baby. And I think Wind Sand can help Alister with his post-traumatic stress—to meet his son after all these years might make him well again. We are hoping to find Wind Sand today. Can you help us?"

"You ask for English nun," Nancy says. "She not here any more, but she know where Wind Sand is. Penelope not her dharma name but she Penelope again now. I give you her number."

There's something she's not telling us. After she pulls out her phone and gives me the number, I ask her what it is.

"Penelope meet Wind Sand at Po Lin. A special ceremony for nuns and monks. She is older than Wind Sand. She know it not right but he is very handsome."

"They fell in love."

"I don't know," she says. "But Penelope leave Chi Lin the same time Wind Sand leave Po Lin. Nuns and monks talk about them."

More gossip. These closed communities must be full of it.

She's given us the lead we wanted. When she leaves us, Derek's eyes are dancing. "What now? Call Penelope and ask her straight out if she's living with Wind Sand?"

"They've broken all the rules," Nigel says. "She might be wary."

"Surely she'll want Wind Sand to meet his father." I look at my watch. "If she's gone back to banking, she may already be at work."

Taking a deep breath, I dial her number.

"Penelope Styles." She spits it out. Professional. Impatient.

"Penelope, this is a private call. You don't know me. My

name is Selkie and I've been given your number by Nancy Long. It's about Wind Sand."

"If you're a journalist, you can hang up now. I've got nothing to say."

"I'm a friend of Wind Sand's father."

She laughs. "That's a good one. He's an orphan. Nancy must have told you he was brought up by the nuns."

I summarise his origins and how we think he got to the nunnery. "He has an egg-shaped birthmark on his left thigh."

That silences her for a moment. "So if you're not his long-lost mother, what do you want?"

I tell her about Alister's 'PTSD'. "Will you help us get in touch with Wind Sand? Nancy told us ... you're a couple."

"Afraid not."

The wall on Miss Tigerlily's map comes to mind. "You won't help us?"

"We're not a couple."

"Oh." That throws me. "I'm sorry my information is wrong. We know Wind Sand ran away from Po Lin around the time you left the nunnery. I was hoping he was staying with you."

"Well, he's not. Anything else? I've got a meeting."

I want to scream, but I keep my voice calm. "It's urgent that I contact him. Today if possible. Do you have a number for him?"

"No."

I don't believe her. She's about to hang up, so I rush to get something from the call. "What about a number for Charlie who runs the secret club? Or an address where Wind Sand lives? Anything."

"Here's something for nothing," she says. "He's fallen for a ghost."

Click.

As I stare at my phone, the boys look at me for an explanation. "Can you believe that? She used to be a Buddhist nun, but she must be reincarnated from Boadicea."

We sit on a bench by the pond, and I recount her side of the call.

"Here's my take on it," Nigel says. "She's older than Wind Sand—and more worldly. She fell for him and, under her influence, they left their callings and set up house. She went back to banking to pay the bills. Then after a few months, Wind Sand ended the relationship. She set him free from the monastery, but that freedom backfired on her and she's bitter."

Derek is nodding. "The woman scorned."

"Bo at the monastery thought he left because of Charlie," I say. "And Nancy says it's because of Penelope. Now Penelope tells me he's in love with a ghost. Which story is true?"

Nigel frowns. "What if it's Fleur?"

The truth hits me. Of course Fleur's been in touch with him. "When was the flu epidemic? Last October. So he ran away from Po Lin in October or November, a few months after Fleur escaped from Rose." I do a quick calculation. "The timing fits with Alister meeting Su Yin. Su Yin says Fleur visited her in a dream, so it makes sense that she'd appear to Deshi as soon as she could. She told him about his history. It probably took a while for the news from a ghost to sink in. It rocked him. He ended it with Penelope."

"The new relationship was possibly shaky anyway," Nigel says. "A young unworldly monk could be overwhelmed by life outside, and living with a woman for the first time. Then his dead mother appears to him with an incredible story about his origins."

"It all makes sense," I cry, "but it doesn't help us find him."

As soon as I say it, Alister opens his right hand and shows us the pebble he's been holding since we left the apartment.

"Carry a stone to the mountaintop," Derek and Nigel say together.

As I throw my arms around Alister's neck, we can't help laughing, even though we have no idea what to do with it.

As we all relax a little, Nigel has a thought. "Some essence of Wind Sand must be here in these grounds. And you've got the stone from the gardens where he played. Try meditating on the stone."

Alister puts the pebble in my palm and I wrap my fingers around it. Just for a moment, its warmth radiates the essence of Alister. Breathing out, I close my eyes and let the nunnery grounds work their magic on my body. Can I hear wind chimes? I was already tense from the pressure we're under, and Penelope's lack of co-operation has added to it. I allow my muscles to let go. The fear that's been my constant companion ebbs away. My mind stills. A vision comes.

"I can see him," I murmur. "His face is hidden, but his orange robes give his identity away. He's climbing a bamboo ladder and his clothing is glowing. Up he goes, all the way to the top of a white mountain. He's stopped. He's pulling something out of his pocket. It's a huge egg. Now he's reaching for a hook that's dangling from the sky on a red cord. He's hanging the egg from the hook. Behind him the mountain reaches to a point just below the egg. The point pierces the egg and it splits open. Something falls out. A baby? Wind Sand ignores it.

"Now he's climbing halfway down the ladder. Out of his

other pocket he's drawing long strips of blue. They flow like silk. There are many shades of blue, and he's draping them around the base of the mountain in billowing folds. The blues are glowing with inner radiance."

I wait for more but the vision fades. I open my eyes.

"The bamboo ladder is a stairway to heaven," Nigel says, and we recognise the name of the forbidden trail on Oahu that's also known as the Haiku Stairs. Both are Alister's nicknames.

"Hanging an egg on a skyhook, that's pierced by the mountaintop," Derek says. "I think that's a Chinese myth about the birth of the universe. That explains the baby. It's a creation story."

"Wind Sand was large and human," I say. "But he was creating the heavens, the mountains and the sea from ordinary materials. Like props in a play."

"We've thought he's a chef," Nigel says. "In your vision he's cooking up a landscape. Setting a scene. For what?"

I think about this. "The egg opened and the sea swelled, then everything became static. Waiting."

"Was Fleur in the vision?"

"No."

Derek says, "According to Robert at the temple, Fleur's waiting. And in your vision Wind Sand's scene seems to be waiting too."

"What if they're waiting ... for Alister?" I whisper.

A ray of sun chooses that moment to break through the clouds. I look at Alister. His face is calm and open, and I start to laugh. I've been pushing so hard to bring everything together in time to rescue his spirit that I've forgotten how magic works. Now my heart fills to brimming and overflows with the profound belief that saving Alister doesn't depend on my wits alone. There's a stronger force at work behind the scenes that's bringing everyone together. I can surrender to it.

We don't have to search every mountaintop until we find Wind Sand, then drag him to the theatre. He'll be there. It's why he appeared just now. He's there, already there on the mountaintop, putting up the props for a puppet show. And although her motives are a mystery, Fleur will be where Alister and Wind Sand are. They've been kept apart for thirty years, but circumstances beyond my control are bringing them together. They are the pieces of the puzzle that will fall into place.

"We're not going to find Fleur and Wind Sand," I say. "*They're* going to find *us*. It's the message of the stone. It waited in the garden till Alister found it. It was in the right place. Tonight we'll be in the right place."

Chapter 33

With serendipity looking after Wind Sand and Fleur, I take Alister's arm, confident that a walk in the gardens will show me a way to reach out to Rose. Together with Derek and Nigel, we cross the footbridge and wander the paths designed to take visitors through a series of traditional Chinese vistas. Two bright red wooden bridges connect to a golden pagoda, the Pavilion of Absolute Perfection. At Fragrance Hill we inhale the perfume of scented trees such as orange-jasmine. At the Blue Pond, surrounded by rocks and water features, we watch koi fish swim. The efforts made by the developers to soundproof this tranquil oasis from the noisy metropolis that surrounds it are working their magic on my mental state.

We stop near the waterfall. Nigel and Derek accompany Alister into the gents' while I use the women's. When I emerge, Derek runs out of the gents' just as Nigel joins us from the direction of the shops. Their faces are strained.

I'm suddenly cold with dread. "Where's Alister?"

"He was waiting for us in the doorway to the gents'," Nigel says. "Then he was gone."

"He was just outside," Derek says.

"Let's split up," Nigel says. "He can't have gone far."

"He hasn't got his phone," I wail. Not that he could use it.

As I run along the paths looking left and right, the vistas that calmed me only minutes ago take on a sinister tinge. Visitors stroll, oblivious to what's happened. With mounting panic, I ask one person after another if they've seen him, but many don't speak English, or when I describe a grown man, they lose interest. I have the strongest sense that he's not here. Why not?

Half an hour later, we meet back at the restaurant and I dial David Butler. "You need to treat him like a missing child," I say. "I think he's been ... abducted."

"By whom?"

"Someone who knows him. They must have been following us."

"Names?"

I give him the names and addresses of Rose, Winston and Su Yin. Then I remember Klaus. But why would Klaus kidnap him? Because he saw Alister with Miss Tigerlily?

"We're watching certain people," Butler says. "We'll know if they've got him. And call me immediately if he turns up."

Nigel is pacing. "There was no-one else inside or outside the gents'."

Derek looks ill. "It happened so fast. He must run straight to the exit and out of the gardens."

"He wouldn't go off on his own," I say.

"Selkie, what if it's ... more sorcery?"

Suddenly I remember what Dr Lee said. "A spiritual hijack! I wanted to close his nape *chakra*, but we've kept it open for his *Hun* to come back." Collapsing on a seat, I look up into their ashen faces. "Someone must have sent a spirit to inhabit his body. It's why we didn't see anyone. They did it remotely.

He's ... in their control."

The sudden loss of Alister's physical presence hits me like his death. Under the prediction of the tea leaves, I feel myself wilt. Then with a supreme effort, I pull myself together. This force hasn't won yet.

"We're going to the lockup in Egg Street." I leap off the seat and head for an exit, the boys catching up to me. "It has to be Rose. She's done this with Su Yin, hijacked her body. Because she can't get into the shrine and have full control over Alister's spirit, she's kidnapped him so I'll take her to Deshi."

"Or it's Su Yin," Derek says. "She's already tried to rescue his *Hun*. Maybe she's trying to unite them by kidnapping him."

"The reward's a strong motivator, DD, but I doubt Su Yin's got the skills to do this. Remember how clumsy she was with the shrine."

"What about Fleur?" Nigel says. "You told her yourself that Alister is separated from his *Hun*. If they're all going to come together tonight, what if Fleur's ghost is using his body to rescue his spirit from Rose."

That would mean Fleur doesn't trust me to rescue him. Something I've failed at so far. As Nigel hails a taxi, I push the errant thought aside.

* * *

The barrier that was blocking Egg Street last night is still there, so the cab drops us almost outside the alley that leads to the gambling den. We jump out and walk around the barrier to the laneway where I had my vision. The roller-door to the lockup is closed and the whole area is oozing portent. The ambience of the thin place puts me on high alert.

We go straight to the loose brick to retrieve the key. Nigel unlocks the roller-door. The garage is empty. No Alister. I get a vision of him tied to a chair somewhere and my inability to keep him safe threatens a meltdown. But when we're returning the key to its hiding place, daylight glints off something metal.

"There's a wider space at the back of this hole," I cry. "I think it's the shrine."

Derek removes another loose brick, but his hands are too big to do the rest. Kneeling in front of the hole, I slip my fingers into the gap on either side of a tiny cupboard. Lifting it up, I tilt the bottom towards us. Nigel and Derek are on their knees to grab it as it comes out. It's a little wooden cupboard about the size of a child's shoebox, with two pairs of doors along one side, each with an ornate brass clasp. Faded motifs too pale to identify indicate its age.

All I want to do is wrap my arms around it and give Alister's spirit a long-overdue hug, but Rose could return at any minute. We replace the key and the bricks, then walk down the lane to the street behind, where I saw the umbrellas on the restaurant deck. The clear air already feels like we're a world away.

"Where to?" Nigel hails a passing taxi.

"The safe in our apartment. I had no idea the shrine would be so small."

We travel in silence with our private thoughts. I caress the tiny receptacle tenderly. The realisation that I'm holding Alister's spirit is so overwhelming that I succumb to a few hot tears.

After a while I say, "It was hidden where I had the vision of the shrine, then another vision of Wind Sand last night. He was standing on the path beside it. I'm sure it's where he was left in the basket, and I think he knew Alister's spirit was there. As if he was pointing the way."

Nigel says, "This is going to sound weird, Selkie. But if Alister hadn't been kidnapped this morning, we wouldn't have gone back to Egg Street. You would have tried to negotiate with Rose. Now you don't have to. You have the shrine."

"You think the kidnapping was deliberate? By someone other than Rose?"

"I don't know. But you barrelled over to Egg Street, and Rose wasn't there."

"We've got the shrine, but we've lost Alister. There's a battle going on to keep him from being whole again. His body is in danger and tonight's ceremony won't happen if we haven't got him back. Where do we look now?"

"His physical self might be harder for them to handle."

I push down another wave of dread. "And easier to hurt."

* * *

Back at the apartment, I go into the bedroom and press my face to the shrine. "Our spirits are together again, Haiku. If you can hear me, tell me where your body is."

Nothing happens. His humming last night, and the fact that the shrine was hidden, reassure me that his *Hun* is still contained here. But before we go out looking for him, I want a sign. I find the Bolero on my phone. When the drum begins beating out its rhythm, I whisper, "Send me a sign."

With tears blurring my vision, I clutch the shrine to my chest and begin a slow dance. The lines of melody soar, carrying my hopes with them. After several minutes, I'm suddenly aware of my bangle getting hot. Alister's still here and able to connect with me. Love and relief brim over, but his separated spirit punctuates his physical absence in a way that nothing else would. Another image of him tied to a chair flashes past, but there's no indication of where he is. I try to see more but it's gone.

After locking the shrine in the safe, I join the boys in the kitchen. Derek has warmed up some buns.

"You need energy food," he says.

"Next stop has to be the old cottage," I say. "Then Winston's place and the empty shops beside it. Alister is tied up somewhere."

"Surely she'd take him to a secret place," Nigel says.

"That's what I'm afraid of, but I don't know where else to look."

Then I remember Su Yin. She hinted at the Egg Street lockup. If she knows where Alister is, will she tell us?

As I'm composing a text, there's a knock at the door. When I open it, I'm looking at her.

"Rose kicked me out." She pushes past me into the apartment. "She thinks I told you where she hid the shrine. As you know, it's been stolen."

"You mean it's been returned to its rightful owner."

"Whatever." She nods to Nigel and Derek, sits down at the kitchen counter, and reaches for a bun. "Where's Alister?"

"That's my question."

She seems genuinely taken aback. "Why? What have you done to him now?"

"He was kidnapped. An hour ago."

"Don't look at me. Or Rose. We were together all morning."

I don't want to believe her, but it makes sense that she'd come here as soon as she saw the shrine was gone. Rose didn't kick her out; she came here of her own volition, thinking Alister is back in one piece and ready to hand over her precious reward. Unless she's sleepwalking again, here to discover where we've hidden the shrine, but so far her eyes and her voice are normal.

"Who else would kidnap him?" I snap.

"If I knew that, I wouldn't be sitting here, would I? Are you waiting for him to ring your doorbell?"

It's all I can do not to hit her.

There's no time to waste, but where the hell do we look? I start pacing when I remember something Nigel said: "If Alister hadn't been kidnapped we wouldn't have gone back to Egg Street." Last night, we couldn't find the shrine, but this morning we found it *by going back.*

"He's somewhere in Egg Street." I pick up my phone and dial a taxi. "Just like the shrine last night, we were looking in the wrong place."

"Where?" Nigel asks.

"The gambling den."

"We're coming with you."

Su Yin leaps off her stool. "Hey, what about me?"

I'm running on adrenaline when we open the front door. Klaus's maid is standing outside her apartment. She's looking in her purse and crying.

"Pia, what's wrong?" I'm aware of the minutes slipping away.

"Klaus ... move out," she cries. "Yesterday night he tell me go away, no more job. He not give me money, not time to pack. I stay at friend, come back now for things. I hope I can open door but,"—she lets out a sob—"I not have money for taxi."

Nigel is already opening his wallet and handing her some notes.

"Thanks Nige," I say. "Pia, check the door."

She tries the code and it works. She beams. "I very lucky. You my friends."

Derek does a quick check of the apartment. "The bathroom cabinet is empty. His clothes are gone. You're safe to get your stuff."

"Can you stay with Charlie till you find another job?" I ask.

Pia nods, not noticing that I know her boyfriend's name. "Thank you."

The news about Klaus feels important.

As we leave Pia and pile into the elevator, Nigel agrees. "It sounds like Klaus is covering his tracks. Does he know the cops are onto him?"

"Who's Klaus?" Su Yin asks.

I text David Butler, telling him that Klaus has vacated his apartment. *Any sign of Alister?* I add.

My phone rings and Butler says, "We know about Klaus. I was just about to call you. I've got some men in the gambling den and they think they've spotted Alister playing mahjong."

"He must be there against his will," I cry. Waves of relief and panic take turns to chill me.

"He came in with a group of Chinese men, but he's the only *gweilo* in the place." The local word for foreigner. "My men can see him, so he's safe for the moment." For the moment. "But I won't do anything to jeopardise our operation—unless things turn ugly."

Meaning he won't rescue Alister unless the men hurt him. Then it will be too late.

As the elevator drops us in the lobby, I hang up and tell the others.

Nigel says, "You didn't tell Butler we're going to Egg Street. What if we barge in on their sting?"

"I don't care. Alister's in danger from those men."

"I won't go in there," Su Yin says.

"I don't like it, Selkie," Nigel continues. "We could make things worse. These guys are ruthless."

"They might be hurting him!"

"Why?" Derek asks. "Why would Alister go to Egg Street—and the gambling den?"

The thought of an evil spirit—and now these men—in control of Alister's body is fogging my thinking. I have to clear my head.

Thinking aloud, I say, "He went there because his *Hun* was in Egg Street. What if the spirit that kidnapped his body—and I'm not excluding Rose doing it remotely,"—I glare at Su Yin who rolls her eyes— "what if the spirit took him to Egg Street to reunite him with his *Hun*—and discovered the four-door shrine was gone?" I stop. Then why is he in the gambling den?

"But if they reunite him with his *Hun*," Derek says, "then he's no longer in their power."

"It's something Dr Lee said. They could force him to withdraw cash or transfer money. The invading spirit would be in control, but ... Alister would need his own *Hun* to remember his passwords and access his bank accounts."

"He'd have the split personality on board, caused by 'fairy borrowing'," Derek says.

"Then something happened," Nigel says. "Keep thinking, Selkie."

Closing my eyes, I imagine Alister arriving in Egg Street

by taxi, his body propelled by the invading spirit. "With that roadwork barrier blocking drive-through, taxis have to drop you right outside the gambling den. What if Alister bumped into Klaus? What if Klaus saw him, right there where he's doing whatever illegal business he's into?"

"Like taking delivery of a truckload of girls in one of those lockups," Nigel suggests. "They might be using the apartments upstairs as brothels. They don't look like residences."

"Possible." I use my thoughts to suppress my fear. "Klaus is there with some of his thugs and he sees Alister, after seeing him in the secret club with Miss Tigerlily."

"Who's Miss Tigerlily?" Su Yin asks.

"What if Klaus thinks Alister is spying on him?" I continue. "Klaus must be under pressure if he's moved out of his apartment. He wants Alister out of the way in a hurry, so he sends him into the mahjong room with some of his men."

"It fits with what we know, and I agree with Butler that he's safe in there." Nigel turns to Su Yin. "How many people were playing when you were there?"

She loses her pout and thinks. "About ten tables."

"In plain view of a crowd is good," he says. "They won't want to complicate things by hurting him. Unless his invading spirit tries to make a run for it."

"I think they've tied him to the chair, but if the spirit wants money, it might make his body do something stupid." I close my eyes and will it to stay put.

"What's your plan, Selkie?" Nigel knows I haven't got one.

I improvise. "Get dropped off on the street behind the lane. Because of the traffic barrier, we can make a quiet approach. Then one of us goes into the gambling den, joins a game, and keeps an eye on Alister. That shouldn't upset anything the police are doing, but it means we're not relying on them. They might have their hands full."

Nigel volunteers. His size will make him conspicuous but also intimidating.

* * *

The cab drops us at the far end of the lane behind Egg Street, and we move towards the entrance to Rose's lockup. On Egg Street, Nigel leaves us and heads around the traffic barrier. A minute after he enters the alley to the gambling den, people start streaming out. A mass exodus. Patrons are being lined up by police in plain clothes, while uniformed officers swarm up the street, pounding on roller-doors. A police car cruises in from the end behind the barrier and guards the road exit.

I scan the crowd, my panic rising. Just as I start running towards the melee, Alister appears, his arm through Nigel's. His expression is as vacant as ever, a sign that the rogue spirit has gone. Relief stops me. He's safe. They're both safe.

But I'm not. Suddenly an arm tightens around my waist like a gastric band. A voice with a German accent whispers, "You're coming with me. Be nice and you won't get hurt."

I'm right outside the side door to a lockup. Is that where he came from? Klaus starts to turn me towards the lane that leads to the back street.

"If anyone follows," he says to the two officers who are getting out of their car, "the girl gets hurt."

As he pulls out a phone with his other hand and orders a taxi, I can see Derek hovering out of the corner of my eye. He's no fighter, and he won't do anything to endanger me. The police are frozen on the spot. A quick look over my shoulder shows

Nigel poised, conflicted about abandoning Alister.

Suddenly a surge of rage racks my body after everything that's happened. To Fleur, to Deshi, to Alister. To all those trafficked girls. With a sudden sucking motion, my spirit rises above the thin place and I look down on the scene just like in our apartment. Then in a flash I'm inside Alister's skin, and taking off after Klaus.

"Not so fast," I hear myself shout.

Alister lets fly with a fist and Klaus goes down, taking my body with him. The two policemen pounce, put Klaus in handcuffs, and march him away, to a stream of verbal abuse.

Back in my own body, I leap up and throw my arms around Alister's neck. "We did it, Haiku," I whisper, not quite believing what just happened.

Nigel, Derek and Su Yin join us.

"Did I just see what I think I saw?" Derek asks.

"That's the creep with the accent," Su Yin says. "Is Alister back together again?"

"Nice one, Selkie," Nigel says. "Are you OK?"

"I think so." But fearing what Klaus's men might have done, I ask Nigel to check Alister over.

Nigel takes his pulse. "It's racing, but starting to slow down. He's been through an ordeal. Then the thrill of the punch." He examines Alister's body as best he can and finds it largely unmarked. "Dr Lee will need to do a proper examination, but I think he's only had his wrists tied." He shows me some rope burns. "No signs of any other physical trauma."

I reach up and brush Alister's cheek, a wave of relief settling in my belly like a soft blanket.

Our little group stands in the middle of the street, guarded by one policemen who prevents us from leaving. We watch the rest of the operation as the queues of gambling patrons are questioned and their mobile phones are checked. Roller-doors are opened and upstairs apartments are searched. A straggle of bewildered girls dressed in nightwear emerges from a stairwell. Uniformed female officers guide them to vans further down the street. At the sight of them, I send out wishes that their families soon welcome them home.

After several minutes, my phone rings. It's David Butler. "My task force leader has just called. Which part of 'stay away' didn't you understand?"

"Rescuing Alister was more important."

He pauses. "It seems that by standing right in front of that lockup, you helped us capture Klaus. He wasn't in the gambling den and we didn't have enough men to monitor every lockup. We put up that barrier and covered the vehicle exits but he was on foot, with a knowledge of the network of alleys. He could have evaded us—but it seems he couldn't resist grabbing you."

The memory of his breath on my cheek brings on a rush of nausea. By disobeying Butler, I played unwitting decoy. "It looks like his men didn't hurt Alister. Just some rope marks on his wrists."

"And bruised knuckles on his boxing hand." Does Butler suspect the spirit swapping? As he blows out a sigh of imaginary smoke, I'm sure he's not going to charge Alister with assault. "You'll see me tonight. My men will be guarding ... the event." He's avoided the word exorcism. I don't blame him.

As I hang up, Alister opens his fist. He's holding the pebble he found in the gardens and I laugh out loud for the first time in days.

"When we slugged Mr Hofmeier," I whisper, "no wonder we packed a punch."

Chapter 34

In the privacy of our bedroom, Dr Lee examines Alister. "He's largely undisturbed. Being back in familiar surroundings is calming him."

It's the confirmation I needed. His body is fit enough to face tonight's ordeal.

"Can you tell if another spirit hijacked his body?" I ask. "We think that's how he was able to vanish from the gardens."

"There's no spirit present at the moment," he says. "Who do you think it was?"

"If Su Yin is telling the truth about Rose, then Fleur's ghost is the most likely candidate. I'm wondering if she took him to Egg Street to retrieve his spirit, but they bumped into Klaus."

Bruce says, "If a spirit took him over, Alister would have been able to talk like a normal person."

I know. He shouted at Klaus before we knocked him down. "I think the invading spirit might have argued with Klaus."

Then Fleur abandoned him. What's her game? If she knows about tonight's exorcism, why did she intervene early? As this evening approaches, I worry more and more about her ability to derail Alister's rescue.

But his spirit and his body are here in this room for the first time in six days.

"Can we reunite him with his *Hun* right now?"

Bruce is quick to shake his head. "Miss Tigerlily is the expert. And with Fleur's ghost flexing her muscles, I wouldn't want to risk it on my own. Especially since it's only a few more hours to wait. Hang in there, Selkie."

On his way out, he prescribes an afternoon of napping for everyone. Even Su Yin curls up on an armchair. Nigel promises to keep one eye open, so I can stop thinking about her.

I close the bedroom door and spend some quiet time with Alister, playing the Bolero and taking him in my arms for some slow dancing. When we lie together, I speak frankly, knowing that Fleur may be listening.

"Do you understand what happened on Egg Street, Haiku? It's all about intentions. I'm sure you were hijacked by another spirit this morning. I don't know if that spirit's intentions were honourable, but mine were. Together we put Klaus out of action."

Hoping he can make enough sense of the crucial details, I outline as much as I know about the evening ahead.

"We'll be working together again tonight. Miss Tigerlily will be in charge. My job is to focus all my energy into calling back your *Hun*. You're trapped behind the fourth door, but with all the love in the world concentrated on your escape, you'll be able to break free." I stress the next few words. "Watch for a wave of light and ride it out through the door of the shrine. I think that's how Fleur was able to escape from the pot where Rose was keeping her. Your moment of intense love gave her the power to escape. It's my turn to do the same for you."

If she'll let me.

* * *

When I emerge from the bedroom, Su Yin is in the armchair with her feet on the coffee table.

She yawns and stretches. "Now you've got Alister and his spirit in the same place, you can put him back together and give me my reward."

After her own failed attempt to open the fourth door, she must know it's not that simple.

"He's been through an ordeal, and all you can think about is your money? That's not going to happen until he's fully recovered."

"I'll stick around."

Better if she's where we can see her. Then I remember her shrine to Fleur.

"We're going to do it tonight," I say. "Using a Chinese medium who knows what she's doing. I know you'll want to help. Have you still got your shrine to Fleur?"

"In my suitcase. But she's never even used it. You want me to bring it tonight?"

"Lend it to Alister, in case the medium needs it."

"You don't want me, just my shrine?"

"It may be intense, Su Yin. Even dangerous. Anything could happen. I don't want to risk your safety."

She sulks. "What about Rose and Winston? They've got a shrine to Fleur too."

"After everything Rose has done, they're not invited."

"How do you know I won't tell them?"

"I don't. But I haven't told you where it's happening. And you're too savvy. If Rose interferes, she'll risk Alister's life—and your reward."

But now that we're in possession of the four-door shrine—and Alister is safe in his bed—is Rose any kind of threat to Alister? Or Wind Sand? The shadow hasn't taunted me since the villain hitting. Rose ran away and hid the shrine, but she hasn't undertaken any effective sorcery since the old villain hitter beat the image of a fox spirit to shreds.

Now that I think about it, the attack in the cable car is more like Su Yin's amateur sorcery. Anyone can light an incense stick and blow the smoke into the shrine. Does it confirm that Rose has lost her power?

"What kind of effigy have you put on your shrine?" I ask. "A doll?"

"How do you know that?"

"My research into sorcery. You tried to coax Fleur's spirit into it, but since she escaped from Rose she's been running wild." And why would Fleur use it after Su Yin started colluding with her mother?

"I suppose. But a doll's not like a funeral pot. No lid. It's just a way of giving a ghost somewhere to visit."

"We'll need the lipstick too."

"Sure. Whatever."

* * *

Returning to the bedroom, I check that Alister is still sleeping. Then with mounting tension, I pack the items we'll need tonight: eight umbrellas, two mirrors. The four-door shrine will stay in the safe until the last minute. Miss Tigerlily's rune-map and my laptop with the transcript of her reading go into my tote bag, along with the magazine of scribbled comments, even though I don't know how it fits.

What else?

Wind Sand. We've discovered his identity, but I've put my

trust in a vision—and Penelope Styles' throwaway line about a ghost—that he knows about his origins and will turn up at the theatre. My confidence is wavering, especially if Fleur's the one who kidnapped Alister this morning. Was she trying to reunite him with his spirit when Klaus got in the way? If she's been keeping in touch with Wind Sand, why didn't she wait until tonight?

She wanted to exclude me.

Are my feelings for Alister going to obstruct his rescue? I've been counting on the power of my love—and Wind Sand's, however new and fragile—to call his spirit back. Fleur's been hanging around in his wedding ring—'waiting and impatient' with 'unfinished business'—but she hasn't been able to rescue him. Or she hasn't chosen to try until this morning.

Because of me?

The real possibility that tonight will come down to a show-down to win Alister's spirit—no longer with Rose, but with Fleur—has me quaking in my boots. My pink boots. I'm going to wear them. Along with my little black dress and my silver bangle. My psychic armour.

Will they be enough?

* * *

When we're ready to leave, Su Yin hovers by the door. She's put all the components of her shrine into a carry bag. I don't think I should touch the doll, if there's any chance of Fleur inhabiting it, but I can't help peering into the bag. What I see makes me gasp. Its arms are attached to tiny sticks.

"A puppet!"

"Yeah. I wanted to make it, like, as real as possible to tempt

Fleur's ghost to visit. Chinese dolls look like children, but I found this shadow puppet of a Chinese woman. It gave me the idea to make a paper screen for the shrine. I light a tealight candle and prop the puppet in a tiny vase behind the screen. Cool, isn't it?"

"She's wearing some kind of gown." A rush of recognition makes every hair on my body stand on end.

"It's an old Chinese story about the concubine of Emperor Wu. She died, but her shadow puppet came to life behind a screen."

"Madam Li," I murmur. "She's holding a little umbrella."

"You've heard of her. She was beautiful and died young. Like Fleur."

The coincidence silences me. Miss Tigerlily was right to ask for this shrine. Did she sense its link to the theatre? And I need to warn her about the scribbled comment in the magazine.

Picking up her carry bag, Su Yin walks to the door. "I'm coming with you."

She waits, confident that I won't stop her. And after what I've just seen, I don't want to exclude her. At the back of my mind, I wonder if Su Yin's rescue of Fleur from the funeral urn, and their lipstick communications during the dream, could smooth the way for me. Perhaps Fleur trusts her. Even though it's not a trust I can rely on.

* * *

We need an extra taxi. Nigel offers to accompany Su Yin, and we travel in tandem over the island, under the harbour, and across Kowloon to Mong Kok.

We arrive at the Shadow Puppet Theatre just before 9.30pm.

Derek takes charge of the props and I hold Alister's hand. A policeman guarding the theatre door lets us in. Another policeman directs us to a room where Miss Tigerlily is already waiting with Superintendent Butler. Tonight she's changed her appearance again. Jeans instead of a business suit, and a sweatshirt with a hood that will make her hard to recognise. Do they think she's still in danger after the Egg Street raids?

"I'll be in the foyer if you need me," Butler says to her and leaves.

Miss Tigerlily greets me, recognising me without the blonde wig. I go to her and shake her hand, then make the introductions.

She nods to Derek and Nigel, thanking them. Then she turns to Alister and shakes his hand. "I'm so sorry this happened to you right after we met. I should have made it clearer that your grief made you vulnerable to psychic attack. I was focused on finding your son, on discovering his connection to the secret club, not on protecting you from his desperate grandmother. I underestimated her."

She turns to Su Yin. "You've been playing on both sides, but you've brought your shrine to Fleur's ghost? Good. Please follow my instructions and don't get creative. You're not a fox spirit, and you're not experienced enough to interfere in an exorcism. Do you understand?"

Su Yin shrugs. "Sure."

"I need your agreement that you'll do exactly as I ask at all times. Or I'll have to exclude you."

"If you don't let me stay, I'll take my shrine with me."

"If you don't agree to my terms, we'll do better without you or the shrine."

Su Yin tosses her hair and lets out a childish sigh. "You have my word."

Dr Lee arrives and greets everyone.

When we're all seated in a circle, Miss Tigerlily begins. "Selkie, David Butler told me your real name. Tell us what you've discovered about Alister's son. Will he be here tonight?"

I outline the clues that led us to discover Wind Sand's identity and my vision that placed him in this theatre. "We haven't met him, but I sense he'll be here. At 11pm. I believe he's been getting messages from Fleur's ghost."

"So she's been playing ringmaster," she says. "If you want to concentrate the powers of a ghost, lock it up for thirty years, then let it loose."

That's what I'm worried about. At least Miss Tigerlily won't be underestimating Fleur.

"And the grandparents?" she asks.

I take the four-door shrine out of a carry bag and push down a sudden rush of emotion about what it contains. "This is where Rose has ... imprisoned Alister's *Hun*." I explain about the fourth door and the missing key. "We found the shrine hidden in a niche near where we think baby Deshi was rescued by the nuns. We took possession of it, so I haven't invited Rose and Winston tonight."

Miss Tigerlily asks, "She knows you have it?"

"Yeah," says Su Yin. "I was there when she discovered it was gone. She was going to use it to, like, bargain with Selkie for information about Deshi. She only cares about finding her grandson, nothing else. That's why I ran away. She was angry enough to explode. She's ... scary."

Miss Tigerlily nods. "Rose doesn't need your invitation, Selkie. If Fleur wants Rose here tonight, she'll be here.

Winston too. Tonight isn't only about retrieving Alister's *Hun.* That's our agenda, but it may clash with Fleur's—not only to reconnect her husband and her son, but also to inflict maximum retribution on her mother."

"Shit." Derek voices the consensus in the room. "Sorry."

"It's why I've called you here early," she continues. "We all need to be prepared. Expect the unexpected. If you don't wish to stay, leave now but you won't be able to return until it's over."

She waits while we all make eye contact with each other. We're staying.

"Good. I'll outline the plan, but things may not go to plan. We must assume that Fleur is with us right now, so she'll know what we're planning. But we don't know what she's planning. This looks like our show, but it's her show. You all need to be ready to do whatever I ask. Without question."

More eye contact and nods.

"We'll use the area in the theatre between the seating and the stage. Nigel, you'll set up the two mirrors at directions northwest and southeast, covered until we're ready with these cloths I've brought. You'll remove the cloths when I instruct you to. The mirrors will open the door to the spirit realm, inviting Fleur to join us."

She looks into the bag of umbrellas. "Good that each has a different pattern. Derek and Bruce, you'll open them and arrange them at the eight compass points, leaning on their stems so their domes point away from the centre of the circle. These will give Fleur's ghost places to manifest undercover."

She inspects the contents of Su Yin's carry bag. "A shadow puppet as an effigy. Perfect. Su Yin, you'll set up your shrine in the middle of the circle of umbrellas, but don't light the tealights until I say so. Do you have spare tealights?"

"I'm not stupid."

"I don't like your attitude. Lose it."

"Whatever." Then she catches Miss Tigerlily's unwavering glare. "I have spare tealights and I'll keep them burning once you tell me to light them."

"Thank you. That's your job for the duration of the session—to make sure that candles keep burning behind the effigy."

Now Miss Tigerlily turns to us. "Selkie and Alister, you'll sit beside each other on the floor in the middle of the umbrella circle, and in front of Su Yin's puppet-shrine. Selkie, show me your bangle." I extend my arm. "On your left wrist."

She turns to Alister. "Alister, I see you're wearing your former wedding ring on your right hand. Good. You no longer believe you're married to Fleur."

She turns back to me. "Selkie, if you sit on Alister's left, you're closest to his fist but he can't reach the bangle. If you sit on Alister's right, the bangle is closest to him, but that puts you next to his right hand—and the ring." She thinks about this. "Fleur is already angry with Rose, perhaps not with you. We'll put you beside his ring. You can also tell me if anything happens to it during the exorcism." Finally she says, "The four-door shrine will go in front of Alister."

Our earnest concentration fills the room. Miss Tigerlily has more to say.

"Those are your positions, but you each have actions too. Selkie, your job is to focus on your feelings for Alister. Imagining your future together is a good way to tap into emotions that may have been buried in grief this last week. With the power of your love, you're going to call his spirit to escape from behind the fourth door. This will be exhausting but wait for my signal." She holds up a small gong, suspended from a rope handle.

"Be prepared for the unexpected," she continues. "Listen out for anything I say, and do whatever I ask. Even if it's scary. Especially if it's scary. If you're unsure or worried about anything at all, call out what's happening so I know."

She turns to Dr Lee. "Bruce, your job is to monitor Selkie's communications and make sure I hear them. The antics of Rose—and Fleur, depending on her agenda—might try to distract me. Use the code word 'Miss T' to get my attention."

"Understood," Bruce says.

"And keep this toolbox with you." She points to a metal box at her feet. "We may need the bolt-cutters—and the hammer."

Miss Tigerlily moves in front of Alister, so he's staring at her. "Alister, your job is very simple. But not easy. Your body must concentrate on your missing spirit. Keep your eyes firmly fixed on the fourth door. Your ring might get hot, and there might be other weird and frightening things going on, but don't be distracted. Don't take your eyes off that door. Your body and *Hun* spirit must work together. Your spirit's job is to escape and fly home. It only has to bridge a very short gap between the shrine door and your body. It's a short crossing but a dangerous one, because for that split second you'll be on the loose. You haven't ever experienced this. Your spirit has spent your life inside your body, only experiencing a kind of spiritual freedom during dreams. Then you were stolen and trapped in the shrine. Some part of your spirit will be tempted by the sudden freedom, but you're in control. Call it home."

Everyone is silent, as what we're about to undertake sinks

in. We've all known how high the stakes would be tonight, but these instructions have confirmed it.

After a few minutes I ask, "Where will Wind Sand go?"

"Good question. When he arrives he'll sit on Alister's left. Bruce, can you make sure he knows where to go? And remind him to focus all his love on the father he never had."

Bruce nods. "Will do."

"He's never met his father," I say, "and his introduction is going to be through an exorcism." It's what I've always known, but it still brings on a wave of sadness.

"His monk training will prepare him," Miss Tigerlily says. "And it sounds like Fleur has been priming him. The wildcard isn't Wind Sand. It's Rose. And Fleur herself."

Miss Tigerlily looks at her watch. "At 10.30 we'll uncover the mirrors and light the candles so we're ready for the arrival of the others. The optimum time for the rescue is midnight, Chinese time. We'll start calling Alister's spirit at 10.45 so we're in full swing by eleven."

We carry everything through to the space in front of the stage, and place the props as instructed. It takes a while for Nigel to get two chairs and prop the mirrors against them at the optimum angle, all the time keeping them covered with the tablecloths. Derek and Bruce open and locate the umbrellas, adjusting the circle to make the central area big enough for Su Yin's shrine, the four-door shrine and three adults sitting on the floor. They also position chairs outside the umbrella circle for our support team—and in the expectation that Rose and Winston have been invited by Fleur.

Miss Tigerlily and Bruce will stand between the umbrellas on opposite sides of the circle, with Bruce behind Alister and me, and Miss Tigerlily positioned where we can see her.

Su Yin sets up her shrine, with the little screen in front of the shadow puppet. She puts several tea-light candles behind the puppet, then adds the open lipstick beside a pot of incense sticks and a tiny vase of flowers.

Above us on the stage, the shadow puppet screen is already lowered for a play, but our play will take place in front of the screen.

During these preparations, Alister and I sit beside Miss Tigerlily, while I update her on recent events.

She turns to Alister. "Was it Fleur who took you from the gardens this morning?"

I didn't think to ask him that myself. I'm expecting him to show Miss Tigerlily his wedding ring, but he stares passively as if Fleur's not here.

"It must have been Fleur," I say to Alister. "The villain hitting appears to have disabled Rose's sorcery. There was no worktable in the lockup and she's only been able to light some incense and try to choke your spirit. I think Fleur took you to Egg Street because that's where the four-door shrine was hidden."

"The villain hitting weakened Rose's belief in her fox spirit," Miss Tigerlily says. "As a villain hitter herself she trusted its power. With Rose feeling impotent, Fleur grabbed her chance to rescue your *Hun* herself."

"But the roadwork barrier meant the taxi dropped you outside the gambling den," I say. "You bumped into Klaus."

Barely above a whisper, I recount how a burst of rage allowed me to invade Alister's body, for the split second it took to land a punch on Klaus.

"Your first time leaving your body?" she asks.

"Yes."

"Now you know that under pressure, you can activate your projection-reflex."

There's a term for it: projection-reflex. Of course there is.

"Sharp has also tried to kidnap me. Twice." I describe the kind of migraine that preceded both times.

"A sign of sorcery. From what you tell me, your little black dress will keep you safe from psychic attack tonight."

I think about my armour and hope she's right.

Next I show her the in-flight magazine, pointing out the comments that have related to our predicament.

"Predictions by a stranger," she says. "Or clues from a ghost."

I gasp. "Ghosts can write?"

"It's one of the best ways for them to communicate because it's visual. You don't have to be psychic to get their messages."

Like the lipstick on Su Yin's forehead.

"Looking at the comments that don't fit," she continues. "I'd say she used the hand of someone who was already writing comments. Perhaps he dozed off with the pen in his hand. He may not even know he wrote these extra ones. Then she guided you to find the magazine."

Bloody hell. I've thought we were being guided but not like this. As unbelievable as it sounds, it makes sense of what's happened. Fleur pulling our strings like puppets.

"So why make the clues so cryptic?" I ask. "Why not just tell us what we want to know. Especially the identity of Wind Sand."

"It looks like she was testing you. You said you're the one who found the magazine. How committed were you to sticking with Alister and finding Wind Sand? In folklore, the hero must undertake several challenges to prove their worth."

Testing me.   As if she believes that she'll decide who can be with Alister, even though she's dead. Still his wife, manipulating things from the afterlife.

And who wrote the words: *Madam Li wants her guy. Watch how she does it?* It's a warning. A warning from Fleur?

The others join us in the front row of the theatre seats. We look at our static tableau, poised to fire it into action. It reminds me of what Dr Lee said. A ringside seat.

In my showdown with Fleur?

Chapter 35

At 10.30, Miss Tigerlily stands up and everyone goes into action. Bruce dims the lights. Nigel and Derek remove the tablecloths from the mirrors. Su Yin lights the incense and the candles illuminating the shadow puppet. Then they take their seats.

"It's time, Haiku," I whisper.

Together we take our positions in front of the four-door shrine. When our legs are crossed, Alister opens his right fist and places the stone from the garden on the floor in front of him.

As our arms touch, I focus everything on my future with him, beginning with our past. I remember the moment in Davina's hallway when my feelings for him first took me by surprise; then our connection in France when he gave me my silver bangle. Alone on a Hawaiian beach, my love for him made me dance; then lessons from my Irish great-grandmother's early life mirrored my commitment to him. All through the long months it took for me to embrace my feelings, Alister was always sure of me. Now I'm returning that sureness. It swells in my chest and bubbles over. An avalanche of love.

Just outside the circle, Miss Tigerlily lifts her hands and hits the gong with a mallet. It creates a shimmering cascade of sound that sends quivers of portent through me. In a torrent of trust, I let go of my sole responsibility for Alister's rescue and hand it over to her.

The ceremony has begun.

"Calling Fleur," she says. "We're waiting for you to join us, Fleur."

The atmosphere is laden with the echoes of the gong—and the silence of our expectations. For several minutes nothing happens.

Now a sudden strobe in a mirror blinds me and a rush of air spins through the space, jostling the umbrellas. Fleur! Then a tall figure slips through the circle and sits on Alister's left. My heartbeat falters. It can only be Wind Sand.

Without warning, Winston's voice calls something in Cantonese. "Choi dai!"

Rose has rushed in and taken in the scene. "Ng choh ah!"

I don't know what they're shouting, but Winston grabs her and pulls her onto a chair.

Above the noise, Miss Tigerlily says, "Welcome Fleur. You've found our entrance portal and brought your guests. Choose an umbrella or the puppet shrine so we know where you are. It's time to retrieve Alister's *Hun*."

Air continues to swirl through the space. The smoke from the incense wafts and twists. Miss Tigerlily hits the gong once more. It's time to call Alister home.

Without planning to, I start humming the Bolero. As I get into the haunting melody, I sense the space behind the fourth door and see the light seeping around the doorway. My humming gets louder and Alister joins in. The sound of his voice is so affirming, I will him with all my heart and soul to ride the wave of love and light out through the crack in the door.

On the other side of Alister, Wind Sand starts to drum. With his hands on the wooden floor he's beating out the rhythm, the rhythm of the Bolero. Fleur must have prepared him, and I can't help crying. Because Wind Sand's love for the father he's never met is harmonising with our music. Together we're doing what I've always hoped; we're singing Alister home.

Miss Tigerlily's voice rises above the music. "Fleur, choose an umbrella or the puppet shrine. Help us rescue Alister's *Hun*."

While Alister and I keep humming and Wind Sand keeps drumming, each of the umbrellas jiggles in turn—round and round the circle as if Fleur can't decide which one.

Then beside me I can smell something. Burning metal. "Miss T, Alister's ring is hot!"

"Fleur," she calls, "you can't do this on your own. After Rose stole Alister's spirit, you could only haunt her and stop her opening the fourth door. You entered Alister's body, but he was kidnapped from you. You're strong but not strong enough. Together we have the power to rescue him. The power of love. Then you can reunite him with your son."

Rose is still jabbering and thrashing in the chair. I'm scared that she's here and grateful to Winston for holding her down.

The fumes from the metal get stronger. "The ring is burning his finger," I shout. "Fleur is still there."

"Bruce," cries Miss Tigerlily, "the bolt-cutters."

Suddenly, Bruce is leaning in between me and Alister. With one deft action, he's snipped the ring from Alister's hand. It falls to the floor where Bruce beats it flat with a hammer.

It happens so fast, our humming resumes without faltering. I keep focusing on the shrine, on Alister's *Hun*, and in my line of sight the puppet behind the screen starts to dance. Fleur's shadow is dancing to the drum beat. She's dancing to the Bolero.

"Thank you, Fleur," Miss Tigerlily calls. "You're in the circle with us. Release your spell on the fourth door. Release it *now*. Everyone, focus everything we've got on Alister."

With a huge burst of humming, drumming and puppet-dancing, we focus all our love on his spirit.

"Alister, ride the wave of love! Call your *Hun* home!"

On a ribbon of light, I see the red cord and sense his *Hun* riding it through the crack around the fourth door. Now it's crossing the space between the shrine and his body. I can't stop crying. It's happening. He's calling his spirit home.

That's when Rose breaks free of Winston, her yellow blouse flashing in one of the mirrors. Like a madwoman she stomps on the umbrellas, then descends on the dancing puppet. In another flash, the puppet stops and Su Yin lets out a yelp of pain. She rushes to her shrine, cutting Rose off from her goal.

"Fleur," Miss Tigerlily shouts. "Direct Su Yin. Protect the four-door shrine."

Before Su Yin or I can intervene, Rose turns and grabs the shrine. She races for the exit, where Nigel and Derek block her path. Turning back, she takes the stairs onto the stage.

"Bruce, turn on the lights."

Suddenly the lights behind the screen illuminate the outline of Rose. Still clutching the shrine, she climbs a high step-ladder just like in my vision. At the top she holds the shrine above her head and shrieks, "If I drop it, Alister fly away. Gone forever. You want him, my grandson Wong Chi Lung come with *me*."

Su Yin cackles out a word-burp. "*You'll never have him. Give up now and save yourself.*"

As total panic pins me to the floor, Wind Sand's tall silhouette appears at the foot of the ladder. He reaches his arms up to Rose. "I am the grandson you lost in the market. Give me the shrine that holds my father's *Hun*."

Rose's shadow looks down. "You not my Wong Chi Lung," she shouts. "You not him. You not ... Chinese enough!" She drops the shrine.

Wind Sand catches it. In seconds he's raced across the stage and down the steps, returning to us on the floor.

But I'm looking at Alister's blank face. When Wind Sand puts the shrine down, the door flops open.

"Miss T," I cry, "the fourth door is open. Alister's spirit is gone."

"It hasn't gone far," she says. "Fleur, catch it."

What? We're relying on Fleur to retrieve his spirit? Suspicion grips my chest like a tourniquet.

Madam Li wants her guy. Watch how she does it.

What if it's been Fleur all along? Has she manipulated this moment, because she stole his *Hun* herself? But Rose intervened and locked it away, then used it to bargain for Deshi. Now that Alister's free of his prison, Fleur can carry him away for eternity, leaving his empty shell behind for me.

But when I look up, I'm frozen by a different terror. Another shadow has appeared behind Rose's head. Just like in my dream.

The shadow of a fox.

"Miss T," I scream, "look at Rose. She's a fox!"

"Selkie," she shouts, "protect Alister's body. Activate your projection-reflex. *Now.*"

Thanks to Klaus and Egg Street, I know what to do—this

time powered by love. Bouncing off the ceiling, with an instant view of our tableau, I'm back inside Alister's body. Just in time, I've brushed his fingers against his nape as the silky shadow circles his neck.

Round and round. Red. Malevolent. Wild with fury.

It can't get in, but stopped from invading him, the fox descends on my empty body sitting beside Alister. I gasp as I see it wrap itself around my neck, looking for a way in.

Am I going to save Alister but lose myself to this predator?

As I watch, it keeps swirling. My little black dress has wrapped me in a protective bubble, and the fox spirit can only churn the smoky air.

"The fox spirit is looking for a host," I shout from Alister's body.

"Fleur," Miss Tigerlily calls, "speak to the fox."

Does she think it's here at Fleur's invitation?

The puppet dances for a moment, then Su Yin wraps her arms over her head and cackles, "*You'll never have him. Selkie will never give up on Alister!*"

Then before our eyes, the one umbrella that missed Rose's stomping flips over and takes off at speed into the rafters. As if it's being pulled by an invisible force, its dome scoops the air in a single movement.

"She's caught the fox spirit. Bruce, open the fourth door."

Bruce races in, opens the door wide, and springs back just before the umbrella drops like a weighted parachute over the shine. With a thud, its stick flips the door closed.

Su Yin cackles, "*It's trapped.*"

In a flash, I brush Alister fingers across his nape and return to my body. We're not done yet.

"Good job, Fleur," I cry. Do her actions prove she's an ally?

"But it's midnight heralding the seventh day. We're running out of time. Rescue Alister's *Hun* so he can be a father to Wind Sand."

The whole room is holding its breath. I've just risked everything. I'm trusting Fleur. As we watch, the umbrella flips onto its back, then swoops up into the rafters again. Beside me Wind Sand starts drumming and I join in, humming the Bolero. With graceful aerobatics the umbrella dances in time with our music, swinging and switching in the incense-laden air.

"She's catching his *Hun* like a butterfly," Miss Tigerlily calls.

It's my dream in action. Madam Li with her umbrella.

As the umbrella dances above us, I pay attention to its pattern for the first time. Pink and black tiger stripes. For Fleur. The room fills with love. The shared love between Fleur and Alister. It's their first dance in thirty years, and tears of compassion course down my cheeks for everything they've lost.

After a minute, the umbrella drops. I jump out of the way as it covers Alister who crumples onto the floor. Now Fleur has both his spirit and his body trapped under the umbrella—with her.

I rush forward, unsure what to do. Then in an outpouring of emotion, I know.

"Haiku," I cry. "I'm here. I'm waiting for you. Waiting with Deshi. Ride the wave of our love back into your body."

"Make a circle of love," Miss Tigerlily cries.

I grab Wind Sand's hand as Nigel and Derek race in, along with Su Yin, Miss Tigerlily and Bruce. Even Winston leaves Rose who's still jabbering from the ladder. We gather around

Alister's crouching form and join our hands together over the umbrella.

"We're focusing everything on you, Alister," Miss Tigerlily says. "Your spirit is with you under the umbrella. We're lending you the power of our will and our love."

"Call your *Hun* home, Haiku."

"I know you are my father," Wind Sand says. "We have some catching up to do. Call your spirit home … Dad."

Under our fingers the umbrella starts to spin. The spinning becomes faster until the pattern is lost in the blur. My heart is pounding so fast, I can't breathe. Alister's fate is in Fleur's hands. Will she let him go?

The umbrella stops spinning and falls over. We all jump back as Alister unfolds his body and gets to his feet. He wobbles a little, steadies himself, then looks around, blinking. I still haven't dared to take a breath, but as soon as I see how his eyes are brimming with radiance, I know.

"Selkie!" He opens his arms and wraps me in a bear hug. "I've got my own voice. I'm back." He throws back his head and laughs. It's the most wonderful sound in the whole world. "You never gave up on me." His eyes shower me with love. "Not for one moment. I saw how much it cost you. You even risked your own soul, but you didn't give up."

I can't speak. I won't let him go. Under the strength of his embrace, the pent-up anxiety of the last six days bubbles over. After our ordeal, he's with me in a way that's new, all the cells of our being mingling into one. As the moment lingers so does the magic, even as we pull apart and share it with our friends.

Alister stands in front of his son. "You must be … Wind Sand."

He opens his fist and proffers the stone from the gardens.

Wind Sand takes the stone and cradles it in his own hand. "My mother's ghost came to me in a dream. Many dreams over many months. She told me my history. It was a shock, but so good to know I have a family. She told me that my father is alive, that I will know him when he offers me an egg-shaped stone. The egg is my symbol."

"Our symbol," Alister says.

They embrace, their hearts touching for the first time in thirty years.

Then Alister reaches out and pulls me to him. "Wind Sand, I want you to meet Selkie."

Wind Sand takes my hand. "We know each other already. We made music together. We played my father home."

Alister starts around the circle, shaking hands and thanking everyone in turn. Derek and Nigel each give him a hug, then hug me. No words are necessary.

Hovering on the edge watching this reunion is Winston. Just as my heart goes out to him, there's a scream. We turn towards the stage in time to see Rose's shadow still at the top of the ladder. The fox silhouette is gone. But as we watch, she wraps her arms around her head as if she's in pain. The action unbalances her. She falls.

As a group, we rush up the stage stairs and behind the screen to find Rose lying on the wooden floor, her arms still around her head. Her glazed eyes stare at the ceiling. Winston runs to her side and cradles her head.

Pushing through to join Winston, Dr Lee asks Miss Tigerlily to call an ambulance.

He bends to examine Rose. "She didn't use her arms to break her fall. She landed on her head." He looks at Winston. "She's slipping away."

Wind Sand puts his hand on Winston's shoulder and stoops to look at Rose.

"She lost her mind," Winston says to him. "She have chance to meet you, but she not know you. She not know her own grandson."

While Bruce tends to Rose, Winston stays. But out of respect, the rest of us return to the staging area.

"Look," Su Yin cries.

The puppet and the lipstick are lying on the floor in front of the second mirror, beneath a drawing of a red heart.

"It's the exit portal," Miss Tigerlily says. "Fleur's gone."

Taking Rose's spirit with her to the afterlife?

Chapter 36

By the time the ambulance arrives, Dr Lee has pronounced Rose dead. For Winston's sake, we form a line as the stretcher-bearers remove her body. Winston shakes Alister's hand and embraces Wind Sand, then leaves with her, his shoulders hunched.

Dr Lee checks Alister over, before taking both of us aside. He wants to make sure our nape *chakras* are fully closed, so together we do the process of visualising a clam. Then the group gathers our implements and clears all traces of our activities. Finding a further use for the toolbox, Bruce nails the shrine door shut and seals the crack around the door. He promises to encase it in concrete where the fox spirit will be forever contained.

We're all exhausted, but also wired. No-one will sleep after what we've witnessed. I'm desperate to be alone with Alister, but he needs time with Wind Sand too.

Wind Sand decides for us. He looks at his phone. "Charlie invites us all to the Fat Waiter. His staff were replaced by police officers tonight and they arrested a few people. The place is now empty. He's going to feed us. A hot pot. He has bottles of snake wine."

The theatre turns out to be just a stroll down a lane from

the back entrance of the secret club. Alister takes my hand squeezing it tight, then I push him forward to join Wind Sand up ahead. They chat as if they've never been separated. I watch their backs, their slim builds similar, but as Bo said, Wind Sand is taller than his father. And he's still shaving his head, making him as bald as the baby in my dream.

When I hear Alister laugh again, it serenades my soul. Every ounce of my energy over the last six days has been focused on this moment. As much as I want to be with him, the red cord connects us, so I savour his reunion with his son.

David Butler has joined us. He walks with his arm through Miss Tigerlily's, showing that they're more than colleagues. No wonder he was so worried about her disappearance before she could contact him.

Su Yin catches up to me. "Is now a good time to mention my reward to Alister?"

"What do you think?"

She sighs. "I know. Wait, wait, wait. That's all I ever do. And I suppose I should be sad that Rose is dead, but now she can't control me any more. Or Alister," she adds, testing out compassion for the first time.

Trust Su Yin to align herself with the winning side, when it's debatable whether she helped or hindered our search for Wind Sand. And she doesn't seem to know that her controller was really a fox spirit. Not a fake one. No wonder Rose had so much power.

"If Fleur's gone for good," she says, "I can say goodbye to the word-burps."

It's what I'm wondering. Does the mirror portal mean Fleur won't return?

Su Yin leans in and whispers, "Did Fleur push Rose off the

ladder?"

"We'll never know."

But I know. It's the prophesy of the tea leaves. *Give up now and save yourself.* She warned Rose more than once.

* * *

Charlie welcomes everyone and we sit at a long table where he pours glasses of snake wine. The snake is still in the bottle to prove it.

When we're all seated, with Alister between me and his son, Wind Sand leaps to his feet and holds up his glass. "Here's to my father getting his spirit back. Thank you all for your help."

Alister is suddenly too choked up to speak. He nods to everyone and looks up at Wind Sand, his eyes brimming. We clink glasses and sip the strong liquid.

Wind Sand continues, "I asked Charlie to open the snake wine because it was part of my rescue as a baby. Merchants at the old Egg Street market used to make it. I hope you like it."

It's sweet with a chicken-like taste. Unusual and not unpleasant.

"Whoever saved me from the child snatchers," he continues, "left me in a basket of eggs at the old nunnery door. To stop me climbing out, the nuns think they gave me some wine. I slept for twelve hours after they found me."

As everyone takes another sip, I imagine the nuns dyeing the eggs red to welcome him and keep him safe.

"And now a second toast," Wind Sand says. "To my mother's ghost. For getting me to the theatre—she insisted that I leave the monastery to be ready at short notice—and you all saw what she did tonight."

He waves the pink and black umbrella. A memento of the strange events—and of his mother.

He's right about Fleur. She's been busy since she escaped her own spirit prison. I've misjudged her more than once, mixed her up with Rose, and attributed evil motives to her. I send her my silent thanks, as we raise our glasses and drink more wine.

"And here's to Selkie," Alister says, finding his voice again and standing up too. "She never gave up on the search—for both of us."

He throws his arms around me and Wind Sand joins him, melting the emotions that I've been holding together for so long.

"Speech," Derek cries.

I stand between my man and his son, trying to find my voice without breaking down. "This moment is everything I hoped it would be. I've had so much help from all of you—you know how much—and this outcome is our reward."

Everyone claps.

Charlie emerges from the kitchen with platters of raw meat, seafood, vegetables and noodles. He lifts the lids on several steaming pots of stock already on the table and shows us how to submerge our chosen morsels in the nearest pot to cook, then dip them into spicy sauces. It's the right kind of meal for a group celebration. We laugh and eat as if we're starving. Exorcisms must create an appetite. Who knew?

There's so much for Wind Sand and Alister to catch up on, but tonight we're all together with many questions about what we just witnessed.

"What about the fox spirit?" I ask Miss Tigerlily. "The outline of its head behind the screen totally freaked me out."

"If you hadn't chosen the puppet theatre, we wouldn't have seen it," she says. "They're good at hiding. But after Rose went up the ladder, the light behind the screen exposed it."

Just like the sail in my dream.

"I thought Rose was a fake fox," I say.

"She was. A confused woman with a lot of grievances. She must have fairy-borrowed a real fox spirit. That's where she got her power."

Robert at the temple didn't detect it. It must have been hiding from him.

"I should have suspected it," Miss Tigerlily continues, "when you told me that the villain hitting weakened Rose, and that Alister's body was invaded this morning. Rose was hosting a fox spirit to do the things she couldn't do. Steal Alister's *Hun.* Invade Su Yin. It couldn't invade Alister because of your psychic activities, and Fleur was trying to drive it away, using Su Yin's voice."

"Like I'm everyone's puppet or something," Su Yin wails.

Miss Tigerlily looks at Alister. "During the villain hitting, the fox spirit was driven out of Rose's body. So when it found you alone for a moment in the gardens, without the psychic protection of your friends, it must have invaded you itself. Was it thinking to get your *Hun* from the four-door shrine and do its own business with your wealth? Fox spirits love money."

"When I thought the kidnapper was Fleur," I say, "I wondered why she abandoned you."

Alister knows what happened. "Fleur tried to get the fox spirit to change sides and work for her against Rose. Then this morning, because of the villain hitting, the fox spirit was on the loose. Fleur got it to invade me and take me to Egg Street, but it turned rogue on her. It was hell-bent on getting my *Hun* back and taking possession of my Hong Kong apartment, but luckily you'd already found the four-door shrine. I got in Klaus's way, and the fox spirit argued with him. I couldn't control what it was saying and it made Klaus so angry that he told his men to take me into the gambling den and tie me to a chair. That's when the fox spirit lost interest and left."

Klaus didn't know it, but he rescued Alister.

Everyone is silent with their own thoughts. We wouldn't believe it all happened, except we were there.

"What was it like without your *Hun*?" Nigel asks. "How did your body experience what was happening? You were present and absent at the same time."

I don't mention how frightening it was.

Alister says, "It was like looking at life the wrong way through a telescope. I could see what was happening but I was far away. Detached. We don't realise how our thoughts and feelings influence what we see. If you take them away, the sounds and sights of life are disconnected from their meaning. I had to struggle to make sense of them. I was aware of some memories, but I imagine it was like dementia, where things seem familiar but you can't grasp the connection. Now that I'm back together, I can interpret the things I remember."

He looks at his son. It's Wind Sand's turn to tell his story.

"My mother came to me in some dreams. I'd never dreamt about her before, so she convinced me that she'd escaped from a funeral pot in my grandmother's house. She told me how she died. It was so shocking, it sounded true. She said that in a few months you were coming to Hong Kong to find me, that I had to leave the monastery or we'd never meet."

"I'm sorry you had to give up your calling," Alister says.

"That must have been hard."

"The monastery was my family, my whole life," Wind Sand says, "and they taught me so much. That happiness comes from inside. That stillness leads to wisdom. How to speak English—an old nun insisted on that, as if she knew I'd need it. But I was ready to move on. And I wanted to meet,"—his voice catches—"my real family. It's weird not really belonging to anyone and being treated like a gift from heaven. I only realised the importance of origins when my mother enticed me away with the promise of meeting you."

Alister reaches out and they hold hands for a long minute, sharing their feelings with all of us.

"We went to Po Lin in the cable car," Alister says. "I remember that. Tell Wind Sand about your search, Selkie."

"We met Bo at the restaurant. He told us you left after Charlie worked there. He said to say hello. He misses you."

"Bo's an orphan. He looked up to me. I'm glad he helped you."

"Then an old monk said something that sent us to Chi Lin."

"A gardener let me have the stone," Alister said. "I got a message from Fleur that I needed one—from the garden where you used to play."

So Alister knew that Fleur was helping us. But without his *Hun* he couldn't tell me. It's why he pinged her ring against my bangle in the cab.

"Nancy at Chi Lin gave us the number of Penelope Styles," I say.

"You spoke to Penelope?" Wind Sand's smile is fleeting. "She's not very happy with me, but she used me as her excuse to leave the nunnery. She wasn't cut out to be a nun. It suited her while she was writing her memoir, then she was stuck.

She liked the idea of a romance as her ticket to freedom. She knew I wasn't in love with her, but she would have let me get dependent on her.

"Then the flu came to Po Lin, and the monks were in quarantine. I didn't get sick so I met Charlie when he helped at the restaurant. He needed a cook for this club, and I took it as a sign. Moving in with him was less complicated than staying with Penelope."

"Penelope told me you'd fallen for a ghost," I say, "so I knew Fleur was guiding you. Her comment helped me trust that you'd be here tonight. I had a vision that you work at the theatre."

"It's a new job. They need someone tall to do the scenery, and I'm learning to make shadow puppets."

As I let the prescience of my vision sink in, Charlie tells us more. "I send Wind Sand to puppet theatre. He work here, but one night he hear German man talk to men about girls. This club nice and private for share photos. German man say how much money he get if girls very pretty. He want men to kidnap more pretty girls. Wind Sand get very angry because he know he stolen as baby, lose his family. He speak to man, they both get mad. German man tell Wind Sand it not his business. Wind Sand want to tell police, but I say be quiet, wait for right time. He too angry to listen. I worry about him, send him away, not tell you when you ask."

I nod my understanding. Then I turn to Wind Sand. "Without your help tonight, I'm not sure we would have had enough love to call Alister home."

He looks from Nigel and Derek to Miss Tigerlily and Bruce, then Su Yin. "I'm not so sure about that. It was an impressive scene when I arrived. I knew you meant business. It's why my grandmother tried to stop it. She knew the real thing when she saw it."

But not her own grandson. Her obsession with a figment cost her her life.

Superintendent Butler fills us in on the police raid. They arrested members of the trafficking ring on Egg Street and at this club, confiscating their tablets and phones. On Egg Street they swooped on three upstairs brothels. They think Klaus Hofmeier is the mastermind, using his knowledge and contacts through The Dove to arrange illegal shipments of girls. They're still investigating how the girls were kidnapped.

I remember the brothel in Honolulu where my former lover had an upstairs flat. The place was always buzzing with clients. "It's always so quiet on Egg Street."

"That's where they've been clever," Butler says. "Patrons had to park in neighbouring streets and use the network of laneways to gain access on foot. Plus the gambling den gave them cover. Brothel patrons were encouraged to gamble there, giving them a reason to be on Egg Street. Trucks brought the girls in from China and parked in garages with interior access to the brothels upstairs. They darkened the windows with heavy curtains. We think they laundered their money at the race track. It's been a slick operation but Klaus got over-confident."

"I saw them here in the Fat Waiter a few months ago," Miss Tigerlily says, "and sensed their connection to child trafficking. But I had no proof."

"We got Charlie to report on them," Butler says, "but Wind Sand accosted Klaus about his activities, so Charlie had to ask him to leave."

"Sorry about that," Wind Sand says. "I was naive. I'm still

learning how the world works."

"I'd decided to avoid the club," Miss Tigerlily continues, "but I sensed a connection to Alister when he phoned me. It was strong but vague so I asked him to meet me here. He acknowledged Klaus and told me his name, but when I returned to my office I thought I was being followed. I decided on the spot to go into hiding."

Butler reaches across the table and squeezes her hand. Was I the cause of her disappearance? We'll never know.

"When you told me Klaus lived in Ocean View," Butler says, "it was another piece of evidence against him. The director of The Dove shouldn't be renting such an expensive apartment. It confirmed he had another income."

"I'm glad I slugged him." Alister waves his fist and looks at me.

"He might have slipped through our fingers if you hadn't," Butler says. "He was about to activate an escape plan."

* * *

Miss Tigerlily, David Butler and Dr Lee say their goodbyes, then Derek and Nigel suggest that Su Yin share their cab back to Ocean View. After farewelling them all, I'm left with Alister and Wind Sand, not sure what to do. I want to give them space but I'm desperate to be alone with Alister.

Once again Wind Sand solves it. "You two need to be alone. Let's get together tomorrow."

He and Alister embrace again and shed more tears, then exchange phone numbers.

Charlie lets us out through the front door. Wrapping our fingers together, we descend to the street and hail a cab.

Chapter 37

In the back of the taxi, we ride in each other's arms. I've got lots of questions, and although we're speaking in murmurs, Alister's clearly enjoying his own voice.

"For a while you had ... the spirit of a fox," I say.

"And it changed my thoughts completely. All I could think about was getting my own way, tricking people and getting wealthy. I lost any sense of compassion; I was totally selfish—and ruthless."

I'm glad I didn't meet him then. It would have tested me more than his empty body. The swirling taunts of the shadow return, but only in my memory. Then I remember my dream. Two fox spirits. Influenced by her mother's origins, did Rose fairy-borrow a Chinese and a Japanese fox spirit? It fits with Winston's story of her history. But the ruthless *Huli Jing* stabbed the gentle *Kitsune*?

With this glimpse into the mind of the winning fox spirit, I shiver at just how close we came to losing Alister tonight. Did Fleur invite it to the theatre, so that we would help her deal with it for good? We'll never know.

"And what about your spirit?" I ask. "What did you understand from inside the shrine?"

"At first it was like a long meditation. I felt enclosed and heavy with sadness. Everything changed when you made contact through the bangle. You reached out to me and in that moment I sensed the red cord and remembered how things used to be. The red cord was a lifeline. Your love ... touched my soul."

We squeeze hands, savouring our touch.

"When you grabbed my bangle," I say, "Rose sent the fox spirit to push me away. You pulled me back."

"That was the red cord. I was only aware of a great agitation. And a cloud of malevolence. But your love shone through like a beacon. It kept me going for six long days.

"After that I started to pay attention," he continues, "to see if I could sense things. I wanted to know what had happened to my body and where I was. I was aware of the red cord and I could feel your love as a kind of warmth. I knew you were trying to help me, but I didn't know how to reach you."

"I heard you speak my name. During our lovemaking. It gave me ... hope."

"I used all my energy to see your face and think your name. I could only do that once, before my energy started to drain away."

I tell him about Rose burning the paper strips.

"When I think about her mental illness," Alister says, "I think Wind Sand was better off being abducted. He's had a life surrounded by love."

I think about this. "That must have comforted Fleur after her imprisonment—to find you both—separated but happy. And what about her? How did Fleur speak to you? I had no idea that she was doing battle with Rose and the fox spirit. At first I thought there was only one of them. Rose. Or Fleur."

"Fleur didn't contact my spirit. I think she was afraid of the shrine, of getting trapped again. She used the ring. She'd been doing that before we left Honolulu, but I didn't understand it."

"It got hot."

"Yeah. But ever since her death, it had never been hot before. I engaged that medium to try to contact her and got nothing. I didn't know she'd been trapped by Rose. Then after I met Su Yin, the ring got hot for the first time—and I dreamed about Fleur. I worried about what they meant, if I was suddenly pining after Fleur because of Su Yin, so I ignored them."

"Then Su Yin told you to come to Hong Kong."

"I didn't know she was being manipulated by Rose. And it's what Fleur wanted too. She was hell-bent on bringing me and Deshi together." He stops. "Not Deshi, Wind Sand. It's a beautiful name, isn't it?"

He drops his head into his hands and starts to cry. I rest my head on his shoulder as the last six days and the last thirty years flow away.

* * *

At Ocean View, we take the elevator to our borrowed apartment and find that Nigel and Derek have moved next door.

We'll exorcise the spirit of Klaus from Alister's place, Derek says in his note.

We've got the rest of the night to ourselves.

The king-size bed welcomes us. In harmony with the Bolero, we move in slow motion, savouring the depth of our connection, the rhythm of our dance, the frisson of our touch. Every sensation is so much more heightened after our ordeal.

We're together on all levels, the physical and the metaphysical. And ironically, after a week of silence from Alister, we need no words, content to let our bodies and souls do the talking. Our limbs entwine, as do our spirits.

And our tears.

* * *

Over a late breakfast we talk as if we haven't talked for a week.

Alister asks about our nape *chakras* and I explain why Bruce closed them.

"It's why the fox spirit could invade my body," he says. "Then after it left—you did it." He knows that's how we slugged Klaus.

What do I say? I'm not sure how he feels. "I—"

"– took an enormous risk. And carried it off. I saw inside your soul, Selkie. I had your thoughts, your determination, your ... love."

He looks at me and I drink in the life behind his eyes like a tonic.

"Well, it was amazing to inhabit your body," I gush. "I wasn't you, I was still me. But for a moment, I was ... a man."

He laughs. "You're a man for a few seconds and you start thumping people."

"Only if they deserve it. And only if I've got a handy pebble in my fist as a secret weapon." Now I'm laughing too. "And it won't happen again. Promise. I'll stick with my female form from now on."

He pulls me onto his lap. "It's the way I like you."

By silent agreement we're not going to talk about this again.

"What about the stone?" I ask. "How did you know to pick it up?"

"After Rose stole my *Hun*, the ring started getting hot more often. It made me pay attention to things around me, even though I didn't understand what I was seeing. When we were talking to the gardener, the ring got hot again. I looked around and I could only see stones so I picked one up. It was shaped like an egg, so it spoke to me."

"Where's the ring now?" I ask.

From his pocket, he brings out the flattened piece of silver, unrecognisable, its engraving gone.

At the sight of it, I risk the question I have to ask. "When your spirit escaped from the shrine ... were you tempted –"

"– to go with Fleur?" He puts the ring down and takes my hands. "Look at me, Selkie. I learned something while my spirit was on the ceiling. I could see all of you working together to rescue me, and there was so much love between you, with you at the centre. I longed to return to the love, to you."

"Fleur loved you too. You danced with her under the umbrella."

"My *living spirit* danced with her *ghost*. A farewell dance. Ghosts want to leave. It's their job, and her departure was long overdue. She whispered to me for the first time—and the last time. She told me to remember her fondly but to let her go, to return to my body and share my love with Wind Sand. And you."

As his words sink in, we stare at what used to be his wedding ring. Last night, Fleur's 'unfinished business' was finally finished.

"Dr Lee snipped it off so Fleur would stop inhabiting it," I say, "but why did he beat it flat?"

"I'll explain when we go out."

He's being mysterious and I let him.

* * *

A text message from Wind Sand arranges lunch, and this time Alister will go alone.

"There's something you and I have to do first," he says. "You'll need your walking shoes."

At Wind Sand's suggestion, I send a text to Derek and Nigel inviting them to a farewell dinner tonight at the Fat Waiter, before they return to Honolulu. I invite Su Yin too, but leave it to Wind Sand to decide when to approach Winston. Mourning for Rose may involve him in funeral arrangements that I don't understand.

It's when I'm getting my walking shoes that I see the in-flight magazine peeping out of my tote bag. Something makes me open it at the page with the shadow puppet. Beside the scribbled comment, three new words have been added crudely—in red lipstick. She must have done it last night.

Madam Li wants her guy to be loved. *Watch how she does it.*

A private message just for me. I close the magazine and send Fleur my deepest thanks.

* * *

It's cool but sunny as we exit the building and follow our road until we come to a walking track.

"Down we go," Alister says.

The trail is well-paved and well-marked. It snakes down the side of the mountain and offers stunning views of skyscrapers and mountain peaks shrouded in mist, of fishing boats and harbour traffic, of islands just offshore. We hold hands and saunter, revelling in the joy of being alive, of being 'spirited', of being together.

The trail switches back on itself several times until we come to a crossroad where we can follow another trail or descend steep steps to the shore.

"This way." Alister leads me down the staircase.

"Where are we going?"

"Aberdeen Harbour."

We've been catching glimpses of it all the way down the path, fulfilling Miss Tigerlily's instruction: *Go down to the sea.*

When we hit the foreshore, we cross the road to the harbour front. Alister leads me with purpose to a spot where the rail is the only thing separating us from the water. In front of us, the bay is full of boats of all kinds, working boats and sampans and pleasure boats alike. I gaze into the depths, glad of the rail to lean on.

"This will do," he says. "You need to be my witness."

For one panicky moment, I fear he's going to jump in. I grab his arm, but he draws the flattened ring from his pocket.

"It's no longer a ring," he says, "no longer a memento of Fleur. It's a piece of scrap metal. Dr Lee said to toss it into the sea."

As I watch, he throws it as far as he can into the bay. Amidst the surrounding noise, it falls with the faintest plop and disappears.

"Thank you, Fleur," he calls. "Goodbye. Your father will burn funeral goods for you, but you don't need them. You're free to fly."

Then he turns to me and holds up his hand. The place where his wedding band used to be is just a strip of pale skin, his connection to Fleur now a warm memory.

As the implications sting my throat, he takes me in his arms.

"Selkie, my love. I'm all yours."

Epilogue

A crush of paparazzi greets us at Honolulu airport. News of Alister's return always reaches the press, who can't get enough of what they hope is a romance between Mr Sloane and his companion, Selkie Moon.

"You're looking radiant after your holiday," a reporter says to me. "Any news?"

"Did you and Miss Moon travel to Hong Kong for a secret wedding, Mr Sloane?" another asks, pressing a microphone under Alister's nose. "Our readers are keen to greet the new Mrs Sloane."

Alister sighs and stops. He's learned that making a brief statement is better than being filmed on the run from the press. I squeeze his hand in encouragement.

"We have spent a week in Hong Kong on family business which I'm pleased to say was successful. We have no announcement to make about our future at this time, but we're pleased to be home. We know you'll respect our privacy. Thank you."

Holding my hand tightly, he pushes his way to the exit where Derek is waiting.

As we settle into the car, I say, "That was easier than I expected. But they make me laugh. A secret wedding?"

Alister turns to me and says, "The press are full of good ideas."

Dear Reader ...

Thank you so much for joining Selkie Moon on her Hong Kong adventure in *The Fourth Door*. It was a wild ride at times—and the thrills aren't over yet.

Where to next for Selkie and Alister—and the rest of their friends?

The next book will take them to Chile for a special event, not to be missed.

While you wait, follow my blog for occasional updates on the series:

http://www.selkiemoon.com/

Author's Note

I wish to thank my editors: Nicola O'Shea, Kendra Olson and Steph Warren for their insightful comments on the drafts of *The Fourth Door*.

The manuscript was also reviewed for cultural accuracy by Alice Chau-Ginguene. I am grateful to her for the errors she identified and the suggestions she made to enrich the local colour. Any errors still remaining are my own!

Also by Virginia King

Selkie Moon's coming-of-age adventures are influenced by folklore in each country she visits. *Leaving Birds* is a collection of adult tales that inspired the prequel to the series *Laying Ghosts.*

Leaving Birds

Murder. Magic. A ghost or two ...

Discover the chilling power of folklore with *Leaving Birds.*

http://www.selkiemoon.com/